Colonial Spy

by
M. C. BECKHAM

A Novel Set In The American Revolution

TRAFFORD

USA ▪ Canada ▪ UK ▪ Ireland

Note for Librarians: A cataloguing record for this book is available from Library and Archives
Canada at www.collectionscanada.ca/amicus/index-e.html
ISBN 1-4120-6296-9

*Printed in Victoria, BC, Canada. Printed on paper with minimum 30% recycled fibre. Trafford's print shop runs
on "green energy" from solar, wind and other environmentally-friendly power sources.*

Offices in Canada, USA, Ireland and UK
This book was published *on-demand* in cooperation with Trafford Publishing. On-demand
publishing is a unique process and service of making a book available for retail sale to the
public taking advantage of on-demand manufacturing and Internet marketing. On-demand
publishing includes promotions, retail sales, manufacturing, order fulfilment, accounting and
collecting royalties on behalf of the author.

Book sales for North America and international:
Trafford Publishing, 6E–2333 Government St.,
Victoria, BC v8t 4p4 CANADA
phone 250 383 6864 (toll-free 1 888 232 4444)
fax 250 383 6804; email to orders@trafford.com
Book sales in Europe:
Trafford Publishing (uk) Ltd., Enterprise House, Wistaston Road Business Centre,
Wistaston Road, Crewe, Cheshire cw2 7rp UNITED KINGDOM
phone 01270 251 396 (local rate 0845 230 9601)
facsimile 01270 254 983; orders.uk@trafford.com
Order online at:
trafford.com/05-1207

10 9 8 7 6 5 4 3

Contents

Author's Note

Some manuscripts come looking for you. They present themselves wearing the innocent look of "coincidence" and "happenstance." They seem to know when to appear. Sometimes they line up so illogically you have to notice them.

Such was the case in talking with Mr. Guy Darby of Chester County, SC in the year 2000. We thrashed out the Revolutionary War and our ancestors …he indulged my talk about the Battle of Beckhamville on June 6, 1780 which bears the family name. We talked, knowing as we do which 99 percent of the population does not, that Tarleton's defeat of Colonel Buford of Virginia at the Waxhaws on May 29, 1780 hurried the Battle of Beckhamville, occurring only seven days later. Mr. Darby said something reasonable… "See the battle site and the monument of Buford's defeat and the historical sign which tells the story." I did and, without my knowledge, the experience would set the backdrop for this book.

Earlier that year, on February 17, Sam Beckham, my dad, had died at age 85. The first coincidence arrived days later in an invitation from Milledgeville, Georgia to "represent" a Beckham relative in a large reenactment. We were to honor the day and those soldiers who welcomed the General Marquis de Lafayette to Georgia after the war. That person, among other veterans, who welcomed General Lafayette, was Cousin Samuel Beckham. Was he called "Sam" by those close to him?

I told only one business associate about the celebration, illustrator Barry Grant, who "just happened" to be a Revolutionary War re-enactor, and he lent me everything–clothes, shoes, tricorn hat, a musket. The complete outfit. We are no where near the same size, so I looked very much the ill fittingly clothed militiaman. Warm, friendly Georgians kept saying, "Have you met Hugh Harrington?" "No," I said to about four inquiries. But at Memorial Hill Cemetery where Samuel is buried, a soldier was standing guard at Samuel's tomb telling tourists and visitors to the event about the patriot, and the speaker was, of course, Hugh Harrington.

Later, I was more informed after Gloria, a Beckham in Maryland, told me about other relatives, all mine, who fought in the Revolution including my great, "to the fourth greats," grandfather William and his brother, my great uncle John "Jack" Beckham. Professional Beckham genealogist, Jim Heidelbaugh of Illinois, added to all this. He indicated great uncle "Jack" was a noted scout and spy for the Whigs (our side). It "just so happened" he was documented in at least three books. I started recording information and was led to being academically encouraged by historian Hugh Harrington, the same Hugh Harrington mentioned above, who indeed is deep in the American Revolution as a writer, published author, and re-enactor.

Almost five years later, the completed novel is the product of the original directive of all those above, and many others, including new friends in different reenactment groups — British, Tory (their side), Continental and Whig.

Dedication

This book is dedicated to four men. All were timely forces in my career with colleges, universities and medical centers. They were exemplary in their professions with unusual courage. They would have been leaders in 1776, and particularly in the foreboding year of 1780.

William D. Huff (1925-1979)-Former Vice President of the Medical University of South Carolina, Charleston. *Thanks, Bill, for your trust and your confidence and then your constant support.*

George M. Humphrey J.D.-Philanthropist and President of Extrudex, Cleveland, Ohio. *Thank you, George, for leading and accomplishing great things by your sterling example.*

Albert B. Sabin, M.D. (1906-1993)-Virologist and discoverer of the Sabin oral polio vaccine. *Thanks, Albert. We still need you. We still miss you.*

William H. Stoneman, M.D.-Former Dean of Saint Louis University School of Medicine, Saint Louis, Missouri. *Bill, you defined integrity and then redefined it to a higher level.*

IN MEMORY
Bobby Lynn Beckham (1939-2003)

VIII

Acknowledgements

There are many people to thank. In the years it takes to write a book, you can buttonhole a lot of opinions and advice.

Special thanks to authors who gave me their time to sit and talk. First among these is Dr. Bobby Moss, esteemed South Carolina historian and researcher and author of *Patriots at Cowpens* and *Patriots at Kings Mountain*, among other works. I spent time in his home sitting in the same chair as the British actor who played Cornwallis in the movie, "The Patriot." (He, too, came to Blacksburg, South Carolina, and to Dr. Moss for direction.)

Mary Eaddy, president of the firm Word Smith, Myrtle Beach, South Carolina, gave advice early on. She advised, I followed her advice, and it was very helpful.

Thanks to Editor Susan Snowden. It was encouraging knowing she labored from six in the morning until noon, many times, living with main character Jack Beckham, his family, and the American Revolution.

Time spent with Tony Scotti, Ph.D., author of *Brutal Virtue, The Myth and Reality of Banastre Tarleton,* Heritage Books, Westminster, Maryland; Rick Boreaum, author of *Young Hickory*, Taylor Trade Publishing, Dallas, Texas; Carol P. Borick, assistant director of the Charleston Museum in Charleston, South Carolina and author of *A Gallant Defense, The Siege of Charleston*, South Carolina Press, Columbia, SC; Charles B. Baxley, J.D., Editor of *Southern Campaigns of the American Revolution*, and Alan D. Charles, Ph.D., *The Narrative History of Union County South Carolina*, of USC-Union, A PRESS Printing Company, Greenville, SC, was invaluable, as was time spent with Rock Hill historian, author, and former Winthrop University professor, Louise Pettus, and Christine Swager, Ph.D., author of *Come to the Cow Pens*, Hub City Writers Project, Spartanburg, SC. Spending part of a day with Donna Johnson, M.D., OB-GYN, of the Medical University of South Carolina, a fellow Furman University graduate, was critical to the writing of a very important chapter.

Thank you to the authors for books written that are "must-reads": *A Devil of a Whipping*, by Lawrence Babits, PhD, University of North Carolina Press, Chapel Hill and London; and *Battleground*, by Warren Ripley, published by the *Charleston Post and Courier*.

Park rangers Scott Withrow and John Robertson of the National Park and Battlefield at Cowpens gave generously of their time and advice, at the site of the key battle.

Much gratitude to York County and Historical Brattonsville historian/author Mike Scoggins, as well as other Brattonsville living history employees: Director Charles LeCount, Jeannie Marion, Kitty Evans, Laura Sterling, and Dorothy McNalley. The latter three also served as models for illustrations.

Living and camping with re-enactors was a highlight of the research, notably observing Kip Carter, leader of the New Acquisition Militia, and members of the "militia" Barry Grant, Mark Hall, John Miskelley, and Joe Hinson. Arlene Mackey and Beth Melton of the New Acquisition Militia made the women's side of the Revolutionary War accurate and educational, and conversing with nautical expert Captain Tom Tucker was deeply appreciated. Barry Grant was one who gave a lot of time to many questions and never tired of it.

Al Pratt of the Great Falls Home Town Association, and one of our own members of McClure's Rangers, was a great help. Hugh Harrington, already mentioned in "Author's Notes" spent a day with me shooting muskets and rifles at predatory trees and it transferred well when writing about firelocks. Then he spent hours and days collaborating with me via email on many technical subjects.

Most of the illustrations in the book were drawn by students in Janice Mueller's senior illustration class at Winthrop University. The students worked with photographs, theirs and others, taken at Revolutionary War re-enactments and in Brattonsville, SC.

I thank the models who gave of their time and skills. In addition to Al Pratt and the women of Brattonsville, I acknowledge MUSC vice president Jim Fisher and Courtney Culbertson (a Winthrop University student).

"Hawkeye," and a host of Revolutionary War enthusiasts photographed at Camden, South Carolina, did a great job at their annual event in November, 2004. I thank, too, "Purple Horse" for his past written inspiration, especially with usable expletives, and Wallace Fennell, III of Rock Hill SC for his expert advice on hunting sus scrofa, the feral hog.

Marilyn Bachman, Edward Lemmon, John Nash, Jodi Weiss Beckham, daughter-in-law, and David Ford, Aaron Klopp, and Janice Mueller provided photographic records for all illustrators. My heartfelt thanks are directed toward each of them. I appreciate the time and the effort it took as well as the "eye" for detail that each of them exhibited.

The students in Ms. Mueller's class took the book as it was being written and breathed visual life into the characters and situations. Experiencing their commitment and talents was extremely rewarding. I owe appreciation to all of them. Those submitting illustrations were: Jason Bunner, Lezlee Elliott, Paul Marshall Jones, Aaron Klopp, Edward Lemmon, Jr., Phhoutong Phimmarath, Woodie Wentworth, and Michael Zuleba. They worked together, encouraging and creatively challenging each other. The results are the excellent illustrations which help bring so many of the characters to life. My single regret is that I could not find places for all of the fine work that was done. And the one non-student illustrator was son Chris Beckham, also a distant relative of the hero, Jack.

Janice Mueller, Barry Grant, and I advised Aaron Klopp about the exciting cover illustration. He realized our suggestions with quiet patience and created an excellent cover. Thank you, Janice, Barry and, especially, Aaron.

And foremost, and to the greatest degree of eternal gratitude, the 21st century Elizabeth Beckham, (Betty), wife and critic, who was a surprising version of the 18th century Elizabeth Beckham. She grieved over the death of her favorite character and worried about Molly Polly.

Thanks for having this book on your mind for the same five years it took me to write it.

As the book was ready for proofing, Dr. Alice Love, retired Winthrop University Professor of English, gave generously of her expertise.

List Of Illustrations

Illustrator

Preface

The Loyalists Pledge To King George Iii

"I do solemnly and sincerely swear on the HOLY EVANGELISTS of ALMIGHTY GOD to bear true Allegiance to our Sovereign Lord, KING GEORGE the THIRD, and to uphold the same. I do voluntarily promise to serve as Militia under any of the Officers appointed over me, and that I will, when lawfully warned by our said officers, assemble at any Place by them directed in case of Danger, in the space of eight hours. I will not at any time do, or cause to be done, anything prejudicial to His Majesty's Government; or suffer any Intercourse or Correspondence with the Enemies thereof, that I will make known any Plot or Plots, anywise inimical to His Majesty's Forces or loyal Subjects, by me discovered to His Majesty's Officers contiguous, and it shall not exceed six Hours before same is discovered, if Health and Distance permit. This I do solemnly swear and promise to defend in all cases whatsoever. SO HELP ME GOD!"

In May 1780, the British and their allies defeated American Regulars and militia in a siege at Charlestowne, South Carolina. It was the worst defeat in the American Revolution, so complete that the war was essentially over in the south. All that remained was for the British to pursue a beleaguered General George Washington somewhere in the Northern colonies and force his surrender. But by pitting neighbor against neighbor, family against family, and American against American, what happened next was the bloodiest chapter in United States history, filled with pure violence.

In retrospect, we can affirm that chapter despite its violence and hatred. Out of that awful time two hundred twenty-five years ago emerged the greatest democracy and the singularly most powerful nation in history. It was worth it.

Chapter One

"Dugma Wa," *Home Never Stays*

As light entered his Grindal Shoals cabin on the Pacolet River one April morning in 1780, John "Jack" Beckham lay alongside his wife Elizabeth. He had been awake for more than an hour in their large feather bed, a bed that had been part of her dowry. First in the dark and now in the predawn light he listened to the thinning crackle of oak logs in the large fireplace used for cooking. He listened to the relaxed breathing of his wife and their smallest children, who slept in the same room and he savored the quiet of these last private, gentle minutes before departing his family.

He was leaving them for a spy mission. In this uncertain time of warring against the King of England, several anxious landed farmers in the upcountry were paying him to be a stealthy eyewitness to the massive British naval blockade of Charlestowne. He would travel by way of his sister's home near the Catawba River to this sizable coastal city, the colonial capital of South Carolina.

Leaning on his elbow, he put the back of his hand gently against his wife's face to awaken her. With her back pressed against him and her waist-length brown hair tucked to the side of her head, Elizabeth was holding six-month-old Henrietta gently between her knees and chest, her arm around the child. He saw with half-amusement, slight consternation, and much affection the sight around these two. At Elizabeth's waist, half under the large quilt were two-year-old Teressa

and three-year-old Sarah, who had climbed into the "big bed" and
draped themselves to their mother's legs. This left four-year-old Nancy
sleeping alone in the bed near the large fireplace. The three had gone to
sleep the night before in their bed six feet away near the wide fireplace
hearth, but these two little girls had wandered sleepily to their mother's
side sometime in the middle of the night.

Up a narrow stairwell beside the main fireplace of the front room
was an upstairs room. There slept twenty-year-old Susan, eighteen-
year-old Elizabeth (known as Lily-Beth), twelve-year-old Mary Leah
(Molly Polly), and eleven-year-old John, Junior, the only boy among his
eight children.

From the front room where Jack's big yellow hunting dog Tobee
slept came the familiar "tic tac, tic tac" of her toenails on the heart-of-
pine floor. That sound always told the story of her nocturnal movements. Many times when the fire in the bigger front room died down,
she would meander into the room with Jack and his children lie down
beside the kitchen hearth near the younger children with a long grunt,
and go to sleep again. But this time Tobee came to Jack's bed and stood
near his head, gently disturbing his feelings of devotion for his wife and
family.

Tobee did not move to lie down, and this variation from her usual
practice caused him to listen more intently. With his body still against
Elizabeth, his arm over her waist touching Henrietta's head, he turned
to look at the dog who suddenly "gruffed." It was not a growl, but her
lips flared out to produce a muffled sound that might precede a growl
or bark. Jack turned and looked into her big soft eyes and whispered
calmly, "Dog, what's it?"

Tobee became more anxious and excited, picking up her paws and
putting them down in the same spot, up and down again in a little
dance and wiggling her back end and tail to the sound of his voice.
She gruffed again, her lips drawn tightly as if she were ready to bark.
She then looked toward the front door. At this obvious gesture, Jack
sprang up. Putting his hand against the bed for leverage, he leapt out
of bed, grabbing the .50-caliber rifle leaning against the wall inches
from his head. Clad only in a long linen shirt, he pulled on his breeches

and stepped into knee-high boots, instinctively fastened his belt, and rammed a twelve-inch knife under the leather. He followed Tobee to the front door and opened it quickly, letting her out as he purposely stooped under the door lock, presenting a smaller target if there were imminent danger.

Jack watched Tobee run into the yard, still not barking but prancing sometimes sideways, sometimes forward in a straight line away from the cabin, looking back to make sure of her master's attention. Jack had seen enough. He ran to get his splendidly trained race horse, "Maw", a marvel of speed standing sixteen hands high. Throwing a rope around her neck as a temporary rein, he quickly cinched on the saddle with its accoutrements of gun powder, lead balls, and a nautical looking glass. He mounted her and followed Tobee.

As he started riding he heard nothing unusual, saw nothing troublesome, but he watched the dog to see if she might stop and bark ferociously. He allowed Tobee to charge towards the noise she alone had heard from the front room of the Beckham home. She was not running dead on and fast and he concluded she was a little unsure of the cause of the alarm, so he took control. Prodding Maw alongside, he said to Tobee "Git back...go home...back! Git back...go!"

Accustomed to hunting, Tobee looked up at Jack's command, slowed to a walk, then stopped and watched him. She began to trot home, glancing back every few yards to watch Jack hurrying in the direction she had been running.

Jack needed to find out the cause of Tobee's alarm. Had Tobee run into the thick woods, the cause might have been a large predatory animal or a single hunter. But she had taken a path leading away from the log home, a normal route for travelers, and a path on which men could ride alongside each other.

The path lay in a southerly direction where the Pacolet River flowed with increasing energy to connect with a larger river. Jack rode cautiously, sometimes trotting Maw so that her hooves did not mask any other sounds. Coming to a brief clearing, he stopped to decide which direction to take. Should he go back toward the headwaters of the Pacolet or continue south? The decision was made for him when for the first time that morning he heard horses and men. Jack listened with absolute concentration to the sound of wagons on the move and the shouts of men driving teams of horses or mules. The sound faded, leaving him aware only of the wind in the trees, the beautiful, calming sweep of sound in treetops that he had known since his youth.

He walked Maw forward and again heard the disharmony of mixed noise. The river carried the sound of men back to him from time to time, and he gauged the men to be less than a mile away. Climbing on Maw, Jack rode toward the sounds that had disturbed Tobee and might threaten him. Coming to a bare spot of ground within sight of the river, he heard the noise of men close by. Looking through covering trees across the river to the other bank, he saw to his alarm that this was a larger troop than he might have expected. A major movement of men seemed to be heading south. It was clear who they were and why they were traveling. They were a group of Tories, made up of Loyalist colonists and some Indians…and possibly some of Jack's neighbors who had sworn an oath to England and King George. With them were a few British officers. This had to be part of the train to Charlestowne, which his nephew Samuel of Rocky Mount had told him about.

Samuel had sent word to his uncle that farmers in the Cedar Shoals area and the great falls of the Catawba had come to him wanting to hire Jack as a paid fifth columnist to determine who might be the victor in the siege of Charlestowne, which was now beginning. Hundreds of rumors had spread throughout the colony of the "awful happenings" on the coast. Men wanted to know in advance who would win in this conflict with the English. Fortunes might be preserved by a choice of loyalty to the Crown or by casting their lot with the Whigs. Jack was known to be a zealous Whig, one who made violent reckoning on those who opposed him.

It was too clear to him what was happening. Close to five hundred men of the colony and perhaps also from the North Carolina Colony were traveling to the siege. He knew he was right when he saw the end of the main body. A party of six to eight "rear" travelers were made up of Cherokee Indians, known to be allied with the British. Jack suspected that "Bloody Bill" Cuningham, a savage American Tory, and his band of followers, many of whom were Cherokee, were traveling with the group.

He waited minutes more for the passing group to fade into the distance. He watched carefully for "side" travelers, those in the group who would ride in a wide arc, even on this side of the river, to protect the larger band of Tories as they passed through. Feeling safer now that this group was leaving the Pacolet for the long trip, he rode Maw home, relieved that they had left but uneasy about their sheer numbers. He now grasped why Samuel had asked him to be near Hicklin's Mill on the large Rocky Creek near the falls of the Catawba. Jack was to meet him there, after first going to his sister Maggie's home, a full day's ride toward the Catawba River.

He needed to get back now, eat heartily, pack his belongings on Maw, and leave for Charlestowne. Once again he was leaving his family, giving weight to the name "dugma wa" – home never stays – given to him by his Catawba Indian friends. The trip to the coast would take eight days, but would start with the shorter trip to see his sister Helen Magatha Beckham Land, nicknamed "Maggie" by Jack himself.

Approaching his cabin, he relieved himself in a ditch latrine fifty yards away. He eyed everything as he walked Maw to the cabin. Everything was in order. The pigs were in their pen. The fenced-in garden had not been raided during the night by deer or wild boar. He walked deliberately along the path to make sure that no disturbance had taken place. He looked around carefully for anything untoward, even broken branches and limbs from a horse or errant cow that might have gotten loose and been foraging nearby. Then he fed Maw and looked her over with pride, for she would take him on this trip on the great wagon trail between the sea and the mountains as well as off trails in the brush. He gave her water and rubbed her down before going into his home in the full lightness of dawn, back into the kitchen room where he had slept with Elizabeth and the baby.

His wife was bent over the fireplace. A strong fire was heating a large iron pot with crushed corn mixed with goat milk that would be the main meal along with bread, recently caught fish, and dried venison. Jack would eat a full meal along with hot cider that he boiled in a pot near the corn and milk. Elizabeth was nursing the baby as she stirred the larger pot.

The smallest girls remained sleeping. Jack picked up Nancy, holding her face against his as he nuzzled her, and placed her in the big bed along with Teressa and Sara. When all was ready, he and Elizabeth would go into the other room and he would stoke the main room fireplace into life. They would eat at a large wooden table with ten chairs. But not before Elizabeth, still nursing the baby, stood at the foot of the stairwell and called up to Susan to get everyone down for chores before breakfast. The two oldest girls always responded immediately, going outside to fetch fresh water, feed the chickens, and hogs, collect whatever fresh vegetables and eggs might be available, and then go back for firewood. Between them, they brought into the house eight bundles of firewood, gathering the fuel from fallen trees and chopping larger pieces of oak from trees previously felled by Jack and John Junior. The girls worked for an hour before they roused their little sisters in the kitchen room and helped feed them. Only then did they eat, making sure the little girls stayed within their sight while they did so.

Jack and Elizabeth sat in silence until he looked up and said, "What does you want from the merchants? I will be bringing you and Maggie roots and herbs and some cloth, but it will have to be right quickly. I am there a short time."

Elizabeth said the main thing was snakeroot and salt, but also the merchants' sharp needles and some cloth. Susan looked up and said, "Cloth, Papa. calico and lace."

"Aye. Mr. Stribling it is," Jack said and teased her. "How is he? Does he be around more when I leaves? Is he hanging in a tree now to see when I leaves?"

"No, Papa. He is right so a gentleman and he will be working his place on the river much this spring and all summer. You may see him before I do."

Jack smiled at this inaccuracy and looked toward Elizabeth holding the baby, wondering if Stribling would be the husband for the attractive Susan. Both she and Lily-Beth, at twenty and eighteen, were

Jack and Elizabeth

past the usual age in the wilderness to be married and have children, but it had not happened.

The others continued to eat while Jack, following his unbroken custom, stretched and went to the fireplace where he put tobacco into a clay pipe and lit it with a stick from the fire. He turned and looked to Elizabeth, and they went into the kitchen and sat at two chairs near the kitchen fire. Jack leaned back in his bent wood chair, put his booted foot on the brick hearth, and looked admiringly at his wife. The half-sleeping baby was interrupted by Elizabeth patting her on the back to burp her.

"I am to be at a barn near Fishing Creek, after I meets Samuel, to listen to cowards and scoundrels who will pay me to go to Charlestowne. They are to know how the Britishers and all theirs will do against ours, and then they will make up their minds as to who they are for.

"Hellfire! They is a sorry lot and not to be trusted. I will take barter, go see and report back, but they has to pay much. I nay trust them."

"Who are these men? Do I know them?" she asked. "Are they known to the Mabry's?"

"Damnation, no!" said Jack. "I fear that Mabry and his family would know these farmers not a whit. These 'in betweens' are betting on who will be the ones who are the best at Charlestowne, and then they will turn against each other. Mabry is on our side and everyone knows it, but ain't no one going against him and his family. They is too honest for these types of men, so I don't think he has any business with them at all."

"So when are you back to the Pacolet?"

"I 'spect when the Britishers has won this thing and run all ours out of town. I ain't waiting to see them and shake their hands…I am back as soon as I knows. I ain't going unless they barter with me well, and Samuel, Kit, and Johnny gits all their paper and notes and anything that has to be carried back on horses."

"Tell Maggie I want her to come visit with me and soon," said Elizabeth. "I miss her sorely, and I fear for her with no husband, even if she does have a big group of hands to help her. Tell her to bring Easter

The Irrepressible Molly Polly

and spend time with me and mine while you are gone. My girls care for her, and I think want to be like her, especially Susan and Lily-Beth."

Jack nodded, and his wife knew he might or might not pass this on to Maggie. He was simply in agreement.

"Where are my two?" he asked, referring to Molly Polly and John Junior, who were inseparable, but always wrestling, fighting, and competing with each other.

"Can you not hear them upstairs?" she asked, with a wifely proud reproach.

Jack tuned his ear toward the stairs and grinned slightly. They were the only two excused from early morning chores, for their job was to clean up after everyone, obeying their older sisters. They put off their first daily appearances as long as possible.

Jack then began another daily routine when he pulled tobacco from his pocket and began to chew on one side. Elizabeth knew that this small act would keep him a little longer at their place. Chewing tobacco was a work habit and Jack would soon get up to begin packing his belongings on Maw. He got up after a period of silence, stealing admiring glances at Elizabeth as she hummed a lullaby to Henrietta. He patted the dozing baby on the back of the head and touched Elizabeth on the shoulder as he moved to the front of the cabin and outside to Maw.

He put his food for travel, his weapons of hatchet and knife and several items to trade in Charlestowne in a side bag tied to the saddle. He took some spices to give Maggie, along with a letter from Elizabeth for her. Jack could not read, but he respected his wife's written words. She came from a family that had much materially and made sure that everyone could read, even the women.

On his way back to the cabin, he stopped and did a gentlemanly thing. He spat out his tobacco and washed out his mouth by a spring. Then he picked mint leaves and chewed them to sweeten his breath. He went back to his cabin, bid Elizabeth good-bye, and held her tightly, out of sight of his children. He kissed her face, her cheeks, and her forehead in an adoring way. He cupped her face in his hands, kissed the tip of her nose, and stroked her long hair. Much between them was left unsaid at a time like this. Finally he kissed her on her mouth and then turned and left. He did not look back, but hugged his children and patted them along the way, as they formed a loose chain to see him off. They followed him on foot and dropped back only after he mounted Maw and rode away.

By this time, Molly Polly and John Junior had arrived in the yard and were clinging to him, one on each side. Molly Polly held his hand before he mounted Maw, and young John walked alongside, wanting to hold something of his father's that he could hand up to him as a last gesture of separation. He treasured holding Jack's twelve-pound rifle and handing it to him at the last minute to be holstered into the saddle.

As the scout and spy headed out once more, he had traveled but a short distance when he heard a noise behind him. He had expected it and it would have been a disappointment had he not heard it. He did not look back except to stop Maw at the last minute. He reached down with one hand and swept up Molly Polly onto his horse. He let her sit in front of him, holding the saddle pommel. Just a few steps behind her in this continuing race of brother and sister, John Junior charged headlong, panting breathlessly into the waiting horse's side. Jack then reached down and grabbed him under both of his arms, and all three rode Maw at a "clip clop" pace for a hundred yards. The young boy sat behind his "pap" with arms around his waist, glancing up adoringly at the back of his father's head. Molly Polly, bouncing up and down in front of the saddle, played with Maw's mane, swinging it from left to right, singing a little girl song, totally content with her strong father protector. And they rode.

"Jack" Beckham was leaving home once again, but not before riding together with these two a little farther. Finally he lowered them both gently off his horse, and waved good-bye.

Riding forward proudly and purposefully, he was several inches taller than most men he knew. At six feet two inches, he easily carried one hundred eighty pounds of lanky body. He had unusually long, muscular arms. His old-looking face had but one feature of "warmth," his blue eyes, and even they became steely and narrow when he was angry.

Jack's looks were distinctive, with his hawkish appearance and twice-broken nose. His thick black, but increasingly white-streaked, hair extended below his neck. Most days he wore deer hide moccasins or brown leather knee-high boots. Twill pants and a black waistcoat over a flax woven linen shirt completed his attire. The soiled black slouch hat that he always wore was a trademark. When his friends saw the hat at a distance, they would announce "surely Jack."

He was in truth a scout and a spy, although he made a living in other ways. He had a reputation as a breeder, trainer, and trader of race horses in addition to being a farmer and a sutler, purveying various wares. He was an ordinary man to his children, who loved him in the only role they knew, but his increasing reputation as a mercenary made him dreaded by many. That reputation, however, was the reason for this trip.

Because of the times, he had become a hated and wanted man by his Loyalist and Tory neighbors, and was distrusted by those who took neither side. They were wary of him from tales they had heard. Accounts of Jack's deadly skills were hotly discussed subjects among some settlers. Everybody along the Pacolet and the hard northern corner of the upcountry seemed to have witnessed his skills or knew someone who had. His wife had heard these stories from their closest friends, such as Mr. Hodge of the Pacolet, but Jack and Elizabeth never discussed the worst aspects of his trade, which involved the life or death of some. Elizabeth could accept the role of her brother, Colonel William Henderson, an officer in the Continental army. But as a spy, Jack had a shadowy side that she did not speak of.

It did not matter what Elizabeth knew for fact or fiction. Tories and Whigs, enemies and friends alike, swore that they had seen "old Jack" kill two men at two hundred yards. These were vagrant rascals who had murdered a fellow farmer and friend of Jack, leaving a widow with eleven children. They killed the man when he caught them stealing his cows. It was said that it took two days for Jack to track them. Hushed and whispered rumors described the scene. He hid in a barn having circled them and was waiting. He leveled his weapon at his first target, a man leading three cows on a single rope. Amidst the noise of cow bells and the rustle of the beasts on the road, the victim seemed to suddenly fall face down, with only a distant muffled sound being heard.

The man's legs were splayed awkwardly on the dusty path, as the men were walking the cows to be sold at a market near Grindal Shoals. Jack patiently reloaded his flintlock while the second thief walked up from behind the cows and looked in stunned amazement at his fallen friend. The second peering man, hands on his knees, was bent over curiously looking at his companion when Jack shot him beneath his jaw, exploding the large artery in his neck.

This story was a favorite of Jack's boyhood companion Randolph Mabry of Turkey Creek, made more believable by Mabry himself, a good storyteller of irrefutable character and repute who used "educated words" gleaned from his constant reading of the Bible. He had been alerted by Samuel that Jack would be in the Cedar Shoals area soon.

Jack would first see Maggie and then wanted Mabry to be with him when he talked to the farmers about their protection in this war against the British. Jack would be comforted that Mabry, a larger landowner, would also have interest in the outcome at Charlestowne, since he was credible and worthier than the malcontents and landholders who were hiring him. Jack dared to think that having Mabry there might influence men who sought easy gain to become more daring to do the right thing, no matter the outcome on the coast. His intuition, however, told him this was a low probability.

These were worried times.

Chapter Two

Maggie, Family, and a Few Friends

Knowing the Cedar Shoals territory, Jack made the trip to Maggie's in just over a day and a half. As he later traveled farther south toward the coast, he would be less familiar with the terrain. He spent a night in the lowlands near Maggie's farm and arrived midmorning, stopping to peruse the farm from some distance with his powerful nautical spy glass. What he saw was reassuring. Everything was in order.

Slave women and men, and children of slaves, were abundant in the yards and land near the main house, most washing clothes in iron pots, some feeding the hogs in a large pen, and others leading horses toward the blacksmith. Jack approached the main house on Maw, watching to see the reaction to his appearing out of the woods. Anxious not to be surprised by belligerent neighbors, Tory or Whig, Maggie kept a fire ladder permanently leaning against the log and wooden shingled house, as well as a ladder on the roof leading to the chimney. The ladders were used to quickly put out any fire on the wooden shingled roof. Also, the first farm person who saw intruders at a distance would climb the ladder and look in every direction and holler to those in the yard and the house.

Jack watched for a reaction as he left the forest line and waited to be seen. When a slave boy, Amos, saw Jack two hundred yards away, he climbed the ladder and waved both hands in recognition, voicing Jack's arrival to everyone within hearing distance.

Jack rode into the farm and was greeted by a smiling Maggie and her closest friend, the wench Easter Benjamin, a slave woman from the South Carolina barrier islands whose age was guessed to be over seventy-five. Maggie looked unusually fresh and happy, not always the case with the burden of doing a man's work overseeing slaves on eight hundred acres of forest and plantation. She excelled at "men's work" and competed favorably with the men at markets, auctions, and the horse sales she frequented.

Maggie gave her usual greeting, "My brother!" and continued. "You are still well and Maw is still beautiful!" Half-grinning as he dismounted, Jack replied, "And you is still pretty but nay as pretty as Maw."

Nodding his head to pay regards to the popular and fabled Easter, Jack walked with Maggie toward the main house. She sat on the front step while Jack leaned against a hitching post near her. People at work bustled around them.

Maggie asked, "Are you carrying wares? I have the need of spices and oil of rosemary, as much as can be had, and oil of aniseeds, jimson root, cloves, and juniper berries. I need prickly ash."

Jack said, "I am in the next days to be at the coast to see what happens with the British who are there…what is to be, or what happens to ours who are defending. I am bartering with some 'unsettled folks' in this place, so I will bring you back all the best from the wives and merchants. I'm carrying things with me now, trading for when I am there…you needing scalps?" he asked, grinning.

"No," she laughed. "Who will be with you?"

"Samuel and the Catawba Soe. I will be at a barn of my choosing on Fishing Creek. Rand Mabry will be there but he does not go to Charlestowne."

"Samuel is to be with you?" Maggie asked.

"Aye, at the barn, but he will be with Soe in traveling and we will meet at the Bay Street Hawthorne Tavern. I needs you to have one of your men ride to Mabry's and inquire about him after I am gone. He is of some courage to be with me at this barn at a night time, for maybe he will be against them men that will be there.

"Hellfire!" he sneered, looking away, "most of them farmers is no good and I ain't agreeing with them no matter what is said. They is all greedy and jest wants to be on the side that wins. So we will talk and I will go to Charlestowne to see what happens, and—"

At that instant the slave Amos shouted, "Men's comin'!"

Jack ran to the front of the main house and looked up at him. "Where? What direction is they?"

The slave sounded distraught. "Lawd, suh, they is coming from all sides…many men's….looks like some has big knives, suh…oh Lawd!…many Tories!"

Jack cursed and ran to get Maw while Maggie called for Easter to get her own gun as well. She had no idea which Tories might be in the group but a large gathering had to be bad. They were sure to be people she knew, neighbors who were getting meaner and more aggressive as the days got worse, with harder feelings among both the Loyalists and those who hated the British.

Amos called in a weaker voice, "Seeing lots of folks, Massah. No ones can't get away." Jack knew he was trapped. He made a rapid decision to get to the large hog shed, nearer the woods, and lead Maw to the other side of the shed where they would be hidden from view by pens that held hogs and pigs. He planned to keep Maw away from the muck and slop of the pens, so she would be on firm ground, ready to run quickly.

He had no choice but to hide in the shed with hogs and surprise anyone who came too close to him. Within minutes, fifteen or more men rode hard into the plantation yard shouting to each other. Maggie stepped with purpose off the step of the house with a pistol in her hand and met the first man face to face. He reined up in front of her and said, "The widow Maggie Land?"

"Of course," she said with scorn, "this is my place and who are you?" even though she recognized him as Hovis Crump, a dirt farmer of little means and a friend of several ne'er-do-well men in the broad community of Cedar Shoals, Rocky Creek, and Rocky Mount.

He said condescendingly, "No place for a woman farm head. Is you one of them or is you loyal?"

"I am loyal to myself and these people," she said sharply and gestured with a wide sweep of her arm toward Easter and the slaves stand-ing in the yard. "I am too busy to be riding around, telling you and oth-ers to do something. I don't care, so git off my place and go somewheres to be bothering someone else."

Peering out through the slats, Jack noticed that many of the men had gotten off their horses and were moving about, going behind the house. Only six men stayed in front of the big house while others were busy doing something behind the house and in the side yards.

It soon became apparent they were rounding up slave men. They appeared with several young slave men and boys and were herding them toward the middle of the yard. Crump sneered and said to Maggie, "We is taking these and you ain't to say nothing. We needs your kind to stay down and be no hindrance to what is going to be happening. You ain't taking no sides but we is, and we are to be with the British when all this is done."

The slaves were panicked. Men were being pressed into slave service by Tories for gain with the British and King. The practice was common and talked about among poor whites and stragglers. The greatest fear among blacks was forced slavery, to be sold on British ships that traded to the Indies. Slave owners like Maggie feared this happening too, for the British had little respect for slaves unless they took up arms against the colonists. All Maggie's slaves were loyal to her and had been so ever since they had lived on the Lands' plantation.

Maggie protested loudly, cursing at this thievery. She now had her gun menacingly leveled in her hands as she talked, but several men had guns pointed in her direction. Easter was looking at Maggie and shaking her head softly and muttering under her breath, "No, Miss Maggie…ain't worth no troubles like this."

The men collected several more slaves while four desperate women clung to their men as they were led away, with children tagging along behind them. This sight made Crump and his men even bolder and they smirked at the idea that more slaves might be sold as a family, including children. Most of the Tories were leaving the farm while Crump and two others stayed and held Maggie at bay. One man said,

"You better put that firelock away, woman, or you will be dead over these peoples."

They did not notice that members of the British Legion, Tarleton's Loyalist dragoons known as "The Green Horse", were approaching, the sound of their coming muted by the Tory men's horses and the cries of slaves being taken away. These sounds were joined by that of terror-stricken and wailing slave women in the yard calling out to those being taken away. Masked by the sound of this calamity, the British and volunteers of the Legion approached closer, still unheard by Tories in the yard.

Jack watched the scene with alarm. Maggie was being detained by Tory irregulars who were more desperate and predatory than Tarleton's experienced Loyalists or those commanded by British Regulars. It would be worse for him with the Legion, for under trained officers they searched farms in great detail, including lofts, barns, smokehouses, corn cribs, and spring houses, looking for anyone against the King. Execution would be immediate and Maggie had plenty of oak trees for hanging. If he were discovered, Jack's only recourse would be to shoot the man nearest him and ride Maw, depending on her great and unmatched speed. His worry would be she might be shot and he would be captured. He was too well known to survive even a trip to the Camden district for a trial.

The dragoons, made up of American Loyalists mainly from the northern colonies of New Jersey and New York, rode into the yard with great authority, surprised and quickly engulfed the leaders of the Tory irregulars.

"Nigh unto twenty," Jack muttered in frustration to himself, guessing at the number of green coats. All of the well trained British Legion were wary of their new surroundings, their horses prancing nervously, and several of them were instinctively reconnoitering the area. Two dragoons started in the direction of the hog pens and smokehouse. Others circled around the house, and three quickly got off their mounts and stormed inside. Jack slowly pulled his long rifle up to his chest, stepping back into the muck to position the gun behind slats. He looked back toward Maw and mentally calculated the time to get to her after firing.

One of the officers, an older man, was talking to Crump who now looked very much a man not in command, but a subservient person taking orders. A much younger Legion officer rode up quickly and joined them. This taller, handsome and distinguished man of bearing dismounted and stepped up to Crump. The three talked while Crump, somewhat defensively, gestured toward Maggie and then toward the slaves who had just been taken. Suddenly the younger officer slapped Crump with the back of his hand with such force that he knocked him to the ground. He drew his sword and swatted the man with the flat side of his blade, across the man's face, with a strike that sounded loud and drew instant trickles of blood. He stepped up to the prostrate man and kicked him heavily in his side. Crump doubled up from the impact and yelled.

"Bind this fool," the older man called to two dragoons, and the men approaching the hog shed turned and ran to lay hold of Crump, one addressing the commanding officer as "Major." They forcefully took the prisoner away from the group to be tethered behind a horse. Jack saw the young officer bow gracefully to Maggie, as if in respect, while the other men joined and bowed with courtesy to her. She and the young Major walked to the side of dragoons and talked.

Jack had heard of general deference to women from the British, but this was unexpected for him, given his present state of dislike for the King's men. Some dragoons, on a hand command from the Major, dashed on their horses to catch the Tories who had left; in minutes Jack saw the slaves returning, many jumping up and down in jubilation as they ran back toward the main house. There was no sign of the Tories who had taken the slaves, just the two left in the yard after Crump had been taken away.

The young officer and Maggie continued to talk and it was clear he was offering apologies to her. The house and yard search had been abruptly aborted and in no time the dragoons had formed up in the yard and were preparing to ride away. Maggie waved with appreciation to them as did Easter and several of the slave men and women.

During this scuffle, Jack had quietly mounted Maw and was in a position to get away. He watched Amos climb back up the ladder and heard Amos call out to him, as the Tories and Legion rode away from the farm. Jack emerged from behind the hog shed, the stench of the pen on his pants and boots, and approached Maggie with a questioning look.

She anticipated him and said, "I am not the enemy of these men. They know who I am…and I am," she said mockingly, "the sister of the rightly well-known Jack Beckham that they have heard of, and would like very much to have 'come to dinner' here."

She smiled sarcastically at Jack with this remark, who looked at her and appeared more grateful, wondering at his good fortune at escaping due to the wiles of his sister.

"Damnation," he said in relieved jest, "Colonel Henderson can use you…you is wasting time on this land."

"Did you bother my swine?" she said.

"They is fine. They could not stand my smell, I am certain," he answered in a practiced repartee with his independent sister and then turned serious. "How well does you know them Britishers?"

Maggie smirked. "Well enough that renegade Tories had nay steal from me…well enough for me and mine to stay alive as well."

Jack sighed a breath of impatience and looked askance, staring at a row of pine trees in the distance. "I am leaving. See to Rand Mabry's health. I will be back and I will bring you spices. Try to stay 'friends' with all these people," he said to Maggie in a last caustic joust with her. She smiled broadly and waved to him as in his mucked-caked boots and filthy clothes he mounted Maw, anxious to meet the men who wanted to engage him to go to Charlestowne.

He did not look back at Maggie and the others as he made his way to choose a barn, one safe enough to have Samuel bring the men he would be bartering with. He did not want them to know in advance where he would be. He would have to measure his time with them and knew that it would be intense hours before he would be able to leave for his winding, dangerous journey to Charlestowne and the coast.

Jack met Samuel later that day at a grove near Hicklin's Mill on

Rocky Creek, recently swollen from spring rains. Their meeting had been planned in advance. Jack approached when he saw Samuel waiting anxiously beside the creek, his horse tied to a young sapling. He looked distressed and hurried to cover the distance between them on foot. He looked fearful when he took Maw's reins as Jack stopped. Samuel looked up at him and spoke rapidly.

"My sister's been attacked by a deserter who tried to take them. Emily has been cut bad in her face and Lucy is crying much and skeered. Mama has them but all is afraid with Pap gone that others will come and do the same."

Jack jumped off his horse and was only inches from Samuel's face. "Where is this man?"

"Gone, sir. He is on foot. Been gone for half a day. He is a deserter from the English, I would allow. He tried to git ours and sell them for sure. I reckon he is trying to git back to a ship and sail, for I hears tales that he and otherns like him kidnap young ones and sell them…particularly boys, but this man tried to take–"

Jack interrupted and spat the wad of tobacco he had been chewing on the ground in frustration. "Don't make no reckoning. He must be daft to try and take young ones. Who would be wanting to have them near here, without no one knowing? Who was he going to?"

"Don't know but he headed towards Farrar's Landing or the Rocky Mount Mill."

Jack almost shouted at this news. "That is headed toward old Oren Stone's. He has been trying to git me and mine for some time. Hellfire! That is the sorry Tory that is up to the devil's mess all the time. That is where this man is headin!"

Jack looked around in alarm as if trying to determine the best way to track this would-be kidnapper and deserter from the English army. He said out loud to himself. "Might be three miles there and the way is harsh with no easy paths. Good!" Jack said as if rethinking it. He looked at Samuel, who was listening and watching his every move. "You gits yourself back to your own. How bad is my brother's Emily?"

"She was cut in her face while trying to git away and Lucy was down on the ground. That man cut Emily with a long pointed knife, and he dropped it…straight and long. I has it here." Samuel went to his haversack, pulled it out and showed it to Jack.

"A dirk," said Jack. "That man is a Scotsman. He is trying to git back to Ulster country for sure. I am sure he is off to Stone's. You are back to yours as of now and to ride to those others who wants to see me. I will meet you tomorrow night. Tell Randolph Mabry where we are to be… and bring Kit and Johnny. You knows the barn at the Pratt's, near Mr. Sherrill's tan yard?"

Samuel nodded yes.

Jack said, "They is good people…he and his own folks, as is the Sherrill's. I will meet you there at the dark. Wait for me and go and tell all the otherns who is paying me to be there – two hours before the dark."

Jack turned Maw toward the great Catawba River, in the direction of the deserter's travel. The tracks to Stone's cabin were not well marked. The old man had always had a hard time getting to auction and market and getting anyone to travel to him. Trails that might have been good in earlier times were overgrown with trees and brush. The craggy sides of the Rocky Creek seemed to have taken over and now dominated the landscape. Jack knew this was to his advantage if the offending man was a blunderer, not adept at finding trails, and not skilled at covering his tracks.

Jack found he was in great luck. The deserter had been running only a few hours. When Jack looked for unusual patterns of broken branches and bushes, there were several. Maw could circumvent most hedges and underbrush and lose less time in getting there than any horse Jack had ever trained. They would be upon this man quickly if they followed his broken trail. The evidence was better than he could have designed himself. The man was walking through streams and small water tributaries and then through some of the greenest foliage, making fresh boot prints and breaking limbs in the woods, moving back and forth, unsure of a straight path to where he was going. The deserter was looking for Stone's house and was hesitant in his steps.

As Jack thought he was drawing closer to the man, he knew he could not move hastily and with as much noise as when he started. Jack became even more cautious when he felt he had closed the distance and might hear or see the man. He frequently stopped and listened for any movement in front of him.

His sense of smell gave him the first sign of a man. Jack smelled smoke from his left by a stream that led into a small opening in the woods. He followed the smell and walked Maw, her reins in his hands, in order to get closer. When he saw the person, he planned to leave Maw on the outside chance she might make noise that could alert the Scot. She might whinny if she were alarmed, or break a branch with her wide and heavy body.

Jack moved closer and smelled a stronger presence of smoke. At a distance of fifty yards he saw a lone man sitting by a fire. This might not be the deserter, but the odds were remote that another lone traveler was moving towards Oren Stone's cabin in this remote section of woods near the Catawba River.

Jack left Maw loosely secured to a bush. He crept forward watching every bit of ground at his feet, glancing up every few feet to stay on course. He covered the yards without a sound that would betray him. He stopped behind a birch tree and studied the man. He was a burly, heavyset and brutish person in his early twenties, standing about five feet five inches with large bushy eyebrows and long stringy hair that looked typical of an English conscript. The man looked to be a dullard, with a gaping mouth and lips, and large brown broken teeth. He looked close to two hundred pounds but his short stocky legs made his upper body look small. Jack thought he might be extremely dangerous, as he was powerfully built and driven by primitive forces – an "animal" easily led by others.

The young deserter was within sight of Stone's cabin, hog pens, and fenced garden. Perhaps Stone knew he was there and was waiting until nightfall to help this man, or perhaps help was coming to escort the Scot to the river and a ferry south toward the ocean. He guessed the latter. Stone would not "dirty" his hypocritical hands for anyone. Jack wondered how many transients, cutthroats, and deserters had paid the old man and been helped.

Jack dismissed these thoughts as taking up too much time. Then he confirmed that this predator squatting in front of him was the man who had attacked Samuel's sisters, who were Jack's own nieces. The man was nursing a swollen arm that from a few yards away looked to have been bitten. The man was rubbing it and holding it up to his chest as he kneaded the area where one of the girls had apparently bitten. Jack had seen enough. He could shoot the man in the back or he could attack him and cut his throat. But Jack wanted Stone to know that he knew.

He walked unseen from behind a tree and into the clearing behind the Scot, crouched and duck walked for several yards towards the man's back. Then suddenly he started running, his boots barely touching the ground as he charged, still bent over, his arms pumping, his long hunting knife in his hand for the last ten yards. He grabbed the unsuspecting, squatting Scot around the neck, pulled the man's long hair back, and held the hunting knife to his throat.

Jack's powerful grip paralyzed the man, who saw the knife blade tip out of the corner of his eye. With that grip Jack forced the man almost straight up and on his heels and marched him forward. The force of Jack's body was pushing the shorter soldier. With the man's long hair wrapped around the palm of his hand several times as if it were strands of rope, Jack made him go forward into Stone's yard. He forced the man's face upward with his powerful grip while he pressed the knife edge into the man's neck; blood seeped onto the blade. He pushed the man to the farmer's large hog trough, stopping at the end of the trough and pressing the knife even harder. The man was stunned and helpless to respond to Jack's surprise attack, a response to his boiling anger about his wounded nieces.

In a mean and slightly higher pitched voice, he called for Stone to come out of the main house. The old widower fairly crept out on command, his knees weak at the sight of Jack holding this big helpless younger man. Jack, glaring and panting hard from exertion, his teeth bared while he breathed in and out, suddenly took his right boot and with great speed knocked the Scot's legs out from beneath him. The Scot fell face-down into the trough filled with dirty water, dead flies, and old feed. Using all his weight, Jack fell on the man's back, pushing the man's head into the trough until it hit the wooden bottom. The man thrashed his legs, the only part of him that could move, and drowned in less than two minutes.

While holding the man under the water, Jack stared directly at Oren Stone, growling a cruel sound that the old man would never forget. As the man's body bobbed in the water Jack got off him and moved to the front of the trough and pulled his head up. He took his knife and scalped him, doing so in the western colony Indian fashion that settlers had heard about but seldom seen. He cut the hair and ears off in one piece, then walked over to Stone and shoved the mass in his stomach. He had never scalped a man before, not until now. And he had done so in an Indian fashion, not seen in his colony, which Jack would deny if ever confronted.

Stone lost control of his bowels in his fright. He was barely able to stand, his knees close to the ground as Jack sneered at him and walked away. Jack called for Maw, who easily broke away from her loose tether and galloped into the yard. With a glance back at Stone, Jack mounted and rode away. As a prize for Samuel, he had taken a smaller knife with a yew handle from around the man's neck, a knife intended for cutting musket patches. He then put this violence out of his mind as he began to think about the men he would meet and bargain with, for they might be even more dangerous than the unfortunate deserter.

The next night, he met the men in the barn near Fishing Creek. He was fearsome company for them. It was purposely after dark so his face was framed by several tin lamp candle lights, highlighting an unusually red raised scar from a recent six-inch cut across his forehead. By that time he had several more days of white stubble on his jaws. Wads of tobacco pulled away his lips showing irregular broken teeth, with their various shades of stain.

In the barn's dim light, he listened to the eight desperate men who had come to talk to him. They wanted to see him up close. Three of the farmers had never seen him, having only heard tales of harsh justice and sure vengeance.

He asked, on his safe return, for one hundred fifty pounds equivalent of barter from neighbors Young and McCalla in the upcountry judicial district of Camden; Matherson and Farrar from the hamlets and farms of Rocky Mount; and Woodrow, Lackey, Sampson, and Walker from the area of Cedar Shoals near Fishing Creek and the great falls of the Catawba River.

Jack Beckham, variously known as Old Jack, Sutler Jack, Mean Jack, and even "that damned Jack," was the only man they had heard of who chewed tobacco, dipped snuff, and smoked a pipe at the same time. When he was untroubled he had a wad of tobacco in each cheek and a bottom lip that slightly protruded with oozing snuff, dripping a trickle down his chin.

Jack listened. He leaned on his long rifle and stared at the men, spitting from time to time not far from their feet, and shifting the tobacco in his cheeks. At one point when three men stepped close to Jack to make an angry point about land and possessions and their best chances with the British, they naively formed a semicircle a little too close to him. He pointed at them once with his finger and they stepped back wordlessly.

The conversation continued among men who did not trust him. Walker had asked, "What if you get captured or kilt at this?"

Jack answered indignantly, "I ain't gonna be neither. Worry 'bout yourself and not me. If'n you that worried, leave now, or keep your scrip or come with me."

Matherson, who had great faith in Jack, sneered at this remark and said, "Jack ain't gittin kilt…others might be, but not him…I ain't asking how many he has to 'walk through' to git back. 'Sides, Jack would never git captured when he has bartering to do…too important!"

The men laughed awkwardly. Lackey, Farrar, and McCalla all questioned, what if something really did happen to him?

"You gits all promises back and you ain't lost nothing…my woman is the one who loses," he said matter of factly.

No matter what was said it would not undo the uncomfortable feeling they had with him. He was simply the best and worst they could find to do this job. They had no other choice.

Jack, throughout the meeting appeared comfortable, but he wasn't. He didn't have faith in any of them, and measured them all as liars.

He had been joined by his invited two companions, boyhood friend, Randolph Mabry, and nephew, twenty-year-old Samuel.

Mabry stood unpretentiously near the back door listening, sometimes leaning against the door and looking out to see Kit and Johnny Beckham, Samuel's brothers, who served as lookouts for an always possible ambush. The two young boys took "watch out" positions fifty yards from the house in the only accessible direction to the barn. If there was an "approach," an ambush, one would fire his musket, mount his horse, and ride away. The other would quickly fire and ride away in a different direction.

Mabry also regularly stole furtive looks at a loaded double barrel flintlock fowling gun near him, in case the meeting turned violent, as well it could in a heated, hate-filled discussion.

At the back of the barn, Jack knew there was a hidden .75-caliber musket, complete with bayonet, behind a hogshead of tobacco that he could grab quickly if he needed it. One of Jack's conditions was that none of the farmers be armed, except with their hunting knives. He had no intention of not being armed. They approved without a word of complaint.

Even more intimidating, Jack wore his twelve-inch hunting knife under the front of his belt, fully visible to the men. It measured straight down in front of his pants below his pewter belt buckle. From time to time he rested his hand on the deer antler handle. He had spent time sharpening it to a perfect edge, the blade obvious in the constricted barn light as he stood, impressive, listening, watching the men's eyes intently, catching them several times glancing at the knife.

Samuel, looking slightly older than his years, stood near and slightly behind his uncle. He leaned against a barrel and shifted his footing, often studying the men's faces as Jack had coached him. Jack and Randolph exchanged cautious glances all evening as the meeting flowed with anger, fear, and irritation. Raised eyebrows and a side glance from Mabry spoke volumes.

After more than two hours of impassioned words from the men directed at each other, but often deflected toward the British and the colonies, all agreed to offer barter. Jack received notes on property with a list of horses, farm tools, livestock, and gun powder as payment. Samuel's brothers Kit and Johnny would collect more notes and deeds while he was gone. He had agreed to tell the farmers what took place in Charlestowne when he returned. He would meet them in a barn that he would choose and tell everything. Samuel would ride to each man's farm to alert them just hours before the meeting as to the place. At that second meeting, Jack knew he would make them wait hours before joining them to make sure it was not an "assassination attempt" on him, as he had forebodingly said to Mabry. It could be a bad meeting one way or the other.

One of the men at the end of the meeting had made the mistake of asking Jack when he would be getting back. Jack had glared at him and said, his voice mocking the man's simple question, "You'll know rightly…but not afore." None of the other men challenged him. They never even looked at the man who asked the question, pretending disdain for the question, although they wondered the same thing. What the hard core colonial scout and spy feared most was that all the men who paid him might turn and declare allegiance to the King if the news was bad. What the men knew, without even discussing it, was that Jack would consider them instantly his enemy. They could lose either way.

As Jack left the man and continued his eight-day journey his mind raced with possibilities of what might happen to him and his family. As he moved at night, he reflected on all the people, white and Indian, on both sides in this war. The Loyalists felt that the British had protected them from marauding Indians from the west and had mollified the Catawba Indians, who populated the forests along the Catawba River. This fierce tribe, decimated in recent years by malaria and smallpox, had been a friend of the white settlers but an enemy of most other Indians.

Along with the constant Indian threat from other areas, particularly the Cherokee of the western colony, not far from the Pacolet, certain farmers and settlers felt uneasy. They were used to people from other places trying to take something from them. Now their very neighbors, friends, and family felt the British were their only hope for security.

However, Jack and many others saw this as just another way of losing their property and their rights to yet another source of "freedom."

It was, in fact, a terrible mix of both bad blood and a poor time to resolve the issue. Reverend John Simpson of the Fishing Creek Presbyterian Church had said heatedly from his pulpit: "Those foreigners would keep walking with impunity over a man's rich farmlands, treading on a family's inheritance."

The Beckham children's first cousins lived away from this area, nearby on Sandy Run, the Grindal Shoals, near the Pacolet. They were the children of Elizabeth's brother, Colonel William Henderson. They formed a riotous group when they came around. But they also provided a veil of safety to his children, as William was a Continental officer in Sumpter's army and just as wary of neighbors' designs of revenge and hatred as was Jack. It was a Henderson-Beckham family that turned inward for fun and play, while always remaining vigilant.

His enemies might have outnumbered his friends for Jack could only see his relatives covertly and he did often, particularly young nephew Samuel, son of his brother, Thomas. Samuel, taught to read and write by a schoolmaster who boarded in Rocky Mount, enlisted with his own brothers Sherwood, Solomon, Laban, and Allen to fight against the British. So did Samuel's cousins, Simon, Russell, and Reuben. Samuel's first cousin, Abner, also of nearby Rocky Mount, had developed a reputation as a fierce fighter who idolized his uncle Jack. Only Kit and Johnny, Samuel's brothers, were not allowed to fight and remained at home. Even Samuel's Uncle William, Jack's older brother, served in the militia.

But more vulnerable than Jack was his sister, Maggie. Her husband had been a prominent young man, Tobias Land, whose family had almost lost their property to a shady Loyalist called Jadrow Eddards. The Land family owned property where a canal had been planned for more access to the Catawba River. It would have been the centerpiece of the family property, but it had not happened. That changed when Tobias was mysteriously killed in a hunting accident and was "found" by Eddards. Tobias was with a party of six, and none said they saw the accident where he was shot by a hunter's fowling gun in his chest.

Ironically, all later turned out to be extreme Loyalists. Tobias, being the only son of deceased parents, left the land to Maggie, who had no apparent way to maintain the land or even pay the taxes.

But the land was kept. A slave family, free slaves who lived on the property, kept up the land. They brought relatives from the barrier islands of South Carolina at Maggie's insistence. Soon, over twenty relatives of the former slaves lived on the property with her. Even after Tobias' death, production actually increased, to people's wonderment and Eddards' frustration .He had offered to buy her property only one day after her husband's funeral at a price so insulting Maggie never even answered him. Later he had tried to get a court justice to change her tax evaluation on the property, even falsely claiming back taxes owed. Nothing came of it after decent neighbors, who felt sorry for Maggie, scolded Eddards.

In 1787, Maggie loaned fifty of the eight hundred original Land family acres to the slave family of Easter, who had helped raise Tobias and many Beckham babies and was much loved. Her family became the first black family to have any direct access to land in the upper Camden district. It almost caused a riot at the courthouse when rumors spread that Maggie would try to sell them land. This gossip caused such anger among many white landholders that it branded Maggie forever as a "troublemaking woman" who did not conform.

It was not only the largest cooperative "work the land" agreement of any kind to a slave family it was done by a woman who had not remarried after her husband's death. She ran a man's farm, hired more slaves, and consistently outbid other men at horse and cattle auctions. She took tobacco and grain to the market herself and, perhaps worst of all, went to church by herself, often bare-headed. She wore a hat only at baptisms, and at Christmas and Easter services.

Maggie was still in her late twenties. She was tall and most attractive, five feet, seven inches tall with auburn hair and the bluest of eyes. She walked with a certain gait that said she was in authority, and with an assurance that might intimidate many younger men. She, as a widow, spurned a lot of suitors, Jadrow Eddards among them. None of her relatives knew how much money or property Maggie had.

Jack had heard, and knew it was true, that Eddards had once attacked her when she went to him in his position as Justice, which he had coveted and finally secured from the local British authorities. Eddards fancied himself a politician, and he secretly longed for a higher role of authority, even governor of the British colony of South Carolina. At the time Eddards was serving in the appointed position, recording deeds on property and notes taken on livestock, Maggie had gone with a slave boy and Easter in the middle of the day to get a livestock note recorded. Alone in the cabin office that Eddards used, with Easter and an older slave man, Bartholomew waiting outside, he caught her off guard and tried to force himself on her.

Maggie spat in his face and struck him with her open hand in his face, stunning him and knocking the glasses off his nose. Leaving the cabin room almost at a run she brushed past the men as they walked down the length of the yard to enter Eddards' door. She heard snickers from the men. She could imagine Eddards, thirty years her senior, grinning with gapped teeth, a red spider-veined face, telling yet another lie to cover himself and his pathetic failed manhood.

He was the worst of those who moved back and forth, with no loyalty, riding on the loss of fortunes at the expense of others; he was neither Tory nor Whig, but a hypocrite and liar. Already it was a bloody civil war, with violence – even murder – widespread within the southern colonies.

Chapter Three

British Siege In Charlestowne

During the journey on horseback, Jack avoided known Loyalist areas en route to the Congaree River and the great wagon road that went up the colony from the low country to Kings Mountain. Later, he skirted St. Matthews, then Moncks Corner, circling impassable brush and trees, even backtracking on two occasions. On May 10, he finally reached a land mass overlooking Charlestowne Harbor. He had reached it by way of barges over inland rivers and finally the Cooper River by ferry, passing Daniel Island and then Lampiers Point before getting safely past Hog Head Channel and reaching land again.

The beautiful capital city was the fourth largest in the colonies after New York, Boston, and Philadelphia. On arriving, he was keenly aware of his need for rest as he looked out over the water and the town. He worked as quickly as possible, fighting fatigue, calling on visceral intuition for energy and survival. He fed Maw wild oats and a bag of corn he had brought, and let her drink from a stream close to the opening of woods. He looked for a place to hide her, finding it in a primitive growth of wild myrtle trees and bushes, and cut a rough opening for her in the thicket. He tore at branches with his hands, cut others with a hatchet, and threw the brush into a pile to use as camouflage for the horse. Maw, carrying Jack's tools of survival, pawed and jerked her head, snorting at blow flies.

Finally, he took her reins, while whispering gruffly but "singsong" to the tired animal. He removed from Maw the saddle bundle she had been carrying. Making a whistling noise with his teeth, he signaled, and she obeyed mechanically and entered the middle of the thicket. She responded quicker when Jack tugged at her reins, saying "shoosh, shoosh" and striking her buttocks. As tired as he was, he went through a trainer's practice with a horse as valuable as Maw. He rubbed her down and checked her hooves, all the time talking to her in a mellow and soothing voice. He brushed her face and mane and checked her tail hair for matted leaves and cockle burrs. As he finished he went in front of the horse and soothed the short hair on her face again.

Jack, this redoubtable warrior with people, was a lover of horses. Unseen to any human outside his family, he then finished his chores with Maw by pressing his face against hers, and with great affection stroked her cheeks as he whispered to her. She butted him fondly on his shoulder and chest as she often did if he did not tarry long enough with her. Jack would pull away finally and mutter "fancy girl" and pat her several times on her side before leaving her; this was a daily ritual in war times or peace.

He carefully disguised the opening with the cut brush and limbs he had piled up. In a short time he had completely hidden Maw. He looked back once at the thicket as he walked away, then made his way to a live oak he had picked out earlier where he would spend the night. This manner of stealth, high up in a tree, was used only when he was alone in the forest with no chance of being followed. It was the most perilous of places to be, but provided him a vantage point to see at a distance first thing in the morning.

He always looked for a tree with no low-lying limbs, one that looked as if it could not be climbed. The horse would stand attentive for over an hour before she would begin to sleep with one hoof lifted slightly.

Looking up at the aged, moss-laced oak, he chose a sturdy limb twelve feet off the ground. He fashioned a tight hemp rope and threw it up and over the limb. It caught perfectly the first time, looping over a sturdy branch. When the other end was in his hands, he threw another lighter rope over the same limb and tied his survival belongings to it.

Now he knotted the heavier first rope and pulled himself up the side of the tree, walking against the huge trunk until he reached the large limb. He sat on the limb and hauled his equipment up with the lighter rope, then climbed to another higher limb, part of the tree where he could not be seen from any ground-level direction.

He settled in for the night, having carried everything he had with him. He placed blankets, hatchet, a tomahawk, and sparse food in the limb above his head. He wrapped a rope around his waist and tied it to his "sleeping" limb for the night, thirty feet high above the dense, leaf-matted forest bottom.

Jack lay wearily against the tree mass, the long hunting knife tied to his belt with rawhide, and a much-used spy glass tucked in at his waist. Across his lap was the long rifle. He would feel the gun between his legs and cradled against his chest all night. His gun was his life and, just as importantly, his reputation. It was a true long rifle, 50-caliber, a special weapon he used as a marksman and sniper without local peer. He had worked with a gunsmith for two weeks, watching Uriah Peden, a man he trusted. Peden also respected Jack for his hunter's skill. The gunsmith fashioned a gun for him, someone whose woodsman's skill was unlike others. It had a forty-inch barrel. He had witnessed the process of rifling the barrels with a steel tooth rod, the cutting spirals as the rifling rod was forced into the iron. Jack had made the selection of maple wood for the stock.

Jack used gunpowder bought from the English through fellow traders. He procured through barter the best linen to patch the lead ball that was inserted into the barrel, greased with turkey fat. He was practiced in ramming in the lead projectile fast with his ramrod. He was often in a position to get off three shots in what most men might think was a very short time. On one occasion, someone had charged him from seventy-five yards away and, not knowing his skill, left themselves open to the second and surprising rifle shot.

Sitting in the tree that May evening before war amidst the smell of wild flowers and pine trees, unseen to anyone who might have passed in the twilight, Jack continued to think about family, although his thoughts were fast-changing and bearing much on what he might find in Charlestowne.

In times like these he always felt comforted, armed with his various fierce weapons, his knife remaining close at hand. He pulled his sweat-soiled and worn black hat down over his face, and listened intently for a few minutes as night insects sang their evensong. A cicada was above his head, chirping an early summer call. Jack whistled softly one last time to Maw. He heard her response, a whinny breaking out of her slumber, very distinctive. But as he drifted out of alertness, his thoughts continued to keep him partially awake.

His last thought before a light sleep was of young nephew Samuel. He might be traveling ahead or behind Soe, and they would meet him in Charlestowne where they would all, secretly if necessary, witness the victory or surrender of the beautiful city. He thought about the young popular Samuel being able to read and write.

The neighbors gossiped that the handsome, affable young Samuel liked people, and that Jack liked to kill people, which was not entirely true. Jack favored killing Tories and foreigners...he always hesitated, if not just slightly, before killing anyone he disliked.

The next morning Jack heard a rumble in the distance. It was thunder-like, but muffled. Quick thoughts shot through his mind. He was safe, another night uninterrupted, away from home.

Resisting an urge to drop his chin on his bunched-up weskit and rest more, he looked around his tree to see what he may have missed last night. He glanced to his left toward Charlestowne and saw an even brighter sun rising than usual in May. The sky was eerie and murky, but there was much light over the city.

Preparing to throw his baggage on the ground he was startled to hear another roar, followed by another. This was not thunder but man-made. It was unmistakable cannon fire from more than one source. Then another and another cannonade, a repeating, and all at once a thundering that meant cannons were firing at one target, and it was Charlestowne.

Jack jumped to a higher tree limb for a view with the mariner's spy glass that he had traded for a knife in this same town two years ago. It had served him well. What he saw in larger image was a city partly on fire with fire bomb "hot shot" projectiles from British ships as well as "carcasses," bombs with apertures in them and flammable material inside set on fire. He watched in amazement as the arch of the shells plumed white, tailing up and then dropping on the streets and buildings with such accuracy that he was reminded that England indeed ruled oceans. The great Royal Navy had no counterpart except a French fleet that had not helped him or any other colonists in the upcountry.

He realized it was still an hour or more before full dawn and that part of Charlestowne was burning. He hurried to throw down his belongings and rappel himself, while he called boldly to Maw. She came at a gallop, up and anxious before Jack, her ears having detected the earlier bombs he had mistaken for thunder. Grabbing all his equipment for pretending to be a sutler in Charlestowne, he looked hurriedly at bags with rye whiskey, knives, and a cache of odd items to be sold on the street. He included hatchets, tomahawks, and three scalps of Indians killed four years ago. They had dried to a smaller size, but would nevertheless be prized by English soldiers who would use them to brag falsely of their exploits.

He planned to meet Soe outside Charlestowne before entering the city. They would become an upcountry "older man" and an Indian with no remarkable features, just a "savage" to English and Americans alike unless they knew markings, horses' brands and hair.

Soe always dressed so that he presented no visible threat to colonists. He kept a deer hide cover around his shoulders to protect him from the weather and only wore ribbons in his hair. He wore shirts and pants like settlers and even leather boots, foregoing animal skin moccasins. He did not stand out.

Jack's nature was to always change to a slower gait when walking in the city, looking somewhat hesitant on purpose, just someone selling goods, and he did not initiate conversations with strangers. The most active gestures coming from him would be showing a piece of merchandise to a passerby with a soft forward thrust of the merchandise with one hand, the other by his side waiting for a comment. Soe would be stoic and sitting down, looking around very cautiously. He and Jack would exchange grunts or Catawba one-word syllables with their voices pitched lower or higher to indicate their level of communication to each other.

Soe understood English, but no one knew it. Jack understood the Sioux variation of the Catawba language. Soe could write several words and Jack never could. They played a role. A practically "mute" savage and a country sutler needing to sell wares and practical objects to men of the city, farmers, soldiers, adventurers, and men who were drunk.

Jack never took full advantage of men drinking whiskey for they could take up too much of his time. But if they talked about what was going on, he listened until he was tired of their loose tongues and had learned all he could learn from them.

The Catawba would have no wares except what would ordinarily be expected of him among all strangers. Soe carried flints for guns, some arrowheads, beads, silver pieces that could be melted, and bags of herbs that still held some mystique, as well as practical use, for white settlers in their cooking. This was his "trade."

He carried no rye whiskey. It was too dangerous for white men already drinking to just try and take it. He never carried scalps. It would be an immediate cause for death, for no one would believe they were anything but white men's, or worse, white children's, scalps. Scalps would shrink after a while and children's scalps and men's scalps all looked the same, especially to drunken men and foreign soldiers.

Jack took four hours to get from his place on the riverbank with a view of Charlestowne. He was looking for an opening into the city that was unguarded and bustling with people and traffic. He took in every sight: people fleeing the city with wagons and sleighs of goods and furniture. He was unnoticed.

As he approached Boundary Street from the west of town, towards the sea wall with the tree stumps and branches of abatis thrown up around the city for protection, he saw a sluggish, plodding Soe astride his horse Sula, already ahead of him. Jack caught up as Soe slowed down even more, not looking back. Not conversing, they rode a few feet apart into the main city boundaries on Charlestowne Road, looking every bit the part of two men needing to sell anything, even in war time.

What he and Soe would see, and report to farmers in the little hills, were English ship cannons roaring; they would hear of ten thousand English, German Jaegers, and Scottish soldiers on James Island anxious to claim the city, anxious to reap its many rewards of booty, food, whiskey, and compliant women. Jack hoped he would learn more from hysterical citizens in all this maelstrom of just how desperate the colony of South Carolina might be against an overwhelming force of men at arms.

Jack and Soe's biggest gamble was to get in the city and stay there without getting killed by the enemy or Tories. They could be thought to be militia if they encountered British, or malcontents sent by the British into the city to do harm to citizens before their advance. Jack stood a chance of being recognized if any Loyalists were in Charlestowne anticipating an English victory. There were already enough Charlestowne citizens doing the same and becoming Tories, but he knew that people would travel long distances to be on a winning side in order to claim land, money, and power.

Jack thought of the kind like Jadrow Eddards and others from the area of the fish dams of the great falls and the creeks near his family's homes. Any unexpected shout of recognition from someone could turn immediately to his getting away or killing the person before fleeing. If challenged by a sentry, Jack would call out "Sutler...trading man!...wares and goods!...trading man!" If stopped and pressed he would disdain Soe as an ignorant savage helper who could speak no English. Generally adults did not pay attention to Soe. Only children laughed and made fun while backing up from Soe or hiding behind an adult.

Soe, as they traveled, only looked ahead if Jack spoke to him. No one cared or suspected that Soe was semiliterate and remembered faces while Jack was talking to prospective buyers.

As they passed the first abatis, with several more to go, a young militiaman sentry called to Jack. "From where do you come?" Jack lied in his best upcountry voice, a harsh sound of vowels, "The Orangeburgh... traveling to sell...we long day's travelers," meaning they had traveled more than three days. The young man looked past them and the goods clanging on their saddles and saddlebags.

No one challenged them thereafter, as Jack and Soe set their sights on where they would end up: on the grass across the street from the Hawthorne Tavern on North Bay Street. Jack and Soe would sit across the street and wait for passers by. They would entertain looks and gestures and then questions from men going in and out of the tavern.

Soe would sit on a blanket mending a blanket with the tools of his trade spread before him, never approaching anyone.

Jack always was putting a handle on an ax or a small handle on an iron hatchet. If it fit, he would look around, take it off again, make small adjustments and "fit" it again. He often "fitted" several ax and hatchet handles in a day's work, all the time aware if anyone watched him at length. All things made by him were for public show and were not fierce or weapon-like; they were tools.

He sold rye whiskey to men who were vulnerable or those that he wanted to stay longer and talk to him; most was sold to younger men. Jack sold no guns but had a flintlock always out of view behind him under a blanket. His best protection was his knife under his frock and shirt. His best weapon for escape though was Maw, who was also nearby.

He could mount her and shoot if he had to escape, but her very fast legs provided his best chance. Hardly anyone ever noticed she had no saddlebags or gear on her, only a small saddle for Jack and her harness.

On this day Jack and Soe would wait for Samuel to show, for he could pass through the city better than they, pretending to be a citizen and always "looking" for a relative or immediate family. He was actually friends with Mark and Julia Hayes, a younger couple who had family near the Coosawatchie, south of Charlestowne. He could always say he was looking for them, and they would confirm it if asked. They lived on Elliott Street in a small town house with their baby girl, Mary.

Samuel looked young enough that his only worry was being kidnapped and impressed into the British Navy. He also could be attracted to a young woman, which would take his mind off being alert. Jack always chided him about young women, and on one occasion scared a young woman away with mean looks when she appeared to have a lingering, flirting interest in Samuel.

Jack knew, however, this was an unusual time in all their lives. Charlestowne was burning in certain sections, and they had to appear to be just merchants trying to take advantage of whatever people wanted to buy in a hurry. Jack felt sorry for families scurrying about, but he could not help them. He was waiting to see the British take the city and then leave to begin the uncertain trip back to the upcountry.

As they sat on North Bay watching crowds come and go, the pace became more furious and hysterical. One woman came by crying for her husband. Trailing behind her were two colored servants looking at a loss to help her. They, too, had heard wild rumors that all coloreds were to serve the English or be sold into slavery in the West Indies. Men came by on horseback hardly glancing at Jack and Soe, with small furniture chests on their horses' backs and guns in their hands. More families rushed by in wagons filled to capacity, with blankets on top to cover their belongings.

The most pathetic were young children looking wide-eyed and lost with parents who tried to remain calmer as they watched the city burning. Young fathers had muskets in their arms and knives in their belts, both now seeming woefully inadequate in light of the British and Hessian invasion that seemed so imminent and overpowering.

Jack saw hundreds now going toward Boundary Street and the horn works where most of the American forces were gathered and pouring through an opening in the city fortifications that no one was now guarding. The city was ready for surrender, or worse, total annihilation from fire bombs, looters, and enemy soldiers from several foreign countries.

In all this confusion, one man started to approach the two from across the street. Jack and Soe both noticed he had been watching them; they did not stare back at him but did watch out of the corners of their eyes. Soe was the first to notice when he grunted one word without looking up and while mending an edge of blanket. "Scatre," he said, meaning "white man." Jack did not respond but looked down the street in the opposite direction when Soe spoke. Now that the man was approaching, Jack dropped his head and muttered in Soe's language a warning word which was "evil man." Neither man appeared to have said or done anything, even to those who might be casually watching them.

The stranger walked straight up to Jack and said, "Mountain man?" Jack raised his head as if just now being aware of him. "No," he grunted, "the small hills...the Orangeburgh and the Santee...we trading men, long days' trading men.

"Mountain man?"

"Naw," growled the man. "I am from the Goose Creek where the British are. I am here to git my horse that was stolen a day or two from since I am here. I think he may be yourn unless you have him stabled, since you are here and can prove he's yourn."

Jack appeared nonchalant. "Nay, she is mine," he said calmly. "Been mine fer three yers."

"I don't think so," said the stranger. "That is my horse flesh. I gots me and six hungry men in that tavern says she's mine."

"Tell you what I do," said Jack in return, almost too casual, for the man smelled of whiskey. "I will sell her to you for yer wife, even though my horse is prettier and can run faster than yer wife."

The man seemed aghast at the comment and leaned in close to Jack and said in a whiskey breath, "I think yer right!" And he laughed so hard Jack thought he was daft. He continued to laugh and put out his meaty hand to him, which Jack took as a sign of even more trickery.

The man, in the middle of a laugh, said, "I jest wanted to see what kind of trader you are. I am Edward. I am a trader too, but I have to inquire of you something. Would you like to git some of this bounty before them English make off with all of it or the pox gits ye?"

"Nay," Jack replied again, sounding singularly bored. Then he inquired casually, "What is it you say? Is the pox here? Is the bounty for sale by peoples who are leaving?"

"Naw!" The man said, looking to the side, spitting on the ground, then addressing the greed of stealing. "It is for taking. Peoples are leaving their homes, and the English and them otherns are goin to take it and leave with it.

"We can help these poor peoples by saving it for 'em and giving some back later. I needs help though." He growled, sounding sorry for himself, "There is much to be seen and packed and left with, and then we has to hide it somewhere before we brings it back.

"And for sure the pox is here, peoples dying from it...some ain't even allowed to take and bury their dead outside the city...they has to burn 'em." Edward laughed a peculiar laugh again.

The man was a liar, but Jack was not sure about the smallpox. He knew he would endure this man just so much longer; then Jack asked him the question that would determine his future patience. "Ain't the people safe and ain't them regulars and all these militia men goin' to help?"

The man looked at Jack almost with pity and a superiority that came with "knowing" more than Jack. He breathed his foul breath and got even closer. "Listen, sutler man, I comes from Goose Creek like I be sayin'. Tarleton and his men has kilt and captured Continentals, and captured over a hundred horses at Biggin's Bridge at Moncks Corner, and taken wagon loads of their bounty...muskets and things.

"Your way out of here is blocked by him, and the north is surrounded by them English, Tories, and Hessians. I knows the way out, and they knows me...I will give 'em some silver plate and candlesticks and tell 'em what I knows about the soldiers in this city. Look at this."

At that, he showed Jack a letter from a Captain Swallow of the New York Volunteers, a Loyalist group. It was a letter of safe passage that allowed "Edward the Trader" to pass through lines of soldiers. But if caught by Americans, it would be cause for a trial if there was time, which there would not have been. It would be a speedy execution if there were not time or patience or sympathy on behalf of the Whigs.

Edward continued his lies. "I knows a house where you will be rich enough to add bounty to your self if'n you are with me."

Jack looked bored, but pretended to be faintly interested.

"I tells you," the man continued, pressing Jack, "this town is for them Redcoats and Hessians."

At this proclamation, the trader was really intent on persuading Jack.

"Already old General Ben Lincoln is so scared he has ordered all dogs to be kilt so as not to alarm his men at night and then them shoot each other." Edward laughed and his foul breath was even more offensive in Jack's face. "People been eatin' nothing but molasses and rice for days and some eatin' dogs too. And I knows that the governor is running for the far street.

"One house, Mr. sutler. I needs your help. You bring the savage too. Only thing I ax is that part of what you and me takes to protect from the English, we gives it back to the peoples we help.

"Some of that will be mine. You and the savage can take much. There's two of you and just one of me. I jest want a little for telling you all this. I'm helping you git out of this city right safely."

Jack knew this man was right about the city. He had learned enough so that he could find his way back to the upcountry and report to the farmers. They could make up their minds which government to support, and he could collect legitimately all his barter. But Jack had not heard from or seen Samuel. He and his young relative had a plan to meet at St. Michael's Church at eight in the evening as the tower bells struck, so they both would hear the same bells and "just happen" to be there. If that did not work, if neither showed, Jack and Samuel would meet at the Scots Presbyterian Church on Meeting Street at nine, listening to the same bells from St. Michael's. If they did not see each other there, then it would be the South Carolina Capitol Building on Broad Street at ten. All of these were within ear shot of St. Michael's bells. Failing that, they would meet at Mark and Julia's house on Elliott Street.

If none of the plan was successful, Jack and Samuel would simply retrace their movements and "casually" meet at St. Michael's on the hour and then the Presbyterian Church on the hour. If they still failed to meet, Jack would leave the city as soon as he determined victory or defeat. Everyone was responsible to themselves. It was a plan that allowed no deviation.

Looking at the man, Jack then queried Soe, who appeared disinterested: "Daduhu?" It was both a question and a statement. Jack did not like this man Edward. He knew Soe did not like him. Did Soe want to go or wait?

Soe grunted back, "Tca." It was a clear answer; he would rather go with them.

Jack turned to Edward the trader after a short time and said, "I ain't interested in your bounty; I jest want to sell, but nobody ain't buying, they being so afraid. I will help you if you shows me a way to go back to the little hills. I will see what you talk about…this bounty," he said distastefully to Edward.

Jack was now finally able to look Edward in the face and challenge him with a statement about bounty, replying to the loose talking trader's boast. Jack, ordinarily impatient, had already tired of the man's bluster. Half-smiling, the man named Edward boarded his horse and began to lead them. Soe followed Jack several paces behind.

The trader indicated they were going to Meeting Street, 37 Meeting Street. With that pronouncement he looked smug and said he would tell Jack whose house it was when they got there. Jack watched Edward with a side glance. The uncouth, vinegary-talking and drinking trader chewed a small stick of wood protruding at an angle from his mouth, and looked arrogant about this accomplishment of having talked Jack into doing what he wanted.

They proceeded down Bay Street, and Jack was surprised when they turned onto the very crowded and even more chaotic Broad Street, where the state capitol stood across from St. Michael's Church. It seemed hundreds of people were in their way and hundreds more were moving in hysteria. Why did the trader pick this street, when Elliott or Church Street or even John's Alley might be less crowded?

At the old Anglican Church, the highest eastern point in the city, a town crier reported from the church steeple what he saw through a spy glass, looking to the harbor and to James Island. He called out every few minutes a report: "Camp fires on the island…more fires…ten ships…still in the harbor…ships still in the harbor."

He was calling out every half-hour, then every quarter hour as he had been instructed by General Benjamin Lincoln, Commander of the city. He had been ordered to call out more frequently to try and calm the people's fears, an impossible task.

The trader Edward turned left at the old Church with the tower crier and started down Meeting Street. As he did, two other men seemed to take up pace with Edward, Jack, and Soe. Only Soe noticed what seemed to be an irregular move, even in a crush of people. Soe called loudly to Jack, "Imbarrah iruire! Bad...they come." Jack turned and looked at the Indian to acknowledge his veiled call. Then Jack saw the movement of the men. He said to Soe in condescending English, "Make haste...make haste!" Then in native language, "Mosapede."

Approaching the Scot's Presbyterian Church and Tradd Street, the trader said, "Know whose house this was where we goin?"

Jack shrugged as if not caring.

"The Governor Rutledge, who ain't the Governor...who is now running for his life. He has a lot to be scared for." Edward cackled and chewed his stick. Then, turning to Jack, the man completely changed character. "When we gits there you leave the savage outside. I want what he carries off on his beast. You can have most of yourn, but I am gittin' you out of this town, and you needs me so it will be rightly done between us."

The trader was now flaunting his position. It was clear he had changed demeanor since the men joined in behind him and they approached 37 Meeting Street. As they got close to the house, the trader told Jack to have the "savage wait across the street until they needed him." He then stopped in front of a three-story mansion with beautiful windows running from the top of each floor to the bottom. It had a handsome set of walnut doors and beveled glass in all the windows. Jack believed this really could be Governor Rutledge's house.

As they neared the top of the steps, Edward turned to invite Jack in, gesturing for him to go in first. Jack politely held up his right hand, flat, in a show of declining, a common motion to allow the person in front of him to enter.

Simultaneously, Soe, who had stopped, shouted from across the street holding his saddle and bridle upward for Jack to see. But what turned Jack around was his cry of "YEP IRU!" Jack accepted the message with a stone face, and then not changing his expression turned to the trader and mumbled something inaudibly. What Soe had said was sobering: "Men, they come." It spoke grave warning to Jack.

At the top of the step the trader pushed at the door as if to open it. If Jack had turned back around at that moment he would have seen a surge of gaited movement behind him. The two men following them had dismounted. They were running deliberately in a cadenced stride down the street. One said to the other in measured heavy breathing tones, "The filly."

As they reached the mansion's entrance on the street, one turned to steal Maw, who was tied loosely to the great iron fence. The other slowed his run to begin walking up the steps as quietly as possible behind Jack, trying to do so without drawing any attention. The man left on the street looked at the silky race horse with chestnut coloring and black mane and reached to grab her reins. At that moment the man trailing Jack was being observed by Soe. Left unnoticed in the calculated flurry, Soe placed his .50-caliber flintlock rifle on the back of his horse and sighted the man on the steps, only thirty yards away.

The discharge from Soe's gun was remarkable in its sound on the street. The man was on the fifth step behind Jack and Edward. He was only eight feet behind Jack, already with a ten-inch hunting knife in his right hand and holding it straight down by his side, pointed directly at Jack's back.

Soe's shot was higher than he had aimed. The lead ball hit the would-be assassin in the shoulder socket, virtually separating his arm from his shoulder. The man fell off the steps onto the grass as the gunshot resounded, his right arm already grotesquely turned backwards from the wound, flopping helplessly by his side.

The other man stealing Maw was transfixed and immobile at the noise. He never looked back toward Soe, but at the ground and his partner. He then heard footsteps, looked up quickly, and saw the Indian running toward him. Soe held a tomahawk in his hand behind his head while muttering, sounding something the man had never heard that did not make sense. It was a guttural sound, a low-pitched voice but piercing, "Ka'i!"

At the same time, even without turning around, Jack had an advantage on the man in front of him. He did not look back at the street. With one motion, he had his knife out of his belt and had dropped into a crouch. It was good that he did. Edward the trader was a practiced man of violence. Looking straight ahead, he had started a wide swift motion of a knife that he had concealed in his shirt. He swung angrily with his left hand in an attempt to catch Jack in the throat with his long-bladed hunting knife. But due to the crouching motion Jack had instinctively made, Edward hit the top of Jack's head with the back of his hand.

Jack sprang up and with one powerful move thrust his knife into the man's abdomen. Using his left arm, he pushed the trader backwards while his right knee slammed into the man's lower stomach. He pushed the trader toward the great doors of the mansion, and held the man against the gray stucco entrance and abutment of the house; he had pinned the man's wrist, knife in hand, so hard the man could not have dropped his blade.

Jack stabbed him rapidly: once, twice, three times, then four times in his chest. Edward was already fading and slumping badly when Jack calmly reached down with his bloodless left hand and removed a paper from Edward's weskit; his passage out of the city, which Jack had not forgotten. He rushed down from the front steps of the house onto the street, partially to help Soe, but also to get away from anyone he had not seen inside the house. Soe had stopped in front of the second man with tomahawk raised when Jack hollered, "Hold!"

The second man now realized Soe was not a white man but an Indian dressed as a sutler. He was also now aware of Jack behind him, and he glanced up to see a very bloody knife and realized he was all by himself. This unsettled him totally. It was clear that the Indian had killed his friend, and that Jack had undoubtedly wounded or killed Edward.

Something happened now that Soe had seen and always thought was the most primitive feeling he knew. Jack became, when faced with great danger, calm to the point of distraction. It was as if he was in the "spirited kingdom" that Soe heard about from other men. He had heard about Jack and King Hagler, the former chief of the Catawba's. It was peace flowing through a warrior faced with death and danger.

Jack slowed down. His speech was different. He spoke to the man almost in a whisper. "Why do you come at me?" Then a stunning question: "Sir, you knows me, don't you?"

The man said, "Nay." All they wanted was Jack's horse and to sell it so they could get away to the Black River.

Jack said again in the same voice, "You knows me, don't you?"

The man nodded his head, now almost child-like. "Aye," he acknowledged, then said they were to be paid for bringing Jack to this house.

Soe heard and understood it all and reacted in a primitive fashion. In an instant, to this admission, he swung a tomahawk from his left side partially cleaving the left side of the man's face. Another swing into the bloody mass of the man's face killed him. He stood over the man, momentarily unaware that Jack was already leaving, but he followed quickly and the two men ran to get their horses. It occurred to Jack that he had not yet seen Samuel, who might be dead as part of this plot. It also tore at Jack that he did not know any of these men. He had been discovered; he would have to leave Charlestowne.

Before departing he was near enough to Edward to notice that the trader was still breathing and moaning, his eyes fixed on the elegant facade of the former governor's mansion. Jack ignored him; he would need now to escape a fallen city.

Chapter Four

Captain Swallow

On the street both men realized they had not even been noticed in all this furor. A large group of Continental forces of the First and Sixth South Carolina marched rapidly toward them, and then they passed them. It appeared there were over five hundred men; slaves followed the soldiers, as well as militia marching in a disorganized fashion.

Jack said to Soe, "Manare," meaning we will follow. It made sense. They would be in the best company if they could be a part of a large group. Jack felt that these were men going to fight, and he would stay with them as long as he could to get to the other end of the city.

In the crowd of men, followed by women, young fathers, some children old enough to walk or run, some dogs and chickens, horses carrying family treasures, Jack and Soe fell in. They blended perfectly into the maelstrom. The wailing, shouting, cursing and praying to God for deliverance added to the bedlam.

Jack saw, as did many of the experienced soldiers, that the shelling of the city had been stopped for some time. He knew the town was about to be occupied, and many other worse things could descend on these people. Amidst all this he had to leave Charlestowne without Samuel. He had to leave alive if possible and not be captured. He would surely be hanged if the English found that he carried a rifle instead of a musket, as the rifle was a weapon of a sniper and killer of the King's forces. He and Soe would have to discard theirs at some point, another alarming thought.

He glanced back at 37 Meeting Street once more and noticed people walking over to see the bodies of Edward and his men. They would wonder if these men were Tories, murdered at the last minute for their treachery. Jack could confirm that for them.

He saw up ahead where the Continentals and militia were going to stop. They were approaching the horn works set up near the great square in Charlestowne near King and Meeting Streets and near Boundary Street, where thousands of tattered blue coats and militia were gathered. The men were in the throes of surrender, not only to foreigners, but to fellow Americans who would take up arms and other weapons against their own neighbors.

Jack saw other disturbing sights. Some buildings and homes had been destroyed and burned. Several homes on Meeting Street were half-burned, empty shells of elegant mansions smoking from fires several days old. It appeared some people had died from something other than bombs or fire. They had surely died of the smallpox. Some slaves' remains were being purposely burned in order to quickly get them into a common grave in an attempt to avoid the spread of the disease.

He heard a man shout incoherent curses about women and children killed in the bombardment, who also would be burned if there was no grave to bury them at Scots Presbyterian, St. Michael's, St. Phillip's Anglican Church. Almost instantly, he saw further results of the man's anger. A grandfatherly looking man, an uncle or relative, seemingly of wealth in front of 45 Meeting Street, was digging a grave for what appeared to be a child, while a younger man sat totally grieved and incapacitated.

The mother and wife apparently were not present. Jack realized why when he saw another freshly dug grave. Was this smallpox or shelling? These people could have been English sympathizers and not allowed to bury their dead in a churchyard with Whigs, formerly their friends and neighbors. The anger and hatred were fomenting and mixed with hysteria.

Rumors were the order of the day. There was no coherent chain of communication, just wild assertions and fears that many men would be hanged for their rebel acts of treason, that many would be imprisoned for years on prison ships in the harbor and die of disease. There were rumors that families would forever be separated and lost, that children would be taken for foreign families. And worst of all, no civil order would be forthcoming for violence against citizens. These were some of the people's fears in this May of 1780, with the war now lost. No one could say that these things, partly or almost totally, might not happen.

The Regulars, the Continentals, from several colonies were also badly beaten. They had been reduced to eating one-fourth rations, mainly rice, rotten vegetables and molasses, and had received no regular ration of beef in weeks. Officers and enlisted men looked worn and defeated from the sleepless nights of firebombing and shelling that had destroyed parts of the city. All looked as if they had been in or near a fire with smudged faces; their clothes were tattered and they carried their weapons haphazardly.

The malaise that engulfed the men was so overwhelming that desertion was a great concern weighing on the minds of many officers as they readied the men for surrender. The sight of Lt. Governor Christopher Gadsden, along with other officials, gave rise to the logic that they would be hanged first. None of the lower ranking soldiers was privy to the actual terms of the surrender, which actually included allowances that would have allayed the men's fears. But it was hard to communicate with them.

Most feared any "good" news was a way of placating them. One rumor was confirmed as true. The men would not be allowed to march out with their colors flying. All expectations among the masses of militia and Continentals were that they would surrender their arms, but it appeared no other honor would be given them at all. This confirmed their worst thoughts about a punitive enemy.

Another rumor was confirmed; they could sell their horses, but no horses were allowed to leave Charlestowne, once it was occupied. This disturbed Jack the most. Maw would surely be taken for her beauty and thoroughbred lines, obvious to many British officers.

In all this mass of men, Jack was actually looking for three people.

He was looking for his brother, Thomas, who was at the defeat of Savannah and had marched into Charlestowne with General Benjamin Lincoln. Although Thomas was militia, he would have to hope for parole in a short time to be able to go home, although in defeat, to his family. It was just a matter of how long.

Jack's brother-in-law was another story. Colonel William Henderson, a member of Sumpter's forces, had distinguished himself as a first-rate officer in the Continental Army, was at the siege of Charlestowne with men under his command. Jack would later learn that William had been chosen over others, including the greatly respected Henry Laurens, to lead a foray of two hundred men, Virginians and North Carolinians, against the English dug in around Charlestowne. There they would capture and kill several British and Hessians while losing some, including General Thomas Moultrie's brother. Still it would be construed later as a victory for the besieged Americans in the face of a great and infamous defeat. Jack knew and feared how his wife's brother, Col. Henderson, would be treated. And there was Samuel, who Jack thought must be dead or severely wounded. He had been missing now for almost two weeks.

Jack approached one American officer and said, "Sir, I am rightly related to the Col. William Henderson of Sumpter's men." The officer looked at him and just walked off.

In all this crowd of men, always moving in disparate directions, Jack felt it was hopeless to find the Colonel, Thomas, or Samuel. He began to make plans now to escape the city with Soe. He would take the Charlestowne Road, the main city route out. He would carry his small weapons, his knife and tomahawk, but as out of sight as possible. First, he would disable and throw away his treasured rifle, a long-range and sniper's weapon, a sure hangman's noose if the British discovered it on him.

Soe was also in great danger. He was expendable as folly for some troops that might just decide to kill him and take his scalp in their crazed glory of victory; a real Indian hair piece as a trophy to show in London.

It was acknowledged that Jack and Soe would protect each other to a point, but both realized their horses were their best hopes of survival. They were probably able to outrun any steeds in the English cavalry, for the men of the King's army had to steal many of their mounts from locals and from farms.

Moving away from the masses was troublesome. They rode away as quickly as they could but found that their luck was even greater than expected. The crowd fleeing the city was stunning in its size and its fever. It was a city of fifteen thousand inhabitants and fear was at its peak.

Jack saw an opportunity and seized it. A family of four was struggling with two horses. One of the horses was so spirited and scared of the noise and crowd that she kept bucking and losing the family belongings. The father of the family was now trying to just ride the horse, and his wife, vastly inexperienced, was leading the other horse by its reins. The children were young and kept falling behind. A carriage behind the family almost rode into the family but avoided them with small room to spare. Jack rode up to the young man and said, "I been a horse trainer …you needs help with her…jest help your woman and little ones."

The man looked straight through Jack. He was clearly in shock. Taking the reins, Jack talked to the horse and walked her around in a circle, but still moving forward and holding Maw by the other rein. Soe watched and stayed close. Jack continued to talk and walk in small circles. The horse looked spooked, but the presence of Jack's horse caused the big change in the skittish animal. Jack could see she was younger than Maw. It took several circles and soothing talk, with Maw walking close beside her, sometimes bumping gently against her. The younger horse leaned into Maw with affection as colts do with their mother's; this continued for a little longer as the horse began to settle down.

Jack said to the father, who looked relieved, "Jest walk beside her, your young ones can ride on Maw and your woman should walk with you." The man agreed with a nod, still without words.

They walked like this for several hundred yards toward the city boundary that was still clogged with people streaming out. They looked like neighbors and friends, with Soe dressed as he was and not easily visible under a hat pulled down over his forehead. However, as they walked and rode, Jack looked up to see what he'd feared most. In the distance dragoons were approaching, and they were certainly not colonists. Moving away from the family, Jack went over to a great iron fence and took his precious long rifle and put it in between two iron posts. He bent the barrel as much as he could, making the tip useless; for extra measure, although it could be easily repaired, he broke off the cock of the gun and threw it away. He then threw the rifle toward a marsh. Looking up again, he saw the British and Loyalists still at some distance. He looked at Soe, who acknowledged everything and had already discarded his flintlock.

The men approaching were triumphant. They were mainly Tories. Jack and many fleeing people would be the first unfortunate people that would encounter this group. Maybe this would work for them in the madness of flight. It could be a massacre, accompanied by looting, kidnapping and worse—whatever men of the opposing force decided to take or do in the face of final victory and occupation.

People in front of Jack and his party, at a distance of several hundred yards, were being detained. A dragoon officer, replete with a blue-green and red Tory uniform with silver buttons marked "RP" (for Royal Provincial) on his coat front, sleeves and collar, was approaching. The silver epaulets showed that he was a captain; he was in his twenties possibly, but he was definitely in charge. He rode his horse swiftly forward, his saber in his left hand, shouting instructions to the volunteers. He rode past Jack and Soe and the young family, but later rode back and then stopped near them.

Jack prepared for the fight that could occur— one violent and unexpected swing with his tomahawk, the only weapon of any great damage he had left. He knew Soe would do the same. They would both try to kill the officer and then gallop to the side of the mad crowd and try to ride forward as fast as they could, hoping to be lost in all the chaos. It was their last hope.

The officer spoke to the young father first and asked him where he was going. The young man could not speak. His chin quivered and he cried, tears streaming down his face. Jack was afraid this officer could pattern himself after the notorious Tarleton, who had a reputation of just "sabering" anyone who refused his command or hesitated. Jack hoped this officer, even a volunteer Tory, would know war and recognize a citizen who was helpless in protecting his family.

As the officer asked again with impatience in his voice, a junior officer rode up to him and said, "Sir, Captain Swallow, sir, we have a Regular rebel officer who wants to be onto our side. He offers help." Jack started to move forward, and the Tory dragoon moved his horse in front of Maw. "Hold, sir" he said, and invited the interrupting officer to address him about the turncoat. "Bring him to the fore," said the Loyalist officer.

Jack had blundered into the one man who had signed the transport paper for the trader, Edward, and now he was about to have to get past him or talk to him. The young officer brought the deserting American forward, and Jack felt a further horrible pain of circumstance and bad luck. The American officer was the man Jack had spoken to at the horn works and to whom Jack had said he was a relative of Colonel Henderson.

Jack spoke furtively to Soe. "Great man danger." No one heard him, and Jack noticed that the young father and his family had moved forward in the crowd and were now getting caught up with others.

The Loyalist officer must have sensed something. Others were streaming around Jack and Soe, and it appeared to the Captain that these two men were the healthiest and strongest of people, more sure of themselves than those now fleeing. Most refugees were older, or infirmed, or women and slaves, or groups of children. The Captain looked at Jack and said, "Who be ye, sir?"

Jack glanced over at the defecting American officer, who had not noticed him. Pulling his black hat down slightly, Jack said." Sir, sutler man, goods and wares."

"Where ye be from?" the officer quickly asked.

Jack started to reply when the deserting American officer saw him and pointed directly at him and said something to the junior officer. Jack pretended not to notice, but he saw the expression on the junior grade Loyalist's face when the defector spoke to him. Jack's hand moved casually to the small of his back and to the top of his trousers where the tomahawk was placed under his loose shirt. Soe imitated this move ever so slightly.

Then Jack took a courageous chance that could cause a fight and sudden violence or stall the officer. Jack wondered with lightning thoughts if Captain Swallow remembered Edward the trader, or if the document signed by Swallow for Edward was only one of many he might have issued.

Quickly, before the American deserter and the other Loyalist officer could command Swallow's attention, Jack said, "I comes nigh the Goose Creek. I am sutlering, but there is no business here. I am fixin' to return to the Goose Creek with wares."

Swallow said, "And you are called, sir?"

Jack breathed ever so slightly and said, "Edward, the Trader." He stared into the officer's eyes, looking for a flinch or the widening of his pupils in recognition of a lie. Swallow started to speak when a shout went up from the American deserter that caused him to turn around.

"This man is part of the militia. I seen him in the horn works."

Clearly the deserter was trying to curry favor fast and deliver a prize to the Loyalists to establish himself as a friend of the British invaders.

Jack recoiled only slightly and with feigned surprise, and said calmly, "Nay."

But Swallow had been alerted. He turned to Jack and said, "You say you are Edward?" Then Swallow smiled a knowing grin before Jack could respond, and he moved his mount closer to Jack. Soe was directly behind Jack, intentionally out of the line of sight of Swallow, but he knew there was danger from the moment Swallow moved toward Jack. Soe muttered a very important message to Jack, "Witkru tcarre," meaning he was "ready for battle," and he instinctively and subtly moved Sula closer to Maw.

Still grinning, Swallow motioned with his right hand, beckoning Jack to come closer. This was not Jack's intention. He clutched the cold metal top of the tomahawk behind his back. If needed, his hand would go to the middle of the weapon's wooden handle. He would pull it out and thrust the blade end, with one quick jab of his extended arm, into Swallow's face. With the greatest of hand speed he would then grab the end of the tomahawk and strike a blow to Swallow's head, while Soe would do the same to anyone close to Swallow who could delay them.

He noticed that Swallow was reaching out to put his hand on Jack's shoulder without any malice in his face. Swallow said as if sharing a secret, "Sir, you did your duty?"

Jack's mind raced. He looked squarely into Swallow's eyes and tried to figure the next course of action. He did not answer, but looked at Swallow's other hand, which was harmlessly holding his horse's reins. Jack wanted to react. He looked at the officer behind Swallow. He was effectively talking to the American deserter, who was being ignored by the Loyalist officer, Swallow. All was not preparation for battle from these Tory men. This made for a strange condition indeed. Who was Swallow to Edward? Did he hire trader Edward or did he sign a pass and was told of Edward?

Jack took a chance with his hand still firmly on his weapon behind his back. He took his other hand off the rein and slowly brought out the pass from his coat that he had taken from Edward. He did not open it out or say anything, just handed it to the Captain. Swallow recognized it but did not open it. He nodded and spoke. "A man is no longer a threat then?"

Jack's face looked empty.

"Good sir, I understand," muttered Swallow. "You will be satisfied. You will wait here for our Colonel to give you merit for allegiance."

Jack did not want to wait. "Where is he?" he asked simply.

"Coming!" replied the Captain hastily and with irritation in his voice at the question. He called back to his subordinate, "Bring the deserter."

Jack's mind continued to race. Now the American officer, willing to defect to the British, was in a situation of reduced importance. Captain Swallow believed Jack to be "Edward." So Jack concluded Swallow did not know Edward personally. This dangerous bluff with people, noise and havoc all around him, had worked. But Jack knew he had been betrayed. Samuel was surely dead or captured, and he himself was now thought to be dead. How did Soe place in all this? Jack was sure of him and no one else. But whoever betrayed him might have thought Soe to be there also.

Captain Swallow beckoned the deserter to be "brought quickly." Addressing the American officer now with little disguised contempt, he asked what were his intentions and information he had to share? Looking at Jack and not the Captain, the American said, "That man is militia…he is a relative of a Continental officer. He said it to me."

"Perhaps sir you have heard of Colonel Henderson of the Rebel 6th?"

"I have indeed."

Swallow said, "Can you tell me this man's name?" and pointed toward Jack.

"Nay, sir, do not know him, but he identified himself to me at the horn works."

"I will tell you this man's name," Swallow said with authority. "It is Edward the Trader. He is a friend of the King and he has performed a duty for his country. You, sir, are a deserter and a coward. What say you to that?"

"Begging your forbearance, sir, but I believe he is militia."

"What would you have us do?" the Captain asked and smiled sarcastically with the question intended for Jack.

In his practiced years of deception Jack could be very cunning and deceitful. He spoke. "He is wrong, sir, but he 'pears to be a goodly man. I would let him ride on with me, and we will take care of him."

Jack said this looking at the deserter with a coldness in his voice that was too obvious to the man. The American deserter saw two men in Jack and Soe with whom he did not want to ride. One was a stoic Indian that he now saw for who he was when he was brought nearer. He had no idea from what tribe this man might be. The other, a white man, had blood on his pants and his coat, and he looked experienced in something other than selling wares. Looking at the Tory officer as people came brushing past and in front of them to get away, he said to Swallow, "I will tell everything to help you, sir. I have no time to argue with this man and this savage."

The Captain, tiring of the conversation, motioned for Jack and Soe to wait for the commanding British officer. Jack replied with a signal of his hands that they would wait on the other side of the heavily traveled road away from the flowing masses of people. The Loyalist Captain nodded his head in permission.

As soon as Jack and Soe were on the other side, there were even more hordes of people leaving, hundreds of them moving between them and the Captain. The two felt certain that they were out of Swallow's sight and moved into the throng, completely hidden by swiftly moving, disjointed people, farm animals, horses, sleighs and wagons. They escaped.

Captain Edwin Swallow, a Tory from the Saxe Gothe region of the Carolina sand hills, officer of the Loyalists' First Brigade, was ready to report to his commanding officer. He sent a Lieutenant to ask the British commanding officer's aide de camp to accept a hospitable gift from his brigade "on this occasion of the fall of the enemy," the fall of Charlestowne.

Swallow had seen a great opportunity handed to him in the very first hours of the impending Charlestowne surrender to His Majesty's forces. He could be promoted for his service to the Crown in delivering up to a brilliant young Colonel, under Cornwallis, these prizes--the loyal and successful mercenary, Edward the Trader, and a deserting American officer of General Benjamin Lincoln's staff.

"Well executed, sir!" he expected the Colonel might say when he explained to the British officer of Edward the Trader's accomplishment and how he, Swallow, had captured the American deserter.

The notable British officer, having now been informed, and having formally accepted this proffer, approached Swallow with interest.

The officer moved forward, his horse cantering and covering the ground quickly between him and the waiting Loyalist Captain. With extraordinary bearing in a forest green uniform, a flowering plume in his distinct hat, a gleaming saber in one hand, and a look of total command and victory in his surprisingly fair, slightly feminine face, the English Colonel advanced. Flanking him rode young, ambitious, and marble-faced Captains of the British dragoons, erect in their bearing.

They had all anticipated this moment of victory and now prepared to enter the city.

The Colonel in command approached. He rode directly up to Swallow, who had dismounted and was standing by his horse. He removed his hat in a sweeping bow and salute to his commander.

The Colonel said to the Loyalist Captain, "Sir, thank you for your courtesy. I am eager to meet these men, for the most part the one who has served the King in our advance."

Swallow motioned for a Lieutenant Hamilton to fetch "Edward the Trader," from across the road. He was to meet Lieutenant Colonel Banastre Tarleton of the British Legion.

Chapter Five

Incident At Mabry's Farm

Jack's sole duty, back safely in his home region after a dangerous journey from Charlestowne, was to report back to farmers who had paid
him. These nights and days just past had been harrowing; news of a total British victory had spread fast, meaning more "backroom" Loyalists
were now evident on roads and in communities.

He had negotiated a trade for a gun, giving up all his wares to a
man on the Wappoo Creek as he made a circuitous route back to the
upcountry. His main concern, however, was the men in the barn who
had hired him to go to Charlestowne. They would have heard rumors
by now, maybe even wild, distorted rumors. For all he knew they would
be waiting to kill him. He had no way of telling. Still, he had to report
something, for some could possibly be friends and had to know their
lives might be in danger. But he and Soe were desperate men. It was
Soe who thought of how the farmers who paid Jack might find out. He
suggested they see Maggie, Jack's sister, and tell her. She knew all the
men through trade as fellow farmers.

They rode one full day into a forested area near Maggie's home,
avoiding known Loyalist areas. Once assured they were not being followed, that her life was not in danger with their presence, Soe went for
Kit and Johnny Beckham to get to Maggie. They would ask her to meet
Jack in the woods. Maggie brought the beloved Easter Benjamin with
her. The three talked, and Jack told them everything. Easter, in her old

age, kept repeating, "Lawd hab mucy...oh Lawd." It was her wonderful way of bearing horrible news.

Maggie "listened" like a man. She never showed emotion, but instead stared straight ahead while Jack talked. Toward the end she said she would let the men who had paid Jack know what happened. Then she would let Jack know the allegiances of the farmers.

"Do you have all that is coming to you?" the always money-conscious Maggie asked Jack pointedly. She knew the answer immediately. Jack would never take this task on without receiving hard promises of barter first. And the men who hired him knew he would report back, even if it was through his sister.

Jack then told Maggie he was going to Grindal Shoals on the Pacolet to his home, but was stopping by friend Mabry's first to tell him that there was no Colonial army left in the South, that the British had won. He and Randolph would now decide how they might live, what loyalties among friends would have to be formed. Maggie was already on her feet preparing to leave. In fact, she left first. Soe himself would go to the safety of the Catawba Nation along the banks of the Catawba River near the Charlotte Towne village of the North Carolina Colony.

Jack thought this was the worst day of his life as Maggie rode off with Easter. They might never have time together again. Easter waved to Jack as he watched without responding He felt his shoulders sagging, wondering about Thomas, the imprisoned father of Samuel. He did not know if their home would even be there or if Samuel was safe.

Jack, when traveling, always approached his friends' homes, as well as his own, with a set plan. With childhood friend Mabry, it was preset that he would always approach from the north farm fields, from a grove of trees. He would, if he had the time, approach at dusk, minimizing the time he might be seen by anyone else. It was also after chores and right before total darkness. The Mabry's could predict how long it would take him to arrive at the long front porch based, on the time from his signal in the grove.

All of the Mabry family--Randolph, wife Hannah and teenage girls, Ann-Marie, Katherine, and twins, Tencie and Plessie--knew the secret of Old Jack's arrival. He had trained the girls to ride, trained their horses, and with their father, taught them how to shoot a long rifle. Jack had taught Ann-Marie how to throw a tomahawk. As children all were better shots than their friends and went hunting with father "Rand," as Jack called him, and Old Jack himself.

If it was not at dusk when Jack arrived, he would study the Mabry home from many yards away with his spy glass. He would watch for an hour or so if he had to. If he saw Randolph, he would strike his heavy rifle barrel with the back of his hunting knife. It was surprising how far the noise carried. It sounded much like an anvil being used and was a common noise in the country. He would then watch for Mabry's reaction. Often, if Rand Mabry did not react, Jack moved yards closer. When the single sound was heard Mabry would nonchalantly go to his porch and put an always polished copper wash pot against one of the wooden posts on the porch. He never signaled back with another sound of metal. He never even looked back. That would be obvious. Jack wanted him to be as uninvolved appearing as possible on the rare possibility that someone was observing his friend. If the copper pot was turned open and empty toward Jack it was a clear sign for him to approach. A pot turned in toward the house, with the bottom placed in Jack's direction, was a sign of visiting company, expected company or uncertainty. In that case, Jack moved on, always to the southwest to continue to Grindal Shoals and the Sandy Run along the Pacolet River and his home.

On this particular clear day, Jack banged the rifle barrel when he saw Rand casually returning from the edge of the yard toward the house with his dogs. Mabry never looked up. He took one step onto the porch and leaned the shiny copper pot against the front of the house on the front porch, the open pot toward Jack's direction; a clear signal.

Jack was over two hundred yards from the house now. He started his slow gallop on Maw toward the Mabry's. About one hundred yards from the house Maw slowed, shook her head up and down, her ears pointed. To Jack this was a serious alarm. He jumped off the horse, grabbed his rifle, and stood listening beside her. Behind him, Jack heard a sound that he recognized, the noise of people some distance behind him.

He was being followed. He was amazed and somewhat bewildered that this could happen. He always stopped when traveling from time to time to catch the downwind and listen. He knew reverberations in the woods. Maw would react but not overreact. Mounting Maw again he started to ride slowly and listen carefully. Maybe it was another farmer or some of Rand's family coming home for the evening from a hunt or a visit. He stopped suddenly in case the pursuer was now galloping, got off his horse, and listened intently. He heard nothing but the wind. Then he heard, from even farther away, human sounds moving away from him.

Perhaps it was someone who had gotten close, but was traveling from west to east and was now moving on. Jack listened for several minutes more but heard nothing. Feeling reassured, he moved toward the Mabry's' farm. Rand would be alerted that Jack should have arrived by now, so Jack hastened his horse's gait. In the distance he saw his friend outside the farm house waiting, still appearing nonchalant and uninvolved, and tending to one of the dog's ears.

At the entrance to the Mabry farm, there was a grove of pecan trees. At dusk Jack picked out the row of trees, still with Rand Mabry in sight, and waved his hand in salute before starting to gallop faster. He had not seen Mabry since that night in the barn, before leaving for Charlestowne, and the news was the most important he would ever have to tell his friend.

As he reached the end of the tree line, he felt a sudden heavy blow to his right shoulder somewhere from his right side and at the same time a hard explosion to his head. Just in time, before his consciousness faded, he saw the two large rocks that had hit him. Instinctively, he knew something completely unexpected and horrible had happened. He struggled to stay on Maw, who reared up and galloped forward with Jack, the suddenly injured rider, holding on.

Out from the last tree stepped two men with guns aimed at him. At the same time he heard running and cursing behind him as he felt someone grab the reins of Maw. He saw Rand Mabry running toward him with a look of fear he had never seen in his face. His red hair was bristling, his blue eyes wide, his teeth bared. He was running hard, taking in deep gulps of air, as he ran headlong toward the ambush.

Jack's senses were dulled. He heard Rand as if Rand were in a cave. His mind drifted. He immediately went back in his mind to a time when he and his friend had run for their lives from a yellow jackets' nest. Rand now had that same look.

They survived the stings of the yellow jackets, but Jack had the same ill feeling that he was now in the greatest danger of his life. He felt a sense of irony in the fact that he might die not far away in a battlefield, but close to a friend that he had cared for so much as a child. Jack was knocked to the ground by two men with rifle butts. One, in his haste, missed Jack completely, but swung again and hit him in the shoulder. The other man struck Jack in the back. Only Mabry's hollering and shouting at them stopped a severe beating.

Now only forty yards from the Mabry farm house, the men, four of them, stood pointing their flintlocks at both Beckham and Mabry. The men stood in a half-circle. Jack stood bent at the waist, looking up, facing all of them, but focusing on one in particular: Jadrow Eddards.

Mabry stood facing Jack and the four angry men. All of them now had their guns pointed at Jack Beckham. All had known Jack for years. All had reason to dislike his family, for at some time they had been involved in selling horses where Jack had advised buyers on the horses' worth. Everyone else had always asked Jack to question these men's prices, and the way the horses had been treated. Jack looked for scars and felt their flesh. He could tell if they were skittish from being whipped often. These men had lost money because of Jack. When the colony rebelled, they had sided with the British, hoping for favoritism. The men were Loyalist neighbors Moffett, Crump, Freeman, and Eddards.

Jadrow Eddards hissed at Jack. He called him a murderer and a traitor. He called his family traitors. He said Jack was a horse thief, the worst insult. He said he was an Indian lover. He began to swear louder and louder. Jack, looking him in the eye, finally said evenly and clearly, "You put your hands on Maggie."

He continued in measured sentences, "You tried to put her hands on your filthy body, you put your mouth on herns...you tried to rape her."

Eddards was completely stunned. He looked the part of a coward. He could not speak. He took a step backwards, his mouth gaping. Jack then growled in a whisper, "I'm going to kill you, Eddards."

Now Mabry and the other men were speechless. Two of the men knew Jack was telling the truth. Eddards, trying to hide behind his "political influence" with the British, had bragged that he was the only man who could make Maggie do anything. Mabry broke the stressed silence by saying to Jack in a stern low voice, "Jack, hush. This don't get us nowhere." Eddards, trying to recoup his balance, said, "You're a liar, Beckham."

Jack replied, seething, "You are a liar and a woman raper." Rand was now only hoping nothing was going to happen quickly and violently with the next exchange of words. All of the men had raised their guns higher, and Jack, weaker from the flow of blood from his head, sat on the ground spouting insults at Eddards.

Mabry turned and looked straight at Eddards. He spoke calmly. It got everyone's attention. "Jadrow, you are a good man." Eddards felt a little vindication, undeserved, but it helped gain back face he had lost with his friends due to Jack's accusations. "Jack Beckham can be a useful man," Mabry said condescendingly, motioning with one hand towards Jack, downplaying Jack's importance compared to that of Eddards. "Good horse trainer, maybe the best I know."

Mabry continued, appeasing the men with the loaded guns. "We need you both when all this is over. Jadrow, what we need now is for both of you to be at rest with one another. You men may never see Jack again. Let's forget this."

The men with the loaded guns never lowered their weapons. They looked unaffected and unconvinced. One of the men spoke. Hovis Crump said with a sneer, "We know you sold your property to Hodge." This was unknown to others as far as Mabry and Jack knew. Seeing an advantage on Randolph and Jack's faces, Crump pressed on. "We know you got young ones too. We know Sandy Run where you live...we can find you and your family." His voice rose. "You damned traitor!" Neither Mabry or Beckham spoke. Mabry was wondering how to break the silence when Eddards said with authority, "Mr. Mabry, we got no bad feelings with you. You are a good man, too."

Mabry thought to himself that Eddards owed him money; in fact he held two pieces of legal paper on land Eddards owned in Turkey Creek Hollow, the only land he owned in that part of the county. In Eddard's greed to own more land and endear himself to the English, he was indebted to Mabry.

Eddards said, "Please step aside, Mr. Mabry. We just want to settle this here and now."

One of the men who had not spoken, guffawed. "We want to settle it now but I ain't sure here…I sort of likes that tree over there myself."

For the first time in the fading dusk, Mabry saw a rope. It was lying on the ground, visible when Eddards turned to grin at the man who had spoken. It was already knotted in a hangman's noose. Eddards continued: "Mr. Mabry, sir. You are a gentleman. Everybody knows you are a friend to all. You ain't taking no sides. You jest want what is right." Sounding as if he were addressing a jury, he said, "Sir, please step aside. We honor you and your family today. Sir?"

Randolph Mabry looked at the man. He spoke very gently to him as he often did when addressing his family. "Men, this is wrong. This man is a friend of mine and yours. He will leave you alone. He will help you if he can. He…"

"No, I ain't," said Jack suddenly. It was as if someone else had spoken. No one expected him to interrupt Randolph Mabry, certainly not at this point. Even Randolph had felt he was approaching some sort of compromise. He was thinking of giving the mortgage paper back to Eddards if he had to, in a swap for Jack. He was certain Eddards would accept, even if grudgingly.

What Jack had said was the last thing Randolph needed him to say. It was a complete surprise to him. He turned and spoke to Jack in a forceful but low voice. "Jack, shut up! Listen to me!"

He was interrupted by Eddards. "Mr. Mabry, we ain't leaving now. You see this man has threatened me. He will try to kill us. I need for you to step aside, sir." Looking at the fallen man, Eddards tried to sound gracious. "Jack, let's us just talk." Eddards lied and everyone knew it when he said, "Let's us just square up and settle whatever it is between us."

Mabry saw that the men's determination was now growing; they were now even more afraid of Jack. They were becoming bolder out of fear. The look in their eyes was different; their expressions resembled animals being hunted. They were indeed worried. They knew this was a time Jack had to be dealt with. They were trapped, not him. They would have to kill him now or not be able to travel freely themselves. Only Eddards seemed to have confidence at the moment. Mabry's fear was the men would do something suddenly without thinking, and that even Eddards could not control them. Mabry knew he could be killed in a crossfire or to keep him from talking about a murder, especially Jack Beckham's murder. He felt a wrench of urgency himself.

Mabry sighed dramatically. "I want to say something to my friend and then I'll go." It was a grave pronouncement. The men now shifted their weight toward Jack. They were even more alert. Jack Beckham was going to die when Mr. Mabry left.

Mabry spoke loudly enough for the men to hear him as he put his hand on Jack's shoulder and said, "Jack, we been friends for a long time.. I'm sorry." Then he leaned in and whispered, his hand patting the scout's shoulder from time to time as if he were a father. He could have even been praying with his friend.

Jack never looked at him. Mabry, looking sad, whispered to Jack, "When you hear the first noise, lay yourself flat upon the ground." Jack didn't answer. Mabry knew he understood. Taking his hand from his shoulder, he said in a louder voice, "And I'll do my best for your folks." Mabry spun around and looked at the men. His voice was stern. "You give me time to get in my house and get my family out the back, you hear?" Eddards nodded politely.

Mabry looked at Jack one more time and turned to leave. Almost as if on command, the men lowered their guns slightly, while Eddards reinforced the ground he was standing on with a shift in his weight. For the first time Jack was completely alone with his executioners. It was clear they would honor the evil deed of killing him with either sudden gun shots or a longer march into the pecan trees mentioned by Crump.

Eddards said triumphantly, "Jack, when's the last time you saw your wife? When's the last time you saw your children? Didn't think we knew about that did you? You ain't never going to see them, Jack. You savage! You going to die tonight!"

When Mabry reached the front door of his home he glanced back and shouted at Eddards to wait. The men turned and acknowledged his command with nods. They began to walk toward Jack, sitting on the ground, apparently helpless. They moved more deliberately now, giving Mr. Mabry time to collect his family and leave the farm house. It was clear they intended to hang Jack, prolonging the taunting. Two of the men were now on Jack's right side and one on the left. Eddards stood in front of him with the hangman's rope.

As the men reached Jack, only a few feet in front of him, Ann-Marie came from the corner of the right side of the house. No one saw her until she raised her hand and brought out a double-barrel musket, a fowling gun, with a shorter barrel length, only twenty-four inches in length, from behind her long calico dress. The men looked bemused, then wide-eyed, when she raised the musket and positioned her stance like a man. She stood left leg firmly in front, her right leg planted back, and she raised the gun, and aimed at the men.

Whatever fleeting thought Hovis Crump had, the next and last sound ever heard by him was her musket as it ripped his face apart, with practically all the smaller lead balls, broken glass and nails with it that she used in the first barrel. She followed by firing the second barrel with larger lead balls, which hit Crump in the face and chest as he was falling. The two shots slightly unbalanced her, and she stumbled forward when Crump's shattered face, splattered Freeman and Eddards with cartilage, blood, an eyeball, and bone.

There was enough shot from the gun fired only fifteen yards away that it struck three of the others in their midsection and chest, doing no fatal harm, but surprising them into no action. The next sounds were thunderous. They were simultaneous. Older sister Katherine appeared from the left side of the house and fired a musket into Moffett's stomach, doubling him up with blood flying from his mouth, along with half-digested food and saliva. His stomach entrails emptied into his hands, his milk-white colored colon spilling snake-like onto the ground.

He was still cursing and screaming and writhing on the ground as Randolph Mabry, who had been standing in the front doorway, aimed his long rifle and fired into Moffett's left side at the same time. Rendered unconscious, he fell almost on top of Jack, who without hesitation grabbed the hunting knife from his belt and punctured Moffett's neck, sinking inches of the steel into his throat.

Hannah Mabry, moving from inside the house to beside her husband, calmly handed him a musket, as he dropped his hunting rifle. With the gun, he shot Freeman with multiple lead balls. Freeman fell instantly, with a shot to his chest and another opening up his thigh to the bone and severing his femoral artery. He fell with a shocked look as if he was trying to determine whether to run or fight. He had raised his gun but it went flying over his head at the impact of Mabry's musket.

The twins, Tencie and Plessie, bolted onto the front porch, and each shoved a long gun into their parent's hands. Randolph raised to fire at Eddards, but the cowardly Tory had already dropped the hangman's rope and started running. The strong and unwavering Hannah fired her rifle at Eddards just as he reached a cedar tree in the yard. It splintered the limbs and trunk, giving the whole scene a sweet smell of cedar, inconsistent with the foul smells of blood and excrement from the dead men.

Reaching Jack, the Mabrys thought he had been shot due to the blood on the back of his head. They quickly realized that a rock of some size had hit him when he was ambushed and had caused the wound.

Jack, looking up, mumbled with a slight smile, and said something that was indistinct. At that precise moment a horseman was made out in the almost dark evening charging straight at them with a musket in his hand. Mabry rammed the rod down his musket and hoped to sufficiently fill powder in the pan and get off a shot.

"Hello the house! Hello the house!' the rider shouted, the always proper greeting when approaching a house unexpected.

Jack sat up on one elbow and mumbled in a voice that was hardly audible, "Samuel."

Randolph, his gun partially raised, said, "Thanks now be to our Lord."

Chapter Six

Ambush At Alexander's Old Field

Mrs. Hannah Mabry was not looking as Samuel, who was talking excitedly, reined in his horse yards away from the family and Jack. Samuel jumped off his horse to run up to them with his news, but it did not hinder Mrs. Mabry's job. She saw blood flowing from Jack's head and was ministering to him with a cloth, unconsciously blocking his view of Samuel.

Jack looked glassy-eyed. Hannah said, speaking as she always did in her strong manner, "John, you have a split head that is needed to be fixed." Samuel had at the same time rushed up to Jack's face to get his attention. Now there were two people who were in front of him and talking seriously.

Jack looked at Samuel and muttered, "Where in hellfire has you been?"

Mrs. Mabry, ignoring all this, called to Tencie, "Get the water."

Jack pulled himself up to one knee and looked at Samuel as if he still could not focus on him.

"Justice Gaston is looking for you!" Samuel gasped, trying to get a breath. "Tarleton and his men done kilt a hundred Regulars at the Waxhaws! They massacred them…hardly any left and some others taken to…to Camden to be hanged!"

"My God," whispered Mabry.

Jack stared at Samuel. Mrs. Mabry remained busy and when Tencie brought her a bucket of hot water she said firmly, "No, it has to be hotter." Her voice now seemed to be heard by everyone for the first time.

"What is it?" asked Jack.

"Your head," she said. "Get the horsetail hair and dress needle," she called to Tencie.

This time the young girl brought a steaming copper pot of water. Her sister Plessie brought a thin needle made of fine turkey bone and several strands of horse tail, which had been boiled months ago and dried to pliable strands about twelve inches long. Mrs. Mabry had positioned herself again in back of Jack, and instructed him to take his shirt off. Jack did so and sat still with this woman in charge.

Samuel tried to get attention regarding the awful news he had just brought. "Jack?" Jack groaned but said nothing.

Randolph Mabry intervened. "Hush, young buck," then called attention to Jack's injury. "Look at his head." Samuel moved around and saw what Mrs. Mabry saw. Jack's scalp behind his left ear had a seven-inch gash that revealed his skull, gray-white in color. The hair was matted with blood, but blood was still trickling down his neck and back.

Taking the hot water and putting a cloth in it, Hannah squeezed it out and washed the wound. She did this three times. Then with her index finger she felt around inside the hanging flesh and, once satisfied, ran her finger over the exposed skull carefully to see if there was more dirt under the skin and hair.

Jack shuddered as she poured the entire bowl over the back of his head and over the wound to remove the debris and blood. "Better," she said to herself with a degree of satisfaction. "Randolph, pull this man's skin back together." Rand Mabry acted as if he did this daily. He positioned himself behind Jack and firmly pulled Jack's scalp back together with both hands.

Tencie, who knew what to do, handed her mother a poultice of black snakeroot and slippery elm. Mrs. Mabry put it on the wound, then removed the poultice after letting it sit for some few minutes. Taking the horse hair, she threaded the needle and then began to sew. She stitched back and forth, drawing the scalp together and dabbing it from time to time to stop the bleeding. After ten times through his scalp, she tied off the hair at the base of the wound.

Hannah stood back and reviewed her handiwork, then said to Jack, "John, you are here tonight…eat yourself something big tomorrow morning at breakfast—"

"No, Mrs. Mabry," Samuel interrupted. "Jack has to go tonight to the Justice's farm! He needs to hear what the Justice has to tell him."

"He can't go," she insisted, not looking at him, and it seemed a closed matter.

Jack pulled himself up and took Samuel by the arm to steady himself. "Where were you in Charlestowne?" This sounded like Jack. He was angry at Samuel.

"I was with Captain McClure and his Rangers. Maggie told me they needed me, and I was to go with them, not you. She said you would understand once I saw you in the city. We never got to the city.

"Captain John made the decision once we gots there we would come back without fighting. It was sure we had lost the city. I ain't never seen such guns from afar. It seemed the whole city was burning. We weren't the only ones not going into the city. Colonel Buford and his Virginians left, too. Colonel Buford took Governor Rutledge with him to gets away. I been trying to tell you.

"Mrs. McClure, Miss Gaston, and other women of the Shoals went over to the Waxhaws and tried to help them Regulars. Over one hundred were kilt and laying in a church…kilt not with muskets but with sabers and knives. They picked 'em up in baskets…most of 'em."

Jack was silent. He first looked at Rand Mabry and then began slowly shaking his head. Mabry walked a couple of paces away and then turned around and walked toward Jack. Mrs. Mabry looked questioningly at both of them.

Jack spoke: "Hellfire, they is going to be killing people that ain't being for the British." He looked at Samuel. "Maggie told you this? Not to join me as we rightly agreed?"

"Yes sir. She said I was needed with McClure and you would understand and we would meet in the city."

Jack did not respond. Looking around him as if he was finally coherent, he said calmly, "We has to go. We has to see what the Justice is saying. I heard of this Tarleton. He is of the devil if what I heard is so." He looked at Mabry. "I knows you ain't going with me 'cause of your family. I will do the same fer mine after I leaves the Justice."

Mabry, who was a strong man of faith, said to Jack as he and Samuel started to walk away, "God is protecting you and Samuel." Jack gave a look of appreciation as he neared Maw. Then Mabry approached Jack, holding out his most prized weapon, his long rifle that had been true to him and had been his weapon since he and Jack had hunted with it ten years ago. It was equal to Jack's rifle and, in fact, had been made by the same family, the Pedens from the Cherokee upcountry. In turn, Jack took from his saddle the gun he had bartered leaving Charlestowne. He gave it to Mabry and then gripped his hand in a warm gesture of appreciation and friendship.

Jack and Samuel mounted their horses and began what would be at least a five-hour ride from Mabry's farm back to Cedar Shoals near the great falls of the river. He motioned for Samuel to lead and to go fast as he could. The two rode as carefully as they could. It was a temptation to "see" Redcoats and Tories behind every tree, but they both seemed resigned to fight sooner or later. Before they left, Jack had filled his canteen with water, and he drank often to keep his strength. He stopped only once to take the poultice off his head, but out of courtesy to Hannah Mabry he kept it in a saddlebag to use again.

With clouds covering the moon, it took Jack and Samuel longer than expected to reach Justice Gaston's home. It was after midnight, and Samuel had said they must be there at midnight. When they reached a ridge where they could see the Justice's home, Jack wanted to stay for a while and observe.

Jack got off his horse and listened. Coming back after some minutes he said to Samuel, "We ride." If Justice Gaston had been taken by the British or, worse, by neighbors, Jack wanted to know, and he knew that if Samuel was captured, he would likely be dealt with leniently. Also Samuel was good enough to get away if confronted.

Jack would ride several yards parallel to Samuel, both in each other's sight. They would ride off in different directions if pursued by a party.

Samuel rode toward the Gaston farm at a careful trot. In view of the house he saw something that warmed his heart. It was a gathering of men, some thirty or more in front of the house, most with torches which illuminated their faces. Samuel recognized all of them. They were neighbors and friends. All were bound to defend their land and not be part of any alliance with the English. They were loyal to the colony.

He looked for Jack who was observing the yard signal that it was safe to proceed. They rode side by side into the farmyard looking ahead to see what would happen. Three men saw Jack and Samuel at once. They murmured, gesturing and pointing at them. A shout of "huzzah" went up, followed by another "huzzah." Two men walked out to greet them and Jack saw they had a bottle of rye whiskey they had been passing around.

Jack and Samuel prodded their horses to proceed faster, and Jack heard, "Welcome, Jack Beckham…Samuel! Old Jack is here." Another "huzzah" rang out and Jack began to feel this was a celebration of sorts. Coming out to greet them was Justice John Gaston.

The old Justice had a good reputation for performing marriages for anyone who showed up at his farm. He was influential there in the Cedar Shoals community, but several people thought he was one of the stingiest men around. Many wondered how much money he had hidden.

For the first time in days, Jack felt a glow of relief seeing so many people he knew. He managed to tease the Justice while he took the reins of Jack's horse. After dismounting Maw and greeting him, Jack said, "Sir! I is already married!" Gaston only managed a slight grin in response.

"Come into the house, Jack," Gaston said. "We needs your kind like we ain't never…" His voice had faded toward the end of his sentence as the old man turned to lead Jack in. They talked one-to-one in a front room of the main house, away from everyone. Gaston sat in a chair pulled up close to Jack, his hands clasped as in prayer. From time to time he rolled his thumbs over and over each other and looked Jack in the face intently.

"'Tis true, sir," he said to Jack. "'Tis grievously true. My wife went with relatives and tried to help them Regulars. We heard they had been kilt. It was nigh unto a hundred men dead and the rest dying. Many prisoners taken to Camden and Charlestowne.

"We also heard about Charlestowne from nephew John McClure, who was there. What you don't know is the Tory Captain Houseman— from the Rocky Mount fort— has been here. He asked me to have folks gather tomorrow morning at Alexander's Old Field and declare our allegiances to King George.

"We has to sign our x's or our names or…" He paused for effect. "Or all of us will be hanged…and anyone, any man that darest not sign a paper to swear to Almighty God that they will be for the British, will be hanged from a tree.

"And, sir, it is worse than that. Houseman is calling for our men to become militia for the British. He asked today for my boys to join them and become Tories. He left this oath of allegiance for me to bring tomorrow and to have it read. He is looking for us to take arms against each other."

"Read it, sir," said Jack gravely.

"I…" The Justice looked up sheepishly at Jack. "…do solemnly and sincerely swear on the holy evangelists of almighty God to bear true allegiance to our sovereign Lord, King George the Third, and to uphold the same. I do voluntarily promise to serve as militia, under any of the officers appointed over me, and that I will, when lawfully warned by our said officers, assemble at any place by them directed in case of danger, in the space of eight hours. I will not at any time, do or cause to be done, anything prejudicial to His Majesty's government; or suffer any intercourse or correspondence with the enemies thereof, that I will make known any plot or plots, anywise inimical to His Majesty's forces or loyal subjects, by me discovered, to His Majesty's officers contiguous, and it shall not exceed six hours before the same is discovered, if health and distance permit. This I do solemnly swear and promise to defend in all cases whatsoever. So help me, God!"

The old Justice let the paper drop to the floor as if it was contaminated. "What say you to this, Jack? Has you heard this already?" The Justice studied Jack's drawn face for a response.

Jack shook his head "no" without saying anything, but looked back at the Justice and said, "I ain't coming here and with Samuel, at that, to says we has to swear allegiance of loyalty of any kind to some King!"

"No!" remonstrated Gaston. "No! I asked you here to see if you would join my nephews, John and Hugh, and all them Rangers and my boys, plus otherns, and go to the field tomorrow.

"Shoot the devils gathered there. Shoot Houseman! No, I ain't asking you here to be no Tory."

"How many men you gots?" asked Jack.

"Don't know," said the older man. "I been asking men to join me here tonight and to stop them neighbors tomorrow that will sign that paper.

"Captain Houseman's only been here this afternoon. We has to be fast. I can't make you be doing this, but I needs all the good men who will not sign anything. Even though you don't live here, your folks do, including Miss Maggie, Samuel, and Thomas.

"And Jack," he said, placing his hand on Jack's arm, "you may be the best shot I ever has heard anyone tell of. I needs you to shoot good and don't miss, so my boys and others will right likely do the same."

Jack pondered, and before he could say more, the anxious Gaston, still seated, turned and called out to John McClure to join them. As McClure walked in, the Justice said to him, "This be Jack Beckham."

McClure said, "A pleasure, sir."

Sitting down close to the two men in a cane chair, the young twenty-five-year-old leader said to Jack, "The Justice tells you what is happened?"

Jack's eyes narrowed, and he spoke to McClure deliberately, aware of being much more experienced than McClure. He seemed to ignore the question and said, "Did Samuel go with you to Charlestowne?"

McClure smiled and said to the older man, "Indeed he did, sir. He would have helped greatly if we had the honor of fighting the King."

"Did Maggie Land ask you to take him?" Jack further inquired.

"Sir, Samuel joined us a volunteer. I supposed he had been directed by someone to join us. I darest think it could have been Maggie, for she might have known we would go there because other men she knew were part of our party."

Jack persisted. "Did the Governor Rutledge get kilt at the Waxhaws?"

Curious at all the questions, McClure, nevertheless, showed patience with Jack; he knew Jack's reputation as a confrontational person. "The good news, sir, is that he did not proceed with Abraham Buford's men that far…he turned off at some point and went to Mecklenburgh and was thus saved. Colonel Buford himself and several of his officers survived Tarleton as well. They was on their mounts at the battle.

"I can report that several men escaped, but the unfortunate ones who were foot soldiers…well… many died."

Jack softened his tone and replied, "What is it that you are requiring of me and Samuel?"

McClure looked at the Justice.

"Well," harrumphed the Justice, interrupting and clearing his throat, "we needs you to join us and engage tomorrow. I can't tell you who will be there, but you can expect some British, a lot of Tories and them Loyalists who will sign an allegiance to the British. I can tell you they will be our former friends and neighbors. You will know when we git there. You will know how many British and Loyalists will be there, but only then."

Jack pondered this and softly said, "Eddards."

Young McClure heard this. "You know Eddards?"

Jack glared at him. "You know Eddards?"

McClure dropped his head and said, "I know he is a hypocrite who says he knows our Lord but is in fact a thief and liar."

"You knows Eddards," Jack said and almost creased his face with a faint smile. Getting up from his chair he said, "Samuel and I shall join this."

At this turn of events, the Justice and McClure walked to the front porch. Gaston said in a loud voice. "Boys! All of you are with Captain McClure. You will leave right soon to go to Alexander's Field. Go! Do your duty with him and return home!"

At that, a man shouted "No quarter!" Some shouted "Tarleton's quarter!" And they all mumbled and cursed as they walked up ritually to pass Justice Gaston on the porch. The old Justice shook each man's hand in a powerful grip and back-slapped them as they walked up to the porch. Each took a swig of rye whiskey from a common jug as was custom. They walked off the porch and began to assemble in the yard for a six-mile ride and walk to the fallow ground of Alexander's Old Field.

That night, McClure's Rangers rode their horses and many times walked through heavy brush along Fishing Creek. They made little conversation. The men were mostly clad in animal skins of deer and beaver, linen shirts, moccasins, old tired wool hats, armed with butcher knives and muskets. They were thirty-six strong.

Among them were seven Walker family members: Charles, John, Joseph, Philip and Robert, Samuel and Alexander. James McClure, Captain John McClure, and brother Hugh McClure serving as Lieutenant, were the core of the McClure's and the heart of the Rangers. All had been to witness the defeat of Charlestowne and gotten as far as Moncks Corner. All also heard of Tarleton's massacre at the Waxhaws, only a week earlier.

John Mills, John Steele serving as another Lieutenant, John Craig, four Gastons--William, Hugh, Robert, and Alexander--and James Johnston and Matthew Johnston were in the party.

William McGarrety, Samuel McKeown, Alex Morrow, and David Morrow rode with them, as did Francis Wylie.

The contentious but ever zealous religious and pious Reverend John Simpson of Fishing Creek Presbyterian Church was with the group.

George Gill and Samuel Houston and five Knox men, James, John, Robert, Samuel, and William, made up the total group who had been waiting in the Justice's yard when Samuel and Jack arrived.

Seventeen of the men had been with Continental groups that had been defeated and now were disbanded. They represented the South Carolina Thrid and the South Carolina Sixth. Most, fourteen of the seventeen men, were from the 3rd, including Captain John McClure and Lt. Hugh McClure and Lt. John Steele. They were trained to fight and were part of the men who would have fought at Charlestowne, had they not arrived too late to be of any consequence.

Still, they were going to a Field where they had no idea how many of the opposition there would be. There could be soldiers of the Crown mixed in with armed Loyalist volunteers and the "new citizens" of a colony for the King of England. It took them almost three hours to walk and ride along the Fishing Creek that night, moving through brambles and brush and open fields to complete the six miles. Once there, they lay in an expanse of woods overlooking the Field just one hundred yards from seven British tents and an equal number of camp fires, with one sentry walking lazily around the tents' perimeter. They would wait for daybreak, but they would have to get closer.

McClure studied the camp for activity and noticed that at dawn's break more people began to come from the roads to the field on horses, some walking, and some pulling sleighs with children, followed by several dogs. It became clear that the British, as was their custom, were cooking pork and beef on a spit over a large fire; on the ground sat jugs of whiskey and baskets of bread– inducements for recruiting. A large tree stump had been cut to serve as a table, where a British officer sat in a camp chair waiting to enlist men to fight for the Crown. Loyalist neighbors were positioned conveniently beside the officer to tell about each family, which would be recorded. They also informed the officer if someone was of dubious character in terms of his affection for the Royal troops.

As McClure studied the Field with a spy glass, he asked others to join him. John Steele, his brother Hugh, William McGarrety, Sr., Jack, and then James "Son" Noland of the nearby Rocky Creek community, whose family had owned the field at one time. Noland had been asked to join them by one of Justice Gaston's couriers earlier that evening; he had done so and caught up with the men as they left Gaston's.

They passed the spy glass among themselves. After one hour of daylight, they saw to their frustration over two hundred people on the Field.

McClure asked quietly, "Who do you know?"

McGarrety, being from the Winnsboro community, knew only three. Noland knew the most and said half of them were scoundrels. Noland said, however, that two others were faithful to the colony. They were young men, Joseph Wade and William Stroud, who lived a short distance from the Field. Noland related that the two had helped him put up a split rail fence around part of the Field only days before; he was sure of their loyalty.

"Do you see Houseman?" said McClure.

Hugh said, "Yes, but he is hid by a tent. Wait until he moves to the tree stump and talks to the crowd or he moves around."

"But that could be two hours," said his brother, John, "and what if a young one wanders up here and sees us?"

Noland said he saw a man named "Wicker," who was a thief and had been caught by neighbors stealing goats and cooking them. He had been missing for some time.

Young Captain and leader John McClure said, "We needs a sure plan to attack. If damned neighbors get shot, then so be it. The men will have to pick their first targets and then choose from among them that fires back."

Jack grunted and cleared his throat as if preparing to speak. Captain McClure, still prone, turned around and responded before Jack could talk. "Jack, you shoots first… and tell me who you is aiming at."

Jack only said, "I has a way to see them from over there." He motioned to his right.

Captain McClure signaled to the others that he was leaving with Jack as Jack started walking away. Crouching and moving around tree stumps, the two quietly walked, still slightly stooped, over thirty yards and then squatted among the trees at the edge of the woods. They were at an angle from the people on the Field. Jack motioned and said, "From here you can see all them, all the time. I can shoot four times before any can shoot back. Samuel will be down here 'sides me with three loaded long rifles whilst I stand. I will drop rifles on the ground after I shoot. He will jest hand them up to me, and I will fire 'em. My rifle will shoot

The British and Tories
turned and fired

first, then three more rifles I gets from ours. I needs the best rifles we has, and then I will git them back after I shoot. Tell them ne'er worry.

"Have ours bunched together; when I shoot all four shots, they shoot and then run twenty yards to their right. They shoot together again and then run twenty yards to their right. Then they do it again.

"In these trees the British and Tories will always be firing where the men just was. But our boys has to shoot and run to their right...ever' time."

McClure, a man used to fighting, said, "You might be in the line of fire back at you, right after your four shots, maybe afore."

"Nay!" Jack spat a stream of tobacco juice. "I will shoot four shots then get behind that big tree there with Samuel. Tell the mens who let me borrow their rifles to git back there, and we will deliver their guns to 'em.

"As them Tories shoot at ours I will git back to the woods and pick my targets from behind a tree. So will Samuel. Hellfire, they don't be more than seventy-five yards away when I shoots...long as they don't run the other way too fast. Our others with me can shoot from behind them trees jest as well when I gives 'em their rifles back."

"If they run, we will charge them," McClure said soberly. "What will you do then?"

"I will see who is on the Field. I might just go home. I ain't going to 'social' with no one here," he said sarcastically. "If there is no one I has to attend to, then I will leave."

"You mean Eddards?" asked McClure.

Jack did not answer.

"It is done rightly then. My men will wait and shoot after yours."

McClure hurried back to his brother, Hugh, and to John Steele. They both got up and passed the word down among all the men. Being experienced, they questioned each man as to what to do, making them repeat back to them. "Shoot once and run to your right. Don't try to reload until you gits twenty yards to your right."

The men all nodded that they understood the orders. Three men brought their rifles to Jack and Samuel, who looked at them carefully. Jack looked hard at the men, still at this last minute trying to assess their loyalty. He told them to each pick the biggest tree they could find and stay behind it until after his shots. He would fire four times and run to their position, and then wait for "British and Tory medicine," as Jack called the deadly lead balls he'd witnessed.

Samuel and Jack went about their duties without speaking. Samuel loaded the rifles; he poured powder from his horn into each barrel, then the lead balls, forcing each one in with his wooden ramrod. Only then did he put black powder carefully in the pan. He did not cock the guns.

Jack carefully did the same; he did not cock his rifle, but held it pointed slightly up, holding it across his chest as he began to walk several yards to his right and them to his left. Samuel stayed put, kneeling on one knee with the three loaded rifles all cradled in his arms. Jack came back, looked at Samuel, and grunted and nodded his head. Carefully, Samuel cocked all three guns, still holding them cradle-like. Jack would be able to simply reach down and take one from Samuel, shoot it, drop it, and then take up the next.

Samuel now stood up halfway, looking forward, planting his feet to stabilize himself. Jack looked at the Field and then back at John McClure, who was watching him. Jack abruptly stopped his motion of lifting his rifle to his shoulder and whispered loud enough to be heard, "Where is Mr. Noland?"

Surprised, Hugh McClure motioned that he was to Jack's left about thirty yards away. "Have him here," whispered Jack to McClure. Hugh left his position and brought Noland to Jack.

Jack spoke to Noland in a warm manner. "Sir, where is them two boys who you said is ours on that Field?"

"Wade and Stroud? They are to the right...the far right," he said, and pointed to two very young men, slouched hats over their faces, both eating beef and bread and sitting down. Jack noticed both had brought their rifles, not an uncommon sight, although most had not.

Jack said to Noland, "Holler at them boys when the shooting starts, if you can git their attention, and tell 'em to stay down, then run to us."

Noland nodded and went to his right to be closer to Wade and

Stroud. Jack waited for him into get into position. Raising his gun again, he aimed at the British sentry's waist and then lowered his gun slightly and murmured to himself, "Wound him."

He fired. The shot entered the sentry's rear end, ravaging his right buttock. This shot sounded loud to Jack and Samuel, but it was muted by the trees for a second. Reaching down toward Samuel with his left hand, he dropped his own rifle to his right and then aimed the second shot at a British Regular who was eating. The soldier simply stopped and looked up at the noise. The .50-caliber lead ball caught him in the calf of his right leg, splintering his shin bone, and he buckled and fell, screaming.

Jack reached down again, and this time noticed that a man on the field had grabbed his musket and was trying to load it. Jack's shot hit the man in his right hand, and separated his fingers and hand back to his wrist, leaving him writhing on his knees.

At this third shot there arose a din that filled the entire Field. There was enormous screaming and running and horses bolting. Above all this, Jack heard Noland hollering at Stroud, "git yourself down." A final shot was being aimed at Houseman, who now appeared and was armed with a sword and shouting to his men, "Form and wheel." Jack, however, shot a Tory who had a musket and was running toward Houseman. Unfortunately for him, he offered an easy target. He was hit in his chest, immediately killed, and fell sprawled at Houseman's feet. Houseman reached down to assist him, while shouting orders.

Jack's four shots had been fired. There followed a volley from McClure's men, from their rifles all at once; it must have sounded as if all creation was ending. The crowd, however, was so scattered it was unclear how many and who had been shot, had fallen down, or stumbled from fear. Then there was a deadly silence for what seemed to be several seconds, followed by the wailing of the first men shot.

Samuel and Jack both had two rifles apiece as they ran for cover behind a pecan tree that offered more protection than pines around it. As they reached the tree they were welcomed by three men standing behind it, all reaching out to help them break the momentum of their run. All grabbed their selected guns and hid behind the tree, waiting for a returning volley from the field, aimed at Jack's just vacated position. It did not come.

McClure's Rangers had reached their new positions to their right and many had reloaded. Some had gotten off shots. Orders were called out, people screamed, and there was erratic firing from the Field. Jack looked up in surprise to see Wade and Stroud firing at the British and Loyalists before they themselves ran for the woods.

Captain McClure's men moved again to the right, those who had shot, and those who had not; some had not enough time to reload and aim. There was another volley from the Rangers and this time little response from the Field of British and Loyalists.

Jack moved behind another large tree to aim for a selected shot. He fired in haste and missed a shot that would have caught one of Houseman's men, but it hit two feet beside him and plowed up earth. McClure called to his men, and it was clear they were giving chase to the Field, trying to capture whatever men, weapons and bounty they could from the British and volunteers. The people who had come to declare allegiance to the King were running quickly with fear that they would be followed and killed.

Suddenly a volley came from the Loyalists and British that was unexpected, and Hugh McClure was shot. All other missiles from the British and Loyalists' muskets had been high or wide and apparently did no harm than to wound William McGarrety, Sr., in his arm. McClure's arm, however, was shattered; bone protruded from his upper arm near his shoulder and he lay on his back in shock.

This injury to McClure, as often happens in battle, caused more anger and hatred to boil over from the men. Now shouts of "no quarter" rose from several of them. This was the worst sound for the Loyalists, who were surrendering, and to the British, who were dispersing on horseback or running beside the horses of those getting away.

Houseman was nowhere to be found. To a keen-eyed Jack, now roaming the Field with a knife in one hand and a rifle in the other, neither was Eddards seen. Looking like a man possessed, Jack called out to Samuel. They both searched frantically. Jack was in a murderous mood, and he ran fast from person to person to find the traitor and molester. He was not found.

As full control came under McClure's command, a single shot rang out. James Noland had killed a Loyalist who was aiming his gun at Stroud. This prompted another sharp report as James Knox shot one of Houseman's Regulars, who had turned to run away. At that, pitiful cries of "quarter, quarter," rang out from the losers that day. All who had come to Alexander's Old Field, fully expecting to be part of a new plan of order, protected by the Crown were now part of a group that had just been routed by American farmers, neighbors, and militia.

But the colonies were perceived to have "lost." The state capital was under British control. All of the colony of South Carolina was under British control. All except, it appeared, this section of the great falls area of Cedar Shoals, the Rocky Creek community, and Fishing Creek.

Captain McClure called out, "Give quarter, give quarter. Go home. Help yer families." He looked for more of his men who might be wounded and saw that Hugh was in great agony and in need of help. He knew the British would surely retaliate for this ambush; nevertheless, he was elated over their victory, and he patted several men on the back as they were all leaving.

"Tarleton's had his day!," he exclaimed. "Remember today! Remember today!"

He looked around again as his Rangers were leaving the Field, but he did not see Jack or Samuel.

Chapter Seven

Meeting Colonel Carrington

After the ambush at Alexander's Old Field Jack Beckham went into hiding being pursued by many British and Tories. Captain Houseman, a local Tory, had received orders to retaliate; the surprise attack on Loyalists and British Regulars would not go unanswered. The British particularly wanted to show support for citizens who might join the war effort as Tories. They wanted to make it clear that anyone who supported the Crown would be protected.

Cornwallis had already reported to Lord Germain--who would report directly to King George – that Loyalists would rise up throughout the south and join the King's forces. Among the military minds and strategists who represented England, it was considered already accomplished that the southern colonies had been defeated. Charlestowne, and to another degree Savannah, had been the prizes. The emphasis was on moving up the other colonies toward the north and finally defeating General George Washington.

The untimely ambush at Alexander's Field by a group of farmer-militiamen was not what the King's men had in mind. A handbill was quickly circulated in the area of Fishing Creek and the area of the great falls. It read:

"Assassins and traitors at Alexander's Old Field, near the Cedar Shoals, and the Fort near Rocky Mount, shall be brought to justice

and hanged if resistance is given, or they shall henceforth be tried at
Camden district to determine their innocence. Named here they are:

William Stroud Jr., Joseph Wade, Hugh McClure, John McClure,
James McClure, John Steele, James known as 'Adjutant' Johnson,
Matthew Johnston, Samuel Houston, Rev. William Simpson, William
McGarrety, William Kennedy, John Mills, John Craig, George Gill,
Samuel McKeown, Alexander McKeown, Joseph McGarrety, Joseph
Morrow, John known as 'Jack' Beckham of the Pacolet River, Samuel
Beckham, James known as 'Son' Noland, William, Hugh, and Robert
Gaston, of the Cedar Shoals community, Justice John Gaston, the Knox
and Walker men of the Fishing Creek community. Anyone harboring
these criminals is subject to the King's laws of treason."

Looking at the bill, Jack felt a sense of foreboding for other people,
including Maggie and his close friend Randolph Mabry. He would not
see Rand Mabry soon except under the most secret circumstances. He
could not go to Maggie's or any of his relatives, including Thomas, and
most of all, his own wife and eight children on the Pacolet.

He sat on the ground in a clump of young sapling trees on a June
afternoon, and knew for sure that Samuel was in the Catawba Nation
carefully hidden by Soe. But even the Nation of the Catawba's remained
a danger for Jack, for Loyalists would look for him there. Tonight he
would stay on the banks of a creek bed. He would be able to hear horses traveling down the stream many yards away. He would hide Maw in
a grove of pine trees, and whistle for her if danger was imminent. He
was only four miles from Cedar Shoals on Fishing Creek, but he might
as well have been a hundred miles away, for the only people he trusted
were hiding or being watched. Most of all, he needed to know where
McClure and his men were, for he wanted to join them for a short time.
He believed, though, that he would be safe in the woods for at least the
next week.

Days later Jack heard that McClure, and many of the men who had
fought at Alexander's Field, had ridden straight to Winnsboro, twenty-
two miles away, to do the same damage to Tories assembled at Mobley's

Meeting House. They had gone at the urging of Tom Johnson, brother of "Adjutant" Johnson, who felt his family was in grave danger.

Jack fingered the heavy paper bills, wondering how they had been distributed. He had picked his from a tree along the Fishing Creek bank near Judge Gaston's now burned-out home. Jack could not read, but he recognized his own name. He recognized Samuel's name and the British seal of authority. The hand bill also clearly was an effort to encourage friends of Judge Gaston to turn against him and his family.

Thinking about someone he could contact, it occurred to him that the schoolmaster, Elberton Chandler, was thought to be above suspicion. The schoolmaster would often spend weeks or months at families' homes and would be provided food and lodging, as well as a small amount of currency. But this organized schoolmaster would have three or four families to meet at one home if they lived within five miles of each other.

In these war-torn times families were in agreement in their opinions of either Loyalist or Whig. All Jack knew was that the schoolmaster was teaching five families, and he did not know their loyalty, particularly since the ambush at the Old Field had dispersed so many neighbors. He did not know if they were angry, scared of the militia, or diehard Loyalists. He would take a chance and try to see the schoolmaster, who he knew was staying at the Richard Carlisle home near the falls of the Catawba River. They were a religious family, honest and approachable people. To Jack's mind they were as neutral as a family might be and still able to have friends on both sides of the conflict. He wondered how long this would last.

The school teacher, Chandler, was from Augusta of the Georgia colony. He visited the Carolina upcountry and spent eight months a year teaching area children. He even taught slaves' children to read on Sundays so they could be more help to plantation owners. Some citizens did not like his progressive ways, but two owners had paid him extra for teaching older slave boys who were being trained to be overseers. Several times, the Reverend William Simpson had invited him to Fishing Creek Church. Simpson was secretly teaching slaves to read and write. He asked Chandler to also teach and to check his work in teaching script to slave children.

On this night Jack would stay safe, and then just before dawn he would move toward the Carlisle home. He heard noises in the night but slumbered well, and at two hours before sunlight, he ate old salted beef and stale bread along with water from the creek. He did not smoke but fed Maw and departed for the Carlisle home.

Seeing the house from a distance with a misty fog covering the ground waist-high, he felt this hurried manner was a dangerous way to approach the farm house. Anyone else would take this easy approach to the house, but Jack would go in downwind. He saw the home and was relieved to see Chandler's horse outside the barn.

He picked a hazardous plan. He would position himself behind a tree and call out to the house. In the ground fog no one would see him if he stood behind the tree and just called out. There was no outward sign of anyone moving at the house. Not even the chickens and guinea hens were visible. He looked for several minutes, but listened harder.

In the distance crows cawed in a field, but that was all. Constantly he feared someone knew he was coming and was waiting for him. This was unreasonable most of the time, but if once he took it for granted he was safe, he would be killed or captured. Being desperate to make things happen was not to his liking, but at the first streaks of daylight Jack moved behind a tree within fifty feet of the horse, who was dawdling on a loose rein. He threw a rock and hit the front door, then called out, "Mr. Carlisle! It is Jack Beckham. I am here. I wants to speak to the school man!"

The mare jumped to one side at the noise, and he found he was in luck when three dogs came running out from under the porch. The guinea hens started squawking, all upset at the disturbance, making enough noise to awaken the whole family. This many dogs howling and barking might indicate they had treed something. It could be a wild animal in the yard. The thought crossed Jack's mind that someone might think that stragglers could be stealing the horse. That could bring guns from several of the Carlisle boys. Maybe they did not hear him. He leaned forward toward the house as the front door opened.

Jack saw Mr. Carlisle come to the door with sons Jebual, James, and Matthew, and began to call the dogs when he noticed the horse was loose. He called back to Chandler, addressing him as "parson." He then called to the yard, "Jack? Are you there?"

A younger man, wearing spectacles and looking prim and properly dressed for such a sudden awakening, came out of the house and hurried toward the mare. As he reached the horse, Jack called in a stern voice, "School man, don't git on that horse or I'll kill ye."

Stunned, the headmaster said, "My word!" He stood frozen by the horse for a moment, as Jack looked at him coldly.

"I wants to ask you, why did that man call you parson?" Jack said.

Licking his lips and swallowing, the schoolmaster said, "'Cause I am also a sometimes preacher."

"Hellfire," said Jack. "Don't you have no real living you can do? Can't you plow some?"

"Yes, sir…but I have to tell you I have been looking for you."

Jack was amazed. He was the one now wondering at what was being said. He took a step closer to the man and said, "You should ne'er be looking fer me." It sounded like a death sentence to the teacher. You be trying to collect some ra-ward or something? You honest or beeve-headed?"

Trying to appear in control, Chandler adjusted his glasses. "No sir. I am true. I have a message for you."

"What you talking about?"

"You are a friend of Mr. Mabry, and he says Mr. Wade Hampton has need of you, and he needs you right away."

Jack was astonished. There was no connection he knew of between this man, the "school man," and Randolph Mabry, and certainly not with a wealthy man such as Wade Hampton.

"All right, what is it? And I will know if you are telling me rightly."

The man knelt down on one knee and began drawing in the dirt. He looked back up at Jack and again adjusted his glasses and squinted through them. "Mr. Mabry says you are to be at Bear Ford near Fishing Creek Church this Sunday night two hours before dark. He says you

The School Master

know the Ford. You and he have been there before. He said to tell you the 'yellow jacket's nest' is gone."

"I think you are right as you say," said Jack. "Only Rand Mabry knows that. What about you? Where you goin' after you tells me this?"

"I am going back to the house and will say nothing. Besides, Mr. Carlisle is a good person, and he takes no sides. If he did, he would be on your side."

Looking at him carefully, and menacingly, Jack said, "That ain't enough."

"What is the reason?" asked the man, feeling fear encroaching again.

Jack glared even harder. "I have lived my time by not trusting people. I ain't starting it now. You are with me."

"What will I tell the Carlisle's?" said Chandler, his voice beseeching.

"Nothing," said Jack. "You ain't going back. I will tell them. Now git Mr. Carlisle. I will ride behind you. Just call him out."

The older Carlisle was still standing on the porch when he saw the two men. Before he could react, he recognized Jack. " Mr. Carlisle, can you come?" said Chandler.

Without hesitation, the tall distinguished man was off the porch steps walking quickly toward the two men on horseback.

" Morning, Mr. Carlisle" said Jack.

"Early morning, Jack!" the gentleman responded with a half-smile.

Jack said, "I knows you understand if I take mister school man with me on a trip. If anyone wonders 'bout him just tell 'em he was with Captain McClure's boys in that fight at the Field…and if they see him they should just kill him."

Jack grinned at his own macabre humor, showing Carlisle more stained teeth than he had ever seen in him. This was his form of wry wit, but it had an ominous ring to it that Carlisle recognized and went along with. "I will have him back if you don't say anything." Jack murmured.

"That is agreeable. We needs his services."

For the next two days, Elberton Chandler spent miserable, fitful times sleeping on the grass at night, with one foot tied to a tree with a rope. Jack didn't talk to him much. Jack never asked him to help him spell, nor asked him any questions. Jack sharpened his knives, cleaned his long rifle, and tended to Maw. Even when they ate there was not much conversation, but at least he was not tied when he ate. Jack mostly stared to the side of him, sometimes glancing away, while Chandler was free from the rope.

When they traveled by horseback Jack always led, sometimes stopping dead still while he listened, for what seemed to be a long time. If they came to heavy brush, Jack waited for Chandler to come through after him. Finally, they arrived at a point where Jack would watch and listen so intently Chandler wondered if Jack was even aware of him. He would talk to Maw, and then circle around on foot and whistle low to himself. He climbed a tree, about twenty feet up, and stayed for what seemed an hour, but said nothing when he came down.

On the Sunday that they were to meet at the ford, Jack watched Chandler for hours, sometimes directly, but always out of the corner of his eye. Chandler quit looking up. He knew Jack was trying to see how he behaved, and he finally tried to sleep, saying he was tired. Jack glared. Chandler actually did sleep, and when he awakened it was later than he thought. Finally after two days of this, Jack said something. "Who am I meeting here?" He honed in on the teacher's face, watching every muscle in his jaws looking for deceit.

Chandler said, "I hear it is someone who has a message for you."

"You hear?"

"Aye."

At just the appointed time, as the sun faded, Jack positioned himself to watch the creek. From the other direction, two men approached on horseback. One was Randolph Mabry. Jack did not make a move, but waited to see what both men would do. Chandler, with his hands and feet bound, was tied to the trunk of a tree behind Jack, who wanted him completely helpless if all this was a trick. He promised him he would "cut his throat" if there was any danger at all. Even with Mabry there, he waited to see telltale signs of treachery. He could believe that

Randolph could be used as a lure. He watched the other man, and he listened and watched the woods behind Mabry.

Jack studied the other man. He was about five feet seven inches and had a straight bearing to his posture. He walked around with his hands behind his back and talked to Mabry comfortably. He gestured, as if making a point and then listened politely, when Mabry spoke. It all seemed natural. But, all the while, Jack kept studying Mabry, who would surely give him the most subtle hint if anything was amiss.

Mabry went to his saddlebags, rummaged through them and returned empty-handed. This relationship between two men that had been born out of times hunting and spending time in the woods had its innuendo and body language. Many times one of them returned from a hunt to pull the kill from his bag – a rabbit, squirrel, quail, or turkey. Mabry had never failed to return with some type of game. There had been a humorous contest running between the friends regarding their catch, and the easygoing behavior was comforting to Jack.

When Rand Mabry folded his arms in expectation, looking somewhat bored and glancing in several directions, Jack emerged. He was fifty yards away, behind the man with Mabry. Jack's closeness startled the stranger. Walking casually toward the man, Jack noticed that he brought his heels slightly together, clicking them in a military fashion, and stood even straighter as Jack approached.

Jack ambled up to Mabry and grunted. Rand bowed slightly, then said, "Jack I would like you to meet Colonel Harrington. He is late of His Majesty's forces in the colonies, specifically the 84th Kings' Regiment of Foot.

"Colonel, this be Jack Beckham, my friend, but a wanted man."

Colonel Harrington looking straight at Jack said, "Sir, I have the pleasure of being your humblest servant on a mission from a very distinguished gentleman, Mr. Wade Hampton, someone whom I understand you know quite well."

"Sir?"

Jack looked at Mabry, not Harrington, for an explanation. "I know for a fact this is a request from Mr. Hampton," Mabry said. "Colonel Harrington is his representative."

Harrington, used to authority, launched into his role. He sounded as if he were addressing an assemblage. "I am here to ask you to do something for the colonies."

"Ain't you on the wrong side, sir?"

"I am not, sir," he answered politely. "I resigned my position with the King's army on condition that I stay in the colonies and not return to England, and that I not serve in an official capacity with your army. I am a barrister and former member of the English parliament. I do not favor subjugation of the colonies. Nay. And I am not serving officially.

"At any chance, however, to be of service, I am now, as you are, a wanted man who will be hanged if caught here today."

Jack addressed Mabry. " Hellfire! I knew we was short of good people—"

"Sir," Harrington broke in, "the request is that you kill Colonel Banastre Tarleton of the British Legion."

Jack, who never hid his sarcasm when given such an opportunity, answered, "Sir, I would be rightly obliged to do so if you would have brought him with you as your guest today…all trussed up as it might be. We could have killed him before supper."

"No! That is not what is meant, sir. You are to seek him and kill him. Tarleton has defeated and wrought the worst form of havoc, and he is credited, wrongly or rightfully so, with undue murder at the Waxhaws. He, alone, has affected the morale of many men; desertion is, in fact, at an unacceptable rate, and you are losing the war.

"Mr. Hampton desires that you have the opportunity to kill Mr. Tarleton; it would help tremendously."

Jack stared at the Colonel. "Is there any other way in damnation to kill him than to do it in battle, or are you asking me to trail him down?"

The Colonel turned away from Jack and walked a few paces. Turning back, he asked Rand Mabry to excuse them. Jack, in his lifetime, had never seen anyone so cultured as Colonel Harrington who could take control of a meeting. He was frustrated. He said for Mabry to stay and not listen to someone who talked so well but didn't have a lot to say.

"You are a fancy person, Colonel. What are you trying to tell me that is so Gawd almighty hard to be saying?"

"Please accept my apologies, sir. I am truly sorry to tell you this, but your sister and a British officer of Colonel Tarleton's staff are in fact having a liaison."

"A what?"

Mabry interceded quickly: "Uh…they are having close relations." Mabry had interrupted with a more mellow voice to keep Jack at bay from the Colonel, who may have just unknowingly triggered a violent reaction.

"Jack…they have been in the same bed. I am sorry, too. Maggie is different."

Jack was stunned. When confronted with news like this, he often dropped his head and looked away. He did on this occasion. But then, looking up, he surprised them. "I will be right back to ye."

At this, both men were puzzled. What did Jack mean? Mabry's mind did a thousand searches. Colonel Harrington looked at Mabry, who did not know how to respond. They didn't have long to wonder. Jack emerged from the brush with Elberton Chandler in front of him, untied, looking confused. Jack said, "This is the school man."

Mabry, of course, knew Chandler; he had contacted him for Wade Hampton, but the Colonel did not know him.

"Now," Jack said with angry conviction, "this is how we will find out the truth."

Not wanting the school teacher to know about his sister, he said, "What we just discussed, gentlemen, can be found out for the truth if this school person can git Easter Benjamin to be saying it. She will know rightly. You don't need to tell this school man nothing, just agree that he will get Easter. I believe her."

Mabry replied. "I think you need to hear more from the Colonel."

"That is right with me," said Jack.

Turning to Chandler, he said, "You go and sit. I ain't gonna tie you."

Walking away so he would not be perceived as listening to the men, the schoolmaster looked back at the three, but he stayed within sight of Jack. The conversation continued.

Mabry said, "Colonel Harrington is telling the truth, and he knows how you can get to Tarleton. When you confirm all this you will be able to surprise him when he is at a farm with the officer who shares affections with Maggie. You have your best chance to get him there."

"What farm?" Jack queried.

"Don't know," replied Mabry. "Tarleton's men will take a farm from a Tory and displace the family, then give it back to them the next day. Somehow the officer contacts Maggie. It is not at her place but someone else's. Sometimes it is in the area of the great falls and sometimes near Cedar Shoals or even near Camden. You noticed Maggie been gone?"

Jack looked straight at Mabry but did not answer.

Jack said, "You know this for true?"

"No," Rand said, "only that Wade Hampton said it and sent Colonel Harrington to tell me. The Colonel is a gentleman. He is what you and I call a man of law, an aide to Hampton."

"Well, I need to hear it from Easter" said Jack, sneering. "If I ain't seen it, or I ain't heard it, then I ain't knowing it."

"May I address the situation?" asked Harrington.

"Go ahead," Jack snapped, and then spit a stream of tobacco near the Colonel.

Colonel Harrington remarked, "Mr. Chandler does not need to know about this, but he does need to know his life is not in danger. What if he goes to secure Benjamin and decides to run away? You have scared him, sir. You need to take him into your confidence…tell him he will be protected and that he needs to ask her to meet you; that is all. Unfortunately, she does know, and she will tell you. But I fear she will not respond to someone such as Mr. Chandler, who has no confidence in the request."

Jack eyed Colonel Harrington as if he was speaking a foreign language. He looked back at Rand Mabry for assurance. Before Mabry could speak, the eloquent Harrington asked if he could reassure Chandler. "After all, I am the one to have brought the message from Mr.

Hampton, and he trusted me to see Mr. Mabry. Mr. Chandler needs to know he is not being used unduly."

"How ye gonna do that?" the perplexed Jack asked.

"I have the same question, Colonel Harrington," Rand Mabry added.

"Let me talk to Mr. Chandler right here in front of both of you. He can make his own decision. You don't want to force him, do you gentlemen? He is, after all, an asset to the community, someone much admired and liked."

Jack, at this point was tired of hearing Harrington talk. He had never met anyone who could say so much and not make himself clear. He motioned for Harrington to get Chandler but then stepped in front of him. "Nay!" He had changed his mind. He would get Chandler himself.

Jack walked to the clearing where the teacher was standing and motioned for him to come over. Jack pointed to the retired British Colonel without saying anything. The Colonel cleared his throat as he addressed the school teacher. "Uh...sir...Mr. Chandler, sir, we have a situation, much as was in literature, that I trust you, being very literate, will understand."

Nodding, Chandler turned his head toward Harrington as if listening even more intently. Harrington went on. "You remember in King Richard III when it was said, 'Go with the task at hand and do it joyfully; no harm will come?'"

Chandler nodded yes.

Jack, looking intently at the two, pulled strings of tobacco out of his pocket and put a wad in one cheek and then the other. Looking distrustful, he asked Mabry, "Are they talking about me?"

"Can't be," teased Mabry. "They look to be too friendly."

The two educated men nodded and continued. Finally, Harrington turned, approached them, and said, "Mr. Chandler will do as you ask. He will fetch the slave wench, Easter Benjamin, and she will confirm this. And Mr. Beckham, sir, I suggest we need to procure her as soon as we might."

Looking somewhat resigned for the first time at hearing this odd news about Maggie, Jack motioned to Harrington with his hands, a Catawba sign that they would be traveling, that the two would leave, and he would show Chandler where they would go. Harrington nodded as if he understood.

Before turning to leave, Colonel Harrington said to Jack that he had heard of his great prowess with a rifle, a tomahawk, and a hunting knife. "You are much admired by Mr. Hampton."

Jack had heard these things before. He just nodded at another compliment and took the reins of Maw to walk her to a clearing.

"But," said Harrington, "I feel as if I might advise you of something about your forthcoming duties for Mr. Hampton, if I may."

Jack looked unconvinced.

Continuing, Harrington said, "Invariably when Colonel Tarleton is amongst his men he rises very early and rides among them in camp. This may not be true when he visits a Loyalist's farm, but it is his custom in an encampment. Often before dawn, he is fully dressed and he has been known to begin a march at 4:00 a.m. He walks among the men, talks to them by camp fires, and eats with them. To say that he has their allegiance would be an understatement. He, among all the officers in this area and colonies, is much admired for a young officer still in his twenties…and may I say loved?"

Jack stared during this discourse. He listened even more intently as he tried to determine the point of all this, but said nothing.

Harrington continued. "As he is inclined to do this, no doubt to prepare them for the day and to maintain their fighting posture, he is what I would say, less cautious than he ordinarily might be. In other words, the sentries are not at their fullest during this wee hour, and it is a somewhat relaxed period. The men are not quite stirring, but Mr. Tarleton is, and he rides among the men. You see Sir, he is many times on horseback. In the dark or by firelight, he is elevated among his men; indeed he is the only one on horseback and an easier target.

"I dare say this may be the most opportune time to kill him. Possibly one shot from a distance you choose, and you are on your steed and away before the men become organized. What say you, sir, to this suggestion?"

Mabry looked around, trying his best to appear nonchalant, at the surroundings of the ford and creek. For him, this was an old habit to see if anyone else was present; he also did it as he did not want Jack to know that he was as interested in the answer as Harrington. He was Jack's friend, but he was enjoying this melodrama and Jack's uneasiness. He resisted a smile at his friends expense.

Jack scuffed his boots in the dirt, spat a stream of tobacco juice and moved closer to Harrington. He saw that the Colonel had a young, boyish look, and not many lines in his face. He also noticed inside the man's buttoned frock a striking brass gorget of intricate markings which was impressive. It bespoke his former service as an officer in the military, although he wore it now as a gentleman and as a symbol, not as a uniform.

Harrington stared intently at Jack, awaiting his reply.

Jack asked casually, "Let me be asking you, how does I know this man Tarleton? What does he look like? You going to show me?"

Before Harrington could answer, Jack shook his head no and said, "Ain't no use is there? If I sees him with Maggie, even with others, then I knows he is the man I aims to kill, don't I? Was you planning on going with me?"

Now the former British officer knew that Jack was suspicious of him. Was this a last minute ploy to see if this was all subterfuge on his part? He felt threatened and more vulnerable. Thinking quickly, Harrington rose up slightly on his booted toes and answered coolly. "No sir, I was not. I can describe him to you, for you will surely see him as a leader; he is unmistakable. If you see him with Mrs. Land, even with others, you will know him in that way. But on the field, he wears the uniform and the hat and plume in a way, with his red hair and bearing, that is quite distinct."

Jack had heard enough. For the most part he believed Harrington, but he was intent on getting to Easter. Almost as if on cue, Rand Mabry said, "We must be about this. Jack, we thank you for your presence. I will relay your best wishes to Mr. Hampton."

Jack turned to walk away, but then held up his hand quickly. He held it up for Mabry to stay and not to mount. In fact, he was telling both of them to stay. Mabry knew this, and by his glance at the Colonel saw that he also understood. Jack would now collect Chandler and move away from them. Mabry also sensed something else. "Colonel," he said, "just stand here for awhile and don't move about."

"Aye," said Harrington, unsure of why he said it and why he would do it. However, after a few minutes he had to ask Mabry, " Sir, why are we dawdling here?"

"Jack just wants to be as far away as he can before you leave. Sorry sir, don't take this as an insult, but I think…" At that Mabry was interrupted by the splintering sound of a lead ball striking a tree several yards away. The bark flew off, and they both looked startled.

"Jack!" said Mabry grinning, looking proud of his friend. "He must be nigh unto a hundred yards away by now. I think, Colonel, you just got a salute, begrudging as it was, from Jack Beckham…I would also say he has accepted what you say."

Harrington half-smiled and said, "Good man Beckham…a bit unto himself, mind you, but a good man."

By this time, Jack and the schoolmaster were already much farther away, headed in a direction to see Easter Benjamin. Jack was already thinking of his words to dear Easter. She had raised Maggie, had made her clothes and changed her clothes. She had chased teasing boys playfully off with a stick when Maggie was thirteen years old with chores to do. She had laughed when she did it, saying, "Git yourselfs yonder 'fore I tans you."

It was Easter who sang to herself and then hummed constantly when working around the farm. Maggie often watched her, feeling safe in Easter's presence. The woman cooked, made favorite pies, and cleaned, talking to herself softly, always with the same declaration of "Lawd hab mucy." If someone died, it was "Lawd hab mucy," or if good fortune came, it was "Lawd hab mucy."

If asked a question that she wished to delay, she answered, "If'n de Lawd be willin." Maggie often teased her and asked a question as a game she played with her. "Will you be back tomorrow morning?"

Easter always gave the same serious answer: "If'n de Lawd be willin."

She had delivered many babies in their family. She had cared for men in the Beckham family, including Thomas and Reuben, who were suffering with racking fever. She had washed their naked bodies in front of their wives with cold spring water to stay the fever. She was, above all else, "Easter," a family legend.

But he had never talked in her presence about what he had to ask her. He had never spoken of intimate matters. It was a scant talked about subject even among white people. He needed words, and he wondered who could tell him in his family what to say. Worst of all, he knew now who had betrayed him when he approached Mabry's farm. He had been betrayed before going to Charlestowne. It was either Samuel or Maggie. Only they knew beforehand he was going there. He now sensed it was Maggie.

He sat upright in his saddle and cursed out loud, so that a startled Chandler's head shot up; he felt for a second that Jack was going to turn around and do harm to him. Chandler felt terribly isolated, bewildered at finding himself in the woods with a violent person, out of the safe confines of a cabin teaching children.

Jack bellowed again and cursed. A very disturbed and confused Chandler began to try and slow his horse down, not to get too close to Jack in this sudden rage. He prayed quietly out of stark fear; he quoted from memory as if hearing a sermon, muttering verses from the Book of Common Prayer. "For none of us liveth to himself, and no man dieth to himself. For if we live, we live unto the Lord, and if we die we die unto the Lord. Whether we live, therefore or die, we are the Lords. Lord have mercy," he whispered.

Jack picked up the pace; Maw began to canter. Chandler did the same.

Chapter Eight

Easter

Traveling with Elberton Chandler, Jack felt a great need to let him go. Chandler was a burden that prevented him from getting to Easter Benjamin as quickly as he could have alone. He decided to tell Chandler that he would "trust him to just go and not talk." His plan was also to use Chandler to obtain information.

"Trust?" Chandler said. "Sir, whom do I have to tell? My instructions are to ride to see the slave woman, Easter Benjamin, and ask her to meet with you. What would I do now that would belie your trust, may I respectfully inquire?"

"Just go and tell her I am looking to find her...that be all there is to it."

They were two miles from Maggie's plantation, so Chandler felt safe enough to ride on, although he looked back twice before he galloped on. He went straight for the Land's farm and began to question those he met as he rode onto the property.

"Where is Easter Benjamin?" he asked of a slave girl. He got no answer. He asked three others who were washing clothes in a large iron pot, and no one knew. He asked a young farm hand about Maggie Land, as well. The boy, Alexander, said he did not know and looked away.

Chandler was frustrated; he knew he had to give a message to someone, or he would not rest easy. He would be waiting for Jack to seek him out. Unknown to him, he was being watched by Jack from a distance with a spy glass. Jack had purposely let him go to see if he would go to Maggie's.

Jack watched while Chandler, doing his duty as promised, rode farther into the pastures and land, now being over-planted in this late season. Jack followed out of sight on Maw from a distance. He knew Chandler would eventually reach the main house, and he would return either with Maggie or Easter or alone. Then he would continue on to the Carlisle home. If he came back alone, Jack would intercept him at some point on his way back and get the answer he needed. He did not have to follow Chandler everywhere he went. Chandler was even now disappearing into a tree line and would have to go through the woods to reach another pasture.

Jack positioned himself in a clump of trees in a rotten hollow of an oak three feet off the ground, and rested while he waited. More than anything he listened. Unfettered, Maw was foraging, eating sweet grass close to Jack, raising her head now and then. When she did, Jack noted her reactions to scents and noises. Maw was part of his waiting and watching; to have her tied was not what he wanted. A whinny from her would be a great alarm. He would mount her immediately and decide which way to ride, for it could be a wild animal or a person.

At dusk, Jack saw a group of field hands, more than twenty in wagons, coming back home for the evening. Many were singing as field hands might at the end of the day. There was no sign of Easter. He determined to wait until all had passed and to use darkness as a "friend" to get into the woods to spend the night. He would move away from Maggie's house in case the worst happened. If Chandler had been taken prisoner and confessed that Jack was looking for Maggie, a posse of neighbor Loyalists, Royal Provincials, or even British Regulars would be searching for him in the area.

Jack waited until he saw in the distance, framed by a setting sun, a man on a mule pulling one wagon and Chandler man riding alongside it. Easter was in the wagon. He knew they would be in full darkness when they arrived at Easter's cabin. Jack would now have to follow them undetected or ride into the middle of them and stop them. The man with the mule pulling the wagon was "old Saul," a trusted widower whose only job now in his old age was to take slaves back and forth to fields and bring food to them during the day. He was not a hindrance.

Jack studied the three and wondered where Maggie was. He decided not to interrupt but wait to see Easter alone. Now he asked himself, "How is the best way?" He followed them at a deliberate pace, knowing they would not be listening for a horse behind them, but rather be intent on getting home for supper.

As they approached Easter's split log cabin, Chandler accelerated and his horse began to gallop away, going undoubtedly to the Carlisle home for the evening. Old Saul stopped the wagon to help Easter out, and then moved on.

Easter's cabin, one room with a brick floor and a large fire place, was behind a row of slave houses. It was quiet there, away from the cabins with families, and had been given to her in deference to her age. Young men moved from cabin to cabin for their recreation in the evening, playing cards, telling stories, singing and laughing, some drinking late into the night. Easter was away from these disturbances.

Although she was elderly, Easter remained the matriarch among all the black women, and was also respected by the men. She was Maggie's favorite as well; no one questioned it. If Maggie wanted her at any time, she sent a wagon to bring Easter to the big house. Many times she slept at the house in a room off of Maggie's, so she was not always in her cabin. This would be more evidence that Maggie was consorting with someone if Easter Benjamin was staying in her log cabin for the evening.

Jack knew this. He waited to see if a wagon would come for her. He waited. He smelled the supper from the kitchen and recognized it as sweet potatoes, fried hog fat back and poured hot butter. He envisioned Easter eating by the fire, humming softly to herself, but determined to wait to make sure she was not disturbed.

At around nine o'clock Jack surveyed around him. He made sure Maw was not too close to make a noise, but within easy running distance if he had to get to her quickly. He walked up to Easter's door, which was closed but not locked, and looked in. She was slumped over in her cane back chair, her head resting on her chest, dozing in front of the fading fire. Her head was wrapped in a calico kerchief; she still had on her field clothes and heavy stockings rolled down around her ankles. In her hands was a handkerchief that she often carried, to wipe around her mouth when she was dipping and spitting snuff.

He entered without knocking, eyes darting around the room as was his instinct. He did not want to scare her and cause a scream. Easter was emotional and dramatic, and had not seen him since he had left for Mabry's farm. He made a decision not to call out, even in a whisper.

He took three long strides and was in the middle of the room where she sat. He deftly grabbed her around her neck, and firmly, but not with major force, put his hand over her mouth, his index finger and thumb tight under her nose. Then he leaned down and whispered in her ear, "Shhh. Easter, it is me, Jack. It is so…don't be sceered…shhh…shh!"

Easter would have bolted up if Jack had not been holding her. She screamed under his hand and trembled, a muffled sound that was high and piercing. Jack continued to hold her and say "It is me, Jack," until he felt her relax and acknowledge him.

He moved around so she could see him, although he did not take his hand off of her mouth. He nodded at her as if to ask if she was all right, then slowly removed his hand. She looked at him and said, "Lawd, Lawd, Massah Jack…oh my Lawd! Why is you here?…don'ts you know so many folks be looking fo' you? Please don't be staying here…please!"

Jack put both hands on her upper arms as if to brace her, and said in a softer voice, "I am going, but I needs to ask you something that I have heard."

"No! No! No! Massah Jack, don't ax me that…no, Lawd. I is afred of what you be saying…Oh Lawd, please spare me dis!"

Jack knew she would be emotional about Maggie, her beloved "white chile," and he had seen her like this before. He let it play out and just kept repeating, "Easter, don't be fearful…Easter."

She began to cry softly into her handkerchief, aware that too much noise, particularly of her in distress, would bring all the slaves in earshot to her cabin. They would pose no danger to Jack, but their clamor would be disruptive to all the cabins and would surely be followed by a storm of noise and activity.

Easter rocked back and forth in her chair, weeping and wiping her eyes. She was, however, a strong and knowledgeable woman who had helped minister to others. She had birthed babies; she had tended to – and often cured – all manner of diseases for so many years, for so many people, white and colored.

Jack knew he had only a short time with her. He stood up and allowed her to rock and cry for a while, but then he spoke to her in a harsher voice. "Is Maggie here?"

Easter looked up at him and just closed her eyes.

"Easter! Is she bedding down with some Britisher?"

She began to weep even harder, shaking her head and imploring Jack to go.

"I can't be going until you tells me," he said. "I needs to know…I needs to know…Maggie is my sister…I ain't hurting her, but peoples been talking so I has to know."

Easter continued to cry, just shaking her head.

Jack said, "I know about Eddards."

At that, Easter spoke with conviction in her voice. "Massah Jack, I knows you lub the Lawd even tho' you ain't no church man…I knows that. I knows that the Lawd will take care of him in his own way…he take care of him."

Jack said impatiently, "I knows that."

Then Easter looked at him for the first time without crying and said, "Wills you take an oath? Wills you promise me sometin'?"

"If I can…can't promise something if I ain't heard it."

Easter got up slowly, walking slightly bent over to her one table in the room. She reached under a beautiful white linen cloth, carefully embroidered, and produced her Bible. She had some reading knowledge, unknown to many people, but Jack knew it.

She said to Jack, "Wills you promise to the Lawd not to harm Miss Maggie if'n I tells you? I lubs that chile and you too, Massah Jack, so's I has to know…please dear Gawd! Promise me you wills take dis oath."

Jack stared at her. He started to say something to reason with

"Swear"

Easter, but her eyes bored into him, and he found himself just staring back. He was a little perturbed when he said, "How can I tell you something if'n I don't knows what you are going to be saying? I ain't in no hurry to kill Maggie…what in hellfire has she done to make you ask me that? What do you be saying?"

Even with Easter, Jack knew or suspected what Maggie had done, but he would not tell her first; he wanted to hear it from her. He had not the heart to accuse Maggie of betraying him to the British and even worse, possibly Loyalists, if he could help it.

Easter saw she had to compromise, so she pressed the Bible toward Jack's hand and said quite firmly, "Don't kills your kin folks, Massah. Gawd is bigger than us…some peoples deserves to be dead…Maggie ain't….she is still my chile and she is still your kin."

"Well?" Jack said with some exasperation, reaching out and placing his left hand on the Bible. "I promises not to kill Maggie, damnation no matter."

For the first time Easter smiled gently.

Jack said, "I wants to know if'n Maggie is been bedding with some traitor or a damnable Britisher!!"

Easter was taken back at Jack's words but said, "Yes, she has seen a man at the house, and he is a British soldier."

Jack said " Is this man…is he…is they bedding here tonight?"

"No, suh."

"What do they call him?" pressed Jack…

"De Colonel's man…he calls him Major, suh, dats all."

"What does that mean?" asked a confounded Jack.

Easter was silent and did not change her expression as she looked down.

"Tell me, Easter, where is Maggie?"

"You knows I don't know, suh. They don't never comes here…it is always other place, and I has seen Miss Maggie so few times lately."

"I am obliged to you," said Jack with some resignation, "but I has to tell you, if'n others find out, I can't be sure what they will do…I fear for Maggie. She needs not be seeing this Britisher, no matter who it be."

Easter, her words catching in her throat, said, "One more things to tell you, Massah, and dis is so…I am so sorry, suh." Jack stiffened as Easter teared up and began to cry again, wringing the handkerchief in her hands. "Massah, she be carrying his chile, his bebe chile. I thinks she seven months, maybe…maybe she be more."

At this, Jack said nothing. He did an about-face abruptly and walked out. He hastened his steps to get Maw and ride off, to where he was not sure.

Where were they tonight? Why had she betrayed him? He was anxious and enraged to carry out the gentleman Wade Hampton's orders. He aimed for the woods away from Maggie's and toward the Catawba reservation. Jack would get as far in that direction as possible before stopping for the night. The one person he needed now was Soe, and possibly other Catawbas who would help him search out Tarleton, this officer, and Maggie. Either one or both.

He might break his oath to Easter if necessary.

Chapter Nine

The Baptism

That night Jack stayed in a trench that was so deep and dense with trees and brush, he felt even safer than usual. Anyone approaching, especially a group of dragoons would enter one end or the other, and he would make a run for the opposite side. Maw would stay close, and after brushing her down and getting feed for her, he brought water to her from a branch.

He made no fire. Weary, he lay down, but did not sleep for several fitful hours. Tomorrow he would go to the Catawba Nation by a circuitous, albeit safe, route to enlist Soe's help.

Jack awoke one hour before sunlight and cared for Maw again. He fed and watered her, massaged her back, and replaced the saddle on her. He carried nothing he did not need, in order to travel even faster. He carried the long rifle loaned by Mabry, and he checked his own knife and tomahawk, as well as the spy glass that he would use to survey the Catawba camp before approaching it.

Along the way, Jack looked for new summer berries and was ever mindful of game to kill if the chance arose. It did not take long; he flushed a rabbit that ran straight away from him, but he knew it would eventually circle back to his original burrow. He took up watch behind some bushes and waited a good hour; then, as his prey returned, he crouched on one knee and fired. There would be no meal there, as he wished to travel on quickly – away from the sound of his shot. A few hours later, he settled down and cooked the good sized jack rabbit over a fire of oak, then buried the ashes.

Near this cooking site was a mature pond, fed by a spring that made the water sweet, an ideal habitat for frogs – and he savored frogs' legs. Cutting a willow sapling to a very sharp edge, he used it like a spear as he circled the pond looking for a frog lazing in the sun. Jack found it and killed it with a clean drive of his spear. He cut the fat legs off and put them into a hunting pouch; they would provide dinner tonight, somewhere near the Catawbas.

At late afternoon he approached an area where he knew the tribe had lookouts. He would not have used it if he had wanted to be furtive, but wanted to make contact with a tribe member who would make his arrival known. Jack saw from a distance what appeared to be a rock formation that jutted out over a path; it was an approach to the Catawba Nation. That meant he would come in contact with someone soon; he would call out once and wait. All Catawbas knew Jack, and several of Soe's friends were close to him.

He came within fifty yards of the overhang, and knew he had already been heard and possibly sighted. Still sitting on Maw, Jack called out the name that Soe had given him, "Dugma wa!" Jack listened and heard nothing but wind, then moved several yards closer and waited. Looking to his left and right, he saw nothing.

He had just started to move forward, very slowly on Maw, when he saw movement above him. An Indian stepped out from behind a tree on the rock ledge. He was watching Jack, saying nothing. Raising his right hand to cross over his left to show friendship of two, Jack made the sign and said, "Soe."

Jack did not recognize this Indian and wondered who he might be. The Indian still said nothing but mounted a horse standing behind him on the hill and began to descend. The man was a young warrior, and he started to move away in a direction toward the Nation and at a speed that invited Jack to follow him. This friendly gesture was all Jack could expect, and he was not surprised, although he wondered who this warrior was. He was dressed in skins and boots and wore a rough cloth weskit over a blue shirt. He wore a floppy hat and carried a rifle decorated with ribbons and feathers.

Jack had seen this on warriors who were part of a raiding party, never on one in peace, but maybe this was not considered peacetime after the battle at Alexander's Old Field. Soe had not been at Alexander's but it occurred to him that Samuel was supposed to be at the Nation; this might be a sign of war because a wanted man was in their camp. Jack continued to follow the man as he plodded ahead.

Jack made a decision. He acted quickly without noise. He reached down and pulled his rifle out of his saddle holster. It was loaded with a lead .50-caliber ball and only needed powder in the pan. Jack filled it and did not pull the cock back for it was a distinctive sound, even as two horses were traveling. He lowered the gun in the cradle of his arm and elbow, to bring it up quickly if needed, aimed at the man. He carried it this way and kept riding for some yards.

The Indian went several yards and suddenly stopped and looked back, but showed no alarm. Instead he said in broken English, "Sunday Man…kode…su kode."

The native had said, "Reverend Simpson come into the house." Simpson was called "the Sunday Man," for he preached to the Catawbas every Sunday and had for years, although no one had converted to Christianity. This might be what Jack needed to know. Simpson had been at Alexander's Old Field as had Samuel.

The two continued on toward the Nation, and in the distance Jack saw other tribal members coming toward them; in the pack was Soe. Jack had lowered his rifle slightly as they rode. Now he holstered it away, gaining confidence about the Indian for the first time. Jack greeted Soe as he approached, stopped, and with an embrace of his open hand clasped Soe's upper arm firmly. Soe returned the greeting in the same manner. First one hand onto the upper arm and then the other. They then turned and started riding back to the Nation without speaking.

Riding with Soe were two warriors that Jack knew as "Kutkin" and "Musi." They were Soe's closest friends, and they both looked at Jack and nodded. This was a great show of friendship, and Jack began wondering what they knew that might cause this nodding of heads.

Something Samuel or Reverend Simpson had said since they arrived in camp?

Jack wanted to speak, but it was most improper to initiate a conversation with a Catawba. Jack would have to maintain his silence until they got to camp, which might not be the main camp on the river, and then Soe could answer back. They traveled for more than an hour before Soe and the men stopped and got off their horses. Jack noticed that the man who had first met him on the path had long ago dropped off. Jack also noticed that none of the Catawbas had decorations like his on their rifles.

Soe motioned for Jack to come and walk with him away from the others. Jack saw the others begin building a fire, so he knew then they were here for the night.

Soe looked away casually and said to Jack, "Big fight at the Field!" Jack could finally speak.

"Is Samuel here?"

Soe nodded.

Jack said in Soe's language, "I have need of you to help me find Maggie and this British fighting man, Tarleton."

He then went into the whole story regarding Wade Hampton and the fancy man, Colonel Harrington. Then he asked Soe if he and his warriors would help him find Tarleton.

Soe did not interrupt, and when Jack was finished, Soe motioned that they had to eat. Jack went to get the frog's legs that all would eat, along with cakes of corn and honey in an earthenware jar that Soe's men produced. Before they ate, Jack went to Maw and led her to a stream and brought some new grass for her. Then he went into his evening ritual of rubbing her down, checking her hooves and tail for briars, and caressing her face while she butted him affectionately. This would be an early night for both, for they were showing signs of fatigue.

Settling down, Jack's hand felt his head wound, which he thought had almost healed. Soe noticed the wound and just shook his head. Jack took this to mean the stitches were still in and the wound had not completely healed, for he had lost some feeling in his scalp.

Soe, Jack, and the Catawbas slept around the fire that night, apparently safe on their own ground with knowledge that other Catawbas had encircled them for protection. Jack had not felt this secure in days. Still, everyone slept with a gun at the ready, the horses close by.

Rising at dawn to an owl that would not stop hooting, Jack and the others went about their business. All ate what they had in their bags and drank water from the stream. Musi covered the remains of the campfire, and then the four started for the main Catawba encampment. As they approached, Jack was in the sight of two white men who were there to see him. Word had reached Samuel and Reverend Simpson, and they both waited expectantly to hear news from Jack. When Jack dismounted he put an arm on Samuel's shoulder and shook the Reverend's hand. Jack said as he grinned, "You both look rightly well…for two men waiting to be hanged."

Neither smiled much at that, and then Jack explained, without mentioning Maggie, that he had been asked by Wade Hampton to get to the British Colonel Tarleton, and that he needed help from the Catawbas in tracking and scouting him. Jack asked Soe to join them, and the four went to a group of fallen trees and sat down.

Jack asked Soe if they could leave that afternoon to try to find Tarleton; surprisingly, Soe said no.

"What be the reason?" Jack asked.

Soe said, "I am waiting to be in the water."

Jack knew Soe did not make jokes. He looked at the preacher, who said he could explain.

"Soe is a Christian now; he is waiting to talk to you about being baptized. We have a difficulty that you can help me with."

"Hellfire, preacher, we all has a problem with being stretched by them British with a rope."

"Sir, come over here with me and let us talk."

Simpson motioned to Jack while Soe and Samuel sat on the trees observing. Simpson, a bandy-legged, feisty man of many words, walked over to a clearing and put his leg up on a rock and rested his arm on it casually. Looking quite professorial, he looked up and addressed the taller Jack. "Now, sir, I am about telling you my problem and how you can help Soe."

Jack grunted a reply of approval and folded his arms in anticipation. Simpson continued.

"Soe wants to be baptized like our Lord, who was baptized by John
in the river Jordan." The Parson said it this way for he thought Jack was
completely beyond understanding concerning the Bible. "Soe has heard
the Word. He believes and he wants to do everything rightly."

"So do it," Jack replied.

"Well, sir, there is a problem…with a white man holding an Indian
under water, and a problem about ghosts…"

Jack began to smile, the grin spreading broadly, a phenomenon that
Simpson had never seen before.

"And," Simpson went on, "I am having trouble with the Holy Ghost
with Soe…he is afraid of ghosts."

"That is not hard to believe, preacher man…where are these ghosts
that Soe is afraid of?"

"In the Apostles Creed, which we all believe in and repeat for our
faith."

"I ain't never heard it," said Jack, and Simpson could easily believe
it. "What is so bad about it?"

"It is not bad," Simpson shot back. "It says, 'I believe in God, the
Father Almighty, maker of heaven and earth, and in Jesus Christ His
only Son our Lord; who was conceived by the Holy Ghost and it says
later that, 'I believe in the Holy Ghost; the holy catholic Church; the
communion of saints; the forgiveness of sins; the resurrection of the
body; and the life everlasting.'

"In the holy Apostles Creed, we repeat what we believe; Soe must
say what he believes."

"What part does Soe like?" Jack inquired, partly for his own curi-
osity but also to irritate Simpson.

"He likes the part of the body resurrecting. He also accepts Christ
as King, being more powerful than King George of England and King
Hagler of the Catawbas. But Soe is looking for ghosts when we talk.
He is looking for them outside his hut… when he is hunting. He is
afraid of being baptized because the ghosts may come while he is under
water. I plainly needs your help, sir, and…"

Jack looked at Simpson and tried not to laugh. He motioned Simpson away from him as if he wanted nothing to do with the conversation…then he burst out with a contemptuous laugh that made Samuel and Soe come over to see what was causing the unusual noise.

Jack was on his feet laughing and walking away, while Reverend Simpson hurried after him. Simpson said in a very serious voice. "Sir, you are hindering a man wishing to become a Christian, and Soe trusts you. Would you stand between a man and God?"

Simpson had his hands on his hips and was glaring at Jack, who looked back at him and laughed harder. Jack continued walking until he saw Samuel and Soe. He waved them away.

Simpson, probably the only man that could challenge Jack in such a manner, hurried up to him and stood only six feet away. He raised up on his toes, trying to make his five foot six inch stature more formidable in the face of six-foot-tall Jack. He had decided to push the issue.

"Sir, God may be using you to help a man, a Catawba, become a believer and thereby help others to become believers also. The Bible says, 'Would a man rob God?'

"You, sir, would you rob God?"

Jack was slightly piqued. "I ain't robbing nobody…ne'er have."

Simpson felt the advantage and said, "The only way that Soe will be baptized is for you to be baptized with him…what say you to that?"

Jack almost exploded. "To hell with it. I ain't going to be held underwater either."

"Soe is an Indian…he has a Spirit to help him and his tribe."

"Maybe, Preacher, that Spirit is the same as God…maybe both are Spirit and Holy Ghost…what say you to that?"

Simpson smiled. "Sir, you are correct. Glory it is! You have it rightly so…God is a spirit and a Holy Ghost. I will tell Soe…and you, sir, just talk to him about baptizing. If'n you talk to him, I will baptize him. But you have blasphemed God, sir. You cannot say "to hell with it" when you are talking about our Lord.

"Will you ask for forgiveness?"

Jack took a step toward Simpson as if he was going to do bodily violence to him, and for a second, Simpson feared he would. Getting in his face, his breath hot on the preacher's forehead, Jack said, "Don't begin no 'Preacher man' talk to me, no 'Sunday man' to me. I ain't the one being saved, Soe is."

"Aye, Jack, but you just described it as it is. You have inspired me to say to Soe what God has instructed you. Now, ask God's forgiveness…you are being used by him in a goodly way."

Jack thought Simpson had gone harebrained. This was the same man who fought with him at Alexander's Old Field, and who disliked the British so much. Jack respected him but knew nothing about him. Thinking about it, he searched for a way to get something in return for acting in a way he was not used to. Jack's main talent in daily commerce was bargaining, and when he had something to offer he tried to find a middle ground. In this case he was talking about something that he had little knowledge about…he did not know religion.

He replied in the way he did when bargaining. "I will trade back to you. I will talk to God of this thing, and I will talk to Soe about his being in the water, but that is all I agrees to do. And…I has something to ask of you."

"Whatever it may be," said Simpson. "What is it he asked quickly?"

"I am thinking…it will be something I need," he said. Jack remembered Maggie and thought having someone pray for her might be good, something he had heard about from Easter Benjamin. This was the deal he offered Reverend Simpson.

Simpson looked at him expectantly and said, "Has you prayed before?"

Jack did not answer but walked away to ponder the process. He had not prayed before. He looked around him and all seemed normal, people and things were in order. Children were running and Catawbas were doing usual things. No one was staring at him except a watchful Reverend Simpson, who Jack thought, as a preacher, was supposed to look as he did right now.

Thinking about praying, he almost decided to forget it all and leave. The one factor in his decision, however, was his honor in horse trading. He had made a deal with Simpson, as with anyone in a horseflesh exchange, and the worst thing that could be said about any man was he was a horse thief and liar. That was more serious than this "praying," but he feared what people might say about him and this praying thing.

He thought for several minutes, sensed Simpson shifting his feet from side to side and watching him. He looked up in reverence and just started, although uncomfortably, to talk way out of the range of being heard by Simpson. He mumbled as he addressed God, looking uncharacteristically humble and out of place. "Sir! It is me Jack…Jack Beckham. I lives on Sandy Run near the Pacolet River on Grindal Shoals. I am trusting you are doing well.

"The Preacher says I am 'blas' something to you, and I am rightly sorry. I ain't never 'blased' anyone and I knows I do not want to rob you…or anyone. If'n you think I robbed you, then don't think that. I am going to talk to Soe about being baptized. I will do my best for he wants to be like you…the Reverend says it. So I will be about it. Thank you…by your leave, sir."

Jack did not know what to do next. He took off his hat and made a courteous bow with his arm, hat in hand. He stepped back, one boot behind the other, and held his hat as if he were greeting and saluting an officer in the ranks.

From a distance the Reverend Simpson saw Jack finishing and said, "AMEN" out loud, sensing a small victory. Jack just glared at him and walked past him to find Soe. He had made a bargain with Simpson and he was anxious to fulfill it. Walking among the Catawbas, he had a strange thought. He wondered if this Colonel Harrington had ever prayed? If he had, would the Lord understand him?

Jack felt he had done a pretty good job himself, and if the occasion ever arose he would tell his dear wife, Elizabeth, but she might think he had been drinking. He put the thought out of his mind.

Samuel was in sight but Soe was not. Jack approached Samuel and asked about Soe. Samuel, in turn, asked about the Preacher man and what was said. Jack asked again about Soe. Samuel pointed toward the hut where Soe lived and said, "There." Jack approached the hut and stopped a good fifty yards away and called out to him in Sioux. Soe emerged with his wife, Ahatha. Using sign language, Jack asked if they could talk and Soe nodded. The two walked to an area away from the tribe, but in view of any exits they might have to use in a hurry; it had become clear that Jack, Samuel, and Simpson would have to leave soon or invite a mass attack on the Catawbas by an organized British force.

Soe and Jack had had many conversations. There was a bond between them that exceeded any that Jack had with relatives or friends. Samuel was a nephew, but Soe was a friend who had great experience, and who could read Jack's mind as could Jack his. They spoke few words but had great understanding. It was common for Jack and Soe to go two days when traveling and never complete a sentence with each other; each going about his duties, each understanding.

On this day Jack thought that Soe had changed considerably and asked him a disarming and unexpected question. "Who was the man who met me on the trail with the feathers and ribbons on his rifle butt? Was he long time Catawba?"

"Long time north," said Soe, meaning North Carolina. "He is back to us. His all killed by British."

All his family had been killed for some reason by the British or at least their deaths were being blamed on them. This, then, was the reason why he had hunting party dress on his gun. Jack thought, "This man is still at war with the British. Good."

Jack looked hard at Soe. In truth, Soe knew this was the serious conversation that the Reverend had talked about and that Jack and the Reverend had discussed.

Jack asked him directly, "Are you one of them Christians now?"

Soe answered, "Patki re," which was equal to a yes in his language.

"You has to be baptized then…be in the water with the preacher to holds you there for a short time, just like the Book said…you knows that?"

Soe shook his head "no," and said he would not unless Jack did. And so what began as a conversation would grow into many conversations in the next few days. Jack and Soe, along with Samuel and Simpson, would stay at the Catawba Nation, waiting for news from warrior scouts that were out daily and back into the camp.

The worst news would have been an impending attack on the

Catawbas themselves; however, no Catawba had been at the Old Field so Jack did not concern himself over that. He thought of a massive attack on the Nation by Loyalists and British but a warning would have come in advance even if it took place at night. Jack was safe but would soon grow tired of waiting and hiding; the issue of Maggie gnawed at him

Perhaps after days stretching into weeks Jack would feel the need to pressure Soe into going into the water, so that he could enlist his help—and other warriors'—in finding Maggie. If it were ultimately only Jack and Samuel venturing out, it clearly would take longer and be more dangerous.

A conversation one day lasted two hours, a long time for Soe and Jack to talk while Jack tried to do his best to be loyal to God and not blaspheme Him. On several occasions Jack wanted to give up and leave the Nation and begin the search for Maggie. He was torn between his friend Soe, finding Maggie, needing more help in tracking her, and now he was caught by a little Preacher who threatened that God would be displeased with him.

In all his days Jack had learned one thing about God. He was greater than anyone or any nation or army and he, Jack, did not know anything about God. This was a complex and frustrating time for him. There was no one to fight or bargain with except Soe.

On one hot day, which must have been July according to the heat, they reached a conclusion, and Jack, fatigued from the haggling, set out to find the Preacher and tell him the results. He motioned for Samuel to not join him.

Jack approached Simpson and, with some satisfaction already on his face, said, "Soe is to be baptized. I will be in the water to stand beside him. He will be naked."

Simpson nodded. "That is agreeable...you will stand there with him?"

"I will," Jack said. "Soe does not want to be held under long, as you rightly knows. He will have his knife in his hand, and he will have it pointed at you between your legs under the water. If'n you has him there too long he will kill you. Or the Catawbas will, for many will be there to see Soe."

Simpson was taken aback and said, "This is an act of faith! He will be immersed a short time. Is this the discussion and agreement you had with him?"

"Aye," said Jack. "It is the only way. He agrees."

Simpson, an educated man who had graduated from an eastern school of some prominence, who saw his duty as minister and missionary as a great calling, said this could not be done.

"It would damage the faith that other Catawbas might have. They might not believe Soe if this condition was on the baptism. Soe is important to all the tribe and this cannot be done."

Jack shrugged. He looked bored, spewed out a stream of tobacco, and said, "Sir, would a man rob God ?"

That afternoon, in front of the entire tribe, all who came armed with weapons of various kinds, including muskets, bows and arrows, and cane blow pipes, Reverend Simpson baptized Soe in the Catawba River. It was undoubtedly the fastest baptism conducted during the entire American Revolution. The Minister gave a witness to all who came and said, with Soe standing beside him and Jack on the other side of Soe, "See here is water...what dost hinder thee from being baptized...if ye believe with all your heart ...you too shall be saved."

Simpson had put his hand under Soe's chin and his other hand and arm around the top of his shoulder and lowered him into the water, just so the water covered his face; then he swiftly brought him back up. Soe stood straight up and faced the Catawbas, who were all silent.

After the ceremony, Soe walked to the front of the water, his knife in his hand, naked, and gave his own testimony. "Wa riwe ye wiko dja. God...one who never dies...man of power."

Reverend Simpson walked behind Soe and looked at the crowd with no expectation of anything demonstrative, and it did not come. He put his hands in the air and spread his arms wide, his palms up, and recited the Lord's prayer. After he finished, he started to leave but noticed that Soe had taken his place in the water; there he stood talking, seemingly to mimic the preacher. Soe spoke to the assembled

Catawbas and recited, from what Simpson could tell, a variation of the Lord's prayer.

Samuel had stood away from the crowd on a hill. He did not see Jack in the crowd, but soon he saw him emerge on the right side of the village, clothes wet from being in the river, knife in hand. So Jack had his knife as well as Soe, Samuel thought. He felt it would not be long now before they all left camp, even Reverend Simpson and the "new" Soe.

Before dark, Soe came to a fire in the middle of a group of men, pointed to three of them, and spoke to them briefly. They all then mounted their horses and rode up to meet Jack and Samuel, as well as Reverend Simpson, who were waiting on the hill Samuel had occupied earlier. The men were Musi and Kutkin and the first warrior that had met Jack on the trail. Jack learned that his name was "Widubo," Catawba for "goat."

Soe looked at Jack and pointed at him with one hand; with the other, crossed over at the wrist, he pointed to Widubo and said Jack's name, "Dugma wa." From this point on they would be considered friends.

Chapter Ten

Searching for Maggie

Seven men left the Catawba Nation before dark to find a new place to camp. Jack would choose where, and he rode first with Soe a few yards behind him. Samuel trailed several more yards behind him with the three Catawba warriors in a loose single file. It was unlikely they would be ambushed, certainly not by the British. The biggest fear was another warring party of Indians from the west of the little hills, the Cherokee "yematra," or a straggling group from the north, who could be Chickasaw, "yemotce"... "people mean...angry."

Many times on a ride such as this, the last person dropped back to see if they were being followed. If he did, he would then ride fast to catch the others. Jack himself would ride ahead to scout any unforeseen dangers before waiting for the others to catch up. Reverend Simpson stayed in the middle, not for protection but because of his lack of experience on the trail. .

Seeing a clearing that was bounded on one side by a stream that would give them water, and would also be a warning of anyone splashing downstream on horseback, Jack signaled they would camp here. Then he fed Maw, rubbed her down, ate with the men, and left. On most occasions, he would not stay the night with this many people. He preferred to be by himself, hidden in his own way. None of them would know where he would spend this night. But a distinct and threatening noise could be heard by him, and, if all were safe, in the morning he was sure to come into their camp first. A "whoop" from him in the night would be a warning, and the men would scatter with their weapons and horses.

Jack and Soe both went their separate ways. The five men, Samuel, Simpson and the Catawba warriors, stayed together not far from a fire, with two men always remaining awake as sentries. All horses were close by, tied loosely to bushes.

Samuel took an early night sentry and circled the camp. He never knew where Jack was. He wondered why this pursuit was so intense. He made a point to ask Jack more in the morning light and take the chance of being upbraided by his uncle, who now seemed to be fiercer in his resolve than Samuel had seen in a long time.

The night passed without incident. At daybreak, both Jack and Soe appeared in the camp at the same time, materializing out of the woods leading their horses. The men ate what they had brought from the Nation, salted beef or dried turkey meat, which would not last long and had to be eaten rather quickly, corn cakes, and then water from the stream. Feeling safe from intruders, they sat at the fire together, and Jack stood up to say something to all of them for the first time.

The Catawba warriors did not understand white man's language, and Jack left it up to Soe to translate. He looked directly at Samuel as they started to talk and said, "We has been sought by Wade Hampton to find the British fighting man, Tarleton, so he will be kilt. He has kilt over one hundred fifty of us at the Waxhaws with knives and swords.

"Samuel!" Jack suddenly said to him, and the young man looked up. "Has you seen Maggie with a British officer?"

Stunned at the question in front of these men, including Simpson, he looked defensive, and he said nothing. Simpson felt for him during the deathly silence that fell over the camp. Jack was clearly mad, and he was turning his frustrations toward Samuel.

In the middle of the night, Jack had become further enraged at the circumstances he found himself in. He was being pursued, he had been betrayed, and his own family had done it. His sister was with child by the enemy, and Easter Benjamin was not able to help. He was away from his wife and family and did not know if Mr. Hodge could protect them. He did not even know if Randolph Mabry was safe. Jadrow Eddards had not been brought to justice for attempted rape and murder—crimes against Jack's own family. The hated occupiers, the British, had defeated his countrymen; everything in his world was changed.

This was the wrath that everyone feared about Jack, who could be under control in the most violent of times, but still had a fury that was well known.

No one spoke. Jack glowered. Samuel felt intimidated. It was as if he and his uncle were by themselves with no one else around. Out of all this tension a voice spoke up, and it sounded eccentric and distant.

Reverend Simpson had until now been ignored. He walked into the center of the group and looked at Samuel, then Jack.

"What I have to say is the truth. I will address what I know in front of all of you, but out of respect to Miss Maggie, I, sir, will speak only to you." He was addressing Jack. "Are you ready to hear what I have to say?"

He waited for an answer from Jack, who made a nervous clicking sound through his teeth, a habit that Samuel knew Jack exhibited when he was confounded. The Reverend's comments had caused a shift in the atmosphere.

Jack turned without speaking and motioned to Simpson and Samuel to come closer; then he moved away from all the Catawbas. The three men were now grouped together, and Jack said in a calm voice, looking at Simpson, "Say as you would."

Simpson said bluntly, "Maggie is indeed keeping company with a British officer…I know it for a fact. She has affection for this man; she and I have talked."

"She is carrying this man's child!" Jack interrupted, raising his voice and putting Simpson again in a defensive posture. Samuel looked astounded.

With pastoral composure Simpson said, "Yes, and she has a deep affection for him as he does for her. This, sir, is not a matter that has arisen out of military influence or even necessity; it is a matter of genuine and mutual feelings. Maggie has been to me, and she has sought help…she has plans to marry this man, and she has asked me to assist.

"I am troubled that I turned her away. I will not perform a holy sacrament in this fashion. I dislike the British, but somehow I wrestle with my Christian conscience. The end result is, I will not be a part of it, although I wish for Maggie that she be done with it."

"So," said Jack, simplifying everything, "this damnable thing then… you ain't marrying them?"

"No, I will not, sir."

"Who is it?"

"It is a Major."

"How do you know this?"

"I have heard from rumors that the British Legion has frequented several farms, but clearly it is this Major who is the father, and the one to whom Maggie has endeared herself, so yes…that is clear."

"What is clear, preacher man, is that I has to find her, and by my honor and my word to Mr. Hampton, I has to git this Tarleton who has kilt so many of us. And he continued. "I will ask Soe and the Catawbas to go to farms where we think Maggie is and try to find her, with or without Tarleton or this Major. Are you prepared for what I has to tell you now?" Not waiting for an answer he said, "Maggie has betrayed me, at least two times, where I was almost kilt, once in Charlestowne and once at Mabry's farm…so she is with the British. This marryin' thing to a British says it all…so if'n I don't git to her, another will, maybe hang her. Do you understand, sir?"

"Aye, I do, sir, and it is indeed sad."

"So let us be about finding her then," Jack said as he turned to walk off with Samuel behind him. After he had walked several paces, the minister spoke.

"I know where she is. She is in her mid-eighth month. She is to have this child at a Tory farm…I know not which one."

Jack turned and looked at him coldly. Before he could say anything, Simpson said as warmly as he could, "Sir, you have never told me of your plans. I thought this a mission to find Tarleton, and as it is, I left the Catawbas with you for protection and to get back to my own. We all are wanted men, sir.

"I cannot volunteer information about someone who has sought my help in the church, and besides, I did not know that you were unaware of these happenings. If I need apologize then I do. But I have a Christian duty to Maggie or anyone who seeks me."

Jack was relieved to a degree to know where she might be, but he practically hissed, "Where is she?"

"Sir, she is either at the Boyd's, the Howell's or the Wilson's place. All are Loyalists… that is the grievous part. She fully expects to have this child and to marry this man and be under the protection of the British at Camden. From there I am sure, as the British expect that they have won this war, she will settle down with this man, not here in this area, but another place. I understand she has her farm to sell, and the Major is arranging a sale to a Loyalist, I am certain of this.

"It is my understanding that the sale of the property will take place soon, the child will be born, and Maggie will be under British protection, so finding her is important to you I am convinced. But I have to tell you, there is more to her character than I have known before and have now witnessed. She was intent on no harm coming to you and yours in this war…this war that she felt was hopeless. She sought to have you detained, yes she did…and through this, she hoped you would survive this conflict. On several occasions she did inform the Major of your whereabouts. I believe she meant well.

"So sir, I will be no part of her being harmed. She is with child, and this has to be respected."

"Hellfire, sir, betrayal has to be respected."

The minister started to reply when Jack shouted, "Cease your whining" and raised his arm in a threatening way. "I done taken one oath to Easter Benjamin not to harm my kin, so you can bring to a close this talk."

Simpson, Samuel, and Jack all looked at each other for what seemed to be minutes, but the duration was shorter. Now Jack knew who had betrayed him and most importantly why. He hoped Samuel believed it. It was time for a cooling of feelings.

Samuel spoke. "I nay knew this about Maggie. Can we jest find her and take care of her? She can be put somewhere to be held, and the baby will be cared for. If this British man is truthful he will be borne out...if'n he ain't, he will be kilt or go back to England."

Jack walked away from them and spat out, "So be it." He went to get Maw to begin the trip to the farms in search of Maggie. Before leaving, he gathered all of the war party and addressed them, spitting tobacco juice frequently to his side.

"Samuel, the preacher and me and Soe knows where we are going. We are going to Tory farms to find my sister and any British that be there. They will be there for some time, especially at night. If'n you find them, don't alarm. Just ride back to tell me and the otherns, and we will gather.

"I am taking this preacher man with me to the Wilson place. Samuel will take Kutkin with him to the Knox farm, and Soe and Widubo and Musi will see the Howells'.

"Do it from afar. I will stay watching at the Wilson place, and you do the same. I will come gits you if I needs you, and you do rightly the same."

The plan was set.

The men left separately. Jack and Simpson left last and began the long trip to the Wilson farm, fully aware that traveling would be hazardous. Jack hoped, even as they started, he would find Maggie first and not have to ride to another farm. Always he wondered if Maggie's staying at any place was a trap for him. He also thought about a very angry Captain Swallow, no doubt questioning where Jack was tonight, just as Jack wondered the same about him.

The first night passed uneventfully on a riverbank near land Maggie owned. They stayed in an area familiar to Jack and one he and Samuel had hunted on several occasions. The next morning, Jack spent time feeding Maw, grooming her and patting her face. "Pretty girl," he clucked and teased her while she butted him with her nose.

In mid-morning the next day they arrived at the Wilson farm near Beaver Creek. Jack and Simpson both talked about how this farm of Tories was close to Camden. It was the reason Jack chose it. It would

"Maggie will go to Camden"

be logical for Maggie to have a new baby and rest for days before going to the British stronghold of Camden, that town of activity, the first built in inland South Carolina. It was a stronghold of commerce and legal affairs, as well as a physical fort built to withstand invaders by Americans, and now refortified by the British. And it was likely the closest headquarters to Tarleton.

Taking a position that allowed them to see the front of the main farm, Jack knew he had come too close. This could not be helped. The farm house and log cabins were all built close to a forest and were well hidden by trees until you were almost upon it.

Jack and Simpson spent the rest of the day moving around the forest listening for sounds and watching the pastures and the main house. They ate what they had on them, old bread, dried beef, and water from their canteens. Maw and Simpson's horse were kept downwind, and they were constantly moved as the winds shifted. It was demanding work, and Jack would only be able to rest completely by moving away from the house. But that would be away from any activity or the British or anyone approaching. They would stay here.

For sure Maggie would be at one of these farms, unless her plans had changed. Jack could ride onto each farm, one at a time, and harass the owners to tell the truth. But that would give him away and shorten the time he would have to find her. No, the plan that they had worked out was best.

A full day passed. Activity at the Wilson's was normal and dull. Jack moved to a new position to see the back of the main house and noticed that horses were being shod in a blacksmith's shop, with several more waiting to be shod. This was a clear sign of slow activity. All work horses and riding horses were up for inspection by the blacksmith. Hardly any were being worked. Also, large pots of clothes were being boiled in iron pots in the yard. None of the clothes looked like something Maggie would wear. All were older clothes, men's clothes, and there were no bed clothes being washed and hung out to dry. Jack had picked a place where Maggie might not be.

He would not move, however, but wait to see if others showed up tonight. He hoped to his highest hopes she might appear and be seen so he could devise a way to just take her.

Night fell, and he and Simpson would have to try and get closer. No fire tonight. Maw was left a good running distance from the house so as not to make a noise. Jack fought sleep as the evening grew older, but nothing changed that night. He wondered how long this could last. What if they had to wait a week? He decided to wait three days and then to go to the Knox farm and then to the Howells'. If all three had no activity, he would have to develop a new tactic.

The wait stretched into two days and nights, and the edginess was growing. Jack and Simpson had the activities of the Wilsons now memorized. Jack thought of ways they should improve and this helped break the monotony for him.

On the third day, time was passing very slowly. Reverend Simpson had taken to sleeping as much as possible, and Jack did not mind. In a rush, he would leave the minister to his own devices, and trusted he could catch up; if not, it would be his problem to solve. Dusk started to come, and Jack resolved that tomorrow morning he would move to another farm and at least talk to Soe or Samuel to see if they had observed anything. Settling down so he could hear at a short distance, Jack covered himself with a blanket, with leaves on top for warmth. Maw was hidden in a thicket. Suddenly, he heard a sound some distance away but coming toward him. Whoever it was was not trying to be quiet. Jack jumped to his feet, kicked Reverend Simpson unkindly, and moved to get Maw. Simpson was right behind him as they both got their horses and began to walk them toward the noise.

Jack heard a distinctive sound, and this time it was recognizable. It was Soe. The Indian made animal night noises with cadence and repetition that Jack would recognize. As Soe and Musi approached, Jack whistled, they still being a distance off and not in sight. He whistled yet again to let them know where he was. He whistled again, and Soe and Musi stayed on the path to him. Finally they came into sight. They were not alone. Samuel was with them, as was another young man.

Jack was now fully alerted to what was going on. He recognized the boy as being Abraham, a fifteen-year-old slave from Maggie's farm. This was unusual to bring anyone to Jack in such a fashion…another person to be concerned about when covertness was crucial. Jack mounted and galloped toward them on Maw. When he reached them, he looked at Abraham.

Samuel said, "We got him when he was going to the Howell's. He has much to tell you."

"Tell me, Abraham," Jack said, trying not to sound overbearing.

"Massah Jack, Miss Easter been taken by them mens who has taken her to Miss Maggie."

"What men?"

"Them Tory," Abraham said. "They is taking her to the Howell place, and I followed them, suh…Miss Easter say try find you if'n there be trouble…and I don't knows there be, but Miss Maggie is at that farm, and Miss Easter be worried.

"Massah Samuel sees me and takes me befo I gets to the farm…so I is glad," Abraham said with a look of pride in his youthful and handsome face.

"How long has this been?" Jack asked .

"We been gone about five hours to get to you," said Samuel, "so they has been there about that long. We ain't seen Maggie, but Abraham says she is there, and Easter is needed there, so I figures they will be there tonight, and then some.

"And that ain't all, Uncle Jack. Tell him, Abraham," urged Samuel.

"Yes, suh, Massah Jack. Miss Easter say that Miss Maggie has tolds her the farm to be sold to a mans who is coming. She don't knows him, but the soldier who is Miss Maggie's beau is bringing him.

"I 'spose he be coming soon for Miss Easter is upset. She don'ts want Miss Maggie to sell de farm fo she is afred of what will happen to us…tho Miss Maggie say we be fine. Still, Miss Easter be upset… she don'ts want Miss Maggie to go."

Jack confirmed, "This man is coming to the Howell farm?'

"Yes, suh. He coming soon."

Jack looked at Soe and Samuel. "We are leaving now, and we will see what we has when we gets there, so let's be gone."

At that, all of them, including Abraham, started out, aware they could get only so far in the moonlight before having to stop. They were determined to go as far as possible, and then leave at first light to get to the Howell's.

They reached the farm the next morning at two hours after daylight and stopped in a grove of trees to watch the activity. The Howell plantation lay stretched in front of the party, and it seemed to touch the horizons from east to west. Maggie was staying at one of the most prosperous farms in the area, the home and lands of Lucius Howell.

Howell was a man known to be a Loyalist but a person of generosity and kindness. At once Jack guessed this man might be the potential buyer of Maggie's farm, and the only thought he had was that Easter and others would be well taken care of. That is, if the man did not lose everything he had to unscrupulous Tories.

They waited to see what to do and how to approach. All eyes were on Jack when he summoned Reverend Simpson to talk to him.

"I knows this man, Howell. He will be afraid of me, but I only wants Maggie. You tells him we are about no harm to him and his family, but Maggie is mine, and we are leaving with her.

"And, sir, I wants you and Samuel to take her to the Carlisle farm. They are good folks, and the school man is there. He knows about this."

"He does?" said a surprised Simpson. Jack raised his hand as if to quiet Simpson.

"Whens you gits there, tell Mr. Carlisle to help Maggie, and he will. Take a wagon for her, and Samuel will go with you and so will our Catawbas. I will tell Soe. She must get there safely--no harm to her and the child--so if'n you has to carry her body across a stream, do it with Samuel."

Simpson was absorbing these directions out of a man that he thought was one of the most cold-hearted he had ever met. He knew not to say anything, or compliment him, but to just agree. Beckham is a strange man, he thought to himself.

Jack talked to Soe, and all was decided. They would ride in as far as they could, not being seen, and then charge toward the main structure, a large imposing house. Simpson would talk to Howell and tell him of their non-threatening plans. Jack, Samuel, Simpson, and Abraham would go first, with the Catawbas behind them.

They started their slow trot into the fields that led to the plantation. They rode for twenty minutes and positioned themselves to arrive at the side of the house. At the last few yards they planned to gallop straight in and dismount in the yard and proceed onto the porch. Jack and Samuel would be calling for Maggie and Easter Benjamin. Jack hoped taking them would be swift, with no bloodshed. Certainly there would be no flintlock fire exchange from a frightened household of Howells.

They rode closer and still had not seen anyone. Jack pulled on Maw's reins and came to a halt. He wanted to stop and survey before riding in quickly. He looked to his left and right and then quickly jerked his head back to his left. In the distance he saw men riding. Jack grabbed the spy glass from his haversack, looked, and muttered one word that electrified the men. "Dragoons."

He peered intently, "The Green Horse it be. Tarleton's men…five of 'em and one man who ain't. If this be Tarleton, let him be dead today, and if it be the Major, he will be too…I ain't sworn to be kind to no Britisher.

"We will wait for 'em to--"

Jack did not finish his sentence but instead turned around and rode back at a fast pace with all the men, beckoning to them to hide in a stand of trees they had just passed. He looked through his nautical glass again and was certain they had not been seen.

"Move that way," he said, motioning to his left. He began to execute a wide circle around the approaching men and to take up position to ambush them as they left the farm.

Jack was firm in his strategy to assault the dragoons from both sides of a road that led to and from the farm. He brought Soe up to him and told him to go to a spot and fire as the dragoons left. Jack would do likewise on the other side of the road. The dragoons would be in a crossfire. Then Jack, Soe, and all of the men, would charge with tomahawks, knives, and rifle butts to finish.

As the dragoons reached the front of the home, Jack and his men were set to do fatal damage to them as they left. He picked up his glass again to see the men as they dismounted, and what he saw hit him as if he had been struck in his chest. To his great shock, he saw Jadrow Eddards as the one man who was not a dragoon.

He looked at Samuel with a wild-eyed expression and exclaimed, "EDDARDS! That Tory pig is here!!"

Samuel was open-mouthed.

Almost at once Jack thought, "Maggie surely does not know!!" Looking back with his glass, he saw that the men had moved from the front of the main house to a two-story brick dependency in back; he also saw Easter Benjamin entering the dependency.

"Damnation," Jack mumbled.

Four of the dragoons had taken up relaxed positions in front of the main house, while an officer and Eddards had gone to the dependency. Jack's party of men were over one hundred yards from the house when Jack motioned for them to go forward deliberately. They would ride as quickly but as hidden from view as possible to get to Tarleton's men before they could dismount and fire.

At this very moment, Maggie was preparing to receive "her Major" in the dependency. Easter said in a singsong voice, "De Major be here," as she left casually to go out of the house.

What Maggie would find out momentarily was that Major Nicholas Apergis, her husband-to-be, a merchant's son of London, and a career officer, now serving under Tarleton, had brought a man with him to talk of buying Maggie's farm. This would hasten her trip to Camden to be sheltered from this war, and then to settle in a new place of both their choosing. However, Major Apergis was bringing the one man he should not have brought. Eddards, filled with greed and cunning, saw this as a chance to buy what he could not otherwise get, particularly with his new-found "British sway."

Immediately upon seeing Apergis, Maggie, lying comfortably on a feather bed mattress, propped up on goose down pillows with covers up to her waist, smiled. This was dashed immediately into a horrible scowl when she saw Eddards entering the door sheepishly behind him.

Maggie screamed, "Why is this man here?!! This man tried to rape me!" She shrieked an incoherent and primitive yell that brought the Major over to her bed. He was unable to stop her from screaming as she pointed at Eddards. She continued to curse and shout, bringing Easter Benjamin into the small house thinking Maggie had sudden labor pains and was in great distress. Easter called for Dolly, a slave girl, to hurry with some water as they ran to enter the door. As Maggie yelled at Eddards, the Major grasped the situation. His face reddening, he reached for his saber to confront Eddards. He had met this man only once and that on Major George Hanger's recommendation of him as a Tory who wanted to buy Maggie's property.

Eddards had already prepared to run. But unexpectedly he turned and thrust his long hunting knife into the Major's stomach, bringing him to his knees, gasping with pain. Eddards grabbed the sword to keep it away from the Major, the knife still cradled in his other hand. Seeing Maggie, now becoming hysterical, sitting up in bed, he moved in front of her. In a blind rage, he raised the sword, and brought it down. Maggie lifted her left arm to shield herself, and instinctively put out her right hand to protect her swollen abdomen. The sword, thirty-two inches of British steel, severed her left arm at the wrist. It cut across her throat, entering her right carotid artery and doing further damage to her chest.

Eddards was brought out of his murderous trance by Easter Benjamin's screams of agony and surprise. At the same time he heard multiple gun shots in the yard, the yell of "rebels" from the dragoons, and a mad scrambling of horses. He ran for the door. Easter Benjamin was wailing, as was Dolly, while other slaves were running to the small house. As Eddards charged out, he dropped the Major's sword, mounted his horse, and fled. He was aware that one of the dragoons had joined him as he rode away, but he saw at a glance in the yard Tarleton's men dead on the ground.

All of Jack's men had fired at the same time and had killed three at once. A dragoon, who escaped the firing, Captain Cosmos Donner from New York, was now riding away with the Loyalist, Eddards. Jack rode Maw straight for the small dependency. What he saw upon entering was devastating. Maggie, with every heart beat, was spurting blood in a stream. She was unconscious. The bed was soaked with blood, and it was obvious to Jack that she was dying. He did not know what to do. Easter Benjamin kept sobbing, "Oh my Gawd! Hab mucy, hab mucy, dear Jesus...dear Lawd!"

Jack started swearing and ran to get his gun, mount Maw, and do the one thing his mind told him to do. Kill somebody...kill Eddards. He heard Easter screaming at him in a begging voice. He looked back once but then continued on. He saw Samuel and said loudly, "Help Easter!"

Samuel walked into the cabin and saw the carnage, including the Major lying face down and moaning. Samuel began to cry and curse at the pitiful sight of Maggie. He grabbed his hunting knife to kill the British officer, kneeling forward still on his knees, his face on the floor, holding his stomach. Easter screamed, "No!" and her voice stopped him cold.

Then, with precise steps, she approached Samuel calmly and took his knife from him. She walked over to Maggie, looked back at Samuel, and directed him. "Help me! We has to take dis bebe...you helps me, chile!!"

With that, she pulled the covers off of Maggie and drew up her gown, exposing her stomach with its watermelon-size protrusion. Then, to Samuel's horror, using the hunting knife, she cut the skin from the top of the abdomen, down through the yellow fat, through the white and glistening fascia, and through the abdominal muscle to get to the cavity several inches below the navel.

Easter's knife entered the uterus, exposing a clear fluid that erupted, frightening Samuel even more. Easter calmly said to him," Is going to be right...it will be so...trust in the Lawd."

With the greatest care and intent on her face, she prayed again and then pushed hard on the top of the uterus, the fundus, to extract the baby. She pushed hard and grunted and pushed again.

"This ain't working," moaned Samuel, who wept in frustration. Easter pushed, and the baby began to come from the uterus into her hands. She pulled straight back, and the umbilical cord followed. She

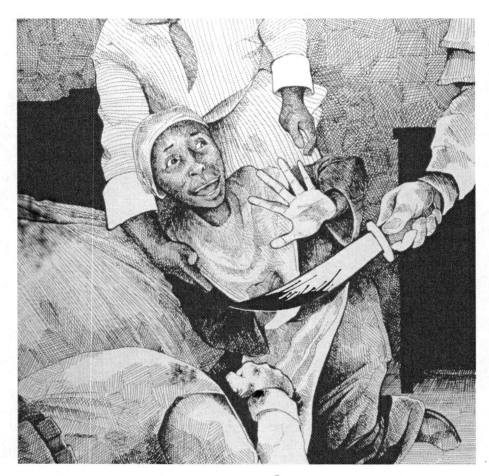

"No, Samuel"

drew it out almost to its full extension and said, "Quick, Samuel, gets me two pieces of cloth."

The baby she had pulled out was blue and bloody and looked dead to Samuel as he used the knife to cut strips from the sheets on Maggie's bed.

"Is it alive?" he asked, his voice trembling.

"Yes." Easter said nothing else except, "Tie them cloths here and here," and she motioned with her head.

Samuel did as he was told and tied two knots to the cord. He asked again, "Is it dead?"

Easter turned to him and said with a look of confidence, "Hold out yo' hand here and feel dis bebe's heart." Samuel did, and through his fingers felt a rhythmic beat of the pulse through the umbilical cord. Then Easter alarmed him again when she took the knife and cut the cord to the baby. She called for Dolly, who had stayed out of the house sobbing, to come and bring water and cloths. She did, and Easter began to rub the baby furiously. She turned it over and struck it on the back with the flat of her palm. "Come...bebe...bebe. Come, bebe. Cry...bebe."

And before his eyes Samuel saw the blue baby began to turn pink, the congestion in its mouth spill out white and syrupy. Easter continued to rub its body. It was a girl.

Easter began to praise the Lord and pray, "Thanks you, Lawd... thanks you, Jesus, oh thanks you, Lawd."

Dolly began to cry again. Then, for the first time, other slaves came into the cabin. Samuel noticed the British officer was still alive but in a very bad way. He wanted to kill him before, and now could not understand his feelings when he said to Easter, "We has to help this man."

Easter said, "Samuel...you done witnessed Gawd's work today...a bebe is born to dis family. Killing ain't good. Help dat man."

At that, Samuel began to turn the officer over and talk to him. Apergis was in and out of shock. A slave woman put a cloth into the small wound to help stop the deep bleeding and wrapped him in a blanket. He was propped up on extra pillows.

"How is?..uh...where is Maggie?...where is she?" he mumbled.

Samuel saw the slave woman look at him hard and shake her head "no."

"I am rightly related to her," Samuel said comfortingly.

The Major tried to absorb this information. "You are?" His eyes closed and his eyelids fluttered as he seemed to pass into shock.

"Gets that man from here," screamed Easter. "Gets him to the big house."

Three men led by a slave named Shadrack picked him up by his legs and arms, and Samuel held the back of his head as they ran to get him to the plantation house. They laid him on a large oak table in the parlor. One of the men just swept things off the table in order to lay the green uniformed officer down. Blood was coloring his coat and trousers and was now moving slightly toward his boot. He was not bleeding profusely, but Shadrack replaced the cloth in his stomach with a silk handkerchief, and the Major groaned with pain. Into the room came Mr. Howell, the plantation owner. "What is happening?" he roared.

"Shot, Massah!"

"No!" said Samuel. "He has been struck by a knife from that man, Eddards. Has you been to the little house, Mr. Howell?" Samuel asked him, choking back tears.

"No," he answered.

Mr. Howell ran out the door to take command of his plantation, which had dead dragoons in the front yard and another wounded in his parlor.

In this furor, Jack had chased Eddards and the Captain and had come within a hundred yards of them when he noticed that all the Catawbas had begun firing again. Another group of Tories, who were undoubtedly part of Eddards' group, were approaching. As he turned toward the men, Jack did not see Eddards and Donner disappear into the woods. He rode Maw back to the Catawbas, dismounted, and filled his rifle pan. His first rifle response to the Loyalists killed a man, hitting him in his chest. The Catawbas had reloaded and were firing again with effectiveness, with two more men fallen.

The Loyalist group began a quick retreat on their horses when Jack made a decision to go back to Maggie. He could not explain it, but pursuit was over for him for now. He rode Maw hard to get back to the farm. There he was hailed by Samuel to come to the big house. Jack burst in the door and saw the scene on the table, with Samuel looking at him expectantly, much like a little boy. The slave men backed up, leaving Samuel alone at the table with the wounded soldier.

"This is the man?" Jack asked angrily.

"Yes, sir, it is," answered Samuel.

"Alive?" Jack asked.

All the men nodded their heads, yes. Jack pulled out his knife and went to the table surely to kill the British officer. Two of the slaves turned their backs and winced, so as not to witness a bloody throat-cutting that surely was to come. Jack got down into the Major's face, inches away from his blank expression, and put the knife blade against his throat.

Jack asked, "Who be ye?"

The Major did not answer, and Jack grabbed his hair in the front and pulled him up violently as if to cut his throat. The Major blinked and came to consciousness. "Who be ye!" Jack bellowed.

"Sir, Major Apergis."

Jack looked at him and hesitated. Samuel interjected, "This is the man who cares for Maggie," as if pleading for consideration for the wounded man.

Apergis said, his voice wavering, and with a thick tongue, "Sir? You are Jack Beckham, Maggie's kin?"

Jack said nothing. Apergis realized he was Beckham. "Quarter, sir, I ask quarter."

"Hell no!" Jack said. "Is you trying to kill me?"

"No" said Aspergis. "Sir, by my word, my feelings for Maggie are to give you safe harbor and exchange…for any other.

"I dutifully agreed to help. My pardon, sir. Please ask her to tell you this…we always meant to preserve you with no harm."

The Major was begging for his life with no knowledge of what had happened to Maggie.

"I am betrayed, sir. Was it Maggie?" Jack queried him.

With adrenalin overcoming his pain and shock, the Major said, "It was not betrayal, sir. I reported to fellow officer Major Hanger and to Colonel Tarleton, and we always meant to intercept you and...and...for the duration of this war, if it was meant to be, keep my oath to Maggie, that no harm would be yours and your family. It is God who is witnessing this, sir!"

Major Apergis seemed to be slipping away again. Howell had re-entered the room, ashen-faced from seeing Maggie. Jack dropped Apergis hard onto the table and walked up to him. "Sir, you is a Tory...you take care of this man...if'n he dies, Tarleton will have you kilt...you better rightly see he don't...you better get him to the butcher Tarleton and tells him old Jack nay did this, but Eddards did."

The only thing Howell could do was nod his head; he feared the enraged Jack, with Maggie, under his protection for childbirth, now dead.

Jack raced to the dependency, hoping that Maggie might somehow be alive. When he burst in, everyone was startled at the sight of him. In her hand Easter Benjamin held steel wire, fashioned by a tinsmith on the plantation. It was as thick as a plant stem, used for hanging up fowl in the smokehouse. She looked up at Jack and answered the question on his face.

"We has to do this, Massah Jack! We has to give my chile a Christian buryin.'"

At that, Easter went about her business. She and a slave woman named "Cat" were standing over Maggie. With the pregnancy, the intestines had been pushed upward in her abdomen. Now they lay spilled out from the wound and on her stomach. Easter and Cat were placing the intestines back in the cavity and taking the wire to pull the stomach walls back together. Other women were tenderly washing Maggie, removing blood and fluid with water and cloths. One woman was caressing her hair and face. Easter said she had to have a dress, and out of a bag brought a calico that Maggie would have worn when she was not pregnant. It was clear that the women were going to lovingly dress her.

This ceremony among women for women at death was accompanied by praying and talking among themselves. They wailed and exhorted God for mercy and called Maggie's name to be blessed. A young, tall slave woman sat in a cane chair, holding the new child of Maggie's acting as wet nurse. She was a recent mother and slave from the South Carolina coast of Georgetown. She was Easter's cousin, already cooing and talking to the new child even as the child's mother was being prepared for a proper burial, not by a childbirth hemorrhaging, but by murder.

"Bless her, Lawd. Bless Miss Maggie, Lawd."

Jack stood watching, touched by the bond and understanding of women for women, and for Maggie especially. He asked Easter, "What is you planning?"

"Bury this chile, Massah. We has to do it for the resurrection day."

"Not on this farm land…never on a Tory land…she ain't been born here, and she not be buried here."

"But Massah, dey looking for you and the otherns…you can't be buryin this chile on her own lands…where is you going and what is you doing?"

"We will bury her," Jack said, and "I will know the place."

He approached Maggie and wrapped her in two blankets, cradled her in his arms, then carried her out of the house. He stopped once and looked back. "Easter you are coming!" he commanded. "You rides with the Reverend." He then mounted Maw and held Maggie close up to him, his reins in his hands preparing to ride.

"Massah, I is too feeble…I can't anymore…I can't ride de wagon, fo' it be too slow…I is saying good-bye to my baby chile, Maggie, now… please, Massah?"

Easter went to Jack and put her head on Maggie's lap. She was cradled against Jack, who held her in front of him on Maw. He had his arms grasped around Maggie, much as if he were holding one of his girls.

Easter sobbed and wailed, patting Maggie's legs with affection. Her shoulders shook, and she kept calling Maggie's name. This went on for so long that Jack finally took Easter's arms away, and whispered that he had to go. He said he would take her to Maggie's burying place some day.

They left, Easter waving and saying, "Good-bye, Maggie…good-bye, chile," and the men heard this until they were out of earshot.

No man spoke a word as they rode. This time would burn in their memories.

Chapter Eleven

British Retribution

Jack and his party traveled southwest, toward the great falls of the Catawba, away from the Tory farm and far from Camden. It was somewhere in the lasting hot days of summer, he thought. He had already spent weeks in hiding time at the Catawba Nation after the ambush at Alexander's, a few days getting to the Carlisle's home, days finding Colonel Harrington, then time seeing Easter Benjamin, and more than a week finding Maggie.

Somewhere along the way Jack had told Samuel they would get as close to Maggie's farm as possible to bury her. The only thing that mattered, for the next few hours, was not to get caught or detained; then they would disperse. Jack led his group toward the place where he had spent time preparing to go to the Tory farm where Maggie was found. They arrived at a spot that Jack indicated was a place to stop. He picked an area not far from a stream of water, but on firmer soil, not in danger of flooding. It was near trees of some distinction, live oaks within view of river birch trees that would give him a point of reference to find the grave again.

The trees might survive a long period of time, save an act of God through lightning and storms.

He and Soe walked over the area carefully, then came back, took hatchets from their saddles and beckoned the others. The men cut younger trees, the trunks the size of a man's arm, and cut the ends to sharp pointed edges and as wide as a man's hand. They notched the tree trunks deeply, twice, two feet apart around its middle in order to get their hands on a place to hold the wood. They used the pointed ends like shovels, to dig the dirt after Jack marked off a plot with his hatchet handle.

It was a narrow trench, only two feet wide and six feet in length. They dug down eight feet, more than they needed, the men alternating with each having a tree "shovel." They scooped the dirt out with their hands and with the blunted ends of the tree trunks, dulled from digging. They also used eating pans to scoop out dirt.

Seven strong men worked hard, taking turns, for over two hours, not conversing much, and at the end Jack dropped into the hole and surveyed this place that would be a resting ground. He heaved himself out of the grave when he was satisfied and walked over to Maggie's body. He gathered her, still wrapped in two blankets, one arm under her knees, and another under her shoulders. In these last few seconds of closeness to her, her head pressed against his face, he smelled for the first time the spice she had put in her hair, anticipating an intimate moment with "her Major." Her hair was still soft, her body cold, but not stiff.

He placed one end of the body in the trench and turned her so she would lie permanently on her side. Samuel had dropped into the other end of the trench grave, to take her from Jack and lay her down. Then Jack reached down with one hand and hoisted Samuel out of the grave. At this point Reverend Simpson came and nodded, as if on cue with courtesy to everyone, and dutifully repaid the favor that Jack had bargained for earlier at Soe's baptism at the Catawba Nation.

He threw some wild flowers that he had found along the river bank into the grave, and took his Book of Common Prayer to read, while all of the men stood watching, some with hands on hips, looking down, others with arms folded or by their sides. Jack stood with hands at his side, his long arms well below his belt.

Simpson looked into each of the men's faces, then read solemnly, rocking back and forth slightly on his toes as he did so, his arm holding the book fully extended from his eyes to correct for his faulty reading vision.

"Almighty God, we entrust all who are dear to us to thy never-failing care and love, for this life and for the life to come, knowing that thou art doing for them better things then we can desire or pray for; through Jesus Christ our Lord. Amen.

"I am the resurrection and the life saith the Lord, he that believeth in me, though he were dead, yet shall he live; and whosoever liveth and believeth in me shall never die."

As he said this Soe said unexpectedly in a loud voice, "Hitarire!!" She is awake. Simpson nodded a fatherly bow of his head at the new convert, then walked over to Jack and said, "I would like to pray for you and Samuel who are Maggie's kin...what say you?"

Jack looked puzzled and remarked, "What are you going to say?"

Patient with a non-religious man, Simpson said, "I am going to read a prayer from this book and ask God to be with you and Samuel."

Jack looked at Samuel, who was affirming with his head nodding slowly yes, and Jack just shrugged his shoulders.

Simpson was doing his duty. He put his arm straight out, his fingers spread open and pointed upward, as if to bless them, and read. Jack listened curiously. No one had ever prayed for him, in front of him, in front of his friends, in front of others, and at a death of a family member such as this. He stood motionless and learned a lesson of humbleness, though his expression never showed it.

"O merciful Father, who hast taught us in thy holy Word that thou doest not willingly afflict or grieve the children of men; Look with pity upon the sorrows of thy servant for whom our prayers are offered. Remember Jack and Samuel Beckham. O Lord, in mercy nourish Jack and Samuel's soul with patience, comfort Jack and Samuel with a sense of thy goodliness. Lift up thy countenance upon Jack and Samuel and give them peace, through Jesus Christ our Lord. Amen."

Simpson closed his book and prayed silently while Jack observed. Soe broke the silence again and repeated, "Hitarire." But Simpson started again. He threw both of his arms into the air and shouted,

"Lord hear our prayer." He seemed to be in the most genuine sorrow Jack had seen over Maggie's death.

Simpson began to pray…a soulful, mournful prayer, with great emotion in his voice. He began to speak in his native Ulster tongue, which Jack understood. With arms still extended, and rocking back and forth even more vigorously on the balls of his feet, he shouted the Lord's Prayer.

"Uor fader quhik I Hevin, hallowit weird thyne nam
Cum thyne kinrik
Be dune thyne wull as I Hevin, sva po yerd
Uor dailie bried gif us thik day. And forleit us uor skaths
As we forfeit them quha skath us.
And leed us na intil temtation. Butan fre us far evil.
Amen it is. Amen, Lord. Amen!"

Simpson dropped his head momentarily on his chest. Soe walked over to Jack with a lively expression, as if ready for a trip…he looked reverent. "Maggie…holy ghost now."

Jack looked at Soe blankly; he could only begin to collect his thoughts for a trip he had to make. He watched as the other men were filling the grave with the dirt that had been removed. His contribution was to do what he had planned all along when the trench was dug. He moved two large rocks himself, pointed and gray and heavy, to put on top of the grave so that it was completely hidden. No animals would get to the body. For all purposes it looked to be a natural rock placement among the other boulders and rocks.

Jack's last instructions to them, for it was obvious he was leaving by himself, was for Samuel to go to a place to hide. He knew Soe and the warriors would be at the Nation, secure after a careful trip back. As for Simpson, he had no idea of his plans and he did not ask. Samuel came up to Jack expectantly and said, "I am going with Abner to the Georgia colony. We go to see Elijah Clarke and his rifles. I will stay with his until Papa is back and can be found. If you see him, tell him Abner and me will serve Clarke, but we are back here soon, when it is rightly well enough."

Jack looked off into a distance as if to see where he was going. "I am to the Pacolet. Elizabeth needs to know her brother is captured in Charlestowne. We has to defend our property with Mr. Hodge."

Jack turned and rode off. He did not look back as Samuel and all the others went their own ways, with the Reverend Simpson himself headed for North Carolina, a sanctuary not yet overrun by British.

He started his long trip. He might bypass Mabry's farm, but it could have enemy camped near it. Mabry himself might remain safer than most, for his reputation as a man of peace set well with Tories who were afraid to challenge him. Doing anything aggressively against Mabry might raise the ire of even more Whigs who respected him. Jack mused over the loyalty to him personally from the Mabry family. Only Eddards might speak of Mabry harmfully. But he had his evil reasons with his three assassins and companions buried in a place that Jack had no knowledge of.

Jack moved in a direction toward the Spartan district and felt it was time to go home. He would have to do so as a "stranger" and he wondered just how much his children had grown and how he would explain what had happened to their aunt Maggie. As Jack traveled toward Rocky Creek, eight miles west from Alexander's Old Field, he thought of another place to go. It was the home of Henry Anderson, a stern Covenanter Presbyterian immigrant from Scotland, much like many of the avid followers of a Reverend William Martin of the Catholic Presbyterian Church nearby. The minister himself, a man of great fire and temperament, more suited to Jack than Reverend Simpson, was a man who liked to drink.

Martin had brought with him five ships of immigrants from Ulster in 1772, all of whom would be given new land. Anderson was one of these who had come. This group of pioneers in the South Carolina colony had formed many of the "hardback" Presbyterians that resisted the English so vigorously. This was Jack's decision, although he felt a dull gnawing in his insides considering a delay in seeing Elizabeth and his children.

Jack rode hard to get away from the area of Maggie's grave and the painful memories. He settled eventually on a sleeping spot that was protected by heavily bunched trees, hard for men and horses to get through easily, especially at night. He camped in a small open space, near oak trees, where he could hide unseen. Maw would be close by during the night, and she faded quickly into slumber after the evening rubdown by an exhausted Jack. He decided to leave before light the next morning and arrive at Anderson's as early as possible.

Looking the next day at Anderson's home an hour after daybreak, he saw several horses in front of the man's cabin, which meant the household was more active than he thought. These horses were obviously tired and recovering from travel. He would wait until someone came from the house or approached it. He did not wait long.

One hour later, out of the cabin door walked five men in single file, all carrying guns. Walking behind them was Anderson. Jack knew them all. They were all Whigs. All had been with him at Alexander's except Anderson. He felt an immediate relief, although they went straight to their horses, and it occurred to him these men had arrived not too long ago; they were in flight.

His decision was to hail them, not frighten them for they were clearly running. He climbed on Maw and advanced toward the house and allowed himself to be seen as they were getting ready to mount, with Anderson standing in front of his house.

"Hold" Jack shouted. "It is Jack Beckham…where ye be going?"

All the men turned at once and grabbed their rifles instinctively, caught unaware as they were. They wheeled toward him before catching their actions.

"Hold," he shouted again.

One of the men, named Joseph Morrow, called to his compatriots, "Tis Jack." At this mention of him they all met in the center of the yard, Morrow, John Craig, David Morrow, Alexander Walker, and Robert Walker.

Now Jack saw the men were terribly haggard. Anderson walked quickly past the men, clearly having more energy than they, and with his emotions showing, said, "Jack…you ain't dead…it is a blessing… where has you been?"

"Beaver Creek at a Tory farm to git my kin and—"

Anderson interrupted him and blurted out. "You ain't been around for some weeks? Since the Old Field?"

"Nay," Jack said. "I been on personal affairs. How is the times here? They ain't good, I speck."

Anderson shook his head and cursed. "It is the hell I feared…you ain't heard then? I will tell you."

One look at the men and Jack thought he understood. They were depleted and gaunt.

Anderson winked, nodded his head and said, "The British did not take it rightly what you and McClure's men, and all these here, did at the Old Field.

"John McClure and these boys here went to Mobley's meeting house at Winnsboro and did the same to Tories there. And McClure and Bratton surprised Captain Huck at the Williamson's plantation and kilt nigh unto forty Regulars of Huck's men. Killed Huck too."

David Morrow interjected, "We got 'em at Musgroves's Mill, Jack… a bunch of Tories went against us and Captain Inman, who was kilt, but they lost sixty-three dead and some'mers about one hundred sixty wounded and taken prisoner by ours.

"But Colonel Brandon was taken surprise at a place not far from the Pacolet River, and he was run off by Tories."

"Well then," said Jack, "sounds it don't fare too well for the Tories, do it? Where is Captain McClure now you figure?"

"John McClure is dead," said John Craig.

All the men seemed to embrace silence, the sobering reality made even worse at hearing these words aloud about their young and intelligent leader. Jack just stared and remembered the young man at Alexander's Field who had allowed him to fire on the Loyalists and who was himself so brave. This young man was now dead in a short time after Alexander's.

"He was wounded at Hanging Rock coming after the battle of Rocky Mount and died," Craig continued. "Young William Stroud who was with us at the old field has been found by Tarleton and hanged… hanged him stripped naked…would not allow him to be taken down, 'cept his sisters did take him down for a burial, five days after he was left in a tree."

David Morrow intoned again, with fatigue in his voice, "Young Joseph Wade has been found by Tarleton and taken to Camden to be flogged. He took too many stripes, and he will live if 'n that is good...I ain't sure it is."

Robert Walker added his description. "We has lost a lot of men... we lost them Gaston boys of old Justice Gaston, three of his boys, Robert, David, Ebenezer, all kilt as well as Captain McClure, who was with us at Alexander's, and Sumpter has been beaten badly at Fishing Creek by Tarleton."

"Damn!" Anderson exclaimed, slapping his thigh with his open hand, " I should say! Sumpter lost one hundred fifty men captured, some kilt, many wagons, and he ran away with almost no clothes on. He had nigh onto eight hundred men and Tarleton had 'bout one hundred sixty and Tarleton ran him off."

Jack held up his hand as if to say enough and just asked, "Is there ne'er good news? Has Tarleton kilt everybody?"

"Well," said Alexander Walker, "we got our measure at Williamson's plantation as said, but it is certain, it is, that Tarleton will send others beside Huck.

"They took over sixty darkies at Area's Iron Works, and they destroyed it near completely. All them darkies has been taken away and nobody has seen them since."

"Gates has lost much at Gum Swamp near Camden...that is the bad news," said Anderson. "We has lost eight hundred fifty of the Regulars both kilt and captured and four hundred men like you and these boys who fought at Alexander's Field. This was the true worst loss for us at Gum Swamp...nay...ever since Charlestowne. I fear we has lost everything.

"And...DeKalb is dead and Gates has fled to somewheres, we knows not."

All the men fell silent again. One sighed so heavily it appeared he might collapse from the defeat and the fatigue. They looked at Jack and

Jack just hung his head and looked to the side. Finally he said, "What else is there? You boys looking for some more fight?"

They all replied, "Yes," but weariness was in their voices.

"Where you going, Jack?" Alexander Walker asked.

"See my farm and family…sees if'n they still there. You heard nothing about the Pacolet or Mr. Hodge… or how about the Henderson's?"

"Ain't heard nothing," said Anderson. "But we has to ask you, Jack…"

Jack looked at Anderson. "What is it you inquiring?"

"We has a copy of this." And he pulled from his coat a bill that had been posted by Tories. Jack recognized the official seal at the top of the page.

"I seen that," Jack said casually. "Has the name of all ours who were at the Old Field, so I reckon we are wanted here and yonder."

"Nay," Anderson said, looking at the other men in wonderment. "It is not so. Has you not seen this?"

"Can't say I has," Jack said, and all the men knew they were the bearer of horrible news to Jack, and they were going to witness it first-hand. The men turned to Anderson, and David Morrow nodded his head at him as if to encourage him to speak. Jack shifted very uncomfortably for whatever the parchment bill had to say.

"Jack," Anderson said somberly, "this bill says you murdered Maggie and a British officer. You is wanted dead or alive, but they is paying more if'n you are brought in dead. They is offering ten gold guineas if'n you are dead and five guineas alive."

Jack gripped his hunting knife subconsciously, completely unaware of it under his belt, and addressed the men. "I ain't kilt Maggie. And no one else 'cept some Tories with Jadrow Eddards. You believe it? That is well with me. You don't? Then we is enemies, for I don't give a damnation…so I am making my way clear with you…it is your choice."

The men were taken back by Jack's composure and his answer. John Craig spoke first. "If'n you say it, I believe it. We are your friends." All the men chimed in with grunts and nods of approval. Jack nodded back at them and said, "Let us talk."

He sat down directly on the ground where he had been standing, and they all sat down with him, cross-legged and at ease, while Jack, not one to talk much, told them the whole story. He left out nothing, including Maggie's pregnancy and the baby taken at death by Easter Benjamin. The only thing he left out was Eddards attempted molestation of Maggie, for that was too hard and too personal. He did tell about the Tory plantation owner Howell, at whose farm Maggie had stayed, and absolved him of any guilt, but he talked harshly of Eddards' escape.

At the end he said. "You wants to know where I am going? I am going to find Eddards, and I aim to kill this Tarleton, and I am looking after my folks on the Sandy Run...so I has enough to do."

Jack picked up a small stick and chewed on it as he talked. He looked at it and said to Anderson, "Can you read that bill to me?"

Anderson patted Jack on his shoulder, an older man's reaching out to another to give reassurance and friendliness, and pulled the paper from his coat again. He read:

"A POSTING AND REWARD FOR MURDER

"By the King's directive a warrant is herby issued for the detaining, alive or dead, of one John "Jack" Beckham a murderer of his own sister, Maggie Land, and a British Officer of the British Legion, Major Nicholas Apergis, serving under Colonel Banastre Tarlton of the same. Deaths witnessed by Captain Cosmos Donner of the British Legion and Jadrow Eddards, of the Turkey Creek. The rebel Jack Beckham is to be brought to the Camden district alive or in a dead state, and a reward will be paid as follows: Dead, ten gold guineas, and alive, five gold guineas. Proclamation this day of August 20 in the year 1780 of his Majesty King George of England."

Jack listened and then nodded his understanding at the men. "What day is it you reckon ?" he asked.

No one answered, somehow thinking Jack was stricken with so much grief that he was just making conversation.

Finally Anderson said to Jack, "You carrying any wares?"

"Rye," said Jack.

"'Tis good," Anderson smiled. "Let us drink."

At that, all the men shared in a swallow from a common bottle that Jack passed around before beginning a trip to another place. Soon he made a motion to the men as if he were getting up to leave and said, "I am going to find Eddards. He is a liar and that is worse than anything he is. If'n any of you find him, kill him. I will pay you one guinea."

The men laughed heartily for the first time in days.

As Jack moved toward Maw, John Craig approached him, hesitating. "I thinks I have lost some of my family…all dead. My pap and my maw I fears and my brother. I needs to see after my wife and my young ones. I would like to be with you till you gits to the Pacolet. I is ready to die, and I won't slow you up none. Can I go?"

"You can follow," said Jack sternly. "If you falls behind I do not wait. If you dies I ain't buryin you. Don't forget Maw is fast, so if I don't see you behind me I am gone."

Craig shook his head yes and went to get his horse as Jack mounted to leave.

Chapter Twelve

Justice Fisher

As Jack began his search for a man he thought a traitor and another search for the cunning British Colonel Tarleton, a course had already been set for him. In November of 1779 two incidents had taken place in Charlestowne that would have enormous consequences on his life and no one could have predicted them.

One incident came with no warning. It dealt directly with a man who was a barrister, Justice William Jay Fisher. At 26 Broad Street in Charlestowne, the same street of the state capitol, Justice Fisher practiced law in an elegant office. The Carolina colony still was unconquered, after battles at Stono Ferry outside Charlestowne in June, where Jack's brother-in-law, Colonel Henderson and friend, Captain Wade Hampton, had fought.

Most major battles had been in the east in New Jersey and New York. The colony was in the process of exerting its authority from England in this war of independence, and Fisher still practiced colonial law, based on the mother country, but not under her heel.

Fisher's mother was the sister of famous lawyer John Jay, President of the Continental Congress in 1778 and elected to the First Congress in 1774. His uncle had practiced law and initially resisted independence, until he grew frustrated with his own fellow members of Congress as well as England, and accepted that his country would soon be embroiled in a war. As a member of the Congress he argued unsuccessfully for a foreign policy that had become disruptive in his Congressional life, so much so that he became the Minister to Spain, an ally of France against England, but not an ally of the colonies.

John Jay felt this a great challenge and on the very same day that his credentials were being accepted by the King of Spain as American Minister, his nephew, Justice William Jay Fisher, was about to encounter life-changing events himself.

The Justice had just returned from one of the famous long midday dinners that Charlestowne folk had perfected through the years, and he had stepped inside his office at exactly 4:00 p.m. He was met there by clerk Thomas Cook, who advised him that several people were waiting in an anteroom to speak to him. The Justice walked in and saw an attractive young woman, then a local couple he had seen on occasion on Broad and Church streets, and finally a black woman of some age with a young black boy, possibly fourteen years of age.

The man spoke first; he said he was Mark Hayes of nearby Elliot Street and also the Coosaw River, specifically the Coosaw Plateau Plantation. He introduced his wife, Julia, who held their young child, and said, "This is our friend," referring to the other young woman. "She is staying the fall months into December with us. She is Mrs. Maggie Land of the upper colony, near the Catawba River."

After the introductions, Mr. Hayes deferred to her and remained seated. What followed was a discussion of drawing a will for the young woman, a widow, but a will also including the black woman, one Easter Benjamin. The woman seeking the will did not want any legal matters handled in her home area and had sought Justice Fisher's assistance in the low country. He found her quite striking and independent minded.

The matter was taken care of and closed within days, but the Justice never forgot the young widow woman, the details of the estate, and her particular wishes.

The second incident related to an invitation that the Justice received from a friend in the upper colony also near Camden. It was an annual tradition for Fisher to visit his close and wealthy friend, Henry Rugeley, in the upper colony not far from the Catawba River, in the early fall. It was an opportunity to get relief from the lingering Charlestowne heat, which generally lasted through September and into October.

Rugeley, owner of Clermont plantation and Rugeley's Mill north of Camden near Grannie's Quarter Creek, would always return the visit with Fisher in the early winter. He usually presented himself after the New Year, to enjoy the warmer low country temperatures. Rugeley had much commerce to deal with in Charlestowne, accounts to settle, and his brother, a successful merchant, lived there. Rugeley's visits were serious business, family business, and pleasant times with Justice Fisher.

Both men's visits lasted a month at least and their immediate families were always included. But not this year, in this time of war and of disruption.

Rugeley had been appointed a Loyalist militia Colonel, but he leaned hard to the middle of politics. He tried to be fair and accommodating to the British, and to his fellow neighbors who were much against the Crown. He was particularly fond of Francis Lord Rawdon, the appointed young and brilliant Governor over the Camden district. Rawdon himself was an Irish Protestant aristocrat and soldier of the King who was very "British" in manners and diplomacy, and an excellent hedge against the ruthlessness of war, real and imagined, by the colonists against the British.

Rugeley, as was the custom, had sent a courier by horse to his friend Fisher, inquiring if he meant to travel to the upper colony for a visit. He would welcome Fisher but cautioned that the trip could be hazardous and that he, Rugeley, still opposed separation from England.

He wrote in the message, hand delivered to Fisher:

"I do not know your feelings toward this unpleasantness, whether Whig or Loyalist or total ambivalence, but I respect you and your decisions. You carry a wonderful and heavy burden with a distinguished family name with your own great influence and character for our colony. Whatever your decision you are welcomed to my home and hearth with the greatest affection and continued loyalty to you and your family.

Please come. We will hunt quail to shoot instead of men, and we will

endeavor to solve our country's problems, you and me, over good wine and
a good pipe and perhaps a good fireplace, if cool enough, in the evening.
I remain, as always, your humble and sincere servant.
Henry Rugeley,
The second day of August in this year of 1780"

Reading the document, the Justice decided to go almost as soon as he could manage, within a month, but he would leave his family with relatives in Moncks Corner as he traveled. He wrote a note and gave it to the courier, promising a visit in the first two weeks of September. His wife Christiana, daughters Genevieve, Rebekah, and son Jonathan, all would be safe and protected by an aunt and uncle of his on the Cooper River. He would leave sometime in September, and would ride to friends' homes along the way. He would never camp in the wild.

His plans were to reach the Camden British stronghold and present his papers of travel, signed by none other than Francis Lord Rawdon of Camden. After hurried preparation and leaving his practice to an apprentice to handle minor affairs, he made his trip on schedule.

The trip to the small hills of the upper colony proved to be uneventful for Justice Fisher. He traveled in areas well populated by British and Tories—Goose Creek, Moncks Corner, Saint Matthews, the Orangeburgh, and he stayed close to the Kings Mountain wagon road that traversed the colony. Still, he met too many men who looked to be adventurers, and their loyalty to the King or colony was always in doubt. On three occasions he showed his transport documents to Tory officers or British Regulars. He was asked to be the dinner guest at one Tory home, undoubtedly for legal advice, and he had to refuse. All his hosts on the trip wanted him to stay longer, but he refrained, telling them of the toils of the length of his journey.

After days on the great wagon trail and reaching the outskirts of the Camden area, preparing to ride to Ruguley's, by necessity he had to go through the Gum Swamp for these final few miles. His thoughts wandered at this time, more from the fatigue of looking for potential dangers than the travel on horseback. He was anxious for the trip to end and to have a satisfying evening at last with his close friend.

What he was to witness next was the most stunning revelation of war, carnage, and death that he would ever see and could never have been prepared for. As he approached the swamp he saw at a distance what appeared to be people picking crops in a field. As he drew closer he saw the extended arms and legs and hands of men frozen, lying on the ground, in grotesque shapes with people picking their clothes from them but also other men trying to control the people. Flitting only two or three feet away were vultures, crows and various birds attempting to get to the carrion. The men in charge were hurrying those "working in the field," who were collecting the remnants of clothes from the fallen.

What affected Fisher next was an overwhelming stench he had never before encountered. He rode closer and fought to reach back to get a handkerchief from his haversack quickly to his mouth and nose. He pinched snuff from a silver snuff box and put it in both nostrils as was the custom against the malodorous smells he encountered in Charlestowne streets. But this was the death of many men, dead now for days. All weapons had seemed to disappear, leaving only black-skinned, bloated corpses in the late summer sun, and a few tattered rags that were left to dangle on the remains. No hats were in sight and no military accoutrements of any kind.

He noticed that horses had been burned to dispose of their carcasses, and the still lingering smoke actually dispelled some of the stench from the bodies. Fisher saw flies. It reminded him of the Biblical plague of flies. These covered men and hovered around them so that the sound of the thousands of wings made their own noise. One figure was so covered Fisher could not distinguish any form to the man. It was a gray stump of a human infested with flies. The stench was beginning to cling to his clothes, and he felt a wave of nausea.

Fisher looked close enough to know the men had been Continental troops, apparently killed in large numbers. He was dazed and trying to comprehend the magnitude of the scene, when two British officers in full uniform rode toward him. They looked extremely healthy and dashing amidst all the death and decomposing bodies. One hailed him and said, "Sir, you are to be the honorable Justice from Charlestown!" It was a statement instead of a question.

Fisher nodded, his breath temporarily taken away. The officer took off his hat and saluted with a sweeping motion. "I am Colonel Perrill, sir, and this is Colonel Heckard."

"My greetings, sir," said Heckard, sounding as cordial and inviting as if this were a Sunday picnic. "We are to escort you to Colonel Ruguely's residence."

The Justice stopped on his horse and ended the motion of being escorted when he said, "Gentlemen...this awful place...sir! What has happened here?"

The officer, Perrill, drew closer to him and said, "Sir, this is what results of General Gates and the rebels who were here days ago. Two hundred men killed, sir, and this is the remains. We are to finish here and let the wild boars and wolves eat the rest.

Heckard asked, "Are you ready to travel, sir?"

Justice Fisher looked devastated. He shook his head as if to clear it of a Hades described in literature and played out here in this field not far from a home where he expected complete relaxation and conversation. He sighed and said, "Yes...let us be gone."

They traveled away from the field of death. Perrill and Heckard's faces did not reflect the carnage behind them as they rode. They looked purposefully forward and smiled only to be cordial if Fisher made eye contact with them during the ride to Ruguley's. As they proceeded, the carnage did not disappear. The road was littered with more dead bodies, overturned wagons, dead horses, and with all this death, more flies, birds eating flesh, and smells coming sometimes in disgusting waves. It continued this way until Ruguley's plantation appeared ahead. Fisher truly was stunned by the hell of war and a defeated army. Now he wanted to know more, and he wanted to get inside away from this nightmare.

He reached his friend's plantation realizing it was still hot, but the lack of low country humidity made it feel almost comfortable. He could count on a welcome from Rugeley, including a groaning board of food that evening, although Camden had been foraged with almost nothing left in the fields and few barn animals. He would take a bath of some length and leisure before the dinner.

The Justice wanted to learn more concerning what he had just missed–the Battle of Gum Swamp, near Camden, where American General Gates had been defeated in a humiliating way. Ruguley's plantation was aglow in victory over the Americans, who had been a menace at several spots and represented a major threat to the British and Tories if their smaller victories continued to mount. The first thing Henry Rugeley proposed after Justice Fisher arrived was a toast to loyal subjects and the King. They talked of the battle at Gum Swamp and Baron DeKalb's death for the Americans. He was a man wounded eleven times from bayonets and lead shot who still lived for three days before dying.

Ruguely said, "He was a good officer and I know he will be talked about in good measure and grace by the Whigs, for he served well and died a hero. Indeed, Cornwallis had him delivered to his own surgeon to see if his life could be spared."

The Justice inquired about the completeness of the victory and was assured the Americans were totally defeated. "You are still under the crown, William, and may it be so for two hundred years. America will become our strongest ally, a great colony of subjects, and I dare say you are to be one we will need to manage this land. Not to be too flattering, but I hope you will consider a governorship or service to the King in a greater way."

Then aside from the transitional courtesy of seeing to his room, Justice Fisher presented gifts he had brought to his host and his wife, Charlestowne silver from the renowned smith Arden on Broad Street. Still thirsting for news and conversation several more hours discussing current events took place before the Justice finally prepared to take the longest bath he could. Then he dressed in the fresh clothes he had left there on his last trip.

Dinner to follow would be a very social affair. Rugeley announced that guests would include the young and powerful twenty-six-year-old Lord Rawdon, as well as the Earl Lord Cornwallis, and three senior officers from the garrison at Camden, including Heckard and Perrill, as well as sisters of Henry Rugeley's wife in the community. All were desirous to hear what news Fisher brought from Charlestowne, and the Justice was just as anxious to hear of progress made by the King's forces in the interior of the upcountry after the fall of Charlestowne. It promised to be a long, informative, but enjoyable evening.

Once around the big table that evening, they ate food from Cornwallis' personal stash of food from his train; foraging had left very little to be eaten from gardens or fields. It was a meal of venison, turkey, vegetables, sumac tea, port wine, bread baked to hold a carrot soup, a sallat of a few greens, and plums with pudding topping.

The men discussed the war and the campaigns yet to be waged. Mainly they focused on the young Tarleton, also twenty-six years of age, and his tactics of waging war that had been so successful. He was, to the greatest extent, the choice of Cornwallis and his favorite to end the temporary industry of rebels that would stand and fight.

Rugeley reminded them that Tarleton had chased rebels to Ruguely's Mill after the Gum Swamp battle and engaged them before the rebels retreated.

"So we have had war here at this place and witnessed Colonel Tarleton, almost as it was from our parlor window." He laughed softly and looked at General Cornwallis, who beamed with pride at his young charge.

The Earl had commented, "The man is so young and eager we have not yet seen the best of him. He makes impetuous moves and sometimes extends his main force from his artillery, even to leaving his cavalry behind, but they catch up well, and they don't stop until their sabers are satisfied."

At all these comments, laughter was the order of the day. It became even more so when the women left the table to take up their conversation. Through the pipe smoke of all the men, more strategy and more accomplishments were reviewed, what was past and what was to come. Justice Fisher was never more convinced that the English and their allies had indeed won the south, and with it the better and faster end to George Washington in the north. His only thought was to rest and visit and be finished with the turmoil and get back to his practice of law in beautiful Charlestowne.

As the evening wore on, the talk became more serious as to what

would happen in the next few months. Cornwallis particularly queried Fisher on Charlestowne and its status from his civilian view. He
brought up only once the name of John Jay and his role as Minister to
Spain. He solicited Fisher with a comment that Jay was "a reluctant
man to go against the King of England and all understood this."

"I would hope," he said "the honorable Mr. Jay would receive a
responsible position in one of the colonies at war's end and continue
service to the King."

All the men said "hear, hear" and thumped their wine glasses on
whatever hard surface was handy. Lord Rawdon took the occasion,
when a pause occurred, to stand and address the men. He turned to the
Justice and said, "I am to convene a tribunal to determine the worst of
the evil scoundrels and murderers from the rebels. I would be pleased
to have you join the proceeding.

"Perhaps you can listen to the witnesses of our Colonels, our
'Council of Colonels,' who will bring up names, and they will either
defend or disparage them as it is." He laughed, "The reasons and names
we will list will mean perhaps one hundred men, who have committed
a felony, are to be pursued, caught, and executed. Possibly you can see
the beginning and the end, with the hanging of one of these traitors."

Rawdon, a man of unusual character and reputation, had just spoken the harshest words imaginable to Fisher, but he made it sound so
eloquent that indeed the earth would be better off, and it was a divine
command, that the colony be rid of these men.

Justice Fisher agreed, nodding his head and saying, "Sir, I am the
guest of you and the honorable Mr. Rugeley. I do as he instructs me
and I am sure he will approve."

At that, they all laughed heartily, but the Justice, a man of facts and
details, gave further thought to the comments and pursued the conversation. "Who and what manner of men do you have to consider, may I
ask, sir?" speaking to Lord Rawdon.

"Oh, my friend, they are the worst kind. Men who are molesters
and women will testify to that account. Men who have in fact broken
their parole and men who have killed their neighbors over a fabricated
property dispute.

"There are men who have stolen horses, and men who have stolen deeds of property and even men who have taken the King's property...gold coins, as it were. Others have been captured in a scrimmage, and others have been caught as spies. It is a merry lot...you will enjoy hearing about them."

This brought even more laughter from the men, particularly the senior officers who would testify against the men whose names would be put forward.

"So," said the Justice, relaxing and lighting his clay pipe, "who might be the worst case of all these scoundrels and traitors?"

"That is possibly too easy a question," interjected Cornwallis, amused and reaching for a clay pipe, eagerly handed to him by a Colonel. "Sir, what crime do you think it might be?"

In a gay mood the Justice said, tilting his head up as if in mock deep thought and for the effect, "I would say...a man who is a spy...yes indeed...one who pledges loyalty to the King, lies about that, steals a horse from a man who owns the biggest land parcel in this area, lies about that, then sells the horse to another man, then lies about that, and says the man who bought the horse, who by the way is his uncle, committed all the crimes!"

The men howled. Lord Cornwallis practically came out of his chair and stood half bent over with glee at the Justice's repartee. "Yes, yes, yes!" he responded. "You have to meet this man. He measures four feet tall, is near-sighted, has a club foot, and weighs four stone."

The gales of laughter at the General's mocking comment brought one of the women to the room, but she just smiled and retreated, shaking her head in amusement. The men had tears in their eyes from laughing, all but the senior officers who now knew they were only allowed so much frivolity, and they smiled mechanically and beamed at the other men.

"Ah, yes," said Rawdon, chuckling and trying to come down from a high-pitched laugh. "It is a duty is it not?...ah yes..."

"Aye!" he remembered, turning to Justice Fisher, "the worst of the lot I would say was a man who murdered his sister, cut off her arm, cut her womb open and murdered her soon-to-be born child, and then killed her affianced a brave British Legion officer lad…an Englishman at that… three murders, mind you.

"That is the worst…and I understand a slave wench will testify that he is not the murderer, but that another man killed them. Of course, the only problem, sirs, is that the slave woman was named as a legatee of the dead woman's estate. She stands to inherit much, several acres and slaves, cattle, horses, pasture lands--some wealth, mind you--all from her young widowed mistress who was to wed the British officer."

Justice Fisher had stopped laughing. He leaned over toward Rawdon and said, "Tell me sir, who is testifying against this man…this murderer?"

"Oh," Rawdon continued, half chuckling, "a British officer who witnessed it…a British Legion Tory from the New York colony who was there, as well as a Loyalist from this area, a farmer who has purchased the property legally; it has been taken out of the hands of this slave woman."

Fisher sat back and put his fingers together tent-like, strummed them together, and appeared to be absent in thought. The men continued the dialogue, but he did not hear them as he reached back in his memory to a story he knew of like this, of a slave being left this much property. He could not immediately recall the details. He was quiet, and the others continued talking.

Then it struck him. He remembered the young woman who had consulted him, who had wished to leave part of her property to a slave wench named…"Easter." This was too coincidental.

He sat straight up, turning in his chair to the men, and said, "I think I know this woman…who was killed…either I know her or this is too close perhaps to chance."

They all looked at him as if he had had too much wine. Two of the officers continued conversing about horses. Out of courtesy, Rawdon, Rugeley, and Cornwallis gave attention to Fisher, who sat looking at them as if he were still trying to piece together details.

"Gentlemen," he said, and at that he excused himself, not coming back for several minutes while he gathered notes he had recorded and had brought with him, on the perchance of meeting this woman and family. Entering the room he said rather triumphantly, "Gentlemen, how many times has a slave woman been left fifty acres to your knowledge? And from a pregnant widow but, to be wed woman, in her twenties…in this area, engaged to a British officer? By heavens help us, her name was 'Maggie' and the slave woman named 'Easter.' Yes! I wrote the will for this woman in my office!!"

All the men were now fixed on the Justice.

"Pardon me, sir, you are such a good friend of Mr. Rugeley," said Cornwallis, speaking with true authority, and a General's commanding tone in his voice. "This is not an attempt at humor?"

Rugeley spoke first, smiling. "No, General, it is not. This is a man of honor, and he does not joke easily. Not nearly as well as he did a few minutes ago," he said, smiling even more broadly and to allay any stress that had arisen.

Fisher said, "Gentlemen, may I have your audience? Please listen to me and see if the coincidence is not too much….nay, if the matter we are discussing is not the same."

At that he started to address the seated officers and Lord Rawdon as if he were pleading a case. "This woman was from this area, and I wanted to remind myself to ask you, Henry, if you knew of her family. I had the notion to call on her husband and her and their new child. She was a fascinating person of independence and charm. This must be the same."

Lord Rawdon stood up ramrod straight. "Tell me, sir, what you know. I have some memory of the details of these murders to be discussed tomorrow, and two of my Colonels here, Heckard and Perrill, are to make statements."

Reading from his scribbled notes, made hastily as he left Charlestowne, Fisher squinted through his reading glasses and said, "Her name is Maggie Beckham Land. She appeared in my office November 7 of the last year. She was with child, and she was to be married to a British Legion officer stationed somewhere near the region of the Savannah. The slave to whom she left much is one Easter Benjamin. Her property is here, near Cedar Shoals and Beaver Creek.

"I remember that Mrs. Land took the unusual step of formally introducing the slave woman as Mrs. Easter Benjamin and the slave boy as Abraham. She accepted my offer to be seated and fairly took over the exchange that was to follow."

At this, Justice Fisher smiled even as he was looking down at the paper in his hand. "She was somewhat brash...she came straight to a point when she said she was aware of my fair reputation, undeserved as it might be, gentlemen."

Again Fisher smiled. "She wanted to secure my services for the writing of a document of will and testament. I said I would transcribe whatever she wished. I have to say I was a little unprepared for her forthrightness when she said, 'Sir, I am a widow now of three years. I am to be affianced. I wish to have a will drawn to disperse my holdings if anything happens to me before this marriage, owing to the times we are in.'

"She went on to say, 'In fact, sir, yes, I do plan to keep my properties if possible, but, if not, I wish to leave them to others and to take great kindness to the woman. Benjamin here. I wish to leave her the legal owner of a sizeable part of property. Is that a problem under our law?' I said, 'Of course not. She is a slave woman I gather.'

"'Woman, yes; slave, no,'" corrected this woman with a scornful smile. 'She has been granted her freedom, as has Abraham.'

"She said she had many slaves like Mrs. Benjamin and sought no more. What she wanted was to make sure of their inheritance. She also stated that she wished to be buried on her farm and that her own family receives the remaining assets.

"What do you have?" I asked as politely as I could.

"She answered that her holdings encompassed approximately eight hundred acres, cattle, tobacco, all of which had belonged to her husband. In the event of her death she wished that Mrs. Benjamin have fifty acres and a complement of cattle, pigs, goats, and horses.

"When I asked as to the slaves, she said, 'They are free. Easter will take care of them as she sees fit.'

"She also urged that I not divulge that she sought my services, rather than in her own jurisdiction.

"I asked if she had in mind contingent beneficiaries, meaning those other than Mrs. Benjamin, in the event that Mrs. Benjamin pre-decease her. To that she replied, 'My husband and my unborn child, sir.'

"I pointed out that because she was not married as of that day, he was not legally her husband. He could be listed with others in the will, but her immediate family could contest the will. I advised that she wait until she was married and then name him. She said that could be months, even a year, as he was meaning to be attached to a force near her, and the marriage would be delayed until that conflict was over.

"So at this point, I have to tell you, gentlemen, I asked politely if we could talk alone. I could tell she did not give in to this easily, but she still said 'yes,' maintaining our trust I am sure. The others stepped into another room, and I asked if she was sure this man would marry her. What if he were sent back to England or, worse, killed or severely wounded?

"She said, 'All this can happen, but we might also have a marriage and family and live in the colony under British law. I am not sure at all if I would go to England, but he is sure he will be here. Still I have no will at all as of today.'

"She asked me who would inherit her property if she was to die today, and I explained that it would be her closest family. She had no children at that time. She responded that her relatives were many and that her desire instead was to take care of Mrs. Benjamin – as well as any others that Mrs. Benjamin saw fit to help.

"I was a bit perplexed, but I took a separate piece of paper and a fresh quill and said, 'Who would be the inheritors, other than Mrs. Benjamin, in your family…and not your future husband?' She recited, and it is all here in writing.'The first would be my child I carry and my husband at the date we marry. Second, Elizabeth Beckham, my aunt, and then my other aunt, Sarah Beckham. Then follows: my niece, Mary Leah Beckham, called Molly Polly, and if it comes to it, my nephew Samuel Beckham.

"'I would wish if my child and husband were not here that the property be equally divided among those named, if Easter is not alive. If Easter is still with us she must have fifty acres in her lifetime.'

"I recall her saying that she believed her brothers, John known as

'Jack' and Thomas, would most likely be killed during this war, and that they would leave wives and many children. Finally, she said that if all of those were dead to sell the 'damn' property.

"Yes, she used those words: sell the property at the courthouse and divide it equally among the slaves on the property.

"I went on with my perfunctory duty, asked her to spell all the names she wanted on the will. I said I would copy it three times and record it and give her two copies.

"In three days she presented herself again at my office, this time to my alarm by herself. She was very pleasant, dressed in a bright green dress, no bonnet, and no hand coverings. After greetings, I handed her the document. Not only did she read it, she read it out loud, and I sat at my desk, intrigued, and listened attentively. I judged that the clarity of her speech and enunciation were good, given her lack of formal education. She read the document with keenness.

"Gentlemen, here is the will. I have a copy among my papers to go over with this young woman on the chance of meeting her again. It reads thus:

"THE COLONY OF SOUTH CAROLINA IN THE NAME OF GOD AMEN

I, Helen Magatha Beckham Land, of the area of Beaver Creek in South Carolina, aforesaid widow, aware of the uncertainty of life and now of sound and disposing mind and memory, do make and ordain this my last Will and Testament, that is to say.

First, I give and bequest to my unborn child all my real property and assets for the benefit during his or her life, to have use of and the slaves on the said property to be of Beaver Creek in South Carolina for his or her lifetime and for his or her appointed heirs on his or her death, and at the time of my marriage my husband to have him share in the inheritance part and parcel equal to my unborn child as described above.... .

"I will not read the entire document out of deference to her and my ethics in dealing with her as a client, but I assure you the will went on to include Easter Benjamin, if she should be alive, and to add all the names of those who might follow in a line of succession. It was an interesting and complicated will of future names and inheritors.

"I did tell her, however, that if Mrs. Benjamin becomes a landowner she will need a will and I took the time to draft one for her to study and read. And that was the last I have heard of this delightful woman, Maggie Beckham Land, until now…and I am practically sure this is the same."

Justice Fisher folded his notes and looked satisfied with his precise note-taking, given the surprise of having produced it on such an occasion as this. Rawdon looked at Fisher; the silence in the room was uncomfortable. One Colonel shifted in his seat, waiting for the response. Rawdon said soberly, "Sir, that is correct."

Rawdon looked at Justice Fisher. "Do you know the officer's name who was murdered?" he questioned the Justice.

"Nay, sir, it was never said to me."

"His name was Major Apergis, a superior caliber officer assigned to the British Legion. Tarleton favored him. Major Apergis died of sepsis from a knife wound from Maggie Land's brother, a devil of a man and a treacherous spy. You just mentioned his name earlier while you were recounting your conversation with her…it is Jack Beckham."

Justice Fisher was searching for the legal response that he knew, while Rawdon looked at him. He replied with a practiced trial question. "Tell me, sir, are there no other witness to this triple murder than two Tories?"

The underlying message and the use of the word "Tories" stung Cornwallis. Both men, Cornwallis and Rawdon, now stood and Henry Rugeley felt obliged to join them. One of the women came to the room, attracted by the sudden quiet and quickly left, sensing a turnaround in the atmosphere.

"Sir," said Rawdon with a measured tone. "We have another witness. Should I tell you his name?"

"Of course," said Fisher gently.

"The wounded Major told his superior officer who knifed him before he died. That man will be here tomorrow to testify to the name of the murderer, and that man, sir, is Colonel Tarleton. He knows and he will testify."

Rugeley looked at Fisher and waited for his friend's reply, knowing it would be deliberate and not confrontational.

Fisher said calmly, his head nodding to all three of the men, "Gentlemen, if the Colonel testifies to this, then the man is guilty. I have no doubt."

"Good, sir," said Cornwallis, interposing his authority as a military man. "Let us have one final glass and be done with the day. I believe, gentlemen, the tribunal convenes tomorrow at ten."

"Correct, sir," Rawdon said, and at that he walked over and shook Justice Fisher's hand and said, "It will be an honor to have you join our proceeding. At least you will see this slave woman again, and you will have the pleasure of seeing the witnesses on behalf of the Crown, including Colonel Tarleton."

"That is well, sir." Justice Fisher shook hands with all around the room and excused himself.

After Lords Rawdon and Cornwallis had left, he walked back to the main room and found Rugeley standing alone, staring down at the floor in thought. "My friend," said the Justice, "pardon my intrusion…the brother may have killed the sister and the child, but the slave woman is an innocent person. I fear she has lost her property to this farmer for no reason."

"William," said Rugeley, "I am sure you are right. Justice may not be done tomorrow. I wish you well at whatever you witness."

Both men bowed slightly and retired for the evening.

Chapter Thirteen

Lord Rawdon's Tribunal

The next day the two men traveled by horseback to Camden, both dressed as the prosperous colonials they were, with silk brocade coats over white ruffled shirts, black necking stocks, riding boots, elegant breeches, and tricorn hats adorned with rosettes of various colors.

Rugeley had a .75-caliber fowling gun in his saddle; two servants rode behind on horses, also with hunting guns for Justice Fisher, in case the men took to hunting game on the way back from the business at Camden . The servants brought food from the master's wife's kitchen in baskets for a later traveling meal, if it was needed. The men would join other town officials at a tavern for a meal as the tribunal would adjourn between 2:00 and 4:00 p.m. It would reconvene if business demanded it until 7:00 that evening. Plenty of time to remain in Camden after legal chores, take in hunting on the way back to the great house, and still arrive in time for a dinner at 9:00 that evening.

Even in war this was a gentleman's life, even in times of courts and tribunal appearances, which suited Justice Fisher's legal training. But what was on his mind was the disturbing conversation last night with Rawdon and Cornwallis, and what might be the final result today.

Camden was a busy district post with British soldiers very much in evidence, with white tents surrounding the village. The fort and the redoubts held the most activity with cannon pointed toward obvious routes and beyond, with a bustle of trade as well as a growing number of Tories in uniform, more than Fisher had ever seen.

The men went straight to the three story mansion on the edge of the village that was surrounded by British Regulars, tents, campfires, men in different stages of war and preparedness, Tories with muskets and rifles close by, and women and children adding to the mix. This was the camp of victors, and today they would judge militia rebels who had committed offenses against the Crown. Already the news had spread of the proceedings, helped particularly by a town crier who had, for the last two days, announced the hearings for today at 10:00 a.m.

Posted on trees and buildings were Bills of Proclamation calling people to hear grievances against offenders, which would result most likely in punishment from the Crown.

Fisher and Rawdon walked up the long steps to the Georgian mansion, receiving nods and bows from civilians and military who perceived their importance. Once inside the large front room, the men were acknowledged by Lord Rawdon, who was sitting in a chair on a platform; he motioned to a junior officer to show the men where they might sit. All around them were senior officers, and three colonels who would witness the discussion and testimony against the miscreants, thugs, robbers, murderers, deserters, all enemies of the King.

For over an hour they listened to several testify and then vote against the men who would be hunted or, if they were in captivity, be judged to die by hanging. One man was sentenced to be flogged, twenty times and then imprisoned. Justice Fisher noticed in the middle of the room a tall black woman with a younger slave woman rocking a white baby. A young slave man accompanied her. Fisher immediately recognized the older woman as Easter Benjamin. He even recognized the young man, who had been with her in his office. In his mind the Justice felt a measure of vindication. He had been right in his memory and deductions.

At the back of the room with an officer in the Royal Provincials was a man with a stocky build, about five feet six inches tall, with glasses and sandy hair. He had a spider vein prominent on his nose, and he constantly grinned at others in a solicitous way and waved a hand of greeting to others across the room. He reminded Fisher of a distasteful politician looking for votes or approval, even among strangers. Fisher thought he saw him foolishly nodding at a condemned man in chains, out of habit.

As Lord Rawdon carried out his role as jury, judge, and designator of the specific punishment, Justice Fisher was impressed by his smoothness of tone. He was a professional, intent on English justice, although the final verdict was as harsh as he knew it could be. A trial would follow the next day with all its formality for several of these men and hangings the next. It would be in order. But the men would be just as dead as if they had been pursued, stripped of their clothing, and hanged, caught in the wilderness of the South Carolina upcountry.

Lord Rawdon, firmly in charge, called an officer over and whispered to him. The man immediately turned on his heel, went to the front door of the mansion, and spoke to an officer who held a musket at the ready. The sergeant at arms then called another officer to fetch someone from the outside. For some reason this caused a rustling among the crowd.

Calling everyone to order, Rawdon said, "We have the occasion to hear witness against one John 'Jack' Beckham of this colony, who is accused of murdering a woman, her child, and an officer of the British Legion. We have two eyewitnesses against this man, and they will be heard as of now."

Walking to the front of the room was the man Fisher had noticed at the back, the grinning "politician" and a Tory officer beside him. They both approached and identified themselves.

"I am Jadrow Eddards, sir," said the shorter man.

"Captain Cosmos Donner, sir," said the officer.

"What have you to say, gentlemen?"

"Sir," said Eddards, "on a day this past summer at the home of a loyal man named Howell, I witnessed the fugitive Jack Beckham take the sword of the officer and kill the woman Mrs. Land, as well as her child, and then stab the officer with a knife, making him helpless to assist the young woman who was to be his wife. I escaped from him and many others, perhaps fifty rebels, after I tried to help the woman who was killed by this man. Only Donner and myself were able to get away from this large raiding party. I–"

Rawdon interrupted him. "Sir, hold your remarks briefly…Captain Donner, what did you observe?"

"Sir, I was part of ours that was surprised and my fellow officers that was killed by the raiding party. I was assembled in the yard when Mr. Eddards ran out of a dependency and shouted at me to escape from the murderer. We both rode away to get more help as we was fired upon by many others. I knows this man Eddards tells it rightly for we was pursued by the man, Jack Beckham, with blood all over him, and him shouting at us and trying to shoot us."

"Did you see this man, Beckham, kill the others?"

"Sir, no, but it seemed likely, for he was the only one to come out of the house to chase us."

"How far away were you when this chase began?"

"Sir, only fifty or so yards."

"Mr. Eddards, you may continue now," said Rawdon.

"Sir, I was in the dependency to visit with the Major, a woman to be married to him…the woman murdered. She, earlier some months ago, sold me the property she owned. I have the legal paper with me."

Eddards approached Rawdon and showed him a deed made over to him and signed in a woman's handwriting, "Maggie B. Land."

"This looks in order, thank you, sir" said Rawdon passing it back to him. "Apparently you…"

Rawdon was distracted as he started to finish his sentence. The slave woman was standing in the middle of the room with her hand raised, saying something. He decided to let her speak and end right now what he thought was a ruse or at least a feeble attempt to keep property of the woman who was murdered, remembering the discussion last night with Justice Fisher.

"Suh," she said in a trembling voice, "I wants to ax you if I has a chance to say sometin'. I begs to say dis fo' my Maggie chile who has been taken away and is with the Lawd."

At this Easter began to cry softly at the enormity of her statement in front of so much power.

"What have you to say?"

"Miss Maggie, fo she died, be leaving properties to me and to others. It is not sometin' I wants forever, but to lives there and be buried there, and to know otherns of mine be allowed to be there and be buried there...dat is all, suh."

"Madam, do you have proof of what you are purposing?"

"Yas, suh. I has dis paper."

"Can you read?" said Rawdon.

"No, suh."

"Then how do you know what you have and what this paper says? It could say anything now, could it not?"

"Yas, suh."

Fisher noticed at this exchange that Eddards smiled and looked at Captain Donner.

"What do you in fact have?" pursued Rawdon.

"It called a will, suh. Miss Maggie leaves it and tells me it is in a hiding place if'n she be dead fo I is, and fo me to fetch it."

"Well," remarked Rawdon, glancing toward the Council of Colonels and preparing to make a note with his quill pen on a large parchment paper on his desk. "We have yet another paper which is legal and has been marked with a seal that says this man, Mr. Eddards, owns this property. What say you?"

Justice Fisher felt the blood and anger in his own face and neck. From his legal experience he thought this woman was about to experience a travesty. He looked once at Rugeley, who was shaking his head sadly from side to side, looking at the floor.

Standing up with his arms straight by his side Fisher spoke in a loud voice, disrupting momentarily the conversation and the atmosphere that had evolved between the wench Easter and the presiding Lord.

"Sir! May I be accorded the privilege of speaking before this distinguished gathering?"

Looking up at Fisher, Rawdon said, "Gentlemen, I have the great honor of presenting the gentleman from Charlestowne, the honorable

Justice William Jay Fisher, a friend of this tribunal, of the King, and our distinguished friend, Colonel Henry Rugeley. So say you, sir?"

"Thank you, my Lord. It is a distinct pleasure to be here and offer my remarks in the hope that they may be accepted as information and material in this matter of a land dispute."

Fisher nor anyone else heard Easter Benjamin gasp, "Lawd hab mucy," under her breath, as she now recognized the Justice from Charlestowne.

"I had the honor of knowing the woman, Mrs. Land, while she was alive. I, in fact, wrote a will for her last year in my office. The will is marked November 7, 1779. It is the same as I imagine the woman Easter Benjamin has in her hand."

"Bring it forward, sir," Rawdon instructed.

"With pleasure."

Looking at the document, Rawdon said, "It appears to be as you say. But Mr. Eddards has purchased this property and paid a sum for it, as his deed has suggested. So the thing I must ask Mr. Eddards is, what is the date on his deed? And, do you, Mrs. Benjamin, know of a record that the land has been sold?"

"No, suh."

Eddards looked at his paper and then back at the presiding Lord and said, "February 12, 1780, sir."

"Can you deliver witnesses to this land sale?"

"Yes, sir. I can produce them," said Eddards proudly. He then walked to the front of the room and handed the deed back to Lord Rawdon.

"Mrs. Benjamin, do you have proof that Mr. Eddards did not purchase this land?"

"No, suh, I don't have proofs, suh."

Rawdon said, "We have a will that names Mrs. Benjamin as owner of fifty acres of this land on the death of Mrs. Land this summer, but we have a deed recorded that the land was sold to Mr. Eddards, and Mrs. Benjamin has no knowledge of the land sale. And we have witnesses that can be produced that the land was sold to Mr. Eddards.

"Incidentally, Mr. Eddards, have you taken possession of this land?"

"No, sir. I have given the wench, Easter, and all the slaves notice that they are to leave the land before this Thanksgiving--if they think they remain free--or I will sell them. I do not regard them as free but that is their choice. I want to do the right thing."

All this time Easter was holding her head down and staring at the floor with her handkerchief in her hand twisting it nervously over and over at Eddards' lies. She bore a great and agonizing burden that choked her throat knowing she had witnessed this man killing Maggie, but her word against his would be foolish and unbelievable.

Looking at Fisher, Rawdon said, "Justice, this looks as if there is no cause for Mrs. Benjamin. Your assistance is greatly appreciated. You are a gentleman. Is there anything else you wish to assist us with?"

"No, sir, these things appear to be as you say. It is clear that Mrs. Land sold this property and never changed her will before her tragic and unforeseen death. I would, however, like to take the privilege of asking Mr. Eddards some questions which just ordinarily intrigue me. Frankly, sir, I miss my law practice."

The men in the room laughed roundly at the Justice's remark, including Eddards, who laughed out of relief at Lord Rawdon's decision.

"First, your Lordship, may I ask that Mrs. Benjamin be removed from the room?"

"As you wish, sir." Lord Rawdon flicked his wrists ceremoniously toward Easter. An officer escorted her and those with her from the proceedings.

Standing across the room where he was sitting beside Ruguley, and with Eddards remaining standing in the crowded court, Fisher said, "When did you and Mrs. Land discuss this sale of land?" Before Eddards could answer, Fisher said, "How much did you pay her for it, sir?"

Eddards was thinking hard and said with confidence, "We discussed it last fall. Last year...several times during the fall...certainly during

November, and at that time it was two weeks before Thanksgiving. We discussed it at her farm."

"Were there witnesses besides the people who signed as witnesses?"

"No, sir, it was something she wanted to do alone. She was quite independent and had a mind of her own."

"So this was in November of 1779, the same month she signed this will and then consummated this sale in February of 1780. You have the paper to that effect showing it as you do now, sir?"

"Yes," Eddards replied somewhat impatiently.

"She was quite independent as you say, Mr. Eddards, quite a remarkable young woman, apparently able to be in two places at one time, for I have witnesses that say she was on the coast for September, October, November, and December of last year with friends on the Coosaw River. I have their names, and they can testify to that, sir."

"I may have been wrong on the date, sir, but it was last fall."

"Mr. Eddards, fall lasts for a few months. Mrs. Land has enough slaves that they can harvest while she is gone; her production on the farm would appear to be quite good. It seems clear she could be gone for some time.

"Your Lordship, may I ask Mrs. Benjamin into the room?"

"As you will, sir."

She entered again, and before she could be seated, Fisher walked up to her and said, "Easter Benjamin, could you hear us talking while you were outside?"

"Naw, suh."

"What were you doing outside?"

"Tending to the bebe, suh."

"Tell me then, where were you and Miss Maggie residing last fall in the months of September, October, and November, as well as December?"

"Where we be living? Where we be staying, suh?

"That is correct."

"We was where we always is, suh, dat time of year...stayin' with friend on the 'coos a watch.' They is the Hayes. We stays dere de last five years. We seed you during that times, don't you remembers, suh?"

"Yes, I remember."

Turning to Eddards, he said, "Sir ?"

Eddards responded to Easter's answer. "It must have been another time. Anyways, I has the deed, and it is legal."

"Is it, sir? How much did you pay?"

"Twelve thousand gold guineas."

"Can you prove that?"

"Sir, I has the deed."

"But you could have paid anything, sir, more or less. Do you not have a receipt for your payment, as well as your deed?"

"Indeed I do, sir. It is in a place where I might retrieve it if allowed the time."

"Sir, why did you not bring it here today?"

"It was not occurring to me. I thought the deed sufficient."

"Well, Mr. Eddards, sir, this is after all a legal proceeding and you are claiming land from a dead woman. So you have a deed signed by this woman, Maggie, with her signature or her 'X'?"

"Her signature. sir," said Eddards, puffing up his chest at having answered so successfully.

"Please indulge me, sir," said Fisher and walked back to his seat and took out a long document with a ribbon around it. "I also have a document, sir. It is the will and testament of Mrs. Land. Shall we compare signatures?"

Taking the two documents up to Lord Rawdon, he showed them, and they were quite different, remarkably so.

"Your Lordship, I think there is doubt here."

Rawdon looked at the signatures and then at Justice Fisher.

"Your arguments are persuasive, sir, but I have to tell you that a written and recorded document is more important to me than a man's memory. It could have been last fall, and it could have been in January that he intended; after all, this deed was recorded in February.

"Also we have two documents with what appear to be two signatures; yours may be the right one, but I have no choice but to say that

Mr. Eddards is to be allowed. Is there any other information you might afford this tribunal? If not, then regarding the matter of whether Mr. Jack Beckham is the murderer, I think he be. But we have another witness who will testify to this murder…or murders, as you know, and I have asked him to join us.

"He is ready I presume?" Lord Rawdon said in a louder voice, looking toward the back of the room at the sergeant at arms.

From the back of the large meeting room the rustle that had started earlier intensified when a young Colonel walked into the room and brought smiles from practically everyone. Eddards, recognizing the figure of Colonel Banastre Tarleton, grinned as he anticipated further vindication from a figure so powerful. He could not help looking around and receiving congratulatory looks from those nearby. He stole a glance at a seated Justice Fisher, who looked on with respect and amazement at the attention given this young legendary and fearsome officer of the British Legion.

Fisher slumped into his seat. He thought he had just been beaten by a distinguished man. He admired Rawdon, and knew that although he was not learned in the law, he was intent on meting out British justice. Fisher studied Eddards intently while Eddards preened and glanced around at others to see their reaction to Tarleton. While Tarleton was moving to the front and greeting fellow officers, shaking their hands and beginning to position himself, Fisher had an inspiring idea.

Without hesitation he got up from his seat and approached Eddards; he then took a seat beside him so as not to intrude on the proceedings and the presence of Tarleton. In a quiet voice he said, "My congratulations, sir. This is a sound decision made by Lord Rawdon."

"Thank you, sir," said Eddards. "This is a fair judgment indeed. I am sympathetic to your point of view for the wench, Easter…I will sell her to you."

Fisher felt a chill at Eddards' suggestion. It would clearly be not just a sale but a way to dispose of a person he genuinely wished to be rid of. Fisher knew, without any doubt, Easter Benjamin's life was worth far less in this man's mind now than it was only minutes ago. He decided to act on his legal intuition and challenge the man, apparently with nothing to lose. Not even answering the proposition about Easter he said, "You are also fortunate to have the Colonel testify against this man Beckham."

Eddards shook his head agreeably.

Fisher leaned in and said, "I know for a fact Colonel Tarleton will testify as to who killed these three people."

"Yes," said Eddards. "It is a fact, is it not?" Eddards was still looking around and not fully comprehending Fisher's words.

"Yes, indeed," remarked Fisher, almost smiling. "The Major who was wronged…Major Apergis lived almost two days and told Colonel Tarleton who wounded him. He told the Colonel this man's name. He identified him. Do you understand, sir?"

Eddards suddenly understood. He turned and looked at Fisher, who looked back menacingly into his face, moving several inches closer as if to strike him if he could. Eddards' mouth was open. Saliva pooled at the corners of his mouth. His narrow pig-like eyes, behind his glasses, squinted at Fisher, and the Justice noticed the vein on his nose was even more scarlet.

Fisher looked into Eddards' eyes. "You wretched, conspiring hypocrite and liar. I know what you are doing. Now the whole world will know…nay!…they will know right before they hang your lying carcass." Fisher was smiling as if they were talking like gentlemen.

Eddards got up shakily, balancing himself on a chair, as his legs threatened to buckle beneath him. He started to walk away, but glanced back several times as he moved to the doors of the mansion, unable to lose the eyes of Fisher following him. Fisher was grinning as he watched Eddards leave.

Eddards slipped out unnoticed by everyone except Fisher, as Tarleton continued to move to the front of the room, accepting handshakes and pats on his back, ready to give answers to his superior, Lord Rawdon. Lord Rawdon rapped a candlestick hard on the table in front of him and asked that the talking cease. He gestured for Colonel Tarleton to come to the center of the room and face the Colonels arranged in a front row and address them with whatever knowledge he had.

The Colonel was indeed a handsome man. He strode to the front with a cadence that was impressive in its manner; this was not a purely military function, but his training showed even in a pedestrian way. It was mixed with just the right amount of impudence and superiority that had endeared his men to him. This, his bravery in combat, and his cunning and tactics, made him a legend already at a young age, even younger than many of his fellow officers that would hear him out to-day. Somewhere, Fisher thought, Lord Cornwallis must be beaming at his young protégé.

Lord Rawdon gave the Colonel the perfect entrée. "Sir, tell us your witness about this incident of Jack Beckham's murders, which have al-ready been attested to by a Loyalist officer and a gentleman farmer."

Turning to the larger crowd, his back to the Colonels, Tarleton said, "Major Nicholas Apergis was a true officer and a loyal soldier to the cause here in the colonies. He was a gentle man, not one of my warriors of any malicious intent, but a man who had great affection for one of the King's subjects and wanted to wed…indeed looked forward to the marriage.

"He was struck down in murder, unexpectedly, by a coward. On the day of this murder, Major Apergis was taking a man of supposed loyalty to see his affianced. She wished to arrange for a sale of her prop-erty to this man, so that she might then be free of her duties as a land owner and be here in this district, under Lord Rawdon's protection.

Tarleton looked back at Rawdon, who smiled and bowed his head in appreciation of the comment. "She would therefore be awaiting a final surrender of the colonies and the peace that was enjoyed before these uprisings. But gentlemen, she was murdered, and her child was murdered by this one man…and it is particularly offensive."

"Thank you, sir," said Lord Rawdon. "We have heard from two other gentlemen about the murders and so Colonel Tarleton adds his expert knowledge. How, sir, did you come about the information you have shared today?"

"Major Apergis died a painful death, sir. He lingered two days with the poison of his bowels in him. He recounted to me on three occasions how this happened and who committed the treachery. He was not taken with delirium at this time, and he spoke clearly.

"To his death he never knew his adored was murdered by this man, and certainly he did not know her child was murdered in this madness."

"For the record, Colonel, who was this man? And I beg your indulgence, sir. Did you say this murderer had come to purchase property from the woman?"

"Indeed, your Lordship! He was to buy her farm and all that is from it. His name, a disgrace to be heard among civilized people, and condemned by an honorable British officer – Major Apergis--as he was dying, was one 'Jadrow Eddards.'"

Colonel Tarleton did not understand the next sounds. A mixture of howls and anger enveloped the room. He heard Lord Rawdon shout at him through the din, "Who, sir?"

The entire room fell deathly quiet.

Tarleton was perplexed. He thought he had been misunderstood. Tarleton turned to the gathering of people, many standing, and said with a louder voice, "Eddards, sir...a Jadrow Eddards, who was recommended to purchase this woman's property by one of my officers and was taken to the Loyalist's farm by Major Apergis. Then the Major was killed in cold blood by this scoundrel."

The next sounds had nothing to do with Tarleton. Rawdon shouted to "hold the murderer," to no one in particular, and soldiers with muskets rushed into the room. Easter Benjamin was startled and weeping, with men rushing to the middle of the room past her and where Eddards had been. One officer grabbed Captain Donner and forced him to the floor, while others clutched his legs and arms.

The formal tribunal had collapsed into chaos. Tarleton instinctively drew his saber as did other officers, all holding them above their shoulders as if ready to strike. Rawdon shouted again above the din, "Where is this man?"

Tarleton looked at a Major Bowers and shouted, "Who? What man?" Then as it sank in, Bowers bellowed back, "Eddards was here... he is still here!"

Tarleton ran for the door, pushing people aside, shouting orders to his men on the mansion porch, and calling them to action. In all the bedlam Justice Fisher and Henry Rugeley were left in their places to look at each other with bewilderment.

The Justice spoke first. "I am afraid, sir, in my eagerness to uncover this snake, I have afforded him a chance to crawl to his hole in the ground. He left from here, I am sure, when I told him I knew what he had done."

"That is to your credit, William," said Rugeley calmly. "He is a dead man as we speak. I would not want the likes of Tarleton on to me. This man has killed a British officer and an innocent woman; he is closer to hell than any man I know."

"Nevertheless, I feel blameworthy. I am indeed sorry…what needs to be done now is to right a wrong in a large way. I have to speak to Lord Rawdon."

Justice Fisher made his way past overturned chairs and men milling about to Rawdon, who stood hands on hips talking to two townspeople, in a room now only one-fourth full. Captain Donner, the Tory, had been taken out of the room and made a prisoner to be interrogated.

Approaching Rawdon, who had a look of great consternation on his face, Fisher said, "Sir, you know what opportunity has now been afforded you?"

Looking questioning, Rawdon started to answer, but Fisher said, "The wench Easter was right, sir. This land was never sold. The deed is a forgery. This man was a terrible liar as well as a murderer."

"Indeed," said Rawdon and clapped his hands together and then raised his voice to its highest level. "Clear this room of all who have no business here…all remaining will be witness to what business is to be conducted…officers clear this room of all who should not be here."

At that, onlookers and men who had come in from the outside began to leave. All that were left were several regular officers and a few townspeople of wealth and bearing who would not be a hindrance but would testify to any further proceedings. In the middle of the room, now looking as isolated as any group of slaves in a house of power, under England's majesty, sat Easter Benjamin. Huddled with her were the slave girl with the baby, and a young slave boy.

Rawdon walked toward them instead of commanding their presence to him; before he spoke he looked over to Fisher and beckoned him with his hand to come to the middle of the room with the slaves. He also motioned for the distinguished Rugeley to approach. These three men of power and the three slaves and the baby were in the middle of the people who stayed at their places and never moved.

Rawdon said in a small voice, "Madame, I represent King George and his court. On his behalf I correct to you and yours for what is nigh unto a miscarriage of the King's justice. I am for that reason to officially grant that you are the rightful owner of the property accorded to you, as indicated in this will. Do you understand?"

"Yas, suh. I is sorry for all dese troubles."

"It is we who are sorry, I assure you."

"Suh, de bebe here has received the Lawd's blessing today."

Trying to discern the attention to the white child and Easter's low country patios, he asked, "How old is he?"

"It be a girl, suh."

"I see. Is the mother of this child close by?" Rawdon asked with a pleasant look on his face, looking around.

"Suh, you knows dis bebe chile, dis Maggie's bebe." De bebe was not killed, suh...we savin' her soon as Miss Maggie died...we save dis bebe, suh," Easter said triumphantly.

Lord Rawdon was deeply moved at this revelation. It was another lie exposed about a ruthless man. The child, in fact, had not been murdered. This was the most unexpected truth. Rawdon, who was unmarried, with no children, was struck by the fact that a child could be an unwilling pawn of a deceitful scheme to defraud, and murder, purely for greed. He was a man of faith, mindful of his power in the Camden district, but nevertheless a man of compassion.

He nodded for "permission" toward the young slave girl holding the child. With her look of approval, he reached down, took the baby, and held it up in front of him, his arms extended, to see her, her little feet now exposed, her toes curling up at feeling the air outside the blanket.

After a brief moment of satisfaction on his face, he was interrupted by a father of three children. "May I?" asked Justice Fisher, reaching to hold the child. "I knew the mother," he said smiling.

Holding the child, he cradled her in his arms and looked into her face. "What is her name?" he asked.

Easter replied, "We calls her 'Little Maggie,' suh."

The baby opened her eyes, began to pucker and cry.

Justice Fisher laughed. "Ah, an independent look about her…like her mother. Is it not so?"

"Yas, suh, she Maggie's bebe."

Chapter Fourteen

Looking for War

At the time Jack was being absolved of a triple murder, he was looking for Jadrow Eddards and considering the possible whereabouts of Banastre Tarleton. Jack was miles between his home and the area where he had fought at Alexander's Field near the Catawba River. He knew it would be difficult to move about and know what was going on. His best source was Randolph Mabry, but getting to him would be time consuming. Instead, he would seek out Elberton Chandler, who must know which neighbors were still loyal.

Jack, along with John Craig, had been moving toward familiar land, his home on the Pacolet. But to Craig's disappointment, Jack suddenly turned east, away from home. His plan was to find his brother Thomas' family; they would know where Chandler was. His mind had been racing to do the right thing for his own preservation, but he was mindful of his family. The still gnawing desire to go to Elizabeth and his children was powerful. But the most powerful consideration was to right the wrong against him, the murder warrant against his life. Did others believe this lie? Would his family hear it? Would neighbors find out the truth, or believe gossip from others who had no knowledge of what happened?

Soe and his people knew what had happened, but they would be far removed from the swapping of conversation and commerce. Jack needed someone to tell him news and that person would have to be the "school man," Elberton Chandler, who traveled in family circles and was privy to all manner of tittle-tattle. Jack was now determined to find him.

The course to find Chandler would be a circuitous one, but he felt sure Thomas' family could direct Jack to him. He only hoped he would find their home still standing. As they rode, Jack considered how his own family was diminishing. Samuel was in the Georgia Colony with Abner, part of Elijah Clarke's Rifles. Maggie was dead. Thomas had been captured in Charlestowne. Jack's brother-in-law, Colonel Henderson, was a prize captive from the South Carolina 6th Regiment.

As Jack and John Craig rode toward Thomas' home, Jack spotted several groups of people. He did not have to engage them for he saw them from several hundred yards away and avoided them. Friend or foe, Whig or Tory, anyone could want to take him for the reward on his head. Jack watched in hiding as they passed, some at a distance but so close he could hear their voices. Craig stayed behind Jack watching him and nodding his head if Jack said something to him. They slept one night there in the woods, Jack in a fitful state, anxious to get to his brother's house.

At one point he saw riders carrying torches and felt certain they were a hanging party. He felt heaviness at the thought of his friend, Rand Mabry, who lived in the direction the men were headed. But then he convinced himself to release this worry. Mabry had more friends than anyone Jack knew of, including the powerful Wade Hampton, who was still a force among both sides.

They began riding again at daylight with great caution, and at mid-morning Jack saw his brother's home. But no one was in sight at the farm. Jack watched for almost an hour and walked the length of the ditch he had ridden into for cover. Maw remained loosely tied to a bush and Jack ranged from one end of the ditch back again to the other, a distance of more than a hundred yards. He listened and watched. He instructed Craig to go to the other end of the ravine and watch until Jack came for him.

From a great distance, Jack finally saw a young slave boy walking casually and stopping to pick at weeds and throw a rock at an imaginary target. This young man had nothing to do. He was alone and walking slowly toward the main house. Jack recognized him as "Cletus," a young man of twelve or thirteen who had played with Kit and Johnny, Thomas' sons. Jack went back to Maw and held her reins while he waited for Cletus to get nearer to the house. Then he rode quickly to get Craig's attention and motioned for him to stay where he was.

Jack emerged from the ditch, his loaded rifle in hand, and rode toward Cletus. The boy saw him, and when Maw went into a fast trot he turned, screamed, and ran. Jack called to him, but the boy ran harder. Jack dug one boot heel into the leather at Maw's side, and she ran at race horse speed to overtake the youngster. The boy would not stop. Jack had no choice. As Maw caught up to Cletus, Jack reached down and grabbed him. The boy screamed incoherently, "Yiiaahhh," thrashing his arms and legs about as Jack held him tightly around the chest.

"Hellfire, Cletus, it is me, Jack. Hush your hollerin."

The boy was wild-eyed and stark crazy with fear. Jack stopped and got off his horse, still holding Cletus around the chest. The boy's legs flailed as he continued trying to get away. Jack grabbed him by the shoulders and shouted, "Where is Kit and Johnny?" This got through to Cletus momentarily. He was gasping for air and trembling. He looked into Jack's eyes and seemed to be composing himself, but then began screaming again. "Don't kill me, don't kill me," he cried, hysterically.

Jack said, "I ain't," and took out his long knife. At this the boy seemed to lose his senses, foaming at the mouth and screaming for his mother. Jack held him with one arm so he could not get away, and with his other hand he handed the boy the knife. "You kills me, for I ain't 'bout to have you kilt." The young man was almost prostrate with exhaustion. He was barely hanging on to Jack's arm, limp and looking wild-eyed, and he did not take the knife. It fell to the ground while he panted and tried to catch his breath.

Jack then did something instinctively. Maybe he had been gone too long from his children. He did what he had to do to calm the boy. He embraced him completely, his arms interlocking around the boy's body. He put his head beside the young man's head, smelling great fear through the youngster's sweat, and talked to him as if he were talk-

ing to Maw. "Ain't going to kill you...don't worry...I has no reason to
hurt you...don't worry...old Jack ain't crazy...I has lost my family, and
I wants to see my young ones, too. I am looking for all my family...I am
looking for Kit and Johnny and any otherns. Don't worry, boy. Don't
be afraid."

Cletus could not speak and was barely able to stand. Maw was
there beside them snorting and prancing in place. Jack reached up and
took his canteen from the saddle and gave it to Cletus to drink. He
gulped the water. He drank so hard the water spilled down his cheeks
and chin and he swallowed hard, all the time glancing sideways, never
directly at Jack. Jack took the canteen from him, let him rest and belch,
and then handed it to him again. "Be drinking slower."

The boy did and began to calm himself; Jack picked him up and sat
him on Maw in the saddle. Jack began a slow walk, holding the reins
in one hand and his rifle in his right hand and just looked back up
at Cletus and nodded at him. Jack started humming, spitting tobacco
juice, as he walked toward the main cabin. Cletus, with eyes wide and
mouth open, held onto the reins and looked straight ahead. They got
to the main house, and Jack helped him down from the saddle and sat
on the ground, picking up some small rocks and throwing them a few
feet in front of him aimlessly. Finally Cletus sat down several feet from
him and said nothing, just stared at the ground.

"Why is you afraid?" Jack said. Cletus did not respond. Jack needed
the boy to talk to him, for it was clear no one was there on the farm,
and he feared the worst. Jack looked at him earnestly and said, "Will
you help me find Kit and Johnny?" Still no answer. His decision then,
out of frustration, was to get back into the saddle, hold Cletus in front
of him, and say, "Jest tells me where you wants to go. I will take you.
You goin' to your mama's? I take you there." Jack then started to ride at
a slow trot toward the slave cabins.

As they approached the cabins, Jack was wary of the reaction the
slaves might have to seeing him with Cletus. He imagined that the boy's
fear had been caused by tales that had reached the area. Rumors that
he had killed Maggie must have been widespread. Riding into their
cluster of cabins might trigger a mass reaction, and Cletus would surely

be affected. At this point Jack felt the need to leave, get away and try another farm, find another friend to help him locate Chandler.

Within sight of the small shanty cabins Jack let Cletus down to the ground and said, "You wants more water?" Cletus nodded yes and Jack handed him his canteen. He drank, and this time nodded his head in appreciation. Jack said, "Boy, I is going, but you mind your mama, and if'n you sees my Kit and Johnny tell 'em I am looking to see them."

Jack pulled back on Maw's reins and started to wheel her around when Cletus said, "Massah? Did yo…suh…did yo… uh…cut off Miss Maggie's head and eat her bebe?" His eyes were big and begging. Cletus, in his mind, had just asked the "devil" a question. The "devil" was a man on a horse several feet above him with a long knife and a gun and a "boogeyman" story about him that had been talked about recently in the slave cabins at night.

Jack looked at him and thought. He had to say something to answer this child's question. "Boy, I has been in the water with the Reverend. No, I ain't hurt Maggie…and Easter knows who did…so if'n you has any thoughts on who, you has just ask her…I tells you rightly…no, I has not done this….do you believe in the Lord as Miss Easter and the Reverend do?"

"Yas, suh."

"Then you can believe me…ask Easter. She tell you."

"I will, suh…uh…cans you rides me a little more? I is tired."

Jack pulled him up on the saddle behind him as he might John Junior, and they rode directly to the slave cabins, with Jack knowing what might await him. But as they got closer Cletus climbed down off the horse with Jack's help and ran toward his cabin shouting for his mama. Jack slowed to a stop and watched as the boy ran away, never looking back.

Starting to leave he heard a woman shout, "Massah! Massah Jack." He turned to see the one person he could have hoped for; it was Easter Benjamin. The reception awaiting Jack was completely unexpected. Besides Easter there were slaves pouring out of cabins and running toward him. Cat, Thomas, Isaac, Lucy, Abraham were there, and several slaves he did not recognize. Easter was jubilant.

"Why is all this glory being made?" Jack wondered. Easter was almost jumping up and down, and at her age.

"Massah, you is here. We knows you din't kill Miss Maggie. Glory to the Lawd…I has to tell you…we is so happy."

Jack got off of Maw and stood beside her, his hand on his saddle, and listened to Easter. Junis, a small ten-year-old boy, came up to Jack, climbed up on a rock three feet high, and bent over curiously looking at him. He peered into Jack's face as if he were looking into a dark hole to see what was in it. He didn't say anything, just looked with his mouth open, fully expecting to see something he had never seen before. A growing number of slaves were coming into the yard, all beaming in admiration.

Jack clearly was not used to such adulation, particularly since he was wanted for murder and was hiding from so many people. And now he was being told something he already knew – he did not do it. He looked up at Easter, who was grinning so broadly she was showing what teeth she had left. She began to clap her hands and started a chant that most of the slaves took up in unison, a pure African continent chant, not discernable to him, high and melodious, beautiful in its blend of voices. "Oh we oh…oh we oh…dear Lawd…oh we oh." A woman behind Easter started crying and singing praises. This only brought louder sounds of "Oh we oh…oh we oh…." Jack stood motionless beside Maw, awed at this reception.

After a time of chanting and dancing Easter shoved "Dan-Man," a thirty-year-old man, toward Jack. Dan-Man, big and sure of his steps, undoubtedly an overseer of the family farm, walked over to talk to Jack while the others backed away. "Massah," he said, removing his hat, "it is good yo is here. Lawd been bringing yo home and dis is a good time, for all us is afred of what be happening now. Don't know what is to come with so manys people don't be kind to no body."

Not ignoring him, but asking the question he had on his mind, Jack said, "Where is the school man?"

Dan-Man knew who he was talking about. Looking toward the east and nodding with his chin he replied, "He staying at the Starnes' house, suh. He has fo chillin he is teachin'…all dem comes dere now and stays all day. But, suh, sometimes the school man be gone for days…we thinks maybe he be daid or lost, but he always comes back even if'n it be two weeks. He gets round plenty, suh…gone and den back…gone den back….he be teachin' a lots, suh, but he gone and den back."

"Can you take me there?" Jack said. "I ain't sure of the Starnes's place." And with that Jack had lied. He knew the place well but he wanted Dan-Man to show the way, for Jack was not sure if the Starnes's place was a Tory farm.

"I cans take you dere, suh. That's what Miss Easter said, suh. She knows you lookin' for him and yo two kin boys, Kit and Johnny. They bees there too, suh, so you can see them at that place."

"Hold!" said Jack, surprising Dan-Man with his suddenness. "You tell me my two kin are there?"

"Yas, suh. Don't make no difference whether they be Tory or us, suh. Massah school man don't wants no one to be afred of being with him. He teachin' all kinds and they alls gits along too…don't be no trouble."

Jack thought it very much out of the ordinary that Whigs' and Tories' children were together in one house. "Don't make no sense," he told Dan-Man.

The man cackled. "Oh, is all right, suh. School mans makes them behave and when they gits too mean he sets them outside and leaves them dere."

Jack turned to get on Maw and just remarked, "Let's go." Then he motioned to John Craig in the distant ditch to join them. Jack did so by twirling his arm and whistling loudly through his teeth. Craig charged from the woods to join them as Jack and Dan-Man had already started riding.

While they traveled Dan-Man looked at Jack with appreciative glances and smiles, riding alongside him until they got to the site of the Starnes home. Once there, Jack saw Kit and Johnny outside the house and Chandler in the yard with them. But Chandler was several yards away with three of the Starnes women, who were cooking over a fire in the yard.

Riding Maw, Jack dashed into the group to get to Kit and Johnny as fast as he could. Dan-Man pushed the horse he was riding to go faster as did Craig, but Jack and Maw had reached the yard quickly and Kit was running toward him; the two met before many in the yard recognized Jack.

"Is all well here?" Jack hollered to Kit. The young boy smiled broadly and shook his head yes. He reached up with courtesy for Maw's reins as Jack got off his horse and reached out to tousle the youngster's hair. Johnny and his black dog came running, and behind them the schoolmaster trotted with a pleasant grin on his face. They all met in the corner of the yard, the farthest from the Starnes's house. The school man said, "Welcome, sir. Where have you been? Where are you going? We have all heard that you are not accused of any crimes against your family, and that it is good news indeed."

Jack noticed the schoolmaster was much more relaxed than the last time he saw him, under pressure, as it was, with a task to find Easter Benjamin for him. He was dressed neatly as always, white linen shirt, white stockings, buckled shoes, his hair pulled back into a tight pony tail. His spectacles were firmly fit on his head, and he was holding a book of some size in his hand.

"You has heard a lot," Jack said, half sarcastically. With that he began to usher the two boys away; they had been waiting patiently, wanting not to interrupt the school man and Jack. He put his arm around both of them and walked to a tree and sat down on his haunches, at eye level with his two nephews. They were sons of his captured brother, and Jack now began to feel sorrow for them. Samuel was away, Maggie was dead, and these two boys were being kept by what might turn out to be Tories.

Seeing the teacher approaching them, walking casually with John Craig and followed by Dan-Man, Jack rose and glared in their direction. This stopped their progress, and began to mill around away from Jack and the boys. Jack resumed sitting on his haunches and talking to Kit and Johnny. "Do you see this school man much? Is he learning you anything?"

Kit looked at his brother and said, "Script and numbers mostly."

Johnny agreed with a nod. "I think he is courting, for he is gone mostly at night and then sometimes he rides off and comes back at supper time. He is fine to us and does not take sides with no one."

"Does you trust him to find me some peoples I need to talk to?"

"I s'pose," said Kit. "He is known right well by so many folks that has children, and he talks to otherns that comes to markets, so he knows many." Jack pondered this and then called out to Chandler and hailed him over to their conversation.

Chandler reveled slightly in being called from the three men to join Jack. This was dispelled quickly when he reached the spot where Jack was standing. Jack reached out and took the man by the shirt front and grasped it tightly. This startled Chandler.

Jack said, "Listen…and listen well…there is peoples that wants to kill me for they don't give a damnation if I ain't killed Maggie…'sides, I have done damage to otherns so they will use that as an excuse. What say you to that?"

Chandler was on familiar territory with an unpredictable and violent Jack, a man who apparently did not understand him or like him, possibly because of his education. Seeking to be of value and to appease Jack, Chandler said, "Sir, I will tell you things to help you. If you believe me, you would do well to go home to your family. Tarleton is away from this area. He is chasing Francis Marion, who refuses to be in the upcountry and fights from savannahs and swamps. Tarleton is out to kill him and arrest all that are with him.

"So much is lost to the British; the Whigs are not faring well…but the Cherokee country, near your home, is also likely to be the worst, for the Cherokees have always been with the British. I hear the British will use them to take down anyone who is not with the King. It will not be good for people in their homes. That is my advice, sir."

All of this was heard by John Craig and also Dan-Man, who was shaking his head up and down in sad agreement and muttering, "Uh huh…dat's so…oh yas, suh…dat's so."

Craig could not contain himself. He rushed up to Jack and said with tears in his eyes, "For the love of our Father in heaven, this is the time to go protect our own. My wife has two babies that are not even walking good, and she has no kin. Will you be leaving? Can'st we go and soon to the Pacolet?"

Jack saw the terror in young Craig's eyes, a man who looked to be no more than nineteen or twenty years old. He knew Craig was wanted for the ambush at Alexander's Old Field and had been running since. He did not doubt that the man needed to go home to his family. They lived miles beyond Jack's settlement in the Spartan district, in an isolated area where attacks by raiding Cherokees and British were more likely.

Jack looked at Chandler, who said the safest route was to go through Winnsboro and on to the Ninety-Six district and approach from the south side of the Pacolet. This would take much longer, and the British were ensconced at Ninety-Six, but Jack could avoid them.

"That is a long way from the Tyger River and then the Pacolet," said Beckham. "Has you been traveling much?"

Chandler stammered and said, "No," but he said he knew from his sources that the British controlled much of what was between Jack and the east, going toward the Tyger. "I suggest the south, with respect, sir."

Jack looked away and then quickly back at Chandler. "I will be taking some of your advice. And I will be taking these young boys with me, as well as Mr. Craig. These boys has got all the learnin' they needs for now. They needs to know how not to be kilt."

Johnny jumped straight up, and his black dog, sensing a change of emotions, started barking. Kit asked, "Where does we stay, Uncle Jack?"

"You stays with my Elizabeth and our young ones. We will git word to your ma that you are not with the school man and nay worry. Dan-Man, you will do this." Dan Man shook his head up and down in agreement. "My older girls can stay with Aunt Henderson for the times being. Mind you though, both of you, you do the big girls' work every day when they is gone to Henderson's." At that, Jack smiled his wry grin, and the boys knew he was accepting them to ride and letting them know he would protect them.

The four prepared to leave immediately without getting any provisions or clothes for the boys. Jack did send Dan-Man for their horses and blankets for the night cold. Both of the boys would ride close behind Jack, and Craig would always ride behind the boys. Johnny looked up expectantly and asked if they could bring the black dog. Jack said, "No, dogs bark at the wrong time."

As they started out, Jack led the group five miles west instead of south, as Chandler had suggested. Then he stopped and motioned for everyone to halt and drink water while he fed Maw, and John Craig tended to the other horses. "We is going to the Broad River past Fishdam Ford to gits to the Tyger River," Jack announced.

"Why?" said Craig, incredulous. "That is not where the school man said to go."

"I knows my country," said Jack. "I pert near knows the Ninety-Six and with many Tories and Colonel Cruger there, it is no place to be social with people you ain't met. What if settlers we run into are with the King? We would have to ride days before we are getting away.

"I knows the Pacolet, the Enoree, and the Tyger better. I can outrun men if I knows where I am going." He turned to the boys. "You two will be close to Mister Craig…and try to stay up with Maw."

At that, Jack said they would travel to find a place to spend the night and try to make the Pacolet by tomorrow. John Craig looked somewhat relaxed for the first time, with thoughts of seeing his wife and two children. It was clear he was particularly stressed. Jack thought him near a breaking point and thus a liability on this trip. He would have to take time to sooth Craig and give him ordinary things to do to occupy his mind. Jack called Craig up to him and said, "You watch my two boys and make sure they is doing rightly and keeping up. When we stops, get them to gather wood and make a fire. You is in charge of them. You is a 'Pap', ain't you?"

Craig smiled and said, "Yes, to two little girls."

Jack shook his head to affirm and left Craig, saying in a strong voice, "Let's be going."

The four traveled hard for the next four hours, even after dark, finally stopping at a stream that was a tributary of the Tyger River which ran into the Pacolet from the great hills in the North Carolina colony. The stream was noisy where they stopped. Jack followed it to a point where it was much quieter but with a strong current. He settled the three in for the night, having them build a small fire for the cold November night. They ate the food he had left in his bags as they sat near the fire. He then told them he would leave them there. This bothered Craig, who looked timid and reluctant until Jack walked over to him and said, "I will be close by and watching. Fact be, I am walking all the time and guardin' you, so I will be around...you is safe."

Craig relented and went back to the fire, where he and the boys stretched out and began to invite sleep. Jack went several yards away and went through his ritual of rubbing Maw down and feeding her more water and talking to her. He then found a clump of bushes after hiding Maw between pine trees and within minutes was asleep. He planned to sleep until dawn unless he heard "warring sounds" – men and horses moving in the night. Jack slept as soundly as he had in days, his .50 caliber rifle barrel propped against his chest. Before sunup, he rose and went to the camp where the others were asleep. Jack went over to Craig and nudged him and said, "Git the boys."

As they prepared to drink water and eat old bread, Jack heard from the east a distinctive noise that he had not heard in over a year. It was the movement of many horses and their hooves in a rhythm that would get louder and louder as they came closer. It would eventually resemble distant thunder, and Jack would be able to tell what direction they were moving by the increasing or decreasing sounds. He was alarmed. He had no idea who these men were.

He looked at Craig and the boys. "You hears that? Many horses and many men. You be ready, for your life may be dependin' on your horse...listen to me and don't go nowheres." With that, Jack jumped on Maw and rode toward the noise, leaving a fearful looking John Craig and two trusting young men behind him.

Jack rode between closely bunched trees looking for a decent trail and listening for the sounds of the horses as he weaved, riding to his left and then back to the sounds and again back to his right. He was looking for a ridge to see as far as he could, or a clearing where he would wait to see the masses that were coming. Finally he saw a stand of pine trees and urged Maw to pass through them. When they emerged he saw a tree line that looked taller than others, and as he raced toward the trees he saw a man on a horse. He was dressed as was Jack, a frock of green for a coat and a black hat turned down, a rifle slung over his shoulder; his horse looked to be smaller than Maw. The man was riding, looking back over his left shoulder toward another man who was over a hundred yards away.

Jack stopped Maw abruptly, wheeled around, and jumped off her. He quickly grabbed his nautical glass and led Maw behind a tree for cover. He watched the men through his glass; both were dressed as militia men. They could be Loyalists or Whigs. Jack studied them and muttered, "These mens are forward scouts. They is trailing ahead for otherns."

It was still a dilemma. They could be from either side. Jack could still hear horses in the distance and now another sound. It was wagons. Men, horses, and wagons. So these men were an army moving certainly for a major battle. His mind could not determine how many there were or what direction they might be going in. He would have to wait until the main force showed itself, but he knew many scouts could precede the main body.

Was this Tarleton, being led by civilian Loyalists as the school man had said? But Tarleton was thought to be chasing Marion in the deeper part of the colony, according to Chandler. Was this Cruger? Worse, was it Cornwallis with a very large group? Where would they be going? To what battle?

Jack moved even deeper into the safety of the woods and waited. At a very long distance he saw a concentration of a moving mass. Even with his glass he could not make them out. He waited and looked again. Then as a column turned to the side Jack finally made out their colors. They were not British or Jaegers, they were colonists, but Jack knew little else. He waited until they were closer, and through his glass judged them to be at least one thousand strong, militia with some officers clad in blue uniforms among them. He made a decision to go back quickly for Craig and his nephews before approaching the oncoming army, for he certainly looked more harmless with young boys.

Jack reached the camp where the three were all standing expectantly, and directed them to follow him. Together they rode to a point where Jack decided he would encounter the group and identify himself. He still did not know this army by name, but he would find out. He moved to a hill and caught the eye of a large column of men and called out, "Hail, boys, where ye be goin'? I am with you!"

Jack waited with some impatience for their reaction, ready to run or be accepted. A man came out of the pack and began to ride toward him as the others pulled up, many with their guns ready for firing. Now Jack and his three were the most vulnerable. Everything depended on what was said next. Jack turned to them. "Be ready to run to the woods and the river…go south."

The man charged up to Jack, who still did not have his rifle in a threatening position. "Who be ye?" he said.

"Farmin'men from the Pacolet, Grindal Shoals on Sandy Run," said Jack. "We huntin' game. Who be ye?"

"You are from the Pacolet?"

"Aye," Jack said, still not knowing if this was good or bad.

The man smiled. "We needs you. You knows this place, I figures, and we can use your boys, too."

"What is the reason for my helping you?" inquired Jack.

"We are Sumpter's army, sir. We are ahead of the British, and they aims to catch us. But we are to fight them. Do you know the plantation of Captain William Blackstock?"

"I do," said Jack.

"Cans you tell us if'n we are close to it or how far it is?"

"I will help get you there," Jack said, glad to join a major force for a while as he headed for his Pacolet cabin. "Why is you to Blackstock's?"

The man answered without looking at Jack. "Tarleton is behind us. He will fight us, and we are going to pick the place. General Sumpter says we are to Blackstock's plantation where we aim to fight the scoundrel."

Jack must have shouted at the man, for he looked greatly surprised. "TARLETON? He is here?"

"Aye, and he will be here right shortly, maybe with cannon along with his dragoons and foot soldiers."

Jack pulled his rifle out of his sheath and let out an unexpected and primitive Catawba Indian war yelp, a hallo that got the attention of the man and many riding close by. He looked suddenly different, with a scowl and menacing expression that caused Kit, Johnny, and John Craig to look at each other. None had seen this before.

The man riding beside Jack asked, "Who say you be?"

"Jack Beckham of the Pacolet."

"You be?" The man stopped his horse suddenly and glared at Jack. Jack faced the man, prodded Maw toward him, and said, "I did not kill my sister and her child. I can be proving that."

The man softened his look at Jack and said, "It don't matter. We has the devil behind us and we needs you to help us. If'n you did, that is between you and your maker. If'n you did not, then all is right. But now we needs to get to Blackstock's, and, Mr. Beckham, sir, I am informing you that Colonel Henderson has been with us and so now is Elijah Clarke. I knows you has kin with Elijah, and we knows that the Colonel is your kin, too. Fact is, he has already stopped these rumors about you killin yourn, so I welcomes you."

At that the man said his name was Sergeant Hill of Bratton's men, attached to General Sumpter. He smiled again, reached out, and offered his hand to Jack. Jack did not shake his hand, which convinced the man even more he was telling the truth. Jack's only reply was, "Samuel is here?" The man nodded, and Jack turned around and shouted to Kit and Johnny, "Your brother is here. We will find him directly." At that, a slightly satisfied and further vindicated Jack rode in front of the Sergeant and said back to him, "You follows me. We can be at Blackstock's plantation in some short hours."

The entourage traveled with much noise and shouting, officers and scouts running fast and furious alongside the moving men, often dropping back and then riding forward at a fast gait. Scouts were constantly riding in and out of the formation, informing the officers of any perceived dangers ahead. The men in the wagons with their supplies broke down often. Decisions about moving the supplies to other wagons or leaving them were quickly made.

Jack circled back a couple of times to see how far the masses reached behind him, and then rode Maw fast ahead to work with the scouts. He informed them where they were, and they traveled back to pass the information. It was a busy and confusing movement, but it functioned. Everyone performed a duty, and in all this Jack never saw General Sumpter, Colonel Henderson, or Samuel. He was sometimes operating alone, or with four to six scouts around him, all on fast mounts similar to Maw.

Within sight of the Blackstock plantation, Jack went back to report and there was a rushing of scouts and officers to get to the farm. Finally, he saw General Sumpter, a slight but hard and gritty-looking man, bent on his mission and looking straight ahead as he rode. A senior officer peeled off as the General's men passed and said, "You are scout Jack Beckham?"

"Yes, to be of service, sir."

"I am Colonel Lacey of Rocky Creek, not far from Alexander's Old Field. I knows what you and otherns did at Alexander's. We are proud of that and you boys. You will be attached to me at this time. Follow me to my Adjutant and stay with him."

"I has my nephews and one who was with me at Alexander's."

"Bring them," Lacey said.

Jack and his three followed until they met Adjutant Thomas, who said they would have their orders directly. They dismounted and stood around looking for Samuel and Colonel Henderson until a soldier came and said, "Sir, you and others are needed to be with the Colonel now."

Jack, with the other volunteers following, walked behind the man for several hundred yards, away from the great gathering of the militia toward a group of some hundred waiting men. Colonel Lacey rode up and said, "Gentlemen, we are to be close to Tarleton as he advances. We will try to get even closer."

Jack looked back at Kit, Johnny, and John Craig. "You," he said to Craig, "stay with me. You boys stay back and down as you can. You will be fine today. Watch old Jack. But if anything happens, go with Craig here to the Pacolet. He can get you close to Aunt Beckham. Don't look for Samuel. I has no idea where Clarke's men is."

They nodded with fear and respect in their eyes and looked at each other for comfort.

Jack and a growing number of men, now close to two hundred, moved to positions behind heavy large fences, sheds, barns and trees, anticipating that Tarleton would have to come down through a narrow trough of land bounded by trees. Lacey went back and forth behind his men and then to the front saying not to "powder" yet. "We has scouts that will ride to us. We will be ready then."

The men nervously checked their guns and looked at their pans, wiped their frizzens, and looked back at their powder horns. A lot of cursing and swearing was taking place as men prepared themselves to be uncivil, to murder, and to give no quarter. These men had seen battle before. Many were whooping and calling out for Tarleton to die. Others were spitting, even with no tobacco or snuff in their mouths.

Jack had a hundred thoughts. At times like this he could use Soe, a great warrior. The Indian would stare off into space and not say anything until battle was on top of him. Then, with an enemy yards away, Soe would become a mad man, hollering and screaming sounds that were indescribable. He could fire his weapon and reload with the best Jack had seen. He was fast with his tomahawk, swinging it as he charged, as Tarleton's dragoons did, with their sabers in a slashing high arc that cut up and then down with amazing speed.

Jack waited and began to pull his rifle to his shoulder in anticipation. He leveled his gun in front of him and aimed. He then took his gun down and looked it over. He knew his impatience would give way to a resolve to be calm. Jack had never been seriously wounded in any fight, and he walked away every time with the other man's blood on him. His thoughts were broken by the shouting of greetings from men as General Sumpter rode up and gave Colonel Lacey a command to move to their left and try to outflank Tarleton. He heard men saying excitedly that four hundred of the Americans, under Few and McJunkin, had been driven back with British cold steel, bayonets, and sabers after firing their guns at too great a distance at the British.

Colonel Lacey then commanded all his men to move quickly, and Jack ran fast with all the others, outdistancing John Craig. He arrived at a spot, breathing heavily from his exertion, where Lacey directed them to be. What they saw was surprising. The British in front of them were watching the battle across the valley where their comrades were taking the measure of the Americans. Lacey, with hand commands, ordered his men closer. Jack and thirty men got within seventy-five yards of the unsuspecting British when Lacey finally gave an order to prepare to fire.

All of the men alongside Jack aimed carefully and fired on command. Twenty British fell at once. This was shocking in its unanimous blow of fire power and in the number who fell quickly. The British were so staggered that Jack and others more calmly loaded their flintlocks and fired again, felling more, while the Redcoats stumbled about attempting to get organized. Jack's intuition was to charge on foot and kill anyone with his hatchet and tomahawk, one in each hand, but the command to charge was not given. He would have been in the no man's land between his troops and the British had he charged. He could have been shot by either side, either accidentally or by British musket. Tarleton, seeing his troops failing, made a decision to rush forward toward the Americans with his mounted dragoons and without his infantry and cannon.

The other militia ensconced behind the broad fence of Blackstock's plantation, though surprised at Tarleton's maneuver, fired at will, and the impressive Green Dragoons of Tarleton's proud force were stopped. Tarleton's men were not able to ride among the militia as they had done at the Waxhaws, killing with slashing sabers on hard-charging horses. There was nothing for Tarleton to do except retreat, for the first time in any battle of any size against Americans. He had gone against a thousand American militia with over two hundred of his best men, but had suffered too much. He would retreat two miles away to get organized and prepare to fight again.

As Lacey pulled his troops back, there was information that

Sumpter had been gravely wounded. He was hit with six rounds of buckshot and would be in danger of bleeding to death. The decision was made to remove him to Blackstock's house and get a lead ball out of him quickly, without anesthetic, to keep him from bleeding so profusely. The doctor said, "You must move him away and to more safety."

At this point in the evening, Colonel Lacey was asked to use one hundred of his best men to take Sumpter, using torchlight, to ford the Tyger River and get him farther away from Tarleton's encampment. All of the officers felt that Tarleton would counterattack, and their commanding General was down.

The group, including John Craig, Kit, and Johnny staying close to Jack, moved across the Tyger in a familiar direction northwest. Jack was with the several men who took the General to Adam Goudelock's house at Grindal Shoals on the Pacolet, only four miles from his home. The scout and spy felt keenly this great twist of irony that had brought him so close to Elizabeth.

Leaving the Goudelock home after midnight, with temperatures below freezing, the horses breathing hard, their vapor wide and visible, Jack and his party began a journey home. He knew the trails and the paths even at dark, and he resolved to be there for breakfast to see his wife and family.

He began the journey with a certain homesickness at being in his familiar woods but joy at being this close to home for the first time in seven months. The heaviness in his chest was from apprehension, with the British so close and what he had just seen so near his cabin. He thought about the safety of his eight children…and Elizabeth.

Chapter Fifteen

Home And Death

Riding toward home, Jack felt something in the air he had known all too well since boyhood. It was threatening to his senses. The wind was blowing from the side and with it traces of cold rain and particles of ice. This was sleet that would continue to get worse. It was only the beginning. He knew he might have to stop, no matter how close he was to his log home with the fires burning. It was a decision bad fate handed to him, but it was too dangerous to go on.

Maw and the other horses stood the biggest chance of falling, with resulting terminal injury. Frostbite was sure to come, for his feet and toes were already numb. He looked at the boys and hollered against the increasing wind and sleet, "How is your feet?"

Kit spoke through chattering teeth and said they were cold. Jack looked back and at that very instant saw John Craig's horse slide off the narrow path and fight to keep her balance. He made the instant decision to dismount and walk the horses to a place off the trail and to a cropping of bunched cedar trees along a shoal. He felt the wind and ice and the temperature dropping even more and knew this was extreme weather.

"We has to stop," he called out, and they all trotted to the trees. In the arbor Jack looked up and saw that a portion of the sleet was being shielded by the cedar limbs, but they were drooping lower with the increasing ice and rain. His torch, a lit pine knot, and the others' torches went out. Standing in darkness with only a faint light visible as clouds intermittently raced past the late November moon, Jack made several lightning decisions. All were made to just keep them alive.

Jack hollered to the others to break branches off the trees. He gave no explanation. They grabbed the lowest lying limbs, and Jack reached up as high as he could to cut more with his hatchet. He had all of them throw cedar brush into a pile, and he told the boys to shake the water off and beat the limbs against another tree. He brought Maw into the middle of the trees with all the cut branches for the most protection from sleet, and he told the others to tether their horses under the biggest tree they could find.

With expertise, he took a stick and coaxed Maw into a horse's most unnatural position. He tapped her on her lower legs, talking to her as he had when he trained her to go forward into a kneeling position. Then, as she had been trained, she lay down on her side, her big eyes wide and looking around while Jack gently talked to her and assured her. Jack patted her face and soothed her while he looked up and instructed Craig and the boys to pile cedar limbs on the ground around her. He continued to sit close to Maw's head and direct them. With Maw pacified, he quickly got up and told the two boys to lie down between her legs on the ground. "Snug up under her stomach and hug her," he said. He piled more limbs, as dry as possible, on top of them after tying two blankets loosely around their bodies. Then he instructed them to put their bodies together under Maw and their heads against her stomach.

Jack went around and told Craig to lie down and put his legs over Maw's back while he did the same, his head near her head. He pulled cedar onto his back while Craig imitated him. He held Maw tight around the neck and talked to her while he was lying with one leg extended along her proud back and one leg over her, as if he were in the saddle. Only then did he reassure the boys and Craig. "We is going to stay alive with Maw's blood and her warm body. Hold her tight. It will do well for her as for us."

He sang out trying to comfort them, "You boys feel old Maw's warm stomach?" They both said yes, but it was a weak response with the temperature now well below freezing. They were as close to death in bad weather as he had ever experienced, and he would not sleep tonight. He would listen for Tarleton's horses, if they dared to be in this weather. Knowing tales about Tarleton, he believed they could be traveling.

It got colder, and Jack feared for everyone without fire. He swore at daylight they would move on foot, walking the miles to his cabin, not only to get there but to keep moving their bodies against the cold. In the night, Jack listened against the wind for movement. When he raised his head, Maw would raise up, and he constantly patted her and pushed her head back down. If she had bolted up all the men would have fallen off of her like firewood from a basket.

Approaching daylight, he felt the wind dying and the sleet dwindling. Jack had not slept. In the night he never heard a sound from the others unless he called out to them to see if they were conscious. Seeing the light breaking at a distance he called out softly, "You boys, you hear me?" They both responded. Jack looked back at Craig, who lay with his mouth open and his head down on Maw's back. He called once, then twice. Craig moved and looked up at Jack with a vacant but distraught expression on his face. He muttered something incoherent, and with that Jack got up immediately and said, "We is going to get shot or freeze to death." He patted Maw and slipped off of her and began to coax her up and call to the boys to get up. They were out from under Maw immediately, stumbling to get away.

Jack said, "We has to drink water and walk toward the Pacolet." His voice sounded hoarse, and he dared not even think about any of them being sick and getting consumption. They all drank water from canteens, gave the horses water from natural scooped out rock formations, and began to lead their horses. Their mounts had survived the night. They were cold and unsure and tended to wander off the path, but they would be steady if all the men held the reins tightly. Jack saw for sure that the ice and sleet had covered the ground, and they would have to walk. This was a strange comfort, for Tarleton and his dragoons could not travel fast. If they also walked, they would be miles behind them.

Maw's blood and cedar branches kept them alive

They walked for a long time, leading the horses, and Jack motioned that they had to stop and eat. Out of all their haversacks came old food, some of it rotten, particularly the bread and some squash they had collected. Jack passed around a big sweet potato, its orange color looking tasty against the harsh bare woods and white ice. Jack ate the peeling and shared the pulp with the boys, while Craig ate a piece of rotten white potato. They all drank water from a stream with ice floes that was running close to them.

Jack motioned that they had to keep going, so they traveled very slowly, walking, looking for enough drier ground to ride their horses. They did not find it, and when Johnny stumbled several times from exhaustion, Jack picked him up and put him on Maw and let Kit lead both of their horses.

Jack looked over at Craig and saw him bumping against his horse, almost falling asleep while they walked. They all were still in trouble. Looking at Kit, he saw a courageous young man trying to imitate his uncle's stern determination, but a youth drained of energy. Jack suddenly cursed under his breath. They wondered what this meant until he motioned for them to walk with him to a stand of river birch trees. With his big hands, and the boys and Craig watching him, Jack got down on his knees and began to dig near a young tree that had roots spread out from it. Jack dug deep into the ground and tore out small drier roots no bigger than strings of yarn. He beat them against a tree then began to gather more. With severely wet ground he came up with only six small strands. He tore strands of cloth from a small silk scarf he had for Elizabeth and took a small rod he had in his saddle and began to strike it with the blade of his hatchet. He was trying to start a fire, and he shielded the roots and small silk mass with his body against the wind. For several minutes he tried. Finally, with a spark and a puff of smoke, with Jack blowing with rhythm on the small fire, there was flame.

He called to the boys and Craig to find anything dry in their saddles, no matter what it was. They brought out paper that was not completely wet that was part of their school work. "Good boys," Jack said. "That learnin' you has is paying you well." Jack seemed to delight in a small book of spelling words that he tore in pieces and also a piece of dry wood that had held it together as a spine.

Craig walked up sheepishly and handed Jack a drawing he had made of three women – his wife and two young girls – that he had drawn on an old hand bill. Jack glanced at him and said, "You be certain you wants to burn this?" Craig shook his head sadly and with second thoughts said no and reached down to take it back. But Jack said calmly, "We needs it," and tossed it into the fire. The blaze began to take shape. Jack stood up and said, "Now we has to make this fire." He walked over to a small cottonwood tree and began to cut it furiously with his hatchet. It was soaked except for a small part in the very middle. Jack split the wood as if it was kindling and took the dry inner wood and added it to the fire. He said to them in a commanding voice, "Be about it. Make haste and do the same." In less than an hour the boys and Craig had split small pieces of wood and used the core of the limbs to make a real fire. The blaze gave off smoke that might be seen, but at least it gave heat that was needed for sustaining their life.

Jack said to Craig, "Look after these boys. Night will come too quickly, and I am to be gone to try and ride Maw and gits to my place. You stays here. Don't travel none. If you burns a fire so it can be seen it 'pears you are not running. Besides, it will keep all you warm. If'n I has trouble with anyone and can't git to my place, I will not be back to you tonight. I am with you tomorrow morning. If Tarleton comes, tell him you are loyal and wishes to be with him. Stay from harm as much as you can allow. I will be back. You hear me?"

Craig nodded, and the boys around the fire looked up and nodded. They were glad to have heat, and they would take their chances being this close to the Pacolet; they trusted their uncle. Jack got on Maw; he would ride her as much in the woods and off the mud trails as he could. He traveled cautiously, and in three hours he had arrived at a point where he saw the clearing that would lead him to his cabin. This was a dangerous time still. He could not ride in openly, even though it was his own home. But he knew the terrain well and would instinctively know if something was amiss.

Jack rode away from the main trail but still in the direction of his home. Darkness would be on him in less than two hours, so he traveled straight as he could to his cabin. He saw it from a distance, looking exactly as it had in April when he left for Charlestowne.

He edged closer and looked for all the telltale signs of normalcy. He saw the barn where Maw stayed, the hog pens and the goats. He noticed the fence around the garden was well kept, and he thought about John Junior and Susan and Lily-Beth, the children who had charge of the fence. He stopped Maw and looked and listened. Within less than a hundred yards he took out his rifle and unwrapped it from its leather cover. He looked at it again approvingly, completely dry and clean. Jack brought out his powder horn, and with no lead ball to ram in, he filled his pan and cocked the gun and held it straight up. With one hand he pulled the trigger and it resounded powerfully. He then rode in. Within yards of the house he called, "Hello the house...hello the house...it is me, your Jack...I is home...."

It seemed a long time before he heard anything. Then a crack of the door and a wider opening and then wider. It was John Junior peering around the door. But bolting past him, turning young John sideways with the force of hitting him on his shoulder, was Molly Polly. She was running as fast as she could, and she did not have all her clothes on, even in this unmerciful cold. Her feet seem to barely touch the ground as she ran so fast and Jack galloped to get her. She was crying tears of joy.

As he got nearer, she was crying, "Papa...Papa." Her face looked uncharacteristically scowling as she cried harder the nearer she came to him. He jumped off his horse and caught her in full flight as she leaped the last two to three yards and flew into his arms. "Why is you crying?" he asked.

"'Cause you is here, Papa." Jack held her tight against his chest, her feet dangling. He reached down and felt her feet. They were very cold. He held her away at arm's length and looked at her as she cried real tears, which he had forgotten she could do. She couldn't speak.

Jack said, "We has to get you back to the fire." With that, he climbed on Maw and held Molly Polly against him, his reins in one hand. With the other he was rubbing her feet to warm them. At the same time most of his family were in the front of the cabin, all chilled from the cold, the older girls hopping up and down to keep their feet off the ground and squealing great sounds of joy at their father's return. Coming to the door and filling it completely, the glow of the large fireplace behind her, was his Elizabeth. She had on her habbit coat, over her bed gown, and she was holding two babies. Jack had never seen such a welcome sight. He was home.

As troublesome as times were, they were temporarily forgotten with children, babies, a wife, and his warm cabin. All the Beckham family went into the biggest room downstairs and John Junior, ever wanting to hand his papa something, rushed to get him a tankard of water and to proudly bring him his pipe. Lily-Beth began to warm the cider that Jack liked so well. From his chair, Jack put his arm up around Elizabeth's waist, she still holding the babies. She leaned down into him and rested her chin affectionately on top of his head.

Jack motioned for everyone to sit on the floor excepting Elizabeth, and he pulled a chair up for her, their knees touching. He reached over and took Henrietta from her to hold while he talked. Molly Polly stood slightly apart from them, not fully accepting the presence of her hero. He pulled her close to him, noticing the stain of tears on her face. Lily-Beth and Susan did not sit down but came over behind Jack and Elizabeth and put their hands on their shoulders. Jack tried to look back and around at all of them, all eight of his family, and drink in the moment. It had been well over two hundred days since he had them this close.

Finally he spoke. "I has much to tells you. But is all well here?" He looked straight up at Susan and she blushed.

"Mr. Stribling has asked me to be in matrimony with him," she said.

Jack countered quickly, kidding. "How cans he do this if'n he has not seen you since I am gone." She blushed a much more violet color, and he laughed. "Well, being he is rightly a gentleman I allow he must have wrote you and is waiting for an answer if'n he has not seen you."

"Oh Papa," she laughed. "He comes around some."

Elizabeth, the proud mother smiled and said, "He is a fine gentleman, and it 'pears he works hard."

"So," Jack said, "you is allowing this?"

"If you are," she smiled.

Jack seemed to reflect, just for show, and paused a few seconds before he looked back up at Susan and said, "Well, I ain'ts the one to be with him…bein' he is so right homely and ugly, so I guess you has to do it soes no one else has to."

All the grown children burst out laughing and John Junior wagged his finger at his older sister in mocking derision and laughed even more. Susan had appreciative tears in her eyes when she hugged old Jack even harder. All the girls hugged Susan, in their sisters' way of congratulating her.

Jack watched them, and invariably all their eyes came back to him, for they hungered for news that he had to tell. All wondered of news of so distant a place as Charlestowne. Most of them had not traveled farther than to the neighboring colonies of Georgia and North Carolina and to Maggie's plantation.

Jack looked up at Elizabeth and got up from his chair and walked over to the fireplace. He had, without knowing it, physically distanced himself from them for the news he would tell. None of the family got up and walked over with him, but all sat as if in an audience and looked at him. "We has lost much at Charlestowne," he said. "The British has taken the town, and they is all around to keep people down and to have no more of this thinking that we is not theirs. We are still as we was under the Britishers."

"What does that mean, John?" said Elizabeth, shifting the two babies in her arms.

"It means your brother William is captured by them; so is my Thomas. I has Kit and Johnny in the woods staying warm tonight with a friend, and I is bringing them here tomorrow early. You, Susan, and Lily-Beth has to go and stay with Aunt Henderson for a spell, whilst the boys stay here." His voice seemed to get softer when he continued. "And it means we has lost more'n that."

As they all looked curiously at him, his eyes narrowed, and he said, "We has lost Maggie."

The impact of Jack's statement did not seem to sink in.

"Is she gone somewheres?" Susan asked, she being the fondest of her aunt.

As Jack's visage looked even more unpromising, they began to comprehend. "Nay, my child, she is dead."

No one spoke, but soft tears began to flow. Molly Polly stood away from her siblings, her mouth slightly open. All the children instinctively moved toward their mother, who just sat and looked sadly at the fire. The flames, crackling in the oak logs, became the only sound in the room. Jack glanced down at the fire in order to take his eyes away from the family. He was waiting to hear someone offer up the slightest questioning that they had heard from gossip that he had killed Maggie. "Has you not heard this?"

"No," Elizabeth said. "We has heard precious little, only from Mr. Hodge that Charlestowne was lost, and you would be returning. We did hear from some who traveled past that battles was taking place and many were now moving toward the North Carolina colony."

"Niece Angela Nott's house has been burned by "Bloody Bill" Cuningham as well, and he warned her that much was going to take place. They has lost all their fences and the top of their place. She is staying with her other relatives. We has not seen it but we fear it as well."

Jack reflected on this when Lily-Beth said, "How did my Aunt Land die?"

"I will tell you later" he said. "I gave her a proper and fittin' burial; we will go there someday soon. But does you know more? It sounds as if many be traveling toward here…it is so?"

None of his family answered. All seemed to be waiting for something else to be said. Finally Jack spoke. "We has to sleep, and I am gone when the light comes to git Kit and Johnny. You, John Junior, is with me tomorrow."

Jack then answered the question he knew was coming. "No, Molly Polly, you can'st go… Susan and Lily-Beth, you has to leave for Aunt

Henderson's. Stay with her till I comes to you. These two boys of
Thomas has to be here with their aunt until I comes back and right
soon. Then I will take them back to his place and their ma. As it is,
they can be harmed...that place is cursed... full of the most Tories I
has seen."

All the joy had been replaced with the sadness over Maggie's death,
but having their warrior father back was the most reassuring thing they
knew at this precise time. Jack said he would tend to Maw and return
shortly. Once outside, he led Maw to her shed and wrapped her sides
in blankets. He fed and watered her and rubbed her down, feeling the
cold numbing of his fingers. He, at last, took her to the farthest point of
the shed and positioned her in a corner between slats of wood, throwing hay between the cracks and patting her on the head as he left.

Jack made one more check to see how cold it really was. He went
down to the river bank and saw to his dismay that a lot of the Pacolet
was showing ice. This was as cold as he could remember since he and
Elizabeth had built their log house at Grindal Shoals on Sandy Run.
His thoughts were that Kit and Johnny and John Craig would sleep
close to their fire just for survival, but it would be well with them.
Settlers and backwoodsmen survived cold with fire, and they knew
what to do. However, Jack knew he had to leave at dawn to get them.

That night, he and Elizabeth slept with Henrietta and the little girls
in front of the kitchen fire. Before going to his big bed, he instructed
Susan, John Junior, Molly Polly, and Lily-Beth to watch from the second floor for three hours and then come get him. He admonished them
to keep each other awake. He would take their place upstairs, watching
through an air hole in the upstairs shutters, but mainly listening. Jack
trusted the guinea hens, the dogs, and himself to watch, but he trusted
his ears better.

As streaks of first light came, looking out over familiar land, his
own land reaching down to the river, Jack saw what severe cold could
do. The fence around the hoar-frosted dead vines in his garden was
white with ice. The rails of the fence held with the weight of the frozen
water but hard wood trees had dropped several branches laden with
icicles. The ground looked as if it had snowed, but it all was ice and

frozen puddles of water. It was treacherous. Jack had nagging thoughts that he might not be able to travel with Maw. If he walked back to the boys and Craig it would take several hours; then they would have to ride two to a horse and very slowly. That meant even more danger if they were in the sights of Tories and, worse, the organized British.

Jack moved from his observing position, which had made his arm numb. His children remained sleeping, bundled up as they were and practically hidden under the heavy quilts. Jack had, throughout his watch, added logs to the fire in their room and stoked it periodically. As he glanced back at them, ready to call John out of his sleep to get ready for a cold journey to his cousins in the woods, Jack caught a glimpse of movement outside in the distance. He grabbed his spy glass, pushed open the shutter, letting a cold blast of air shock his face, and he looked.

In a fog of white ice on trees and land, he saw a horse's breath in the distance clouding the air. He saw riders that he could not identify. He had been concerned that he would not be able to travel and now men on horses were heading straight for his farm and cabin. Adrenalin brought him wide awake. He reached for his rifle. It was ready.

Getting up quickly, he took a musket from the wall and checked it. It was clean and ready to be primed and loaded. Now he had a weapon for a longer shot and a weapon for killing at closer range, forty yards or less. He looked back out the window and saw that they were approaching dead on to his cabin. Through ice-laden trees and fog, he could not tell anything of their description. He made his decision. He walked to the bed and shook John and Susan and Lily-Beth. He said to them, close and into their faces, "Gits your fireboxes. Men's coming." All three bounded out of the bed immediately, fear and questioning on their faces. All had their own guns and knew how to use them. Jack looked quickly back at Molly Polly and gave thanks that she was still asleep.

Jack said to them, "Make plenty haste," as he walked down the stairs to the shed to get Maw. If the men were recognizable neighbors who were enemies, he would shoot them from behind a tree of his choosing. John and his sisters would wait in ambush at the house, and then fire if need be. Jack went first to the room where Elizabeth slept and called to her to get the children ready to ride to the Henderson's or to the Hodge plantation.

He walked fast to get Maw and get a quick saddle on her. Jack checked his hatchet with a quick look as it was tied on his saddle bag. He was now moving as fast as he could walk as he led Maw by her reins out into the cold. He mounted her and began to ride away from the cabin, staying behind trees. "This has to be damnable Tarleton's men. They is the only ones to do something as this," he thought. Jack wondered how many horses had been lamed during the forced ride that the dragoons might make in order to surprise him.

He gave a distinct signal to Susan, Lily-Beth, and John to hide behind a heavy fence. He called out to them, still out of hearing range of the intruders, "Shoot only if mens ride into the yard…and only if I shoots first." He told them to then ride with their mother "to where she would go."

Jack rode and weaved carefully behind trees. He saw three men and then he positioned Maw behind a pine tree. "This is a scout party," he thought. "They is ahead of Tarleton's men." It made sense. Jack would fire at these men and then charge them before they could fire. If they were scouts he would have time to harm them and to go back and tell his children to ride away with their mother.

He waited until he could hear them. Their horses were laboring, with wheezing and snorting sounds coming from their mouths and nostrils. Jack peered from behind a tree and then quickly, like a predatory animal, darted on Maw behind it. He leaned down to look over Maw's head again from just around the tree trunk to get another glance, in case the riders saw a "movement" in the forest.

Jack watched the men coming and led Maw to another tree. He waited, trying to stay resistant to the stabbing cold. The men were not talking and Jack did not hear what he was listening for behind them – masses of horses and wagons, or men shouting and moving. These were indeed scouts or stragglers or men robbing people to stay alive in the winter. It didn't matter.

He waited until their movement was so close he could hear one of the men coughing. Jack dropped the reins from Maw, grasped his rifle firmly in his hands, and ordered her forward. She dutifully walked to her left and with Jack nudging her harder with his boot in her right side, she turned suddenly straight into the path of the men. All three riders had their heads down in the wind. Jack raised his rifle and took aim at the first man, an older-looking man than his companions. Jack did not recognize them with their faces obscured in the fog. He aimed straight at the man's chest, and as he prepared to shoot, the man looked up straight at Jack.

It was John Craig. Jack, with his gift for his trade of staying alive, already had his finger on the trigger of the gun. Then he pulled the trigger and the lead shot went over Craig's head by three feet, shattering the tree limbs above his head. Kit, riding behind Craig, was so stunned that he fell partly out of his saddle and was hanging on to his horse with one hand on the reins and one foot in his stirrup. Johnny's horse was spooked and began to run into the woods, while he tried to control her.

Once Jack knew their identity, and his resolve for murder quickly went to anger at Craig. "Are you beeve-headed, you fool? Why is you here? You is supposed to be where I left you!"

Kit was the first to respond. "Uncle Jack!!" His relief was great at seeing him. "We has to leave…men traveling in the night even in this cold. Some came right to us and our fire. They were friendly…stayed with us a while, but they said others were traveling too and they is Tories trying to catch those at Blackstock's.

"We ne'er knew who was coming. Even those who came to our fire…they left us after a spell…they said they was fixin' to find their homes…they was trying to stay ahead of the others."

"Is these men Tarleton's?" Jack shouted.

"Nay, sir, they is renegades as far as we can tell. They is part of those that are Tories… maybe part of Bloody Bill Cuningham's."

"Good Gawd," Jack said. "Bloody Bill is the worst. If'n he is coming here, we has to choose our ground. I hears he has many mens with him."

"'Tis true, sir. We knows he has been to Cousin Nott's house and burned it and all her fences already, and she now is staying at Aunt Henderson's."

Jack met them as their horses came together, and at that time Johnny, being hailed by his brother to come back, reemerged from the woods with his horse in control. Jack maneuvered his horse close to Craig and said to him, "You should have not ridden as I told you…all you could have been kilt.

"Hellfire. This cold is worse than these men's trailing…you knows the cold will kill you, but you ain't sure 'bout none others killin' you.

"I tell you," Jack said in a voice that sobered Craig, "I wants you gone as soon as you is warm enough to do so. Kind of people like you gits others kilt…so you has to be on your way and out of my company." Jack was dressing him down and Craig only looked sad as Jack talked. He did mutter one "Indeed, sir" before Jack said, "We are back to my place…follow me as I go."

Jack traveled a short distance before he stopped and held up his hand to them to stop. He went a few yards farther before he called out. "Young uns. John! Susan!…'tis me, your pap. Hold your fire…we is coming in. I has your cousins Kit and Johnny with me." From a distance he heard a whoop of joy from John at the mention of his male cousins.

As they approached the cabin, he saw Molly Polly among them. Jack smiled at seeing her on her horse with her fowling gun in her hand, wrapped in blankets from head to toe.

It was a reunion of cousins. They sat looking at each other for only a second, astride their horses, when Jack said, "It is cold," and made a gallop to the cabin, followed by this entourage that had grown to seven. Once at the cabin in the large room, Jack motioned John Craig to everyone, and Craig bowed gracefully. Jack and Elizabeth treated him with back country courtesy and offered him as much as he could eat of stew of rabbit and cider and bread. He ate, looking up every now and then at this room full of people, they being ten Beckhams, boys, girls, babies, and Jack and his wife.

Three dogs were also in the room, lounging lazily near the fire, and Craig winced with homesickness at the closeness of this gathering in a warm home and the thought of his own wife and two girls. He also was struck by the social and fatherly Jack Beckham, a man whom others swore was the most cold-hearted and unkind man they knew. He now had a grudging respect for the man who had just told him to be out of his company and on his way.

Jack walked among them and made sure Kit and Johnny felt welcome. He said for them to be close to John and Molly Polly and learn their chores from them. Jack reminded the oldest girls they were off to Aunt Henderson's and he would go with them on the trip. Jack began to relax, taking his pipe in hand for a smoke, even though he knew Craig was anxious to go at the earliest time. He had asked Jack to accompany him, discovering that the girls were traveling to the Henderson home.

After a time of conversation with Craig and Elizabeth, Jack said he would ride Maw to the Hendersons' and take Craig with him, then ride with Craig part way, stopping to visit his close friend William Hodge. Elizabeth said to Jack, "You have to eat something, and I have more parcels of food to take with you as well as for the girls."

Jack hugged her when they were in the kitchen alone and said, "I will git Maw….just hand it to me through the window as I am on her, and I will take it. Have the girls ready; I will call them directly."

Jack and John Craig went out the door, and both spent some time feeding their horses hay from their hands and then watering them from a trough after Jack broke the ice with his hatchet. The two men rode around to the back, and Elizabeth, staying out of the cold, handed Jack meat wrapped in a deer skin, along with bread in a calico bag. He reached down and took the food. "Have the girls tend their horses, and then we is gone. I am back, but not before two days."

He smiled at her as he said this, but Elizabeth's head snapped back when she heard fierce growling from the dogs in the front room, then a chorus of all three barking loudly and trying to get through the front door. Their barking was unrelenting. One tried to leap through the front window, and he rattled it almost open before falling back to the floor and running back to join the other dogs at the door. Elizabeth was shouting at them to "get out of the way" as she tried to open the front door to let them out. Jack was taken aback momentarily at the chaos and turned to see the cause of the noise. He wheeled Maw around, and she reared up. Jack suddenly realized that men of war had to be coming.

"Bloody Bill," he shouted back at John Craig. Only fifty yards away, charging with sabers drawn, riding fast even on the frozen ground, was Banastre Tarleton and the Green Horse. Thirty or more men in green on horses, their swords drawn and glinting in winter sunlight, were bearing down hard and fast on Jack and John Craig.

Jack Beckham was momentarily frozen, unable to react until Tarleton and his men were only twenty yards away. The dogs came rushing at the horses, running beside them and yelping. One of Tarleton's officers swung his magnificent sword up and then down, killing one of the dogs and never breaking stride. This startled Jack into action; he turned and shouted to Elizabeth, "Git to the Hodge's place," and to Craig, "Ride."

Maw led Craig's horse out of the yard in the only direction that was possible to escape. Jack's mind raced with dire possibilities – mainly that Maw would fall at this breakneck pace on the ice. Craig shouted something primitive, guttural, and full of fear. He instinctively leaned forward in his saddle, a futile move to get his horse moving faster. He looked back over his shoulder wide-eyed at Tarleton's men, who seemed to be on top of them.

Maw stretched her great legs to a full length and left everyone behind, including Craig. But Craig's horse began to pull away from Tarleton's men and trailed Maw by twenty paces as they made headway toward the Pacolet. Jack steered straight to the river and then suddenly turned onto a path that was obscured by a cluster of saplings. Craig had to slow and wheel around to follow Jack. When he did, six of Tarleton's men cut across a thicket and made up ground on him.

Maw came to a sheer drop and Jack did not cause her to slow down. He knew this junction of the river, and he let loose of her reins, releasing the pull on her head, and with that she jumped the precipice without hesitation. Into the deadly freezing water they went, and Maw pumped her powerful legs, fighting to reach to the other side. Jack turned to see what the British would do. At that instant Craig made the decision not to jump the crag and he turned, leaving the enemy behind him to run alongside the river bed.

Several of Tarleton's men followed Jack on the opposite river side, choosing not to plunge into the water, clearly surprised at his decision. They rode on, following Craig but watching Jack and shouting at him. Jack and Maw emerged on the other side and scrambled up the embankment; Jack jumped off Maw and led her quickly into a clump of trees. He took his gun from his back and checked the pan. It was dry. He poured powder from his horn, knelt down beside a small cedar, and fired, hitting the lead officer square in his stomach. The man fell instantly from his horse, crying out in great pain. With that, all the dragoons dismounted and began firing their muskets at Jack.

Jack felt a fit of fury. He stepped from behind the tree and moved forward several yards and shook his fist and cursed the men. He called…"shoot and be damned." They quickly reloaded and fired again, every one of the men getting off a shot that fell short, as Jack knew they would. He was reloading his rifle and seemed to be deliberate in filling the pan after he picked open the firing hole with a thin piece of wire tied to his gun. He raised his gun and fired and again hit a dragoon in his thigh, felling the man. Jack gave a scornful laugh born out of the fiercest loathing.

It occurred to their leader now that Jack was much too far out of their range, that he was mocking them. The dragoon leader called to "be back in force" and they regrouped as quickly as possible, but not before Jack sent another lead ball whistling past them with accuracy too close for the dragoons. They cursed and shook their fists at him. Jack ran back quickly to get Maw and to ride on, putting more space between him and the men. As he did, he noticed a flurry of activity on the other side of the bank. Several dragoons had flanked Craig and cut his route off as he traveled straight down the other side, looking for a ford to cross over to Jack. They surprised him coming upon him fast. He had a decision to make, to fight or try to outrun them, but his fear caused him to hesitate. Craig jumped off his horse and began to run to the river. One of Tarleton's men anticipated his panic and rode right into him with his horse, knocking him down and spilling Craig helplessly on the ground. He lay spread out on his back, looking up at the eight men who surrounded him.

Jack saw all this from a distance. He rode Maw along the side of the bank for several yards at a fast canter to get the best view of what was to take place. He saw a dragoon officer instruct men to ride in Jack's direction and take up a position against him from their side of the river bank. At that very instant, Tarleton himself came riding up to Craig. What Jack saw next confirmed tales of what he had heard of British justice. He saw one of the officers of the Legion call other men to Craig, who grabbed him and began stripping him of his clothes. Craig looked to be a rag doll, his arms and legs jerking and pulling. Jack heard Craig's wails and cries for mercy. Sounds carrying over the water bounced back and forth in their clarity, and Jack heard a distinct mournful cry from Craig, as if Jack were standing next to him, "...to go home to my wife."

A young dragoon had a noose around Craig's neck, and three men forcefully dragged him to a tree and threw the rope over a limb. Craig's feet were still on the ground when the dragoon pulled the rope taut and rode away on his horse, jerking Craig off the ground and into the air. His neck snapped, his head falling unnaturally to his left side hanging limp and lifeless.

Jack then was aware of gunfire as all the men watching him fired at him in unison, with none of the shots coming close. He angrily retaliated with a shot from his rifle that did no harm to his assailants. Tarleton was already mounted and was riding away as his hanging party began to mount and follow him. Jack was in a quandary. Should he follow them to cut Craig's body down, or go back to Elizabeth? Should he take Craig's body to his young widow? He just stared at the scene. Now the dragoon who had hanged him had come back to the tree and wrapped the rope around it several times to secure Craig's body five feet off the ground.

Jack had a strange feeling that he knew the Tory dragoon. The man had scraggily hair and much youth about his face, but a wicked and scornful expression. It appeared that he had enjoyed his murderous act. Jack strained to remember where he had encountered this man, but he could not recall at this distance. He also noticed that four dragoons had stationed themselves near Craig's body and were setting up a guard to keep him from taking Craig. This was usual with the British. They hanged partisans from the colonies and dared anyone to take the bodies down. Jack remembered that young William Stroud had been hanged and that his body had dangled for five days before his sisters could remove it for burial.

He decided he had to get to William Hodge's plantation to warn him and to get his daughters and family who were going there. He circled in a wide arc on Maw around the guards at Craig's body, and they never saw him ford the river. Jack headed Maw as fast as he could to Hodge's plantation. He felt he was racing against Tarleton to get there first.

He was to find out he was absolutely and tragically correct.

Tarleton would indeed get to Hodge's plantation first.

Chapter Sixteen

Hodge's Plantation And Beyond

Jack, on the opposite river bank from the Tories, was being carried by a superb horse that moved guardedly, her legs searching for firm turf among icy patches. Such was the inbred blood lines of Maw, whose skill would save him in a time like this. Jack instructed and urged Maw in the direction where he knew he could cross the now forbidding Pacolet's "walking shoals."

In the summer, at that bend, the river offered rocks easily navigated to get to the other side. Rocks ten times as wide as Maw and protruding out of the water. They were seldom flooded in summer or winter and could be walked across, but not today. In this late November it might be impossible to cross, due to the glassy sheets of ice.

From what would later be recalled, from old timers on the river, this storm of killer sleet and cold would be seen as freakish. Jack knew it today only as another delay between him and his family and close friend, Hodge. Eyeing the rocks, he feared the river was impassable. But he recalled that right beside the crossing was a shallow ditch made so by the crashing water. Maw was into the icy water at his command, the bitter cold water up to her knees as they crossed over, out of sight of Tarleton's men.

He went in the general direction of Hodge's plantation, which took him very close to Craig's body, a spot deep in the woods. It was rarely traversed, except by occasional hunters and pilgrims moving down the river to the Georgia colony. His intent was to bury Craig quickly to keep his body from wild animals.

Within an hour from a secluded spot, he saw from over two hundred yards Craig's body twisting ever so slightly from one side to the other. Four dragoons were sitting around the hanging tree huddled beside a large fire, alternately holding their hands open, then rubbing them together close to the blaze. Jack watched and remembered the British brutal practice of leaving a body hanging for days as a warning for others; then a thought struck him as if he had been completely wrong in his judgment. The British, and particularly Tarleton, as he had heard, left guards where there were people, in a village or in a large town, such as Charlestowne. Victims were left hanging for people to see so that they would be frightened. Craig was in an isolated area. There was no reason to guard his body except to hinder Jack from chasing dragoons or to follow where Tarleton and others might be heading.

Jack cursed himself for being delayed by Tarleton. He tested his point by edging closer to the Tory guards and dismounting Maw. He got even closer to the men unseen, and then purposely stepped in plain view of them only seventy-five yards away. He stared at them. They were momentarily frozen until Jack fired his rifle into a tree near their camp. They seemed totally unprepared for this action. Jack saw them run for cover and wondered if they expected him to try to steal Craig's body. Were they thinking he would circle to avoid them, taking more time away for him to pursue Tarleton?

He made a calculated move to see if they would follow him, although he hoped to a grand level of dread they would not follow him, for he had to go straight to Hodge's. He appeared in plain sight again, knowing he was too far away for their muskets. He loaded and fired twice at the men, who had retreated to a clump of trees. He continued to draw attention to himself, loading his rifle in their sights, mentally preparing to ride Maw away after firing once more to see if they followed.

What happened next almost cost him his life. He heard their first gun fire back at him and recognized it as the crack of a rifle shot and not a musket. A lead ball turned up the ground to his right only feet away from where he had just stepped. It was a shot from other Tories who were hiding in bushes and behind trees and not seen by Jack on his approach. He realized that their plan was to lure him closer into their camp and to take a sudden and surprising rifle shot at him from the fewest yards away as possible, to kill him with a weapon that he himself carried.

Maw had moved several yards away from the sudden noise, and Jack ran to get her. He held her steady to mount, and once astride circled around the men and away toward Hodge's home. His "duty," as he saw it, would have to wait concerning John Craig's body. He looked back several times and listened intently. They were not following.

It took him an hour to reach Hodge's plantation. He did not need the spy glass to see the main house, and initially saw William Hodge's wife in the yard, pacing and looking very distressed. Behind her he also saw the handiwork of the British dragoons. The fences were burned and the main house had been set on fire, but it was not lost; he could see furniture and bedding that had been dragged into the yard as well. The house structure was black, and timbers stood where walls had been. The smoke was still thick, but the fire had subsided.

He saw dead livestock and a ravaged yard with overturned barrels, and clothing scattered. Pigs had no pens, goats had fled, the spring house had been destroyed, and curing houses had been looted and burned. The main barn had been set ablaze behind the house, and Jack saw Hodge's cows walking aimlessly about.

Jack called to Mrs. Hodge from quite a distance. He did not move from his position sitting on Maw. As the woman ran toward him, he watched the woods to see if anyone emerged. Mrs. Hodge was a stately woman, and even while running she was holding up her long dress with one hand and a handkerchief in the other; she looked dignified and in control. Today, however, she and her husband had paid a price for their perceived loyalty to the Carolina colony. Now she called to Jack. "John, John, they have William…Tarleton has William."

He called back to her and moved Maw forward. "Is you alone? Are mine here with you?"

She was shaking her head no as she ran, and Jack took this to mean she was alone and his children were not there. He met her at the point she was almost exhausted. He jumped off Maw and held her hands in his. He then put his arm around her shoulder as she leaned on him, and they began to walk to the main house.

She clearly was not used to this kind of horror and was in shock from seeing the capture of her husband and the leveling of her property. She was still gasping for breath, but she never gave way to tears as she looked down at the ground and said sadly, "Why? Why are they taking William to Camden? Tarleton told me himself they will hang him there if they don't hang him from a tree sooner. He swore they will rid this place of your kind and William, too.

"John! He said your name. What are we to do as of now? What has happened to make this thing be on us?"

Jack looked at her, and she still looked at the ground as they walked. He said nothing. He let her breathe deep breaths and become calmer while he patted her on the shoulder in compassion. She finally looked up at him questioningly. He saw innocent eyes for such a strong woman, and he searched for an answer. He finally said, "We has fought Tarleton at the Blackstock's, and he was whupped there…least he did not fall on us as at the Waxhaws and other places we has heard of him. So he is countin' on being on to us, and he ain't goin' to stop until all is not against him."

Mrs. Hodge looked puzzled and still in shock. Jack asked how long they had been gone. She shook her head and looked down again in disbelief and said, "Maybe three hours or so…seems so long a time without William."

Jack continued to pat her shoulder as several slaves appeared from their cabins and began to form around the two. He asked her again, "Has you seen my family here?"

"No, I have not," she said almost absentmindedly.

Jack said he was going to see what was at his place and then try to get Mr. Hodge back, although he wondered himself how this was to be done. "I has to ask you," he said, "will you have some of yours go to the Pacolet near the 'walking' shoals and look for a man's body hanging from a tree? He is John Craig of the farms near the Broad River. They

needs to bury him and let us know where. I needs to let his widow
know where he is laid, so she can have him fetched for burying."

Jack had said the wrong thing. For the first time Mrs. Hodge began
to lose her composure. She collapsed into Jack, and he held her up
while she cried, shaking hard and clutching him. Jack motioned for
a slave family to come and take her to a place to lie down. "Gives her
something to eat on," said Jack. "It will help."

As they started away, Jack said to one of the slaves, a man named
Hobber, "I am gone to my place. But…I has to ask you…you knows the
place on the Pacolet near walking shoals?"

"Yas, suh."

"Would you see to a man hanging near there in a cottonwood tree
and bury him? He is a friend, and we has to let his widow know." Jack
told him the story briefly. "I don't think there are Tories there. They is
hoping to see me back there, not you, or they is trying to catch up to
Tarleton right now as we speak. At any count jest see if they is there,
and if not cut him down and bury him close by that place."

"I will rightly do so, suh. I am taking son Henry with me and we
will be back right soon to take care of Mrs. Hodge…don't worry none.
We go to Sandy Run after the buryin' to let your family know where
Mr. Craig be."

Jack thanked the men and then as an afterthought said, "You has
not seen my family and girls here, has you?" He had started heading
Maw toward the path to his home when Hobber said, "Yas, suh. They
been here."

Jack spun around in his saddle. "Where are they now? How long
has they been from here? Who was with them?"

"Gone, suh. Jest not long ago. They mus' had seen all these mens
here so they hid and comes out after that Tarleton left. And they was
with Samuel, suh!"

Completely taken back Jack repeated, "Samuel was here?"

"Yas, suh, and he been axing for you too. He gone with the girls…I
'spect they back at yo place if'n Tarleton not be there."

"Almighty!" Jack said. "Samuel is likely to be strung to a tree!" He
was genuinely afraid for his nephew and his girls, fearing if vindictive

Tories were in the party what might happen to them. Jack had heard rumors of women molested by Tarleton's men at Moncks Corner before the siege of Charlestowne, even that Tarleton had hanged one of his own men for taking complete advantage of a woman. All this churned in Jack as he stormed out of the plantation on Maw.

Jack knew if there was to be an ambush for him it would be at or close to his own cabin by Tories who knew him well. This was a great possibility after the battle at Blackstock's plantation, where Tarleton had seemingly lost more men than at any time heard of by Jack. He rode Maw, prodding her, while watching trees and overhangs, as he searched for Susan, Lily-Beth, and Samuel. Jack had one hand on the reins, and his other on his .50-caliber rifle. As he came into view of his own farm, he saw a joyous sight: Samuel and the girls. Jack, out of character, but with instant release of his feelings, called to them with a "whoop." This caused all three to turn around and look in his direction. All beamed and started to come to him as he shouted for them to stay. He was as happy at this sight as he had been in weeks.

The girls dismounted and were skipping toward him over the frozen water as he reined in Maw. He dismounted and hugged them both at the same time among the girl's joyful squeals of "Papa." Samuel observed from yards away, not intruding. Jack walked with the girls, who were asking many questions. He just nodded and said, "Everything is well…we has to be to Mama's now….she is with ours at the cabin?"

They shook their heads yes, and with their manner assured Jack that Tarleton's men had not harassed them. Neither asked about John Craig, and Jack let them assume for the time bring that Craig had gone on to his wife and his home.

As the four traveled to the cabin, Jack looked to Samuel and said, "What has happened after the time with Tarleton at Blackstock's? Did you not get to Mrs. Hodge before them Tories?"

Samuel was clearly in charge of his cousins, and the question was asked of him as if he were directly in command of a military force. He had not seen Jack in weeks, although he knew by now that they had both been at Blackstock's.

"Nay, sir. We was there and hid while Tarleton and his men made waste of Mrs. Hodge's place and took Master Hodge away. Both Susan and Lily-Beth was hid real good. They saw it and was skeered, but they did not make sounds, and we waited till all was gone from there. We could not help Mrs. Hodge."

"I am understanding. They would have taken you too, and left my girls, I am sure. But you would be stretched somewhere. How many were at Hodges?"

"Seemed like more than forty, sir. Tarleton gave many commands and orders, and all his acted quickly. Mostly they fired the barns and fences and killed the animals. Mr. Hodge has been taken, tied up as it is, and walking. He is of an age that he won't be able to walk far. They may hang him soon."

Jack nodded agreement as they came into the edge of the Beckham yard, which had been spared in the futile chase that ended at Hodge's. Susan, with the news of her returning father, had ridden the last hundred yards to tell her mother of their reunion. All the Beckham family came tumbling out of the house into the cold, and again Jack prepared to be with them and determine what might happen next. The answer to that came quickly and unexpectedly from Molly Polly.

"Pap" she said, and ran right into him, not stopping as she thumped into his body and wrapped her arms around his waist. Jack grinned as she did not turn loose, and for a few steps he was walking with Molly Polly wrapped around him. "Pap," she said again, "you are to be safe here…a man has come and told us you will be safe and not to leave… He is your friend."

Jack looked with a furrowed brow at Elizabeth. She nodded and said, "It is true…but a strange happening it is. A man by himself, who says he is a Tory, came to us maybe one hour ago…he appeared friendly. A young man at that. He said he was loyal to the Whigs and felt he was to be one of us and to protect you as well."

Jack stood still and did not continue toward the house but motioned for the others to go inside. Molly Polly nevertheless stayed, and Jack allowed her to, pulling her to his side and enveloping her with an arm to keep her warm. "A man?" Jack said. "He came here right after Tarleton's men chased me to the river, and he is a Tory?"

"Yes," Elizabeth said, smiling. "I am thinking there are many like him…they are not to be sure whose side they are, and this young man is one of them."

Jack felt a momentary sense of order at Elizabeth's comment. Then abruptly he inquired, "What does he look to be? Old as Samuel? Is he as tall as Samuel?" Jack's eyes narrowed. "Does he wear the spectacles?"

Elizabeth was trying to be as exacting as possible in her description when she thought and said. "I have never seen this man…he seems to be older than Samuel and Abner as well. Kit and Johnny were not here to see this man, only me and the girls. I talked to him by myself. He was very friendly and helpful. But he looks to be not as well in keeping with himself as is Samuel.

"He has looser hair, not tied, and his clothes are not that of a man who has a wife to care and sew for him. He looks like many young men who are in this place who are not of a family.

"Do you think you know him?" she asked, trying to determine the reason for Jack's overly concerned questions.

Jack looked at his cabin, with all his family inside, and then back to Elizabeth. His eyes widened, and he said calmly, his eyes boring into hers, "Elizabeth, we are to be kilt."

She gasped. Jack grasped her upper arm and began to lead her with as much respect as he could. He held Molly Polly tightly by the hand and brought her along. Elizabeth gasped again. "John, tell me…my Lord!…have I done something greatly wrong?"

Jack did not look at her. "Git the girls to put big logs in the fire…all the fires." He started shouting at Samuel. "Git Kit and Johnny! Load up them fireplaces with the biggest you can find!" It was clear that Jack sensed great danger, and no one asked why. Once inside the cabin, he first charged up the small stairway to the large room over the cabin and grabbed all the rifles that hung on the wall. Now he was calling to John Junior and the rest of the children to get their firelocks. Elizabeth had Henrietta, Nancy, and the other two girls as Jack hurtled down the stairs, jumping over the last four steps shouting, "Clothe them so's they don't freeze."

The whole house was in confusion, depending solely on what Jack knew and did not have time to tell. All listened to his commands as he went into the kitchen room and told Molly Polly, Susan, and Lily Beth to "get bags of meat and hard tack." Jack went back into the great room and shouted to "build the fires higher…put all big logs we has on the fires…it don't matter if we burns the house with it." This statement alarmed everyone. Their collective hopes and fears meshed into terror, particularly Elizabeth and the oldest girls. They began to gather any clothes they could find with a look of stark fear on their faces.

At this instant a man rode up into the front yard, unheard by any of them. When they were finally aware of him, Samuel shouted, "The yard." Jack, with his hunting knife, the only weapon ready to use at hand, had no choice. He bolted through the front door shouting a guttural indistinguishable cry and charged straight for the rider. He came face to face with Mr. Stribling, the suitor of Susan. The man was stunned, paralyzed with fear. He shouted something defensive just as Elizabeth saw him and shouted to Jack. "It is Mr. Stribling."

Jack still grabbed him by his shirt and said, "You are with us. Git your horse." Stribling did as he was told, and at that all the Beckhams seemed to be in the yard, with their horses and guns and clothes and food. Susan had no time for Stribling. She acknowledged him with a look. Jack said to them, "We is riding east…hold here." He ran back into the cabin and with a gourd filled with water went from roaring fireplace to fireplace and doused all the flames. The result was immediate. The fires continued to burn, but smoke billowed in massive clouds up the chimneys. It would be seen from some distance.

Jack sprinted back to his family and Stribling. He led them, still without explanation, calling Samuel, Kit, Johnny, and John Junior up to the front of the pack. Riding alongside John Junior was Molly Polly with four-year-old Nancy sitting behind her holding onto Molly Polly's waist. Jack just motioned to all of them and shouted, "Don't stop till I does…Elizabeth! Come up to me."

Elizabeth had baby Henrietta cradled in her arm, holding the rein of her horse, Derrick, while Susan held Teressa. Stribling rode close by her, and Lily-Beth rode with Sarah holding on. All moved in one direction with ease with Jack glancing back at them and calling the trailing dogs to come. Fourteen in number, they headed east toward the Pacolet. Jack would lead them for some time before giving an explanation. All of the older children had some idea of the danger, and the small children felt the tension that was generated, but none cried or whimpered.

As the Beckhams fled, the young Tory who had reconnoitered, and implored Jack's wife to keep Jack at the farmhouse, safe on his word, had already met up with the rest of his compatriots in the British Legion. He wore no Green Horse uniform. But he also was a Tory with a reputation among the British military elite as one of the most effective spies in the Carolina colony. He had been responsible for several clandestine deaths among Whigs and had ridden with Tarleton at Blackstock's and had led them to Jack Beckham's home as well as to the Hodge's plantation. He and his group, led by a Captain Kittel, saw the smoke from Jack's home and had ridden in that direction. They were sure he was there by now. The young spy was awarded a look of appreciation from several of the men, including Kittel.

The young man had been among those who chased Jack from his own home hours earlier. He was the one who had hanged John Craig in a brutal fashion. Jack knew this man but had not been able to recognize him from such a distance. They rode, all fifteen Tories, to hidden places in sight of Jack's home with the smoke now curling softer from the chimneys. They were confident that all in the cabin were staying warm from the cold.

Kittel looked at several men including the young spy and muttered, "No quarter to any man...no matter who. Do not harm the others, leave them to be, but no man is alive!" The word passed among the green-uniformed men. All nodded. They began their advance from an overlooking hill through heavy brush, spread out and encircling, ready to charge at Kittel's command and to kill rebel men.

Jack's entourage had already traveled toward the east and across the Pacolet, crossing at Waterloo Dam. He still had not explained to his family, but no one questioned him. They were a desperate family no matter the reason. Jack had made his destination decision as soon as they had fled his yard. They could not go to Colonel Henderson's. He

himself was a wanted officer under General Sumpter. Hodges' plantation was in ruins. The home of Angelica Knott, Elizabeth's niece, was
also burned according to travelers they met. Jack needed the best and
safest place no matter the cold and the distance. He had set his course
for Randolph Mabry's farm. It would take almost two days to get there
by himself. With his entire family it might take more.

That evening before sunset, several miles from his home, he motioned that they would stop. He told Susan and Lily-Beth and Kit and
Johnny to help settle everyone down while he talked to Elizabeth. She
came up to him with an inquiring face and one that said she needed
to know what was happening. Jack knew the look on her face. It was
demanding and uncompromising. He owed an explanation. Jack and
Elizabeth were alone. He stooped down and put a blanket on the
ground for her as she sat down, and she pulled her cloak up around
her. The wind had picked up and the feared night cold was upon them.
Jack looked around at the activity that assured him that the small ones
were being cared for and the boys were making fires.

He said, "We built those fires in the fireplace to make others think
we was there. They was coming for us."

Elizabeth reacted with open-mouthed alarm. "They would have
hurt this family, these children?"

"Aye," said Jack "In some way…you were to be a widow for sure. I
has no idea who comes to you and says I am to be cared for, that no
harm is to me. And that from a Tory. What am I to do?" he said sarcastically. "Wait and welcomes them to my hearth and then determine why
they is there?"

He looked into her face and said, "We are off to Mabry's tomorrow.
It is likely we has no home no more. It is burned as is others." Jack then
walked with her silently back to the others and said to them that they
would visit the Mabrys as soon as they could get there. He gave no
other explanation except to nod to Elizabeth, who would inform all the
others with varying degrees of information for older children and for
those with younger ears.

Jack and the men and boys made sure the fires were burning well
and that wood was plentiful. They ate what had been snatched from

home, and they drank water and some cider that Jack had. Elizabeth nursed Henrietta, and Susan, Lily-Beth, and Molly Polly assumed the chores of seeing the other girls bedded close to the fire. Jack told the men what they knew was coming. The oldest would not sleep. They would walk the camp that night, and Kit and Johnny would serve as sentries away from the camp.

Jack and Samuel would know where Kit and Johnny were, and they would check on them throughout the night with a preplanned signal. If the boys fell asleep, they would take the chance of being discovered, not only by Jack and Samuel but, worse, Tories. Jack had told them the frightening stories about Tories killing or kidnapping young men and selling them on distant islands. The boys fought to stay awake, a hundred yards apart from each other, during the night.

At Jack's home on Sandy Run, the British Legion fell on the cabin in full force. Fifteen men, all surrounding the main house, from all directions, had entered the door and secured the windows at the same time. The Tories searched the house and yard for almost an hour, insisting to themselves that Jack, at least, was there. They not only missed him, but they saw that all weapons were gone and much food was taken, along with bedding covers. Not even a hunting knife was left for the intruders.

Kittel convened the Loyalists in the yard. "They have gone, and they knew we were to be attending here. Jack Beckham is of the devil. We will burn this place down and with it will be a reminder that he will face a hell the same as this, for his treason." He was livid at being outwitted by a man that was so pursued. Kittel had literally tracked this man to his own door and had been denied. He looked at the spy who had assured him Jack was here and said, "Colonel Tarleton will be spared news of your failure here, sir." Kittel deftly moved the guilt to the young man and away from himself. "He will know nothing of this until this man is caught and hanged. You are understanding me on this matter?"

"I am indeed, sir."

"Then you are to be away from here and back to where you may more usefully gather information and only then relay it to me....nay...

or moreso to my Lieutenant. We are no longer in pursuit of this man. We do not know where he is. That is your duty, sir. Now, be away!"

A Lieutenant observing the conversation said, as the young man was leaving, "May I, sir?"

"And it is?" asked Kittel.

"Why not leave this cabin here and in time it will invite this rebel to come back. I think it more likely that he will do so if it is still standing. No one knows we have been here tonight. We will lure this animal back to his own lair and catch him again, I dare say."

Kittel, ever an opportunist but still savagely angry, said, "That is not a worthy suggestion, sir." He then turned to the other men and said, "Fire the place…kill the stock…burn the fences, and take the poultry with you.

"You, Manderson and Maxwell, will stay near here, unobserved, four days and report to us at Ninety-Six if he returns. And you will do it speedily."

The other men under Kittel began to put fire to the house gathering any cloth to burn in the rooms and to gather broom straw to bundle, light, and toss on the roof. Three men set fire to the beds upstairs and opened the shutters to hasten the flames inside. There were three horses left that were taken for booty by the dragoons. All other animals, cows, pigs, and goats were shot by musket. Poultry had necks wrung and were thrown over saddlebags to be eaten. Six cattle were slaughtered and two enterprising dragoons quickly cut sides of meat and threw them into a haversack. After the razing and butchering, the group traveled south. Jack and his family were headed east.

The man who had so surely thought that he had trapped a colonial spy was a solitary figure on his horse, leaving the dragoons with not even a farewell. None of them saw him, once out of sight, completely change clothes, stripping naked in the terrible cold, and hurriedly putting on stockings and buckled shoes, a gentleman's clothes and waistcoat under his great coat. He then tied his hair back with a ribbon and put on glasses, which held plain glass in them. He was assuming a more subtle role to begin a ride back to the Carlisle or Starnes homes near the great falls of the Catawba River to become once again a schoolmaster.

It took Jack and his family two-and-a-half days to travel to the Turkey Creek region from the Pacolet and Grindal Shoals. The children were worn down by the cold, and all took turns being with their mother and baby Henrietta. Jack longed for, but never got, a smooth stretch of ground where he could have made a sleigh of wood, bound with rope he had so as to haul the children behind a horse. They all rode horses, sometimes two girls with a rider, one in front and one behind, to spell their sisters and mother from a heavier load to carry, for all older ones carried baggage of bedding and food. Jack did not have to hunt and kill for food in the last day and a half, but they all arrived at the Mabry farm hungry and tired.

Jack followed his prescribed course for his arrival. He rounded the farm and approached from the north and banged heavily on his rifle barrel with his knife. He was hoping for a quick response, and it came. Both Randolph and Hannah Mabry came through the front door of their large house as Jack banged on his gun a third time. Both tried to look as nonchalant as possible, turning the copper pot inwards and then turning around and looking into the woods.

When Jack and family emerged, there was a shout of recognition and a call back to the home by Mrs. Mabry to her family. All Mabry girls came running and at a hundred yards all the Beckhams rode into the yard. Hannah Mabry and Elizabeth found each other first embracing, knowing without asking that the family was displaced and that children were at risk. They moved quickly into the house, helped by Randolph and his girls, and began to fetch food and drink for all to have as soon as possible.

Randolph gave Jack a jug of cider and several sweet potatoes with hardtack, and they sat down, two men with many stories to tell. They talked for two hours with the cider energizing and warming Jack. He left out nothing, and Mabry, ever the gentleman, asked no questions. He let Jack tell the details, only smiling and claiming wonderment at their journey, a flight from being harmed by the British in this bitter weather.

Mabry was keeping a secret from Jack but fully intended to tell him after listening to his friend's discourse on his troubles. He knew Jack would have to rest and would need even more energy for what he was about to tell him. It was not until three hours later, after much conversation, that Mabry told him.

Chapter Seventeen

Wade Hampton's Visit

It was mid-evening as Jack and Randolph continued talking in the great room of the plantation house. Jack was as relaxed as he had been in weeks, lounging in a large leather chair in front of the fire. He sat listening now as Mabry spoke of happenings over the last months. Mabry named the people who were known as Tories and those as Loyalists who wanted to remain friendly. He talked of those who were ardent Whigs, willing to fight and lose house and belongings, because of their passion. He mentioned Wade Hampton now serving under General Sumpter for the Whig cause, saying that Hampton was firmly against suppression by the British.

Jack's mind wandered as he was feeling marked fatigue. He could have easily sat down with his friend Mabry and worked out a solution to his problems, particularly those facing his family now. He would have preferred to leave with his family for either the Virginia or the North Carolina colony, the latter from whence his wife came, where reported atrocities were not what they were in South Carolina. But he himself had contributed to the tumult between neighbors and the English, and he had done so, in his mind, because of the unjustness of the British occupation.

He sat with a bottle of rye in one hand that he shared with Mabry, passing it back and forth, his long clay pipe in the other, his legs fully extended and crossed over at his bootless ankles. The conversation was punctuated by Jack's questions of, "Who was responsible?" for an action described by Mabry. "Where are they now? Does you trust them?"

Mabry was preparing to tell Jack the news that he had being withholding all evening, looking for the correct timing. He turned to Jack who was looking straight ahead, his chin on his chest staring, tranquil, into the fire. Mabry said casually, "We are to be joined by Wade Hampton tomorrow. He is to be here at our place, and he has the greatest news – nay, I fear, the worst news – about Tarleton."

Jack turned to Mabry with a questioning look that he seldom used with his friend. "Has you known this long?"

"No. I think it 'fore planned by God himself. Wade did not know you were coming to our place. I received his message late last evening from his rider. Your being here is of importance for he desired to get to you a message as he did before with his aide, Colonel Harrington."

Mabry said this casually, almost as an afterthought, knowing Jack's impatience with Harrington. "By the by, Colonel Harrington and others are to be with him."

Jack answered with a creased brow revealing his frustration, "I has little news to tell him of Tarleton excepting that he is now on to me. I am trailing him and he is doing the same. That is my report to Wade. I am of the feeling he will be disapproving."

"Sir, I have the feeling the news from Mr. Hampton is more important than just Tarleton. I am certain it bears news of him and others."

At this Jack was fully alerted to what Mabry was trying to say. "He must have grave news then…things are not well with us so we will be fearful to hear what he has to say.".

That night all slept as well as could be expected. The children had long been asleep from exhaustion when Jack finally gave in to fatigue. He slept fitfully with Elizabeth in a large bed that was too comfortable. He found himself up and walking around in the wee hours, observing four of his girls who were in the same room asleep on the floor. Sometime later, as light approached, he went into a slumber with many thoughts still in his head as to what the day would bring with Wade Hampton.

Jack heard an awakening call from Tirzah, one of the slave men, shortly after dawn and he hurried to get his boots on, the only part of his attire he had discarded for sleeping. He walked toward the voice of the man who called him and heard him say, "Massah Randolph said I calls you. He is looking to see his guests shortly, sir."

Jack was happy and surprised at this news. Hampton was early in the day. He must have stayed a short distance away last night and ridden in at daybreak. Jack followed the man to the front of the main room where Mabry was standing and motioning to Jack to come with him. When they went through the heavy front door of the house, the yard was full of men on horseback. Jack was momentarily startled. He had expected to see the energetic and charismatic Hampton on one of the fine horses Jack had bred and trained, and possibly three to four others accompanying him. Instead he saw what appeared to be over two hundred men.

This was a small army. Why were there so many men and why were they here? Mabry had given no indication of this mass of armed militia. Jack looked to get a clear view of the twenty-nine-year-old Hampton, somewhere in the middle of the assembled horses. Strangely enough, the men were making no clamor, and no one was shouting instructions. They looked organized but seemed ready to dismount and none looked ready to fight; their rifles were slung over their shoulders or on their saddles.

Hampton came forward out of the mass accompanied by four men and Harrington. All were older than the young planter who was held in such esteem by Carolinians. "Good morning, sir." Striding confidently in the manner that came with his reputation, Hampton addressed Mabry first and then Jack. He bowed gracefully as did the men with him, and Jack eyed Harrington but made no comment to him. He instead acknowledged Hampton with a bow of courtesy and said, "Welcome, sir. I hears you has been made a Colonel with Sumpter."

Hampton smiled back and said, "I am just getting used to that rank. Call me as you wish."

"I will do as you ask. You are 'Mr. Hampton' for sure, so if I forgets, please endure me."

Hampton laughed a good hearty laugh, slapping his riding crop against his right boot for effect, enjoying this early morning verbal joust with a friend, and then he beckoned an officer to join them. "Gentlemen, this is Major James Thorn Clayton attached to General Daniel Morgan. It is my pleasure to introduce him as he is the commander of these men you see before you."

Clayton bowed gracefully and said, "Sir, I will be about my duties. We will camp near here. Please have the dispatch fetch me as when you are ready to be moving."

Mabry then stepped forward and said, "Gentlemen, we are to eat and discuss what our honorable Mr. Hampton, that is, Colonel Hampton, has to say to us."

The eight men went into the main house and were led to a large table. They sat down to bread and wine with pork and duck that had been roasted the evening before and corn that had been roasted quite early that day. All respected the seating arrangements that Mabry pointed to, with Hampton at the head of the table. Jack and Mabry were seated on either side of him. The other men filled the remaining seats. Those men turned out to be not aides at all, but land owners from farther south in the Ninety-Six district that Hampton had collected on his way to Mabry's. This then, as it turned out, was a meeting to be held in secrecy, and Mabry's was the chosen place. Jack did not recognize any of the farmers; they did not introduce themselves but deferred to Hampton. In all this Jack was assured all were Whigs who were dedicated to the defense of their property and the government of the colonies.

As they ate robustly, with Hampton drinking a good portion of wine, two drinks from a cup with each bite of food, the men looked to him expectantly to hear his news. He began, looking at the men he had brought with him from the Ninety-Six district. "Gentlemen, we are being pursued by Colonel Tarleton, who aims to conclude this business with us as soon as he is able. We are at the head of a train of many men ourselves, all under the command of General Daniel Morgan, truly an accomplished military person in whom General Washington and our Congress have entrusted much.

"I have to tell you with the greatest faith in our God that we will

Mr. Carrington,
Aide to Wade Hampton

either do well in the days to come or we will lose all we have. As I look at you now in the peace of Mr. Mabry's home, I am looking at men who either will be dead or imprisoned, or men who will win the day with the largest gathering of ours against perhaps a thousand or more British and Tories. This is all in God's hands, but we need for you to do your duty and to enlist those who will help.

"I am here to tell you our circumstance and to warn you or enlist you. That is your decision, but as we leave today you are either against us or with us. It is your fate…do with it as you wish."

All the men responded as if they were loyal to Governor Rutledge and would not be here today if they were not fully committed. One man stood up and gave a toast to Governor Rutledge and Lt. Governor Gadsden, who both had left Charlestowne, the Governor escaping and almost being caught by Tarleton, and Gadsden imprisoned in the Florida colony by the British.

Hampton turned and motioned to Jack and said, "Gentlemen, we have a man who you may have heard of. I have not mentioned his name to any of you as we traveled. He has served well and on many occasions. I have the pleasure of presenting Jack Beckham of the Pacolet River and Grindal Shoals."

Jack had never been introduced before and he was not ready for what followed. All the men stood and acknowledged him and hit the table with their open hands and palms in applause and raised a toast to Jack. Hampton looked at him and smiled, and Jack said, "Hellfire, sir, this is a pretty way to announce a man to be dead soon. Should I say I am pleasured to be here or should I just leave to join the Tories?"

The men laughed with delight. Jack smiled too, assuring one farmer that had traveled with Hampton and others that Jack was not entirely deadly in his actions. The man remembered having heard tales of Jack murdering his sister, a tale he dared not mention at this time. Instead he just looked on in both amazement and horror that this man was Hampton's friend.

Jack looked up at the men and then with courtesy said to Hampton, rising to his feet as he addressed him, "Sir, with the greatest respect, I has nothing to say to these men. I do not know them."

A silence of several moments passed, then Jack spoke again. "If'n my life is somehow to be part of theirs I has nothing to say…I am right honored you asked me to do it." With that Jack sat down and started eating again.

Not taken back, the polished Hampton said, "Gentlemen, I respect Beckham. I asked him to say something to you and he has done so. I am going to ask you to take your leave, if you have had enough to eat. Thank you for your presence. We will continue as you wait on the outside. And we will continue to do as we planned with General Morgan, but I have to hear and to talk to this man at this time. Good morning to you."

Hampton had spoken. The men, disappointed at not being able to converse more with this leader, filed out of the room. Hampton motioned for Mabry to make sure they were not lingering, and that they could not hear what was being said in the room. Mabry went to the window and looked out; then with a nod he came back to the men at the table: Hampton, Colonel Harrington, and Jack. Hampton looked straight into Jack's face, and for a second his youthful face was contorted. He looked as if he were about to burst to say something. Jack casually looked up from eating, and Hampton got close to Jack's face; he then let out a riotous laugh.

Mabry and Harrington looked puzzled, but Jack smiled knowingly at Hampton, and then chuckled with him. "Be damned, Jack, how did you know?"

Mabry could not contain himself. "Know what, Colonel?"

Hampton looked across at him and said, "That every one of these men who were brought here are as Tory as Tarleton is himself a British. They are some of the most dreadful."

"Then why did you bring them?" asked Mabry.

"To control them! I wanted Jack to scare what evil there is out of them. I was prepared to tell them to be with us or be in a stockade! I wanted them to join us or get out of our way. I wanted to get them where we can see them. I would rather have the devil where I can see him than to not know where he is. They would have been recruiting men behind our backs and this cannot be allowed.

"But my friend here has deprived me of that opportunity so it will have to wait until we are through talking."

"Well, Colonel," said Mabry, "I offer my apologies for doubting you. You are indeed worthy of your commission."

All the men expressed amusement at Mabry's comment, which lifted the veil from the strange moment. Hampton looked at Jack only half-smiling, and said, "Sir, you have not answered my question. Did you know anything about these men?"

"Colonel, only that they is not known to be with us; otherwise, I would have heard about them, and I has tried to git to know all who is loyal. 'Sides, they look too fat. All ours is pretty lean, I tell you."

The men enjoyed this conviviality for a minute before Hampton said to Harrington, "Sir, check the door again."

Harrington did so, this time opening it and looking out. No one was near the door. The yard was full of men milling about, and tents were being set up at the edge of Mabry's forest. The four men asked by Hampton to leave were in a knot of other men gathered by themselves, and Harrington remembered the comment about their being Tories.

Hampton now was deadly serious. "Jack... gentlemen," he said, his eyes moving around the table at them. "We are about to fight the biggest you have ever seen." He let this sink in. He looked first at Jack and then to Mabry and Harrington, to guarantee that his words had struck the chord he intended. "Tarleton is aiming to catch us, and he wants more blood for his dishonor among our people. He is gathering his for more war. Cornwallis is coming too. Nay! More than that! Many British and Tories are coming from the North Carolina colony. We hear Leslie with a thousand, maybe fifteen hundred, men...and cannon...are hastening to get here from Charlestowne. But we have a man in this General Morgan.

"He has gathered the most I have heard as of this day for us. We may have a thousand men, as it is, mostly militia, the Over Mountain Men, Andrew Pickens, John Edgar Howard's Continentals, Lt. Colonel William Washington's dragoons, many Georgia boys, Maryland and Virginia boys."

The silence prevailed. Hampton was giving grave news, a warning, and the three men were waiting for him to finish. Hampton measured his words as if telling a story around a campfire. "But this Tarleton, this 'Benny' as Morgan calls him, is out to fight and fight soon. You know he has captured many of our Continentals and has given them a 'right' to be imprisoned with a good chance of dying of disease…or fighting with him. We hope they will not fight, and with not much spirit if they do.

"But we know the damnable Tories and the regular British will fight us, and I tell you this battle, wherever it takes place, will decide much. I need for you, Jack, to join us. Help Morgan! I need you to gather as many of yours to us as you can. Are those boys that was with you at Alexander's Old Field still with us?"

"Quite a few are dead, sir, including McClure himself, and his brother is helpless with a wound. I know Craig is dead and several of old Judge Gaston's boys are dead too…at other places like Hanging Rock, which I hear was a fierce fight…many dead.

"Many others are home. I don't know about them. I know Soe and his Catawbas and Samuel is with me."

For the first time Colonel Harrington spoke. "May I make a suggestion, sir?" He spoke directly to Hampton. Jack felt he had heard this type of inquiring and declarations before from Harrington; he unconsciously put his hands on his hips even while sitting, and turned and looked at the former British officer.

"Aye," said the Colonel.

"My suggestion, sir – being you need to know who is loyal, and you need men to rally to Morgan – is to ask the school teacher, Chandler, from the Cedar Shoals and Catawba great falls to join us and tell who is loyal. He knows them all from that place, I dare say, from teaching in the homes of Whigs and Loyalists.

"This man Chandler has fetched the wench Easter in regard to your recent command to Mr. Mabry and to Jack. He has heard of you and respects you. I believe he knows much about the loyalty of the people in that area, and it will save us much time to know who they are."

Harrington looked at Mabry, who was nodding his head, acknowledging that he remembered Chandler very well.

"What say you to this, Jack?" asked Hampton.

"I don't rightly know, sir," said Jack, glancing away from the table. "I knows my two nephews, Thomas' boys, knows this fancy school man. They feels he is knowing many people, and he comes and goes a lot. Maybe if'n you lines up all the people he knows, like those farmers who came here with you, and he tells us who is our friend that would be jest fine."

Jack said this sarcastically, and all knew it. He then added, "But that is too near for me in time." Jack continued to speak, and the men paid attention. "I am to leave and git Soe and any others I can and git back to Daniel Morgan, with as many as I can. I can git 'school man' and bring him back to us, only if he's at the Carlisle's or Starnes'. I is not spending time looking for a dandy who ain't likely to know how to shoot a gun."

Hampton without looking, and in a grim voice, said firmly, "No. I have not had the time yet to tell you all I needed to say...and that is Morgan needs you to join him now. He needs a scout who knows the Grindal Shoals and the upper and middle Ninety-Six for Washington's Light Infantry boys.

"There are two hundred Tories that may be closer than Tarleton is – we don't know where as we sit here – threatening to slow Morgan down. If that happens Tarleton may catch Morgan. You cannot go to the great falls of the Catawba. You must leave directly." Hampton moved closer to Jack for effect. "We have two spies that are with Tarleton, and you know one of them well."

Jack looked surprised, and Hampton noticed his manner. Hampton continued with Jack's fullest attention. "They will, at least this one person, search you out, and you are to be camped with Morgan when that person looks for you. She will have much to tell about Tarleton, the number of men, and his camp." Hampton pressed Jack. "You have not forgot," he gently chided him, "that I have asked you to rid us of Tarleton...and I know you have tried. This may be the best person, as of now, to help you do that, sir, in this battle that is surely to take place."

"Who is that person...a wench it is?" asked Jack.

"It is indeed…and allow me to shield her." Hampton got up at that comment and Jack followed him to the side of the room, a courtesy to the anonymous person who was a spy – not a slight to Mabry and Harrington. "You know her well, John. She is from the community near Alexander's Old Field. She is the wench Arlee McCormick, who is well known for her cooking, so much so that many do not know she can ride a horse as well as others and can fire her rifle with much good aim.

"She is a camp follower with Tarleton, unattached as she is to any man since old McCormick died."

Jack just nodded. "What is it she tells me and where?"

Hampton breathed deeply. "Morgan is to be camping somewhere on Grindal Shoals before traveling on. He will ask Washington and his horsemen to meet him at a place near there. I don't know where. He will certainly be on or near the property of the Chesneys, Tories as they are. But Morgan himself, I know, travels with our best and remaining men. That is why I need you to gather as many where you can.

"When we fight, and I think that to be near or in the North Carolina colony, it most certainly has to be where roads meet. We will need to know much in advance and fight harder.

"General Morgan has to know how many men Tarleton has and where Cornwallis is!" Hampton had raised his voice and his eyebrows at the mention of Cornwallis. "The wench, Arlee McCormick, will tell you as much as she knows. You have to look for her." Hampton had edged even closer to Jack, talking as secretly as he could, and at the same time ordering him, a scout and a Whig older than him, to look for a woman among all those that would be gathered at a final destination and battle site.

Jack said in reply, a quick sense of obligation in his voice. "I needs Samuel to be here." He stepped to the side of the room and hailed Samuel from the upstairs and asked him to bring Kit and Johnny. The boys appeared almost instantly from the room over the great room where the meetings had been taking place with the men. With them, trundling along, was the irrepressible Molly Polly, again uninvited, but not scolded by her father. Smiling, Jack introduced her to Wade

Hampton as "our Captain who is in charge." She beamed and lined up with the boys, all waiting in a line to hear Jack's instructions.

Jack said to Samuel, "You has to go to Soe. We has to have all his he can bring. Tell him I needs him, and the Colonel needs...uh...tell him Mr. Wade Hampton desires his to be with us to help in the big war with this Tarleton."

Samuel nodded soberly at this command. Jack spoke again. "You, Kit and Johnny..." Both boys stiffened and looked military in their bearing, as they had seen others do. "You must both go with Samuel and leave him as you is traveling and go to your Ma's house and inquire about this school man, Chandler.

"Go to Carlisle's or Starnes' if you has to, and tell him the 'honorable Mr. Wade Hampton' has need of him to help us jest as he did with fetching Easter. Tell him he can nay stay there...he has to come."

The boys snapped their heads forward in agreement, and Jack asked them in a fatherly way if they had eaten enough. Both nodded yes. Molly Polly had felt her part – she sensed being included – and left the room to go back upstairs as the boys prepared to leave. Then the men were alone in the room again when Jack and Hampton began discussing his leaving and where to join Lieutenant Colonel William Washington.

"Go towards the Grindal Shoals again," said Hampton. "He is moving there with so many that you will encounter scouts on the way." Out of his waist coat he took a ribbon-tied parchment dispatch bearing the family crest of the Hampton family. "I will read you what this says. I have had it with me now several days. You are sorely needed to help know the way from the Grindal Shoals toward the North Carolina boundary.

"I dare say again you will only get so far before Tarleton and his will engage Morgan. But Washington's cavalry has need of you now."

Hampton held the dispatch at arm's length toward Jack and looked him straight in the eyes. Hampton sounded ceremonial.

"To the Honorable General Daniel Morgan.

"Sir. It is my duty to inform you that the bearer is Jack Beckham of the Pacolet River, Grindal Shoals. He is an honorable man and loyal to our colony. I plead to place him completely in your hands to use in our cause. He will direct any force, or forces under your command in a speedy way to wherever you will be and he will advise you well. I am too at your service.

In great assurance and prayer to almighty God, I am, and I remain, your humblest and dutiful servant, who has the honor to be,

Colonel Wade Hampton

Serving under General Thomas Sumpter

The tenth day of December in this year of our Lord, 1780."

Hampton was assisted by Colonel Harrington, who anticipated his needs and handed him a lighted candle with wax. Hampton sealed the document, and it became a precious dispatch as he handed it to Jack. Jack took the document as if it were a holy writ. He placed it under the shirt under his walnut-stained frock and tightened the strap that held his powder horn so that it pressed down more firmly on the parchment. He nodded at Hampton and then shook his hand as the gentleman slapped Jack on the shoulder and took a bottle of rye from a table. They would drink a toast to the job to be done. Mabry and Harrington joined them.

Before leaving, Hampton said to Jack, "There is still a task at hand regarding the men I brought here." He then went to the door himself and called in a commanding voice for the men he had collected while traveling to join him. He looked back at Jack. "Sir, you know what to do?" Jack nodded, and even without thinking, loosened the hunting knife under his belt.

The men walked in. Hampton said, "These gentlemen are Mr. Post, Mr. Garrison, Mr. Longmire, and Mr. Pierce, all from the Ninety-Six district. They have traveled with me, as all know in this room, and all profess to be loyal to the colony."

"Aye," they mumbled, watching Colonel Hampton. He then informed them of what they had not heard while they were outside the room. "Gentlemen, we have made a decision to engage the British and specifically Mr. Tarleton. Jack Beckham will now speak to you as to our planning. What he says is of his own choosing."

Jack walked to where the men stood and came close to them. He motioned for all them to come closer as if he desired to tell them something of military importance. They stood only two paces from him, surrounding him. Jack's voice lowered, and he spoke so softly one man, Andrew Pierce, moved even closer, getting one foot in front of Jack's body and then looking at the floor, his hand cupped to his ear ready to receive the important news. He stared at the floor listening.

Jack said, "You is all loyal?"

All the men shook their heads yes and looked satisfied with their answers, waiting for more news and possibly instruction.

Jack said, with a harsh cross tone that staggered them, "I think ye may be all liars. I don't gives a damnation if you is lying to Wade Hampton. I will kill ye if'n you leave here and I sees you with Tories." Jack pulled his 12 inch knife out. "You ain't worth even a one antler buck if'n you is lying. Better you gits your story straight now and off'n this property 'cause I don't care for you. Is you truthful?" he asked again.

Jack had moved into the only space remaining between them so that they had to step back. The men seemed to take a breath and stepped four to five steps backward, all out of reach of his arm and the knife he held in his hand. Playing his role to the fullest, Colonel Hampton intervened. "Sir! Sir! I feel all these men are with us. There is no need to carry this further. Are you men indeed willing to assist and recruit?"

The men looked like they were in church. They raised their hands reverently, and two of them swore an oath to God and to the colony. They were most agreeable. Pierce stuck out his hand to shake Hampton's hand and said, "Sir, I swears my allegiance."

The others grunted, and Jack began to move back and allow Hampton to talk to the men. Hampton then said to them, "All of you are to go and join Morgan and help him. If you have to go back to your home, leave here to get others to join us and then be with Morgan. You must go and return within three days. Are these terms to your liking?"

Only one of the men said "aye." Pierce said he had to go and collect his relatives and others, that it would take him four days, maybe more. The two remaining numbly agreed with Pierce without saying anything. Hampton looked at Jack and Mabry, and Jack just shrugged. "Sirs, if'n you are not back as you say, then you are a Tory."

"It is not so, sir!" Pierce protested. Jack held up his hand and glared to silence him. Pierce insisted, and said he would honor his word to return. As Hampton offered his hand to the men, and they all collectively took a drink from the bottle of rye, Jack and Mabry left the room. Their language was clear. Hampton could trust these men.

After the four farmers had left the room to mount their horses and leave, Mabry and Jack re-entered to talk again with Colonel Hampton and Drury Harrington.

"What think you?" asked Hampton.

Randolph replied that it would be another day before they found out the truth. He allowed that they all could be against the colony. Jack nodded his agreement while he was moving toward his gun, which had been conveniently by him in all this dialogue. He said he was leaving as soon as he saw Elizabeth and his family to find Colonel Washington's dragoons. And he confirmed again, he would send Samuel and his two nephews on their way to fetch Elberton Chandler.

Jack and Elizabeth were parting in a different place, but their separation was once again painful. They went to a corner of their bedroom and said intimate good-byes. Jack then called his children, and they all trooped in and stood around him and Elizabeth. He announced, "We are to celebrate Christmas with the Mabrys. We are to return to our place when I am back to you. That will not be long and then we are to the Pacolet.

"First we has to ask the Tories and the British to leave us. I am part of that asking in the next days to come. Samuel and the boys are off to the great falls and then they are back here."

Susan asked, "What of Mr. Stribling and his family?"

Jack said somberly, "He has a choice to go with me or to find his own and be with them. They do not know where he is as of now."

Stribling looked at Susan and said, "I will go with your father and then leave him to be with mine. I am back here, I promise, as soon as I find mine, and they are safe to my knowledge."

"Papa?" Susan started to speak and Jack smiled and said," I will see Mr. Stribling is off to his family as far as he can go with me." He did not elaborate. As he left, the tribal tradition among him and his family was played out. He touched each of them, and his girls hugged a part of him as he passed by – some on his shoulder and some clutching and caressing his arm or hand. Molly Polly and John Junior were already standing up to follow their "Pap" as he left. Young John grabbed Jack's rifle and carried it proudly. Molly Polly took his hand and placed both of hers around his one and held it tightly as they walked from the house to the yard.

Jack turned to them and said, "Don't be following me this time. I am taking Stribling, and Samuel is leaving with Kit and Johnny. Stay here."

They nodded sadly. Jack's last sight of them as he looked back that day was their standing close together watching him and Samuel ride away. Now he turned his attention to the west and Grindal Shoals.

Chapter Eighteen

Gammond's Store

Samuel, Kit, and Johnny rode with the greatest amount of freedom. They had heard enough to know that major battles were shaping behind them, and they were riding away from organized harm to their own homes. Samuel told the boys as they rode that he would go to their home first before going to get Soe. They should go to the Starnes' home and then to the Carlisle's to try and find the schoolmaster. They would all meet at their home in hopes their father might be there. They would meet again in two days even if Chandler were not found, and then report back to Rand Mabry's. They might even get to spend Christmas at home. This encouraged Kit and Johnny, and for the first time in days they smiled with anticipation of something good and cheerful.

When Samuel arrived at his home he was met by all his family except his father, and all appeared fit and well. He stayed only long enough to eat and take food with him as he headed to the Catawba Nation. The boys went to the Starnes' but did not find Chandler. They were greeted by no one and assumed all were staying with others during this season. Even the slaves did not know where the Starnes were, but there was no apparent alarm.

Kit and Johnny then rode directly to the Carlisle home and found Katie Linn Carlisle, the wife of Richard, who welcomed them. As they dismounted she approached them with anxiety in her voice. "Boys," she said, "has you heard all the brothers Wagner are dead?"

"No," they exclaimed.

"All are looking for the men who did this," she said in response to their looks of surprise. "All mine, my husband, my boys, Matthew, Jebual, and James, are searching for these men. You seen any party riding?"

"No," they answered again.

She looked uneasy and invited them into the house as if to protect them. "We hear it is murder of these men and their horses. Their houses have been burned, and their families are not to be found. We have not heard others are harmed." She clearly was distraught.

Kit told her they had to find Elberton Chandler. He was being asked to meet Wade Hampton on important matters, and the boys appeared more eager to find Chandler than to discuss the killings. She interrupted Kit. "Mr. Chandler is here. He was the one to hear of the murders as he was traveling to the Starnes' home to teach the families there. He was to get the Starnes children, and they were to be with him on the way to the Wagner brothers to teach other children gathered there.

"Mr. Chandler is much afraid and in his cabin. He found all three Wagner men dead and their stock as well." At that instant they heard horses approaching, and it was with heavy hearts that they all peered out of windows. It was the Carlisle men, and they soon heard even more details of the sordid murder that Chandler had reported. According to Mr. Carlisle, he and his men had been riding for hours with other neighbors to find any trace of the murderers.

"Mr. Starnes has been with us," said Jebual, answering the question on all their minds. "Their family is safe."

"Where is Mr. Chandler now?" asked Mr. Carlisle.

"He is much afraid and in his bed, I fear," his wife said.

"Sir," interjected Kit, owing to his command from Jack. "My uncle and Wade Hampton has great need of him now. They has sent me and my brother here to git him. He is needed at the Mabry's plantation, for Jack and others say two thousand men are to fight near there. Tarleton and Cornwallis, too."

The news was almost too much to hear for the peaceful and religious family, after the killing of close neighbors. Mr. Carlisle showed much anger in his face when told this news. "I fear this is like the Bible tells us...the ending of the world before our Lord returns. What is to happen if people are killed as this, and Tories and British do what we have witnessed today?

"Chandler has to go to Wade Hampton! Maybe he will be of some service. He cannot hide and be afraid at a time as this is."

To Mr. Carlisle, this was a decree that had to be made. He mounted his horse, and all followed him on the short ride to the small cabin in back of the Carlisle home, which Chandler had occupied often. They found him sitting on his bed reading. Mr. Carlisle burst into the one-room home and said, "Sir, you are much needed by Beckham and Wade Hampton...you are to be gone from here to see what help you can provide."

Chandler appeared surprised and said, "Sir, I am tired and unaccustomed to the tragedy I have seen. I beg to have rest. May I travel tomorrow? I would like to read the Bible and pray and rest."

"Sir, no!" Carlisle thundered. "What you have seen must not happen again. This is against God. If you can be of service you are to do so."

Kit intervened. "Sir, Mr. Hampton, he is now Colonel Hampton under Sumpter, has much to tell you and ask you about how you can help. The British and Tarleton are marching, and he would have you into his confidence."

Mr. Carlisle took over. "Matthew, get his horse."

Chandler protested and said he would fetch the horse. Mrs. Carlisle said she would get food for all of them, and she left to gather it. Chandler started after her, but Mr. Carlisle stood in his way, acting with grace and concern, and told him to stay. Food and his horse would be brought to him. Kit and Johnny followed Mrs. Carlisle. Chandler was left sitting on his bed with Mr. Carlisle standing in front of him talking about the three men murdered in their own yard.

All of the Carlisle boys went to get the horse from the stable to make sure the animal was fed and watered. When they reached the horse called Taber, they were somewhat taken back by his condition.

He had been ridden in the last hours and not rubbed down. His hair looked matted and rough.

"The schoolmaster," said James with some annoyance, "is not even a horseman. We have to do it for him."

Matthew rubbed Taber, and Jebual fed him while James checked his hooves. The horse had not been cared for. Quickly they refreshed him and led him from the stable to Chandler and the boys in the yard, with Johnny waiting with Kit, still chewing venison Mrs. Carlisle had given him. In a short time, the Beckham boys, with Chandler, left the Carlisle home to ride back to their home and await Samuel; they would all then ride to Mabry's. Chandler seemed more relaxed now that he had gotten away from the Carlisle home place. Kit said they would ride even in moonlight to get back to Mabry and Hampton, and they continued on.

Two days later, Matthew and James went to the stable as they were required to do every day to attend to their horses, Tot and Jupiter. They did their chores, and as they were leaving James stumbled over a hay bale that was displaced. He turned it over to put it in a bin and saw dirt freshly dug beneath it. His foot pressed something as he turned to leave the spot, and he felt a hard object – a knife. He picked it up and saw that it was caked with blood at the hilt, very thick, but not so dry that James could not rub it off. Underneath dried blood was fresher blood. He looked questioningly at Matthew, who shrugged.

On impulse, and with some wariness, they looked at the bale itself. Feeling with their hands, there, in the middle of the straw was a musket. A Brown Bess. They smelled the sulfur smell from the discharged gun powder and knew immediately it had been fired, maybe several times, recently. Both boys had the same idea. They ran to tell their older brother, Jebual, and their father. It occurred to both of them that Kit, Johnny, and Chandler had been gone for almost two days.

Jack and Stribling traveled for some time before Jack saw him off. Stribling waved good-bye as he traveled toward his family home. Jack turned south, away from Grindal Shoals toward the middle Ninety-Six district to look for Washington's dragoons. His skill and practice as a scout would prove him correct, as he saw in the distance camp fires on his third day of travel. He was on the Beaverdam Creek when he saw them and began to use his looking glass from three different vantage points to confirm the fires and the men around them.

He followed the creek toward the Saluda River and then back-tracked up the Little River. There he saw more men coming together. These men were dragoons with sidearms and sabers and carbines. They were Washington's men or Continentals from another colony.

Jack used a practiced tactic to make sure he and they were not being tracked. He waited and watched the men and their fires from a point that others would also watch from. He looked for places that would logically be a sight point. He circled the men at a distance and saw that their pickets were also circling and riding to see the same. These were the men Jack would contact – as he had at the Blackstock's. He picked a rider that was riding to the side and away from his fellow scouts. This man was the point and the most vulnerable. Jack decided to attract attention and do it in such an obvious way that others would come as well. He decided to boldly fire his rifle into the air and shout, "hallo," a war cry he knew the dragoons recognized.

Astride Maw, he raised his gun and fired. He quickly reloaded and watched in the distance, not looking closely at his flintlock as he reloaded but keeping a watchful look at the man he could see. That scout was quickly joined by three others. Jack shouted an Indian cry and waved his gun. At this point he was the most likely to be fired upon in error. He moved Maw carefully toward the men as they cantered toward him, not at a breakneck pace, for they also feared a trap.

As they approached, Jack yelled again. The men scrutinized him, his clothes and horse, his gun, and what might be behind him. Jack waved his rifle across his body and then waited. He did not recognize the men, but they clearly were Washington's men. He was relieved and hoped they were comfortable with his appearance. As they drew closer, he saw serious looks on their faces. These men were hesitating, and that was not good for him. Three of them held their guns in menacing positions, and one carried his saber by his side, gripping it firmly. Jack concluded he only had a fleeting time before he had to run, depending on Maw to quickly put distance between them. Jack decided on one last move. He took his rifle and held it high by the end of the butt. This was the exact opposite of someone surrendering as had been done in Charlestowne in May, when the British siege brought over five thousand Americans into captivity; there, many of the Continentals had held their guns high by the barrel, upside down.

The men started to gallop to Jack. They were bunched together, not spread out to surround him. This was the defining signal. They would be friendly. Still not smiling, however, one dragoon called out, "Where are ye from? Who are ye?"

Jack confidently answered, "From Grindal Shoals...I am Jack Beckham...to do service for Colonel Washington by order of Wade Hampton."

As they came very close, one man said, "Release your gun." Jack still had it, but now by the middle of the butt holding it in the air. He could easily slide his hand up to the trigger and fire. He replied in a non-threatening way. "Nay, I am friendly. I am to scout for Colonel Washington. I have a dispatch from Hampton."

"A dispatch?" The man repeated with more interest and respect in his voice.

"Ride here then; we will take you to Washington." But yet another man said warily, "Show the paper."

Jack took the parchment from under his frock and handed it to the man, who apparently could not read. He handed it to another, who looked at it and nodded affirmatively. "Good it is. I will hold this dispatch."

The five traveled to a grove of trees that looked unguarded. It looked similar to the tree line bordering Mudlick Creek that ran parallel to the Little River. They stopped, and Jack assumed that he would be taken to Washington on foot or on horseback into the grove. Instead, a distinguished-looking man stepped out from behind a row of pine trees by himself. He approached Jack and said, "I am William Washington."

Jack had actually looked past this man to see who else would emerge; then he recognized the officer's markings. He took off his hat as he dismounted and saluted Washington, who was almost as tall as Jack. "I am Jack Beckham, sir, of the Pacolet and Grindal Shoals. I am to be here on command of Colonel Wade Hampton." Without a word, the man accompanying Jack handed the dispatch to the Colonel. Washington read it and looked up at Jack.

"You are welcomed. You know the odds against our force? You are aware of the Tories? That Tarleton and Cornwallis are in this area?"

"Indeed, sir. I has been chased by Tarleton, and I am seeking him out as well. I have been in this area many yers with wife and children, and I has recently been with ours at Blackstock's, where I was pleasured to kill some of Tarleton's. I was at Alexander's Old Field where we run Tories off. So I am back home as it is."

"Aye, then you know much of the upper Ninety-Six and the North Carolina boundary where we are to be if we do not engage Tarleton and Cornwallis sooner. In fact, we must not. We need more men to fight off Tories under Thomas Waters from Georgia."

Washington then led Jack to a small campfire and sat down on his haunches and invited Jack to sit. He drew a line on the ground showing where he was, where he knew Morgan was at this time, and the band of Tories under Waters; he guessed them to be to the south, maybe twenty miles from Morgan. They were moving constantly and gathering recruits. "We are between Water's Tories and Daniel Morgan. Tories must be two hundred or so. I needs you to help find them. I am sending Lieutenant Colonel James McCall to engage, but we has to know we can fight them with all we have."

"How many is that?" Jack asked.

Washington intuitively hesitated to give an exact number to the scout, but he said, "I have my dragoons, seventy-five of them, and I can muster 'bout two hundred militia, all horsemen. We will meet the Tories with all these. But I displeasure at the thought of these Tories being onto Morgan and we not getting them afore that. You are to be with other scouts and find these scoundrels."

Jack spent more time with Washington and several men who joined them, all who would be scouts, fanning out to find a mass of neighbors who were for the King. And now it seemed likely there would be Tories from other colonies, particularly Georgia.

Jack declined the offer to have another scout travel with him. He said to one of Washington's men, "I will find you if I sees the Tories." He spent the next days camping and searching in different directions, oftentimes riding back to the east. His main ploy was to enter a farm and innocently inquire as to directions, directions he already knew. This was his game with those he encountered. If they told him a way to go that was obviously wrong, they were Loyalists to be sure, lying about directions out of spite, not fear. If they told Jack the truth he would ask them about any bands of men that were moving and who they were. If the people were very helpful, he asked "Which direction?"

He did this often, but separated himself from those with whom he talked by as many miles as possible. He did not want to arouse too much suspicion about a traveler looking for other men. It was surprising who told him the truth. Many did. Those who distrusted him were obvious, and as he left these people he rode watching his back.

Jack talked to slaves he met on roads and in adjoining fields of farms, and he talked to stragglers who were fed up with being chased and part of the war, whether they were Whig or Tory. He learned much, but he learned more by listening to what was said. He never took anyone at his word. In all this he had lost track of time. He was sure Christmas had come and gone, and he wondered many times about his family. It would have been easy to ride to Mabry's to see if they were there. He resisted this urge, and this made him even more diligent in finding the men Washington was looking for.

Jack, on one of his longest days out, traveling on Maw since dawn and seeing no one, stumbled onto a group of men who were traveling together on a trail, all on horseback and four of them traveling two to a horse. They looked unkempt. Several had their heads down and were traveling at a very slow pace but in sight of others.

He decided to act as if he were lost and hail them from a distance. Jack circled and intentionally came out of a wood break, out of musket range and at a distance that he could dash back into the wood covering. He called. "Hello! I is lost and looking to find a safe place to be...and stay for some days...where is you traveling?"

A very weary man replied. "Home to family. We are traveling away from war." Others grunted an approval and kept riding. "Where is you from?" one called back.

Jack hollered, "From the great falls of the Catawba. I am finished hunting and going back."

It occurred to Jack that even as he said this, he had no deer meat or any other game to show. He hoped they thought everything was in a haversack. They were too weary to ask or notice. Another sojourner called, "Do not go behind us for naught. Scores of men are there…they is looking to fight."

Jack appeared appreciative. He hailed them with his waving arm and started Maw on a faster jaunt back into the woods. He waited undetected until the stragglers had passed and then rode in the direction the men had just traveled. What he saw was what he had been asked to find – men in front of him traveling in the same direction. Then as he rode between trees and behind them, moving in their direction, he saw campfires of men who seemed to be gathering. Jack spent hours circling them and saw so many camp fires that he began to count them until he was satisfied this was a military gathering of some importance. From time to time he saw the Royal Provincial uniform of a Tory, but to the greatest extent they were all dressed as he and Tories in their allegiance.

Jack started to make his his way back to Colonel Washington to a general location where he knew he would be, and after only a few hours came upon an advance party of McCall's men. The leader said they had heard from other scouts of the Tory massing, and Jack confirmed it. They rested while Jack told them of the location he had come from, while fresh scouts went back to alert Washington and McCall. They would wait for the army to catch up and talk of things they mutually had seen. It would help to know numbers and how fast men were traveling.

The men of McCall found Jack and the advance party. They showed up with almost three hundred trailing men who would now move as dragoons and mounted militia to engage Waters and his Georgia Tories. Jack was unaccustomed to being in an army. True to his calling, he had scouted ahead with several men who spread out and kept coming back to report. What they kept seeing was a group of Tories moving away from them, some two hundred or more. On this advice Washington decided to advance rapidly. At his command, three hundred men on horseback, most of them experienced fighters, began to go forward with strength and purpose. Jack was among those in front who signaled when Tories seemed to change directions. He rode up to one of his counterparts and said, "You sees what I do?"

"Aye," the man said, "they is running and looking not to fight."

Jack and others motioned for men under McCall to make haste, and the chase continued. This hunt would take place over forty miles, and it would be a hunt that would beg eventually for a place to stop and men to fight. All sensed, on both sides, this inevitability after days of hard riding.

At night, Jack would venture as close to the camp fires as possible and count again. Always the count was nearly the same. The Tories were running and could not collect new recruits while they went at such a pace. Jack did notice with some alarm that they were running in the direction of the fort at Ninety-Six. This would mean many more men and even cannon. He did not know how many reinforcements might be at the fort.

Jack went back and talked with scouts and McCall's men for an hour over a fire. He stood the entire time. Jack told one officer, "We has to ride harder…they is going to git to their own, and this battle will be more than we is bargaining for as it is now."

The officer listened intently. "But" he said, "we are moving them away from Morgan, and that is Colonel Washington's purpose."

Jack responded to him angrily, respecting the man's authority as much as he could without dressing him down. "We is also getting further from Morgan. We is way behind the Tories and Britisher's lines. Does us no good to chase the Tory to their den and git kilt doing it. We has to face them sooner rather than later."

The officer walked away, and Jack wondered what effect this conversation would have. He was joined quickly by other men in authority. One asked, "Beckham, what are you putting forward?"

"Ride harder, sir. Leave at light and chase them down. They is too

close to the fort at Ninety-Six. Already they has sent scouts for rein-
forcing, and they may be coming to meet up.

"We is all good riders, and we is getting too much better at riding…maybe 'forgetting' how to fight if we continues this sallying."

"I will direct this to Colonel McCall," the man said.

At the first light, Jack was roused by sounds of men moving. An officer hollered to him, "Lead with the others…we will catch them today
if the Almighty allows."

Jack ate quickly. Having prepared Maw as he did every night,
he rode out with seven other men to reconnoiter. They rode as hard
as they had before, and all noticed that the mass of men in front of
them appeared much closer. Hundreds of men were in a train behind
him, and the thundering noise was impressive. It was impatient men
on horseback that had heard of the Tories' brutality, and they would
not be stopped until they met the men in front of them. At the late
morning, Jack and his were overtaking the scattered and slowest of the
Tories. Jack glanced back once and saw that the men under McCall
were catching and killing some men savagely. Their sabers were making
the fastest work, and he did not see any prisoners being taken.

All at once, the scouts saw that the Tories were gathering around
a building and preparing to put up an organized fight. "Where is we?"
one man called to Jack in the melee of noise and horses' hooves, men
swearing, and Tories seeming to die all around them.

"Looks like Hammond's Store. Hellfire, we is only ten miles or a
little more from the fort."

Jack gave a primitive "hallo" and charged into a small group of men
who had their backs to him, preparing to make a stand. He caught them
before they were ready to meet the onrushing dragoons of Washington
and McCall. He tomahawked one man in his neck, and with an upward swing hit another in the back of his head. Jack was aware that the
dragoons of McCall were catching up, and now were all around him.
He saw more of Washington's cavalry; they were merciless in their attack on the Tories.

Jack saw men falling and being chased and hacked to death, sometimes by more than one Whig. Some men had dismounted from

Washington's force and were finishing off any man that was wounded. This was a massacre. Tories continued to ride away, but dragoons rode them down and killed them without any mercy. Jack had a sudden thought that he was witnessing what might have been Buford's defeat by Tarleton at the Waxhaws, excepting this was his colonists exacting great revenge.

Out of the corner of his eye he saw a man he recognized. Who was this? Jack charged at him with his knife in his hand holding Maw's reins, and his red-stained tomahawk in the other. The man recognized Jack and screamed at him in a shrill, pleading voice. It was Pierce, the man at Mabry's who had now sided with the Tories. Jack, with boiling hatred, rode him down and cleaved his head from the top of his skull to his neck. Blood flew on Jack and Maw while Jack hit him again as he was falling. Going back to Pierce, Jack looked down and saw his eyes glazed, his body convulsing. He dismounted and went over and put him to final death by puncturing his throat.

Jack was being passed by practically all of his fellow riders. He mounted again and saw that the men taking refuge at Hammond's Store were fleeing, among them the officers of the Georgia commander. They were cut down as well. The massacre continued. Only after the field had been won and dragoons had administered the worst killings Jack had seen did they begin to take prisoners. Men were screaming "quarter" and lying on the ground with no pretense of fighting. Others were on their knees begging for mercy. Washington's force was cleaning up the Tories, still with some being killed who resisted slightly, and others being herded to the side while their weapons were piled up.

Jack saw no hangings. What he did see were the dead and dying. Some of the dragoons were counting for a report to Morgan. Jack heard a tally of one hundred fifty Tories killed and wounded and another forty or so captured. This had been the most complete defeat and worst killing that Jack had seen. He felt greatly encouraged. He began to move back toward the north and Grindal Shoals. His job was complete. He thought about the scrimmage at Alexander's Old Field and how quick and decisive that was. It was nothing like this, however.

He felt a measure of revenge against Tarleton, and he prodded Maw to a greater speed to be on his journey back.

He was leaving Hammond's Store and the slaughter to get back to where Morgan might be and to eventually find another spy, Arlee McCormick. He still had not engaged Tarleton himself. Jack rode away from the others, as he was accustomed to traveling alone; but he was aware of those around him. He had not been with this many men, all dedicated to a cause, since Blackstock's. He became used to riders of Washington's cavalry in his side view; others seemed to always be in the distance behind him. All were going back towards Daniel Morgan.

It was two hours before he was completely alone on Maw, picking his way to the north and toward Grindal Shoals. The closer he came to very familiar territory, the stronger the urge became to go back to Mabry's and his family. He had fulfilled his primary duty and that was to scout for Washington. Besides, all had agreed, including Hampton, that Elberton Chandler was to be fetched for whatever he knew and could report on in his dealings with Tory and Whig families. He would need to see if Chandler had been found.

Jack turned to the east. He would report to Wade Hampton if he was there, and if not, he would send a courier to Hampton by Samuel. He was more fatigued than he had ever been, and he began to count the months now since he had left Grindal Shoals and the Pacolet to go to Charlestowne in April. It had to now be 1781 and the tenth month of war and travel and killing and the loss of Maggie, Craig, and many who had fought at Alexander's. He did not know that Kit and Johnny had reached Mabry's two days before and that Mabry had detained Chandler in hopes Jack would come back that way. Jack was to discover that Samuel had recruited Soe and six Catawbas to join him for Morgan, and they were traveling from the Nation.

Mabry had made sure Chandler was secure by having two militia men keep him company. Mabry felt the importance of Chandler, for what he might know about Tories. Chandler, himself, felt comfortable, believing he would have unique access to information for his own purposes. He knew he would be safe. He was to have an audience with a military leader and a wealthy young planter in the Carolina colony.

Kit and Johnny had been gone for several days back to their own home for the Christmas they hoped to have. Elizabeth and her children were guests of the Mabrys, as were her extended family. With the Mabry girls and Elizabeth's seven, it made John Junior the single male of the families in the house. But he and Molly Polly were even closer as they continued their competitive sibling relationship. Somehow John Junior felt he had a "brother" in Molly Polly, and she was quick to assume that role.

Jack saw the Mabry house and the friendly militia men, serving as guards, and he did not employ his usual cautious approach. He was welcomed at some distance by men who knew him, and he waved a sociable reply and rode in. He was almost immediately greeted by Elizabeth, who had been alerted by a slave woman. Behind her came all the family. Out sprinted Molly Polly. This time Jack hoisted her onto Maw and they rode in together.

In the afterglow of being back to friends, Jack sat down with Henrietta and Nancy on his lap, surrounded by his girls, and began to talk with Rand Mabry. Mabry mentioned that Hampton would return "on the morrow after he tended to personal affairs." Jack, recounting what he had seen at Hammond's Store, purposely raised his eyebrows as a signal to Mabry that he did not want to discuss specifics of war.

At the same time, heading toward the Mabry household for a meeting with Mabry, and he hoped, Hampton and Jack as well, was Mr. Carlisle and his oldest son, Jebual. He had ominous news to tell whoever was there about the school teacher. Mr. Carlisle had doubted himself several times as he traveled. Elberton Chandler was a "proper man" who disdained violence in his conversations and in his manner. He prayed sometimes with the family at meals and was a good instructor. Carlisle had never seen him with a weapon. He had never seen him shoot, and when they hunted together for larger game, Chandler helped load the meat in bags, but he had never cut a deer or turkey or rabbit in preparation to eating. He always stood back and watched.

Carlisle wondered if Chandler had brought the knife and gun back to the horse's stable to protect someone. Was he hiding it so a young man or a neighbor might not be discovered? But who would have killed the Wagner brothers and try to hide it? The brothers were no harm to any citizens and were not known to take sides. And there was no plundering of their property…just slaughtered livestock. It looked to be the evil labor of men in a party or cross- country stragglers or even British deserters.

Jack and Mabry continued talking as circuitously as they could about what had happened at Hammond's Store. The girls, Elizabeth, and John Junior stayed nearby. From time to time the Mabry girls came in and out, and Hannah Mabry moved pleasantly about with two slave women who were doing chores at her direction. Finally, with most of the children beginning to drift away, Mabry said, "We have the school man, Chandler, here. He is in the cabin to the back side of the smoke- house."

Jack's face brightened. He seized this moment to get up, hand the babies to Susan, and walk away with Mabry to talk about things Mabry needed to know. But Molly Polly and John hung onto his side, and they left with Jack to go to the cabin to see Chandler.

The first thing Jack saw were the two militia men of Hampton standing outside the cabin. Mabry smiled and said to Jack, "I was not going to allow any harm to come to Chandler. He is already afraid, and I thought he might fare better with people around him. He is expecting to see Wade Hampton, so you can tell him your mind, and then Wade can do so. You might want to wait for Wade to come back."

Jack nodded to the two men as he prepared to enter the cabin after motioning for his young ones to wait outside. He waited until Mabry announced to Chandler, "Sir, someone important is here to pay re- spects." Chandler turned immediately and got up from his bed. He had started smiling before he turned to face Mabry and was still smiling as Mabry made this pronouncement. Chandler unconsciously brushed his hair back and tucked in his shirt to meet Hampton. Through the door stepped Jack Beckham.

Chandler's face went slack. He recovered nicely, however, and said, "Sir, a pleasure." He tried to look cordial to Jack when he said, "Mr. Hampton is gracing us with his presence?"

Jack looked back, a gesture of sarcasm, and eyeballed Chandler with a sneer. "Hellfire, is you expecting a crowd? No, I am here, and Colonel Hampton is to join us. I has much to parley with you as it is."

Chandler tried not to appear shaken with Jack in his presence, this man who clearly had positioned himself, in Chandler's mind, to be his adversary. Jack sat down on the bed, and Chandler remained standing. Mabry crossed his arms and listened as Jack spoke. "We just kilt about a hundred and fifty Tories and ran off some, and some are prisoners of ours. We are 'bout to fight Tarleton and Cornwallis; they has over a thousand, maybe more, and we has almost a thousand. This thing may be settled soon, or we are to be dead or on a prison ship... soon to die I 'spect. Wade Hampton needs your help. Is you understanding me?"

Chandler paled; he shook his head up and down but said nothing.

Jack continued. "I am off to be with General Morgan with as many of us as we can muster. I needs from you, and Wade needs from you, as many of those you know are loyal who are in the great falls of the Catawba. We needs names. We needs to know who ain't.

"We will fetch those who are to be onto our side, and we will hunt the otherns down with Hampton's men outside, and we will do with them as what we allow. Rand will write the names."

Jack picked up a feathered quill and handed it to Mabry, who already had a piece of parchment in his pocket. He sat down at the lone table in the room and looked expectantly at Chandler. Chandler hesitated. "Sir...uh, gentlemen...this is God's will...that only he knows what is in their hearts. How can I judge another man? I have no--"

Jack interrupted him. "I ain't interested in what's in their heart...I is interested in what is in their hands...is it a rifle, a musket, a knife, and who are they loyal to? Shut up this mouthing...gives me names, and I will decide who is loyal and so will Wade Hampton. We ain't asking for you to be no prophet, just give some means so we begin to know...we needs names."

Jack's insistence was enough to make any man lie about what he knew in order to satisfy the man. Chandler stared at the floor. "I can tell you those I have met and names of people's children I have taught. I have a feeling, but am not sure of their allegiance."

Mabry said one word, "Speak."

Chandler said, "The Carlisle's are loyal to the colony. So are the Starnes. So are the Pratts and the Fords. The Cope family and the Kane families are related and appear loyal. The Mathersons and the Nolands and the Glasscocks. So are the Hicklins and Collins near Purity Presbyterian Church. There are the Spratts and the Hayes families, who have been to Charlestowne to the capitol for legal affairs many times, and they are most certainly Whig. They are friends of Governor Rutledge.

All these I am sure, as are the Flanagan and the Long family, as well as the Givens and the Percivals near Little Rocky Creek. There are the Ligons and their children, long time in the area."

Chandler hesitated again. Mabry glared at him, and Chandler purposely avoided eye contact with Jack. All these are from the great falls near Rocky Mount. "I feel the Pinkhams are Tory...they have not long been here from England. The Shakeltons are possibly loyal to the King, as are old Oren Stone and Thomas Rist of Cedar Shoals.

"I am most certain young Louis Sorrow is of the English, as well as George Woods of Rocky Mount. That is all I am sure of. Again I beg you, gentlemen, I cannot judge another man. Please tarry as much as you can with those who may be loyal to the King. I do not want blood on my hands because of my feelings."

Jack looked disappointed. Mabry had been writing and just held up his hand to stop the flow of conversation until he finished the names.

Jack said to Chandler, "Is that enough?"

"It 'tis, sir."

Jack then did something unusual. He asked Mabry to excuse them. He would do this to coerce Chandler into more information and to have just the two of them in the room. Jack got up and stood in front of Chandler, making him look at Jack squarely in the eye. "A big battle, school man, is to happen right soon. I am taking you with me. You will not leave my side. I wants you to tell me if any damnable Tory shows up when we are with Morgan that you knows they is lying. I will deal with them."

"Sir, I beg you, I am frail when it comes to these matters. I am of no use or good to you. I pray to stay and go back to the great falls."

"Nay," Jack said and dismissed him with a flick of his hand.

Chandler looked at him pleadingly, and this apparent weakness made Jack even harder in his resolve. He spoke directly to Chandler of his plans. "You remember that Colonel Harrington, that 'fancy,' and how he allowed I can kill Tarleton?"

"Sir, yes, I do remember. But refresh me, I beseech you, on the exacting of how you intend to dispose of Tarleton."

"I aims to do as the fancy Colonel said. Track Tarleton down and wait until the daylight when he walks among his men and then make waste of him. I will git close enough to do so. When all this is done you are to be gone."

"But, sir, what if Tarleton and his win the day at this battle that is to be? What then?"

"It ain't goin' to be. If'n something does happen to me, then Samuel and others will track him down. Tarleton will die somewhere in this colony. He ain't back to England, I swear it."

Chandler probed more and tried to do so cunningly with a man devoted to covertness. "What if Tarleton gets away? Will you track him from this battle?"

Jack looked impatient. "Try to be of some reasoning, sir. If Tarleton comes to this battle, at least I knows where he is. As of now I don't where he or Cornwallis is. Just allow him to git to my front and I will not lose him!"

Chandler appeared to be tired. He slumped his shoulders. Jack got up to leave, but said as he got to the door, "I am calling you before the night. We will travel after dark."

If all this was not threatening enough to Chandler, he heard Mabry call to Jack from several yards away. "My men say people coming… scouts say it is Mr. Carlisle… and one of his boys. You will want to ask them many things I am sure."

This staggered Chandler. He felt a foreboding, and he looked out the crack of the door to the distance and saw several men riding in from the east. As the Carlisles came into view, Jack and Mabry rode out to meet them. Molly Polly and young John went back to the main house. When the four men met, a tale of murder and woe followed. Jack listened with a growing sense of disbelief. Mr. Carlisle produced the gun and the blood-caked knife. "Jack," he said somberly, "the Wagner men did not have a musket. My family does not have one. Whose would this be 'cept some Britisher or Tory? It was found in the barn in the place where Chandler had been."

They continued to talk. Jack and Mabry asked many questions. They had all dismounted and stood talking about the murders. After an hour of questions, the same questions that the Carlisles had asked themselves many times, the four began to have periods of silence and uncomfortable shifting from one foot to another in the gathering cold day. Jack made a proposal to Mr. Carlisle. "What you are now saying, sir, needs to be said in front of this school person. He owes an answer to you and your family."

All the men mounted and turned their horses to the trip back to Chandler. As they approached, Mabry said to one of the militia, "Fetch the man." He went inside and quickly came out. "Sir, he is not here."

The men rushed inside, and there behind the bed, at the foot of the logs to the cabin, was a trench that had been dug, wide enough for a man of Chandler's size to squeeze through. They looked at each other and then ran through the cabin door to behind the cabin wall. The hole was barely distinguishable from the outside, but Chandler no doubt had escaped. "Coward!" said Mabry.

"Aye," said Mr. Carlisle.

"Maybe," replied Jack. "I hope he is a coward."

"You tracking him, sir?" young Jebual asked.

To their surprise he said, "No. I figures he is a coward and will not do well in this weather. If'n he is more than that, I will git him in my own time…it is a far way to Augusta if'n that is where he is from. 'Sides, Wade is here tomorrow, and we has to report to him, and I has to find Morgan…and, most of all, this butcher, Tarleton. I think Wade Hampton is more important than what we has seen today."

Hampton arrived the next morning and was briefed. Like Jack, he knew the battle in front of them was more important than tracking Chandler. Still, Hampton decided to send two scouts to catch

Chandler on the chance he went toward Grindal Shoals and the gathering of Morgan's men. If he went back toward the great falls, it was of no consequence.

Hampton then told Jack and Mabry what information had been sent to him from General Sumpter via Morgan. The news had been delivered by Hampton's aide de camp, Colonel Drury Harrington. It was overwhelmingly good news that Hampton shared. Hampton smiled as he reported it. "We may have the British outnumbered at this battle to take place." He let this sink in. "We are gathering men in good numbers. Still, we need more.

"We hear that Cornwallis may be delayed with much bad weather, and if this be true, Leslie as well. Then Morgan will want to choose his field carefully and to his own great advantage. So it is of much importance that you move on to be with Morgan and Washington and others. This battle may be to our liking and sooner than we expect."

Jack and Mabry both felt a sense of urgency at Hampton's remarks. Mabry inquired of Jack, "What will you do about the ones Chandler mentioned as Tories? Are we to see them?"

"Nah" Jack growled, and spit a stream of tobacco in disgust. "Chandler is a liar. They may all be Whigs by the time we gets there to Morgan. For sure, they will be if'n they hears about Hammond's Store."

Chapter Nineteen

Battle Near The Boundary: The Cow Pens

Jack and Mabry had to decide who they would have to go toward Morgan. The good news of many Whigs expected to fight for Morgan could diminish in numbers if the battle was put off too long. Jack felt it might happen within days, and he was impatient to get to Morgan. He asked Mabry to stay and have Samuel and others who reported to Mabry to meet him at Morgan's flying camp. The news of Washington's terrible defeat of the Tories at Hammond's Store had to encourage and inspire all Whigs and Washington, who by now would have rejoined Morgan. Jack felt even more eager to finally get to Tarleton, albeit in a major battle.

It was decided that Mabry would await Samuel and others who would come to his farm. They all would go to join Morgan. Both Richard Carlisle and his oldest son, Jebual, volunteered they would go. Jack talked to Elizabeth and gave the impression he would be gone only a short time. John Junior and Molly Polly rode with him a short distance before he left them, but in all respects it seemed he would be only gone a few days.

That evening Samuel arrived at Mabry's. With him were Catawbas Soe, Kutkin, Widubo, Manahe, and Sohane. These men brought their number to nine, including the Carlisles and Mabry. Hampton, however, had one more surprise that he had not shared with Jack. He assigned Colonel Harrington to go with Mabry's men. He wanted Harrington to report back to him as he, Hampton, rejoined General Sumpter. Hampton did this without Jack's knowledge, for he knew the uncomfortable feelings that Jack showed toward Harrington. Still, he needed to know as soon as possible the results of a major battle, and he secretly feared Jack would be killed.

The men then traveled to join Morgan, and somewhere along the way to meet Jack. Washington's troops had been given a predetermined place to meet Morgan, as Morgan retreated. Burr's Mill on Thickety Creek was chosen, and the dragoons made the rendezvous.

Jack sighted men of Washington's cavalry as they rode toward the grand meeting with Morgan, and he joined them. Jack had never seen this many men gathered for the cause for the colony. He could not estimate the number. One scout rode up to him and said, "Sir, I am Henry Isaac Stroth from over the mountains west of the North Carolina colony. How many men are here?" Jack shrugged. Stroth said, "These are men from my territory, sir. We fought Ferguson at King's Mountain." Jack gave him a welcome salute and Stroth then joined the many others like him riding in.

Jack began to ask questions of men about the camp followers, and he was directed to them, now a large gathering of women, slaves, and children that would closely support Morgan's troops, at least until the battle itself was imminent. Jack went through the camp – with all the campfires and cooking and chatter – asking questions. He did this for two hours until he was directed to a woman who knew Arlee McCormick. "She has only been here near a day or two…she has been traveling," the woman told him.

Jack saw Arlee and hailed her. She recognized him, a man with ties to Rocky Creek and Cedar Shoals and the great falls of the river. He walked up to her and asked, "Has you news of Mr. James Noland since Alexander's?" They made small talk, discussing the surprise attack at Alexander's Old Field on June 6 of the last year. Arlee joked that Jack and others had made sure she could not go back home again until all this was over. "You shot most of my neighbors, Jack…they is still mad at me and still looking for you." She laughed, and it would have seemed to be a cordial meeting of acquaintances had it not been such a serious occasion.

Jack changed the tenor of the conversation quickly. "I am supposed to see you here. Wade Hampton has ordered it. You is supposed to tell me news of Tarleton's camp."

"My Lord, Jack! It is you? I was only told someone would ask me the question you just allowed about that devil, Tarleton. I am glad to git this off myself and tell someone else. All these women know not that I have been with Tarleton and all his. I was afraid they would find out and report me as a traitor."

Arlee appeared delighted to have the burden removed. She waggled her index finger as an invitation to talk privately, walked several paces away to a fire with a pot of stew, and invited Jack to sit and eat something. As she sat down across from him, her back to the masses of followers, and with a look of satisfaction on her face she said, "Cornwallis is miles behind Tarleton. He is having trouble traveling and waiting for another Britisher from Charlestowne with many cannon. His men is having some troubles with high streams.

"Tarleton wants to push on. He is traveling as fast as he can, but Morgan is staying ahead. Tarleton will not slow himself. He will drive his horses into the ground, and many of his men is riding two to a horse to make up ground. They is coming."

"How many you 'spect?" Jack asked.

"At least a thousand of his, more if Cornwallis and others join him."

"Damnation," said Jack, looking straight into her face. "How many you think we has?"

Arlee smiled broadly. "I hears fifteen hundred, maybe two thousand. Old Morgan is a fright to these Britishers, only they don't know it. Tarleton don't know it." She laughed a hearty laugh. "What are you to do with this fact?"

"Tell what I learns from you to one of Morgan's officer men soon as I can find them. I am sure Wade has a reason for this. I ain't questioning what it is."

Jack went on his way after finishing the stew to find an officer to report to, but his timing was off. A command was circulated that all men and wagons were moving, and rumors were running rampant. Jack heard Tarleton was close on their heels. He heard Morgan was going to link up with another major force from Maryland and Virginia; he heard Morgan had made a decision where to stand and fight; he heard they were moving to make a stand in the North Carolina colony.

Jack was a small part of this movement and did what made him comfortable as always; he rode Maw to get out of the masses and to the side of the great train. He was not under direct command, and he chose to play the part of a scout. This was his territory. He soon found himself looking at the movement of humanity and horses, and he talked to others in the train who shared information with him. He learned that Morgan had linked up with Washington. He would join with troops from other colonies, including Georgia, North Carolina, Virginia, and Maryland. The only question remaining was where Morgan would choose to engage.

Jack also learned that Morgan was pushing forward and their travel now might be shorter. He prepared to eat in his saddle and not stop except on direct command. He was passing landmarks he knew well from Grindal Shoals and the Pacolet. He also knew they would not fight here. They had passed Duncan Creek, crossed over the Tyger River and Thickety Creek. He guessed they would be traveling directly to the boundary of the North Carolina colony.

He heard from scouts that Morgan was turning west on the Green River Road. This meant he was six miles from the Broad River, and would undoubtedly reach an area known as the Cow Pens. It was a well-known crossing of roads and a large area of primitive pasture land. The field of grass and pea vines had been eaten down by so-called "beeve" cattle that were allowed to forage there before being driven to market on the Carolina coast. The land offered Morgan cattle that could be slaughtered and eaten, as well as provide forage for horses.

The information from Arlee McCormick was proven to be accurate when a scout rode into Jack's view late that day and hailed him to stop. The scout, named Peeples, told Jack that Tarleton was a little more than a day behind Morgan and that he was pressing hard. It appeared that the British Legion had been joined by many Tories, but not Cornwallis. They talked about the truth of this information and agreed it was as close to accurate as they could hope for. It seemed to hold true when they heard soon after that General Morgan was ordering a camp that night. It gave Jack comfort to know that this is where they would fight.

There were many campfires, and Jack circulated among them look-ing for Samuel and all of theirs from the area of the great falls. It was dark and breakfast time on January 17 that he found Samuel and the others who had traveled with him. They were camped with men of the upcountry, the New Acquisition Militia, all who knew the Catawba River and the western area near Mabry's farm. Mabry was talking with several of them as Jack approached Samuel. "Does you recognize where we be, Samuel?"

"Nay, Uncle. Seems to be a lot of land and a lot of men, and I hears the Broad River is behind us."

"Aye," said Jack. "You has never been here, but we are in a pasture land. This is a cow pens herding ground. I has been here twice with old Tom Crim to help him drive beeves to the low country. This is a big place. I thinks old Morgan has picked it pretty good. 'Cept we has no place to go backwards, so I figure we better beat Tarleton or else join him."

Samuel caught the macabre humor in Jack's voice, and he smiled slightly. Jack then went among them shaking hands and greeting Soe and the Catawbas in their fashion. He made an arm grasp greeting to Widubo, his new friend since the baptism of Soe, and he met Catawbas Manahe and Sohane.

Jack was not prepared to see Colonel Harrington, who was sitting at a campfire. Jack came straight to the point when he asked Harrington what he was doing there. Harrington said he was there on direct com-mand of Wade Hampton, and he would fight with the Americans for what was "his colony" as well. Jack asked with disdain, "Can you fire a gun as good as these farmers?"

"No" answered Harrington. "With all respect I feel I may do better than they. I have had the experience of doing so, and I believe I am accomplished."

Jack did not look convinced, and he moved on as Harrington continued to clean and inspect his rifle, a French Charleville .69-caliber musket without a bayonet. It undoubtedly had gone up against the British Brown Bess musket, a .75-caliber. It was Harrington's most used gun and one Jack did not prefer to a rifle.

As Jack walked on, talking and listening to others with Samuel by his side, he saw Soe and the Catawbas; they had prepared themselves for warfare. Soe had one circle of white painted around his eye and one circle of black dye from tree roots around the other eye. All the Indians had feathers hanging from the butt of their rifles, and their tomahawks were clearly honed sharp, their polished metal catching the glimmer of the campfires. Jack also noticed for the first time that Soe wore a holy cross of tin around his neck along with a bear claw.

Jack asked Samuel about his family and was reassured that all was well and that Kit and Johnny were with them. Their father was near the Orangeburgh and was safe, traveling with a contingent of Hammond's. Jack's brother, William, had taken charge of watching after Thomas' family, and at his age of fifty-five was hunting more and spending more time with Kit and Johnny. Jack also asked about Chandler.

"He is not seen," said Samuel. "Many think he has gone back to Augusta…many others think he has gone to a colony to the north. We has no proof he is in any of these places."

Jack continued to walk until he encountered an officer of some rank, a Colonel, and asked where he might give a message that one of Sumpter's men had asked him to deliver. The man smiled and said, "Why not give it to the Old Wagoner?"

"Who might that be?" Jack asked.

"Why, old Daniel…old Morgan…has you not met him?"

"Nay" said Jack.

"Be with me then," he said.

They walked to a group of men, and Jack heard one man talking, imploring others to "fight tomorrow and give me two shots." He was speaking in a friendly way and slapping them on the shoulder as he walked away. "I aims to beat Benny…I ain't lost before and old Morgan will win this one too, boys."

"Hellfire, this is General Morgan," Jack thought, and in a moment he was face to face with the ruddy-faced general.

"Well, sir, here he is," the Colonel said.

"Good" said Morgan. "Son, you have information for me!"

Jack was somewhat taken back and looked at the Colonel, who was smiling at his good fortune in stumbling onto Jack. Apparently Morgan had been looking for men like Jack who had information to be relayed. Jack bowed with courtesy and said "Sir, I have the privilege to be…"

Morgan interrupted and said, "Jack Beckham."

"Aye."

"Thank you for your duty, sir," Morgan commended him. "You are a friend of Sumpter's, Wade Hampton, and a marryin' kin to Colonel William Henderson. You was a help at Alexander's and Blackstock's… and with Colonel Washington a few days ago.

"I hear you knows this area we are in."

"Aye. I do, sir."

"Well then, tell me, Beckham, how long 'fore Tarleton gits here?"

"Pert soon, sir. I figures now he will be onto us in less than one day; that is, if 'n you figures to fight here…he travels faster than most."

"Don't you have a message for me?" asked Morgan.

"I do, sir, and that is Tarleton is traveling with about a thousand men. He is directly behind you. Cornwallis may not git here fast enough because he seems to be dawdling for some reason and 'cause of them streams of high water. Sir, you may have only Tarleton and his to fight because of that."

Morgan looked at Jack with piercing eyes. "Yes, I know all that. Thank you again, sir. You are confirming all I know, and that is what I need. We will indeed fight here. I want you on the first line. I 'spect we will fight 'Benny' fairly soon, and I has a plan for you to fire with my best rifle boys. 'Cept I desire you to fall back to Washington's cavalry, as you can, and be prepared to ride with him."

"What else is there, sir, for me to know?"

"Son, you will fire first with our best boys that can shoot a possum in a tree right twixt his grin, and then my militia boys behind you will fire two times and that is all. They will fall back, and my Continentals in their positions will be in the third line, and they will fire.

"Washington and his Virginia boys will wait until needed and ride into Tarleton's horses. We are picking the ground, and we are picking the fight. The Colonel will tell you where you are to be...and Beckham!"

"Sir?"

"Pick some of them boys you know to fire with you. Jest make sure they can fire just a hair 'slower' than you. We will be just fine, for I hears you are good and straight." Morgan grinned at Jack.

Jack then went back and brought several men to be with him, asking Soe about the two Catawbas, whom Jack did not know. Soe only nodded yes.

Along with Jack and the Catawbas, Samuel, Mabry, and the Carlisles joined a thin jagged line of about one hundred fifty men; they would be the first to encounter Tarleton, firing from behind trees. Most had been shooting rifles for food during their lives, not shooting at men.

As Jack walked forward, he saw Harrington in another group. "It's a fine day to skirmish, is it not?" Harrington cheerfully called to Jack and Samuel.

"It is if you shoot forward," replied Jack. "You should be able to remember what a red coat and a green coat appears to be...you has seen more of them than any of these boys."

Harrington waved his gun high in salute, and this bizarre dialogue between them trailed off as they both prepared to take orders and to receive Tarleton's men. It was still early morning and in the distance Jack heard the haunting sounds of bagpipes and muted drums. The men around him were deathly silent. It stayed this way for minutes as the sound came nearer.

Jack finally hollered out, "Sounds like the birthing of a calf, boys."

Men chuckled and others took up swearing and cussing, and a "hallo" went up. The Colonel came behind his men and yelled, "Patience, boys, and don't holler them to death...aim and be fair in your shots. Hold close until you can see 'em and shoot for them officers."

Jack and others peered down the Green River Road where the British troops were advancing. With such a battle about to take place, no one seemed to notice his own breath blowing wisps into the frigid January air, and as Tarleton continued to advance, the men fell silent.

What appeared first on the Green River Road was Tarleton's Legion. They would ferret out the Americans in front of them and rout them if possible, followed by masses of red coat infantry and artillery. Behind them, waiting ominously was Fraser's tough "give and ask no quarter" Highlanders. All Jack's men knew was that the most hated and talked about enemy was in front of them and they were anxious to shoot.

Jack became calmer as Tarleton advanced. He looked for the British Colonel but could not make him out. He saw other officers and sergeants, and they continued moving closer. He looked down a line of his own men behind trees and caught Soe's eye. The Catawba was beginning to show more anger and resolve in his face as were the others standing with him. Jack casually dropped his rifle down in his hands and adjusted his hat while he called out to no one in particular, "Anyone sees Tarleton?"

Samuel, standing near his uncle, continued to look ahead. Mabry and the Carlisles stood near each other, from time to time lifting their boots and stomping them on the ground in a reflex against the cold. All the men were focused, with their hands on their rifles kneading the butts and fingering the brass trigger guards, purposefully, but not touching the trigger. The green coats came closer and closer, and some shots rang out from somewhere among the Americans; none of Tarleton's men fell.

The militia commanders called again to wait. Over one hundred fifty militia were poised to fire. As Tarleton's green coats came within fifty yards, their expressions clearly visible to the Whigs, the commanders took a deep breath and bellowed the order, "PRIME AND LOAD...MAKE READY...TAKE AIM...FIRE!"

The results were remarkable. It seemed that one-third of Tarleton's Legion dropped. Many were sergeants and higher-ranking officers. Still, the Legion advanced to the command of "PRESENT... AIM...

FIRE!" Jack and all the militia mechanically refilled their pans with black powder, jammed in the lead balls, and cut the linen patches to prepare and fire. Jack and several others fired again and again, bringing down many more men.

It was time to break and run back to the second line. All did so with precision for militia; it appeared that they had rehearsed this maneuver many times. They fell back to Andrew Pickens' line of militia, who fired once, then twice, and then fell back one hundred fifty yards.

The third line – John Eager Howard's Continentals – was next, and they fired on Tarleton's men. Jack ran back toward Maw, who had been left in the company of Washington's cavalry, and mounted her as the dragoons prepared to act on command. Almost as soon as Jack mounted, the command was given, and the dragoons charged into a scattered group of Tarleton's dragoons and took their measure of them.

Tarleton had pursued with all his who were left, and they had been joined by the 71st Highlanders, his magnificent reserves. But the British sensed that the Americans might be finished with their aggressiveness when they saw the Continentals, as well as the militia, begin to leave the field. They charged with blood-thirsty abandon into the Americans at the same time that General Morgan called for his troops to turn and fire. The result of that action was devastating to the British, who never expected a turnabout of such magnitude.

Many Americans then used the fiercest weapon that the British had perfected against them. They charged with bayonets and took lives and wounded several British who were overwhelmed when they realized it was the Americans, not they, that had more numbers and had inflicted more casualties, and who were still attacking. Their position was made worse by a militia that had regrouped, and with Washington's dragoons, having tasted victory in a murderous way at Hammond's Store, were now on top of them with slashing sabers.

Tarleton and his troops were close to being massacred in such a turnabout that Jack and many militia, as well as Continentals, were now fighting with deadly self-assurance in the remaining minutes of a battle that they knew they had already won. They fought with a "joy" of battle knowing that they were defeating an enemy, particularly Tarleton, who was too well-trained to be taken for granted.

They pressed the issue. They attacked standing wounded British Legion. Two of Washington's cavalry hacked to death one Legion dragoon, catching him on each side and severing his arms, then striking him in his head and chest as he fell. One British officer surrendered too late and was struck in the face as he raised his arms and dropped his saber.

Washington's men fought to inflict pain and death, and not defensively. It was a grand and glorious feeling for them to see green coats and red coats on the ground bleeding and dying, and in front of them, the same colors running away. Jack was brought back to a harsh reality when he saw Colonel William Washington himself going against Tarleton and two British officers in a saber duel. An officer had raised his saber against Washington when a young Whig fired a sidearm at the Englishman and ended the fight. Tarleton and his turned away and rode away from the field.

Jack looked around. This battle, with over two thousand, had lasted only an hour. It was a victory that Jack never anticipated. He had never fought with this many men against so many of the enemy and won so decisively. He relished the gore and the accomplishment. He, along with others, scoured the field and counted over three hundred British dead or wounded. More than five hundred British were captured. Morgan had lost only twelve, with some sixty wounded.

This was a great and stunning accomplishment for the colony, and Jack rode Maw fast from man to man to revel in the battle and to look for all his that had been with him. He found them all, and they came together and talked of the battle, slapping others on the back and passing around a bottle of rye whiskey.

Jack had forgotten about killing Tarleton himself, and it occurred to him that Tarleton may have been captured. He sought out officers to see if this was so. He spent much of the early afternoon asking questions and riding to and from pockets of men and officers asking for information.

Jack encountered Harrington, who looked business-like when he

announced that he was leaving to go back to Wade Hampton and report what had happened. He invited Jack to ride with him, but Jack
declined; Jack wanted to meet with several British officers. He per-
suaded and detained Harrington to get his assistance in learning about
Tarleton. The aide-de-camp to Hampton agreed to help obtain the information so that he could report it to Hampton. Together they gained
permission to talk with members of the British Legion and Tarleton's
foot soldiers, but learned nothing. They tried unsuccessfully to inter-
rogate members of Fraser's Highlanders.

Frustrated that no one knew where Tarleton was headed, or if he
had been captured or wounded, Jack asked to speak to a British officer
who had been wounded in his head and his arm with a saber. The officer was being cared for by several camp followers. This officer appeared
to be very young and fresh-faced, a red coat and part of the infantry.
Jack looked for and found Arlee McCormick and asked her to be with
him as they talked to the officer. Jack wanted to bargain with the man.

Jack kneeled down beside the officer and said to him in a frank
voice, softly but matter of fact, "I will git you food from this woman,
and you will be rightly cared for. You needs to have water to live. Some
of you is going to die. Many of you is dead, as it is, and is being buried
in a wolf pit. Does you want to see yourn again? Does you want to
live?"

The man nodded, yes.

Arlee played her part. "Jack, don't kill this man. He is young, he
has much to live for. He don't have to die." She took a canteen and held
his good side up to drink and then gave him a piece of newly cooked
beef sinew to chew on. She rubbed the part of his arm that had been
cut badly and began to refresh the bandage. Jack watched from directly
in front of the man, as if he were skeptical. He then took out his knife
and held it dangling in his hands while he knelt again in front of the
officer--close to his face--and asked again. "You wants to live?"

"Aye, sir, I ask quarter."

"Much as you boys gave quarter at the Waxhaws and to old
Buford?"

"Nay, sir. I was not there."

"I don't rightly know that for a fact, do I?"

"It is my word, sir."

"Don't care…there is over three hundred of you dead and dying. One don't make much more, does it?"

"Sir, I am a Christian. I implore you. I ask for quarter and to be relieved of my duty as I am wounded."

"I train and swap race horses," Jack said, surprising the young man. "I will trade with you. Where is Tarleton, do you allow?"

The man understood. Jack wanted to barter. He thought and said with clarity, "I feel he is looking for General Cornwallis, sir, and that would be to the south and east…toward Turkey Creek. I know he is traveling back down the way he came. The streams are bad, and he will be slowed…that is all I know."

Jack acted forgiving. "You has quarter. I hopes you live and you spare the life of one of ours."

"Thank you, sir."

Jack left and mounted Maw. Harrington, who had been standing by watching, got onto his horse as well. Together they rode back to the camp site to rejoin Samuel. There, Jack took an accounting of who was going back to their homes. Mabry and the Carlisles felt they should be of service if needed, but Jack encouraged them to go home.

"What are you to do, Jack?" asked Mabry. "Elizabeth and all yours are waiting for you. Stay with us as long as you are able to do so."

"Nay," said Jack, "I am trailing Tarleton."

For some reason, the news seemed to shock some of those there. "Why?" asked Mr. Carlisle. "We should be diligent to protect our own now that Tarleton has been beaten as badly as he has. Cornwallis and his will surely not allow us rest. Our homes and our families all are in more jeopardy now than before. We, in fact, need you more now because of this happening here."

Jack again surprised them. "You is right. But we both are right. There is no wrong in this. Tarleton will do more now than he has before. Many of us will be kilt, I fear. But I also has to honor myself to Wade Hampton and see that Tarleton does not make for revenge. We has to protect our families, and we needs to git Tarleton to do that. I am leaving to find him." Jack looked around and said to Soe, "Is you back to the Nation…or are you with me?"

Soe crossed his right arm over his chest and said in English, "Going with you…all going," referring to his fellow Catawbas.

"Samuel, you are back to your home," Jack ordered.

"I choose rather to go with you, sir. The sooner we do, the best it is I can go back."

Jack nodded agreement and began to shake hands good-bye with the Carlisles and Mabry.

"What are we to tell Elizabeth?" Mabry asked.

"Tell her Samuel and me and Soe and his Catawbas are hoping to tell Mr. Tarleton good- bye. But we are back to her sooner if'n he runs to the other colonies." Jack turned to Samuel and said, "We needs more to go with us, so let us see who will that be."

Motioning to Harrington, he said, "Colonel, sir, you are with us as we travel. We are going toward Sumpter and Hampton. Is that agreeable?"

Harrington shook his head a tentative yes. Jack had started to adjust his saddle on Maw and did not see the slight gesture.

Jack and the Catawbas, Samuel, and Harrington then began to make their way into the camp to look for those militia that chose not to be part of Morgan as he started toward the Broad River. Jack was looking for men that were going home. His intent was to talk them out of it.

Chapter Twenty

"Catching" Tarleton

Jack went back to where Arlee McCormick and others prepared to follow Morgan as she and several women tended to the wounded. Without making a sound, he motioned her to join him. She left the pot she was stirring and walked over to listen to Jack.

"How's the Britisher?" he asked.

"Lot o' blood lost, and he is gaining some infection. If you is betting, don't bet on him." She looked tired and resigned to caring for several of the wounded, including this dying man.

Jack said, "I needs your help. I am to be following Tarleton. Can this red coat travel with me? I needs to talk to him as we go. I am going down the river and hoping to catch stragglers or deserters from Tarleton…deserters I reckon I need. But this man can help me find Tarleton. Can he travel?"

"Yes" said Arlee, "at least one mile, and then he is dead." She had given Jack some of his own "medicine," a dose of sarcasm wrapped in the truth. He did not look too surprised at this man's condition.

"I then has another question. Who do you know among them New Acquisition boys is meaner and has not too much to lose?"

She laughed. "Just ask their captain. He is Huel Carter. A leader he is, and he seems to be in every backwoods fight that there has been. He can recruit them boys. He is the only one here who has more fightin' for him when the smoke ends than when it begins. Damn, sir! One fight, he lost six and picked up ten volunteers. Went home with four more than when he started!"

"What backwoods fights?"

"Aw!" she said with feigned consternation, "you ain't never heard of them? I mean backwoods! He and his whupped the Baxter brothers and cousins…Tories all…and all their kin…near the Waxhaws and the Jackson home when they all fought inside a house. Only eight people came out of that house, and there was fifteen that was in there. Huel only had seven when he went in, so I figures one of the Baxter boys decided to join him in the middle of the fight.

"And he and four others kilt three of Bloody Bill Cuningham's scoundrels when they caught 'em in a tavern way up in Charlotte Towne. So, like I say, talk to Carter. I allow he will leave here with more than he brought in."

Jack genuinely laughed, but Arlee turned more serious. "I will ask one thing and I mean right well by it. Don't take me for no fool, you hears me?"

"I figures I owes you anyhow, but remember, I is married."

Arlee let out a belly laugh and said, "You is too scarred up for me and you has the most woman in Elizabeth that I knows. But hear me."

Jack assumed a serious manner.

She said, "I wants to go with you. I was with Mary Gaston and all the women from the Cedar Shoals and the great falls that went to the Presbyterian Church at the Waxhaws. We was there to help Buford's boys. They lost a bad fight. Tarleton's boys just kilt many cause Buford did not have his boys ready. Tarleton's boys don't come to be sociable; they will do as they are told and they ran Buford off and kilt many.

" But there would not have been a fight at the Old Field, where you was at, had there not been such a killing at the Waxhaws. It was bad, I tell you. How bad? I tell you again. They was all laid out in that church and all died. We picked up pails of body pieces…fingers and arms and even heads. Lot of them boys died two days later and some died calling their kin to help them.

"One asked me if I was his ma all the day, and he died late, after it was dark. He was in great pain…not have much of his stomach parts left. They was on the floor, mind you." She looked down and shook her head on remembering. "Know how he died?

"Don't know" said Jack somberly.

"I kilt him. Choked him with bandages. Stuck 'em in his mouth so he can't be breathing, and I pinched his nose shut and he passed." Arlee sat back on the ground, her legs crossed and looked straight at Jack. "I can shoot and ride…I has seen Tarleton's handiwork, if you please."

"Don't have to say more," he said, getting up and stretching, looking almost bored. "We be sorely pleased to have you. You probably knows all these boys anyhow. Let us go find Mr. Carter. I am anxious to shake his hand if he is as mean and bothersome as you allow."

For the third time they had a mutual laugh, and both mounted their horses to look for the New Acquisition militia among the hundreds of men left in the camp. They looked for several minutes and inquired from some Georgia boys who listened and just pointed. Jack and Arlee saw a group of men standing around a fire, and she grunted slightly and nodded her head as they approached. One man recognized her. "Arlee it is. Did you use your iron skillet with Tarleton?"

She ignored him.

"Huel!" she called out to a group of men.

A distinguished-looking big man, over six feet tall, walked out of the crowd and approached them. Jack said under his breath to Arlee, "Hell, he is as strapping and handsome a man as old Morgan had here. Is you sure he is not a gentleman?"

Carter smiled at Arlee, and she motioned to Jack. "Huel, this is Mr. Beckham, who has relatives near you in the Cedar Shoals and the great falls and Rocky Mount.

" I heared of Mr. Beckham," Carter said. "Sir, you is also kin to Abner and Samuel Beckham and Maggie Land too, I figures. All is from near me if you count the miles a little short.

"How is they?"

"Samuel is with me, Abner is with Elijah Clark, and Maggie is dead."

Carter took off his hat at this news, a gesture of courtesy, and said,

"I am most sorrowful. I did not hear. Please accept true feelings of regret."

"You is kind, sir. Arlee says you are a man who don't tolerate fools too well…you also sounds like a gentleman. I thank you again."

At that, Carter bowed to Arlee. She smiled and seemed to enjoy more than anyone this conversation of civility between two men who had distinguished themselves with violence.

Jack continued. "Sir, I am to track down Tarleton and kill him. I would like to enlist you and any of yours to help me. I can offer a bounty and the pleasure of doing this honorable thing for Governor Rutledge.

Carter looked surprised, interested, and tired. Jack pressed him. "How many of yours would join us?"

"Not many, I am afraid," said Carter.

"They are long away from either their family or a tavern. Some have already lost money betting some others of them would be killed here. They is penniless and mad at those that collected this wager."

"Then these are the men that might be interested, sir."

"It may not be so, sir. The men who won the wager are leaving, and the men who lost are tired. The men who are left here might not stay with you for long, just might tire of looking for Tarleton…don't know if you can count on them. They has been fighting not only here, but among themselves and in other places."

"How many you reckon?" Jack asked again.

"Let me parley with them, sir. Be at rest for awhile. I will return directly."

Huel Carter started his round of talks with the men as they stood around the fire. They were warming themselves and preparing to return to their homes. None were going with Morgan, and all felt they had accomplished much with this rout. Some felt the war was over, at least in the upcountry. Others told Carter they wanted to join forces with Francis Marion in the low colony and fight in warmer weather. Jack overheard one man say, "The women is prettier near Georgetowne and the Santee, and there is more taverns." That brought laughter from the group, who had appeared solemn and fatigued.

Then Carter spoke to five men, and they all shook their heads in an affirmative manner and began walking toward Jack. He noticed they all looked similar to Carter in their health, well fed and with some girth, except one. Jack commented, "I wants to be with you boys no matter…seems as if you eats well." They laughed at this remark, and it made for easiness in the conversation.

Carter motioned to them and said, "These boys will listen to what you has to say."

"Pleased I am to meet with you, sir. I am 'Bear' Grant from near the Catawba River."

"Sir," the second man said, "I am Marcus Hall…from the same."

"I be James Simpson, sir, a kin to Reverend William Simpson of Fishing Creek. I understands you and my uncle was at Alexander's Old Field."

Jack smiled as broad a grin as he had in days. He walked up to the man, put his hand on his shoulder, and said merrily, "I knows more about your kin than I wants to know…we has been many places. Is he alive?"

Simpson said "Yes, sir, the last I heard. He cannot go back to his church, but he aims to do so as soon as he can."

Jack grinned. "If you sees him, tell him Soe is still baptized." Jack laughed, and Simpson, out of courtesy, did the same, although he did not know the meaning at all.

"Sir, I am Walker McOwen from the North Carolina colony… Charlotte Towne, it is. I am a long time friend of Captain Carter and much pleased to serve with him."

"Was you at the fight with the Baxter kin in Charlotte Towne?"

Jack's question surprised Walker. He shifted his feet and looked at Carter when he answered, "I was pleased to be there, sir."

"And you, sir?" Jack said to the last man.

"MacKenzie Burton, sir, from the Orangeburgh. I heared about this fight, and I traveled to be part of it. These boys here are some that I fought with at the pasture. I am pleased to be part of them and to hear what you has to say. I has no family now, so I am looking for all this to be finished so I can be farming again."

Jack addressed all the men, including Carter, about his directive from Wade Hampton. He recounted what he knew about Tarleton. He motioned to Arlee, and she told her story of the Waxhaws and Buford's men. Jack told of being chased and the death of John Craig, as well as the battle at Blackstock's. Jack said the battle they had just fought might make Tarleton more "murdering" than he had been. "I figures he owes old Cornwallis more of us strung up on a tree than before…we needs to catch him afore he gets too many men and tries to run us down again."

Hall asked "How much is you paying?"

Jack answered, "Did you lose a bet at the battle?"

"Everything but my horse and what I has on me," he grinned. "Two green-eared boys that can't shoot too well should have been kilt. I thought for sure they would. I should have kilt them myself…would have saved me some coin."

"I will give you gold guineas and more of them if you be the one to kill Tarleton. If he is captured we will take him somewhere that I won't tell you. We will ask Cornwallis how much he is worth to trade back to them."

Grant said incredulously, "You would trade him back? Let Tarleton live?"

"For gold I would. Then I would follow them and try to kill 'em all. I believes in doing the honorable thing and tradin', but after the trade I would kill them, and you could be part of that as well." Jack smiled a hellish grin.

Grant said, looking with questioning, "Let us talk to ours. Huel? By your leave, sir," he said to Jack.

The militia men walked a few paces away and began to talk in a closed circle. Grant said, "This man is as cold and mean as I has seen. I like him right well."

"And that is two I say," said Hall. "He 'pears to be part of the devil that we needs if Tarleton is to be had."

Burton volunteered to say he had heard of Beckham, and everything heard was bad, including killing his own sister who had been with the British.

"Huel? What say you?" asked Simpson.

"Damned good man! He is honest, and he is one of us. I heared much about his blood lettin'…let's throw in with him and find this scoundrel. If'n we miss him, we will all know it. We might catch him, and after a time we are all back to our homes anyhow."

They all walked back to Jack and Arlee. Carter said, "We are of your party."

"Good," said Jack and shook hands with all of them. "We are leaving right soon. I has to care for my horse flesh so I am back to you, and we are leaving to go south. They is fifteen of us. Five Catawbas; my kin, Samuel; Wade Hampton's man, Mr. Harrington; you six; me and Arlee."

Jack spent more time with Maw than he had since he stayed at Mabry's. He groomed her and fed her fresh hay and water and wild oats. He rubbed her face while she ate, and he talked to her. He noticed a raw place on her face from the bridle, and he tenderly applied a mixture of water and oat paste to her sore spot. He checked her thoroughly for cockle burrs and small pebbles in her hooves. He noticed she needed two shoes to be tended to, so he did the work. Then he gathered all the men who had come with him and went to get Carter's men.

All collected, they rode out of the Cow Pens that afternoon, leaving behind a camp breaking down, dead men littering the field, many wounded being cared for, and Morgan moving north with his own men and hundreds of captured British and slaves that had been with Tarleton. Jack secretly marveled at the success of Morgan and all those that had been part of the one-hour crushing defeat of the British. He fumed under his breath that he could not go back to Hampton and report the demise of Tarleton and that he could not yet go back to Elizabeth and his own family. The thoughts of his children kept him company for the first five miles as they rode…the babies, his grown girls, ready for marriage, and Molly Polly and John. He was only brought back to the reality of his trip when he heard Widubo, the lead scout, call back that men were ahead of them. Jack moved quickly ahead on Maw to see for himself.

Widubo pointed Jack, Soe, and Samuel to the site where he had spotted the men. Behind a clump of trees they observed these men sitting around a small fire beside a swollen stream. They were four stragglers, red coats trying to catch up with Tarleton's men, with only three horses. Jack saw that the horses were some fifty yards away from the fire, grazing while the men huddled under a tree for protection from the wind.

"Hanaure," said Soe. "We shall go." He and Widubo would cut the horses off from the stragglers, and Jack and Samuel would ride straight into the men. They would be unable to get to their horses, and they would either run or try to stand and fight. At a signal, the Catawbas raced toward the horses, and Jack and Samuel rode just as hard at the British. Soe and Widubo were between the men and their mounts before they could grasp what was happening. When they looked up, they saw more men racing toward them and saw the futility of their situation. All four of the soldiers raised their hands in defeat. One had the presence to grab a white cloth from the ground and wave it in surrender. They all called for "quarter."

"Be down," Jack hollered at them, and they all sat down by the fire with their hands still raised. Soe and Widubo jumped off their horses and stood menacingly close to them with tomahawks in hand. The men were stunned with fright. All seemed to be very young and inexperienced.

Jack began to talk while the Catawbas circled them, looking as hostile and predatory as the men may have feared in their worst nightmares about "savages." Jack said, "We is not going to kill you 'less you try to hurt us."

One soldier with trembling voice said, "God bless you, sir."

"We only wants to know where Tarleton is."

"We know not," said one of the men.

"Has you not seen anyone?' Jack asked angrily.

"Nay," said another soldier.

The first soldier answered, "Only one man traveling by himself. He said he was back to the Georgia colony...that he was a schoolmaster, and he was afraid of war...that is all."

Jack looked at Samuel. "Quick! Get that Harrington here."

Samuel rode back and met the others as they were riding forward to join Jack around the stragglers. Jack motioned for Harrington to join them and to ask the British about this man they had seen. Harrington surprised them with his English accent, but it seemed to put them at ease. They all conversed with him as Jack listened. Harrington asked them to describe this man. He asked them questions about their travel, what they had done at Cow Pens, and where they thought Tarleton might be.

In the course of the conversation, he assured them they would not be harmed, and one man did brighten and say the schoolmaster told him he was trying to get to the fort at Ninety-Six. The same man said Tarleton would have to be traveling down the streams to rejoin Cornwallis, who was last reported on the other side of the Broad River and the rock hills south of Charlotte Towne.

This told Jack much. Cornwallis might indeed want to be moving toward Charlotte Towne, but he and Tarleton could decide to retreat back to Winnsboro if they joined together. If Leslie joined Tarleton they could still have a large force in the South Carolina colony and at Winnsboro. What they did as an army depended on where Morgan was going. Jack thought that if this man was Chandler, as described, he might feel more comfortable with the British; he also might have been guilty of what was suspected of him, the murder near the Carlisle's.

Jack had a hard time believing Chandler was as dangerous as might be suspected. He still thought of him as a weakling and a coward. But he would track in the direction of Ninety-Six to overtake Chandler until he found differently and could determine Tarleton's location.

The men left four grateful British infantrymen, but without their horses. Jack said, "Let 'em walk." They would take their horses with them a long way before turning them loose and taking anything of use from their saddles. The fifteen traveled and saw bands of stragglers, but they simply went around them. Each time, however, they perused the men, some who were walking with no weapons; others were wounded and riding. This was a beaten string of men, and Jack scanned them to see someone who looked to be Chandler.

Jack and the men camped for the night in a spot that was well known to him. They picked an area near a shoals on the off-chance that men and horses trying to cross in the night would alarm them. As always, they took turns through the night as sentries. At daylight, they began riding again, noticing that the water had not frozen in the night. Without rain, they had the best chance to catch Tarleton, who had to cross still swollen streams with many men.

Tarleton had abandoned his cannons at Cow Pens and was traveling as light and as fast as he could. His infantry would lag behind, and this would interrupt Jack's forces if they tried to go through them. Jack's plan was to sight Tarleton from a distance, circle around any British infantry, and attack under moonlight. Then they would all divide into small groups and ride away. All was planned, but they needed to find "Benny," as Morgan had called him before Cow Pens.

The Whigs under Jack and Carter crossed the Pacolet and progressed down toward the Broad River, where the river flowed from Ninety-Six to the Camden district. Jack felt certain they might catch Tarleton before he reached Cornwallis, probably camped beside a major stream that would be treacherous or impassable at night. He asked Harrington to come alongside him as they rode.

As a scout and a spy Jack's greatest job was to catch Tarleton, but he wanted to find Chandler as well. He summoned Samuel, and they all three rode together. Jack asked Harrington if he knew where Wade Hampton was under Sumpter. Harrington gave an irritating answer.

"We are predisposed to meet at a certain place and time, sir. I feel I might not say where, as per Hampton's request. But I have time to be with your train before I leave. Is that to your liking?"

Jack's face said it was not. "I wants you to go toward the lower Ninety-Six. Take Samuel with you. If you see this Chandler as you travel, you go to him, and Samuel comes back to me and tells me where. I will tell Samuel where we hopes to be as we search for Tarleton. He will get back to me by the by. If it is likely that I can, I will come for this school man. I do not see you after you leave here… you journey on to Hampton…wherever he be,"

"Are you to think Chandler will trust me?" asked Harrington.

"Try and make him. You is both met…tell him you favors the

British and you has changed your mind. How many days does you have before you goes to Wade?"

Harrington pondered. "Two," he said.

"Be gone then. Samuel ?"

"I understand, sir."

Jack and the others took a turn at that point and moved directly east. Harrington moved on toward the fort at Ninety-Six. Samuel said to the Colonel as they rode, "Sir, we have to be as fast and quiet as possible I am sure…I reckon we do not want this man to see us first."

After a full day of travel, Jack was fortunate. What he hoped for happened.

He was looking for men coming toward him, or traveling to the west, not south or east, which were routes for Tarleton, and he was looking for men that were obviously British soldiers. He was not looking for Tories, although he felt bands of them would seek revenge once hearing of the total defeat at the Cow Pens. Most of all, he looked to avoid Bloody Bill Cuningham. He would try and kill him and his kind another day.

Jack saw two men on horses approaching. He gathered all his, and they rode hard and thundering into the two men, Soe and the Catawbas leading. They made for a terrifying sight, and the British, who were deserters, did not know if Jack and his were Loyalists or Whigs.

Jack decided again to play another deadly game of pretense. As they approached he yelled, "British! We are looking for rebels. Where is you from? Has you seen any?"

The men looked haggard. "Sir" one said, "we are finished with this war…we…"

"Makes no mind," said Jack. "We are of Cuningham's men…we are to help Tarleton and any others after the bloody fight at the Cow Pens. We are looking to engage and help."

Jack reached back for water and for hard bread to give the red coats. He patted one man on the shoulder as he gave it to him. The other companion eyed the Catawbas warily and Jack said, "They are friendly to the King. How are we to help you? Do you know where you is going?"

"Sir, we do not. We are looking for Loyalists that will hide us and help us to get back to Charlestowne along the way. We have lost much, and we are not soldiers. I am a tailor and my friend is a merchant of wares. We were both impressed, and we have been in the colonies…it is almost two years. We want to be back to England."

"You are among friends, as it is," Jack lied. "We can tell you a place to ride to. Where is your major force? We needs to join them, as we fear they needs guides and men with weapons."

Both men looked at each other. One said, "Sir, we are not traitors… we are tired and we respect our Colonel Tarleton. We would not want you to say of these things we have told you."

Jack sensed a barter. "I will nay tell him nothing. We are tired too, and if Tarleton loses again we will not easily come out of our homes to help. We will keep our word with you as friend of the English and you on your English honor." At that Jack reached out to shake their hands.

One volunteered, "We think the Colonel is trying to cross at streams that are high, and he threatens to shoot any that do not cross on his orders. This is another reason for our leave. Men may be drowned trying to escape. We last heard he would try to cross on Fannen Creek, near a shoals there. But water is too high, and the shoals are not seen well. He could well try at another creek."

"How long is this you are gone?" Huel Carter asked.

"We are gone one full day and night, sir."

Jack said, "Go three miles to the west and look for cabins on Lawson Fork. All them are loyal to the King. Tell them Cuningham's men sent you."

The men looked dazed but thankful.

Jack turned to leave, and spoke quietly to Carter. "We is ahead of Tarleton…hellfire, we is out- running him. He either has many men and is slowed or he is stopped many times by water. We has to double back."

They later crossed Mill Creek to continue their search. At the same time, on the way to Ninety-Six, Samuel and Drury Harrington were being hailed at a distance by a lone man who did not recognize them. He looked to be desperate and with a lame horse. He was walking the horse, that was in pain and going very slowly. Harrington turned to Samuel. "Look! Can this be? Look! That man appears to be Chandler."

Harrington took his eye glass and sighted the man, who was over a hundred yards away. "It is! By ancient gods, this is a wonder," said Harrington, "Where were you to meet Jack Beckham?"

"On the Broad River...way above the Tyger on the side where there is Lynch's Tavern. The man there is a friend of Jack's...his name is Nelson. He was to tell Mr. Nelson where he would be if'n he left there. I was to meet Jack there at the early dark time tomorrow and if not, then the next day. After that I am to meet him at Mabry's farm when I can."

All the time Samuel was talking, Harrington was looking ahead at the approaching man. "SAMUEL! I think it is him! Be gone back through the woods. I will bring Chandler with me to Lynch's Tavern as a friend."

Samuel turned and melted away, unseen by Chandler. Harrington then spurred his horse. "Hail, sir!" Chandler said. Harrington did not answer but continued riding...he did pull his hat down to not be recognized at a distance. As they met, the smiling Chandler, looking unkempt, stopped dead in his tracks when Harrington reached him.

"Sir! It is you...Colonel Harrington! Sir, I did not expect to see a friend. Why are you here?"

"Indeed," said Harrington, "why are you here? Are you not still a master for schooling at one of the homes near the Catawba?"

"Yes, I have been and as of late. But I am on my way back to my family in the Georgia colony. I am not of this war, and my students are distracted...nothing can be learned until this is over. Sir...tell me...are you still with the Whigs?"

Harrington's mind raced. He now suspected Chandler to a great degree, but the man seemed to be such a mystery. He replied off-handedly. "I feel I am for the right...and a peace for both sides. I am restless that all be settled so I can make a permanent place here, possibly in the Georgia colony. Tell me, sir, is Augusta a livable place?"

"Oh, there is no doubt...however much warmth in the summer...

but the winter is mild as Savannah and Charlestowne. You might try the interior of the colony."

"It would be a pleasure if you were there."

Chandler looked uncomfortable and confused as Harrington continued. "You asked why I am here. I am seeking to get away from the warring...I am not attached to Mr. Hampton or anyone at the moment. I was in fact traveling to see friends in the lower Ninety-Six, but I think I am inclined to go back toward the coast. You spoke of Charlestowne...I feel as if I can still be a citizen there as I have not declared myself formally against the colony. I certainly do have friends there. What say you? Would you care to travel to the east?"

Harrington knew the answer even as the question was asked. He was probing Chandler. Chandler was in flight to get to the post at Ninety-Six. But Harrington wanted to hear it and confirm it, then devise his plans to deliver him to Jack Beckham or to Mabry's, and then make him face whatever legal hearing there might be concerning the murders discovered by the Carlisles.

He started to walk his horse and suggested to Chandler that they buy a mount from the nearest neighbor, or ride two on Harrington's horse until they found a cabin. To his surprise, he heard Chandler say, "It would be my pleasure to travel to the coast! Certainly! We can talk of literary things. I have Shakespeare in my possession. Do you know Anne Bradstreet? I dare say she may be the poet of greatest comfort when I am alone."

Going along with this unusual and unexpected turn of events, Harrington said, "What is your favorite then?"

"Oh that would be the essays of Locke. I read them often. I find them thought-provoking, more intellectual than poetry, for it is more instructional."

Chandler stopped and rummaged through a set of papers and brought out a sheaf that looked worn. Out of the same haversack he brought out a knife and seemed to absentmindedly put the knife in his belt. He did not look up as he did this. He was smiling and talking to himself, seeming to be intent on producing something to read to

Harrington. He wanted to read some works, and he had found a "pupil" in Harrington.

"Ah, here it is." He almost gleefully thumbed through the pages and had the satisfied look of an instructor about to give a lecture. Harrington thought, "this man is certainly a teacher...he enjoys his work." Harrington motioned for them to travel while Chandler found the essay he was looking for, and they began to walk their horses.

Chandler began, "This is an essay named 'Of the Division of the Sciences.' Chandler held the book tightly to his waist, his hands almost resting on the knife handle, looking straight down to better read while he walked. "Science may be divided into three sorts. All that can fall within the compass of human understanding, being either. First the nature of things, as they are in themselves. Their relationships and their manner of operation: or secondly..."

Chandler looked intently at the page and only glanced up to see the path they were taking. He read on as Harrington seemed to be interested. In truth, Harrington began to relish the tranquility of the moment. They were two men in a winter forest, one with a healthy horse, another with a lame one, talking of philosophy. They were entertaining beautiful words in the middle of a war that had seen unspeakable death and violence. Harrington's mind began to wander even more. Chandler had a melodious voice; undoubtedly he was used to talking to children of all ages and capturing their attention.

Harrington was enjoying the reading, so much so that he turned to nod with appreciation at Chandler. As he turned, he was dumbstruck. Chandler had his ten-inch knife out of his belt and in his right hand; his eyes were wide with hatred, his lips curled up in a grotesque sneer, and his teeth were bared. He was coiled, about to strike Harrington, but he had not changed his voice as he said, "It is aptly enough termed also logic...the business whereof..."

Harrington did not think, but acted. He grabbed Chandler's arm and stumbled backwards. Chandler was now cursing and sweating. He called Harrington a traitor and swung wildly. Harrington was knocked even farther back by the force of Chandler, who set upon him with unusual force for such a slight man. Harrington looked down and saw that his frock had been cut, but he did not have time to assess if he was injured. He had to ward off a mad man that had gone from reading poetry to being inches from killing him.

Harrington heard a voice. It was a man hollering, "Hold!" It came like lightning from the woods behind him. He heard the man scream this time, "HOLD or I will kill you!" He dared not turn and look while Chandler was so close and so possessed.

Chandler suddenly said, "Samuel!" His voice was accommodating and soothing. It sounded as if he were talking to Samuel as a student. Harrington glanced quickly over his shoulder and then back to Chandler, who was still smiling at Samuel even as he held the knife he would use against Harrington.

As Samuel came closer, he said to Chandler, "Let loose the knife."

"Samuel," Chandler cooed, as he placed the knife on the ground at his feet and motioned toward Harrington. "This man is a spy for the British. He has caused much death to be done. He has been waiting to kill others...and your uncle. He is responsible for your aunt's death. He only pretends to be with Wade Hampton. I know this to be a fact...I..."

"End this talk," Samuel said.

"My Uncle Jack has never trusted Mr. Harrington, and he always thought him to be a traitor to both sides."

"Yes," said Chandler in quick agreement trying to woo Samuel, "he is insightful, your uncle..."

"But he will know better, sir. You are a liar and a traitor and not to be trusted."

"Samuel, I..."

"Enough of this tripe. You are a fool, and you have taken the wrong side. Colonel, bind this man with what you have...we will take him back to Jack and the others."

At Samuel's words about Jack, Chandler's expression changed dramatically. His face clouded, and his eyes were filled with hatred.

"My God," said Harrington, "look at this man. This person is mad.

I have never seen the likes of two people in one person's body. Sir," he said, looking at Chandler, "you are an evil spirit."

Chandler screwed up his face as if to say something, but he spat in Harrington's face and moved menacingly toward him before Samuel stepped between them. With his rifle fully extended, he jabbed it straight into Chandler's forehead. The end of the rifle barrel snapped Chandler's head back. As he was falling back, Harrington grabbed him and held his shoulders down on the ground. Samuel dropped his rifle and pulled his own knife out and placed it hard against Chandler's throat.

But Chandler resisted, and Samuel's knife dropped dangerously close to him. For a brief time they wrestled him and hit Chandler, looking for submission, until Harrington struck him with such force with his fist in Chandler's nose that it stunned him. Samuel grabbed his rifle and stood up and placed it in Chandler's face, against his jaw. He pressed down hard and, enraged, said, "Is this your day to go to hell, sir?"

Chandler's eyes "cleared" for a moment. Harrington grabbed his hands and forced them behind him, as Samuel placed his booted foot against his neck and dared him to move. The schoolteacher heard the cock of the rifle and knew he could be killed by this young man. He did not resist while Harrington tied his hands with the raw hide from his own powder horn, cutting it loose and using all the string to bind him.

Harrington, ever the gentleman, asked Samuel as he held Chandler down, "Did your uncle truly think me a spy?"

"Indeed he did, sir. He almost convinced Hampton and Mabry of the same. I think this man on the ground, this lying dog, has just saved your life. My uncle will believe you now."

"Then let's find your uncle; I am anxious to be vindicated. But why did you not leave? Why were you in the woods? Thank our Lord that you were."

"As I said, sir. My uncle thought you might be against us. I'm afraid I did not trust you. I stayed to see you and this man together."

Harrington mulled this over and the turn of events that had just happened. The three started back toward the place to rendezvous with Jack. They traveled with Chandler's hands tied and a rope to his waist, walking behind the two men on horseback. They traveled this way until they bought a horse from an accommodating Whig, who marveled at the sight of a man being bound and made to walk. They reached the tavern after hours of travel and met Nelson, who greeted them warmly. "You are young Samuel! Welcome, and who are these gentlemen?"

"One gentleman, sir, and one scoundrel."

Harrington made his greeting to Nelson and put Chandler in a small room. He tied him to a beam of wood that traversed the ceiling. Chandler would have to stand the entire time as the rope held him up by the waist, his hands still tied behind him. "Looks like a place to hang a man," Harrington said. "Do you agree, sir?"

Chandler looked sullen and did not answer. They had to wait only three hours until Jack and Huel Carter arrived with all those that had started with them. They were hungry and looking to eat at the tavern as Samuel and Drury Harrington told Jack the story about Chandler. Jack's eyes blazed.

Samuel did not fear for Chandler; he was beyond that. He just wondered how Jack was to kill him. Jack went into the room with Chandler, walked up to him, and stood three feet away with hands on hips. "You kill them brothers near the Carlisles?" Chandler did not answer. Jack said almost in a gracious manner for such an occasion, "You a spy?" Still no answer.

Jack, even in times like this, bargained. "You wants to be hanged here or back at the place where you was a teacher? We can gets a bigger crowd there. Why don'ts I just cut you loose and close that door? Why don'ts I leave all my weapons outside and we fights with our bare hands till one is dead? That is what we will do."

Jack began to cut the rope from Chandler, and at the same time rip at Chandler's clothes. Chandler had always felt he was in the presence of a madman with Jack, and this time he was truly frightened. "Nay," he cried. "Wait, sir, let me go back and be accountable. I will present my case. I am not guilty. I beg to go back and face my accusers."

Jack glowered at him and then hog-tied him with a rope; to it he attached another rope, which he threw up and over the ceiling beam. Chandler would choke to death if he struggled to break free.

As Jack and the other fourteen who were traveling to find Tarleton were filling up the main tavern room, a rider came into the yard; he was recognized by Mr. Nelson. The man was alone and out of breath. "Sir!" he panted, talking to Nelson. "I has just seen the British. They is the most I has seen. They are fording the Broad River near Bullock's Creek on Hamilton Ford. It is Tarleton himself."

"Has you not heard, sir?" Mr. Nelson said. "Tarleton and all his has been beaten badly at the Cow Pens, twenty-five miles away from Hamilton's Ford. They is riding away, not to us. How many were there?"

"Too many to count, sir…I am too much afraid. I thought for sure they were looking for Whigs. I feared for me and mine."

Jack and Huel Carter were standing nearby with Burton, Grant, and Hall, and they all rushed to hear the message again. They questioned the man, and he repeated his story.

"Damnation," said Jack with delight in his voice. "We has him!"

"How far and how long has you traveled to be here?" asked Grant.

"Two hours, sir, at the outside. He may have forded by now and is moving."

Jack called to Samuel and told him to have Harrington bring Chandler and to guard him. "Tie him to his horse…if he runs, just kill him…we has little time now." Chandler heard all this and watched big-eyed as he was cut down and taken to his horse. Only his legs were untied; then a rope was placed around his waist and tied with his hands to his saddle pommel.

That night, Jack and the Cow Pens victors watched across the Broad River as the campfires of the British Legion burned. Jack asked those around him how many men they reckoned were there. They could not estimate, and there seemed to be too many to count. Samuel said, "There may be more stragglers coming in and joining Tarleton across this ford, so we might be seen."

"For sure we has no fire ourselves," Carter said with resignation.

"We has to get closer," Jack said.

"We can best get Tarleton as he walks around tomorrow morning, and he may leave right early."

Harrington replied, "'Tis true. He has been known to force march at two in the morning."

Jack stared into the distance at the flames dancing in the fires and wished to not only be closer but warmer. He dismissed the thought. "We are crossing now," he said , "but we has to watch for pickets."

Harrington offered, "His sentries are close to the camp but he will send out scouts in all directions during the night. That is what we look for, and we have to avoid them."

Jack motioned for all to get ready to cross, and he said to Samuel, "Tie Chandler's mouth."

The fifteen crossed the river and took up their places overlooking Tarleton. He had camped on a hill on the other side, leaving a valley between them. It was certain that, being in flight, Tarleton would have sentries riding and walking the camp perimeter. The only way to get to them would be in the early hours, when guards might be tired from a night watch.

Jack went behind his group and tended to Maw. He kept her at some distance with the other horses and where Chandler lay, tied to a tree with a Catawba guarding him. After caring for her, Jack went back to the front to join Samuel and others as they carefully watched Tarleton's men in camp. Huel Carter approached Jack, and they exchanged thoughts. Carter said, "Tarleton is going as fast as he can to get to Cornwallis. He will leave early. We heard from some of his who was captured that they were greatly tired when they got to the Cow Pens. They were marching and riding straight on for days to catch Morgan. And they left at two hours after midnight, as it was, to ride into Morgan on the morning of the fight. I figures he will do the same here."

Jack nodded in agreement. "I has to git much closer, and I am leaving now. I hope he is the only one walking around afore they travels. I will shoot that person and be hoping it is him."

Jack crawled forward after he had walked some distance toward the Legion. By prearrangement, Carter and the New Acquisition moved closer as he went forward. Kutkin stayed with the horses until the men moved up, and then he joined them. Chandler was left tied and by himself.

Jack watched the campfires; he would be able to judge when they would leave by the flames. They would not put new wood on the fires in anticipation of leaving soon. He estimated that the men would be here at least three more hours. He then edged farther in the grass and began to look in earnest for the scouts riding outside the camp.

He saw two that were riding toward him, and then they turned to complete a circle around the camp. Jack moved in even farther and saw that two other scouts came from the other direction, crossing the first two but circling away from him. He watched for standing pickets and for those walking the camp edge. The fires still burned high, and he began to think they might stay until daybreak. This was not what he wanted. He did not want to give Tarleton daylight; he needed to make his shot and escape through dark. All the rest of the men and Arlee would ride after his rifle had fired.

More time passed, and he saw that fires were burning down. The cold in the early morning was particularly chilling, and Jack looked at his rifle often to see if dew was misting the pan. He wiped it constantly and repeatedly touched the barrel to feel for moisture, which told him to check the pan and touch hole, the frizzen, and the cock again. As time passed, Jack became more attentive and on edge. He noticed that the sentries had slowed their walks, and the men on horseback were cutting their circles closer to the camp, no doubt to make their tour faster. He looked back to see if he could still see his own men. All were out of sight.

Jack turned back to the British and saw a figure moving. It was a figure that went to one spot and stayed there on a horse. From what he had seen of Tarleton on two occasions, this was him, but he was not moving. He looked through his spy glass in the dark; it was no doubt an officer, and it appeared to be Tarleton.

Had Jack known what had happened that early morning he would have abandoned his position. Two hours before, Elberton Chandler, working frantically on his bound arms and wrists, the rawhide old from long use, had managed to get free. The Catawba guard had joined the others to fight or watch Jack's shot. Chandler had circled the British camp and was now inside.

Jack waited longer. This was a dilemma. Should he shoot in the dark? Should he wait until the camp began to break up? Should he follow them and wait until another day? All his hunter's instincts told him to be more cautious. He waited still longer. Then it occurred to him that this might be his last shot at Tarleton. Better to chance it now than to find out later it had been his best chance...one that was lost.

He looked back to Huel Carter and raised his hand in the gaining light in hopes Carter could see it. Carter, the closest to Jack, did see and whispered back to Grant, who then told it to Burton several yards back, and Simpson who passed it to Hall and the rest of the assembled. "Jack is going to fire." They were ready. Jack raised his rifle – clean and with new powder – sighted Tarleton's head and dropped down to hit his chest, to be sure of the shot. He fired.

It was a clean shot at some seventy yards. The figure drooped and seemed ready to slide off the horse. Jack calmly prepared another shot, counting on the panic and confusion that would follow. He would not have time. Much to his great alarm and disbelief, men on horseback seemed to come alive at Jack's right side and to his left flank. Men were moving fast toward him on both sides.

It appeared to be twenty to thirty men on each side, and they all were apparently armed and ready. They had reacted within a minute of his shot. Jack stood up now. Stealth was lost, and he hollered back to Carter and the militia to fall back to their horses. He ran to get Maw as Tarleton's men closed extremely fast. They were strung several yards apart, hoping to envelope Jack and all his, and they were doing so.

As Jack ran he saw Samuel leading Maw toward him, holding her reins and riding his own horse. Soe was beside him on Sula. All the New Acquisition boys and Arlee were running to begin mounting. Out of the corner of his eyes he saw, to the left and right sides, Tarleton's men closing fast. Jack knew he could not ride out. He also saw it was later than he thought. Daylight was breaking. He called, "Form and fire together... one time!"

Carter and his men, and Soe and the Catawbas, jumped off their horses as they all came together at once and knelt in the grass, side by side, and fired with one great volley. They fired at the closest right flank of the dragoons with much effectiveness. Six British went down at once, and two horses stumbled under the shock of the barrage. Reloading quickly to fire back to their left, Jack saw Maw, Sula, and Samuel's horse all bolt back to the horses that were milling around in the confusion.

As Maw started she was shot in her midsection and her legs in a crossfire between the two groups of fast closing dragoons. She went down on a leg that was shattered and almost in two. Jack's heart seemed to stop at the sight of the great horse down. His worst thoughts about her were about to be realized. She was in great pain. The sounds from her were excruciating. He was driven to call out, "KILL THE HORSE! KILL MY HORSE!!"

Grant, Hall, and Carter rose out of their positions. They stood, full up out of the grass, to aim at the stricken horse. When they fired and shot Maw, all the shots were accurate and any one would have done fatal damage. They suffered for their actions. They were shot point blank by dragoons who had closed to almost on top of them. As they were hit, six more of Tarleton's finest closed on them; with sabers high and flashing from atop their horses, they cut downward ferociously. Grant, in dying, pulled from his belt a sidearm and fired it before a dragoon reached him, killing the man who fell headlong into all three of them.

Hall and McOwen never saw the eight dragoons behind them that cut with their sabers without mercy and without breaking stride. Both died without turning around, but pitched forward under the weight of more than one saber striking them. Firing from her position as she calmly loaded three shots and got them off, Arlee was shot by several dragoons firing their carbines at her lone figure. She died quickly.

Soe and the Catawbas reached their horses before any of the Whigs, and they rode back directly into the fight and tomahawked every man they met. They were lashing out with abandon until the first group of dragoons from the right regrouped and fired at them. It seemed that all at once Kutkin, Manahe, and Sohane were shot. Kutkin clung to his horse, struggling to stay on, while Manahe and Sohane were on the ground. Widubo was also shot in his stomach, and he held the wound with one hand as he swung his tomahawk at two dragoons.

At this point, Jack's Whigs had been reduced to seven. He, Soe, Samuel, Harrington, Simpson, and Burton were not yet wounded. But Widubo was barely alive facing over twenty dragoons and more that were about to reach them. In all, over fifty dragoons were about to descend on them and they planned no quarter. Jack and his were bunched together. This was their worst position to invite all the dragoons to ride to them and butcher them.

Jack called out in all the maelstrom and death around him, "Fire at them to our rear. Run to any horses."

They seemed to fire together, and they cleared out a group that was riding toward them. Jack and the others without horses now ran as hard as they could to get to any horse and try to get away. It was not likely. As they reached the confused horses Jack mounted the first he saw as did others, except Soe and Widubo who were already mounted. They all broke for the river with the dragoons chasing them, thirty to forty yards behind, holding their sabers high.

The only chance they had to leave alive was playing out. They were able to get some critical distance between themselves and the dragoons and to plunge directly into the cold water of the river before Tarleton's men caught up. They went straight in, and their horses stayed up. The animals plunged in and, high-stepping, made their way to the other side.

They were followed closely by the dragoons, who also forced their mounts into the water. But they hit holes in the river bed, and several horses stumbled and threw dragoons off. Jack and Harrington got to the other side before the others. Jack was cussing from frustration. He took his rifle from high on his back and reloaded. Harrington followed. Jack shot at the first man trying to cross and killed him immediately. Harrington did the same to another. As Burton, Samuel, Soe, and the stricken Widubo reached the bank, Jack hollered out to Harrington, "We has a chance to load and fire. We can'ts outrun them."

So these two men loaded and fired. They did again, mechanically and coolly. There would eventually be a flash in the pan after so many firings, but they kept at it. Each time they fired, a dragoon was wounded or killed. The water slowed the British. One by one, as they dared to cross the river, Jack and his men all fired their rifles – deadly at this range. Widubo was hanging on his horse in shock, his eyes glassy, but on their side of the river.

The dragoons' carbines would not reach, and the toll began to mount, even though other dragoons joined on the other side and threatened to cross the river. Jack and his men now rode to try their best to get away. But at this interval more dragoons went in the water to try and reach them. Jack took a position on a higher rock and cleaned the touch hole in his rifle. As methodically as he ever had, he filled the pan and fired. He did this again, seemingly to dare them to cross. Then several British made it past a point that none had been able to reach. Jack fired his last shot, and a man grabbed his leg in pain. As he fired, Soe, Samuel, and others mounted their horses and fired at will.

Jack jumped back on his horse and rode away, following them. They rode to escape, but Tarleton's men pursued. As the Whigs rode they made up distance, and then Jack hollered, "Be for yourself," and they all split and rode in different directions. On three occasions, Jack stopped and shot at men of Tarleton's Legion as they came distantly within his range. Soon, none followed in his sight.

Back at the bloody remains of the battle, a man walked among those Whigs who were dead and did so with a wicked smile. He kicked the bodies of the fallen Catawbas, Carter, Grant, and Hall. He scoffed at Arlee McCormick, her long blood-matted hair now revealing her womanhood. Elberton Chandler was about to join the British Legion on their flight. He would be thanked by Tarleton himself for warning him about Jack's early morning sniper shot. The cloth stuffed "straw man" with the gourd for a head lay mockingly on the ground with Jack's rifle ball embedded in the stuffing.

Tarleton was still alive.

Chapter Twenty One

Back To Grindal Shoals

Jack rode to get back to Mabry's. He could not help but try to rehash what had happened. What had gone wrong? He mentally checked off what he did not know. Where was Chandler? Probably released by the British to go back to his colony. Was Chandler riding due south to Augusta? He was not worth chasing.

Maw's remains would be picked clean by wild animals. Soe would want to bring the dead Catawbas home and might go back. Would the British bury Carter's men and Arlee? Jack had prearranged a meeting with Samuel at Mabry's, but Samuel might go back to his home if Jack delayed.

Harrington knew where Hampton and Sumpter were supposed to be, but the defeat at Cow Pens could dramatically alter Sumpter's plans if he could engage Cornwallis. It was certain that Morgan was off to the North Carolina colony, but if Sumpter and Morgan combined they might hurt Cornwallis. Burton, Jack assumed, was back to the Orangeburgh district.

As Jack weaved his way to Mabry's, he remained alert for remnants of British stragglers and deserters from the Cow Pens. He and any Whigs would be a choice target for irate Tories in bands. Would "Bloody Bill" come east and look for those known to be at the Cow Pens? For the first time in his memory, he wondered if Mabry's plantation would not be a target for an attack by an organized group of Tories.

Jack constantly looked for Samuel and Soe. He did not look for Harrington, who might have gone back another way, depending on his plans with Hampton. Jack did know one thing for sure, that he was tired and uncertain, even in the face of an unexpected good result of the battle near the North Carolina boundary in the cow pastures.

Jack also noticed, while carefully feeling the hide of the horse he was riding, that this was a well cared for animal. It was Huel Carter's horse, and it raised his appreciation of the man he had met and had lost quickly. A sense of remorse came over him. He could not report what had happened to all the New Acquisition who had been with him at Hamilton's Ford unless he met militia who knew Carter, Grant, Hall, and Simpson; only then could he get word to their families. Jack would make sure people in the Rocky Creek area knew about Arlee McCormick.

On his second day of travel, he saw Mabry's from the direction he always traveled. Jack watched very carefully from a tree line. He took his knife and hit the barrel of his rifle and waited. For such a large farm there was no one in sight, not even farm hands. Jack hit the barrel again, a very distinct sound, and moved closer on his horse. He tried again. This time a slave boy and Rand Mabry came running to the front of the main house and looked fleetingly in his direction, then put the copper pot on the porch facing out.

Jack rode in confidently. He was met by Randolph, who welcomed him with an invitation to keep riding to the back of the large house. "Come quickly, Jack…we have a surprise for you." Jack had no idea what this might be. He had not been welcomed by Elizabeth, if they were there, and Mabry had clearly been occupied with something of great importance to hurry Jack to the back. Around the corner of the large home, Jack saw a gathering in the backyard near the dependencies. All his family was there. All the Mabrys and Samuel too. In the middle of the families was Easter Benjamin with Abraham, and in their midst was a small package that everyone hovered over.

"Massah Jack," Easter said, as she saw him and rose, holding the object of everyone's attention in her arms. It was a baby. Easter laughed, showing all her teeth, and pronounced with noble affection, "Massah, this yo niece child…this Maggie's bebe, suh."

Jack looked and saw the girlish pride and family possessiveness of another Beckham baby in his own girl's faces. Susan and Lily-Beth beamed. They were of age to have children, and he knew they felt this new addition in a motherly way. Molly Polly stood with her hands behind her back grinning, rising on her tiptoes with anticipation at her father's meeting this baby for the first time. Elizabeth smiled with a look that Jack had seen every time she had delivered a child.

Jack got off his horse and walked over to Easter holding the baby, arms extended out to him. Strangely everything seemed quiet. Why all this attention? Jack looked at Easter; she seemed to expect him to say something special, and he finally took the baby in his arms and held her. Elizabeth walked over to Jack, shrugging up her shoulders in a feminine way and smiling broadly. "We are taking this baby home with us. We have another child."

"Good Lord," Jack said.

This was Easter's sign. She was hearing something good and Godly. She had never heard Jack mention the Lord. She expressed great joy toward Jack. "Praise the Lord…Jack and Miss Liz Beth has 'nother chile…it's Maggie's. Thank you, Lord!"

Jack looked half-amused and half-bewildered. This was the first time he had seen this child. It took him back to Maggie's death and her burial. Even as they were leaving that day to take Maggie to be buried, he had not seen the child much at all. He asked quietly, "What is her name?"

Elizabeth turned to Easter, who was still grinning. Easter said, "Little Maggie."

Jack said, "Good…let us go home to the Pacolet."

Molly Polly jumped straight into the air and said, "Can I hold the baby whiles we travels?"

"No, don't think that is so. Easter will hold it, I am sure."

Easter, still smiling, said, "Naw, suh, Massah. I am back to Maggie's place. I wants you to be having this bebe. I know it help heals you,

Massah, fo what peoples say about you. Now everyone knows it not true. This bebe ain't been dead by you. Naw, suh. You is helping raise this chile."

Jack handed Little Maggie to Elizabeth, and she let Molly Polly carry her as the Beckham's began the process to gather their things for the ride back home. No one had mentioned war or death. No one had mentioned Cow Pens. No one had said anything to Jack about Maw's death. Samuel had already told them, and no one was yet ready to hear about the awful loss at Hamilton's Ford. Everyone was drained from death and war and the times they lived in. The new baby had displaced all that with the sweet mysteriousness of a new child.

Jack, Samuel, and Randolph held one last meeting together. With the look of days-on- end fatigue in their faces, they talked about Hamilton's Ford. "Where is Soe?" Jack began.

"Back to the nation."

"Widubo?"

"Died, sir. He is taken back with Soe."

"Sorry I am about the otherns of the Catawbas, too," Jack mused on hearing the news.

"Soe has them, Uncle."

Jack looked surprised.

"Soe and me went to git them. We saw Tarleton had gone, and we tied all them on horses, and Soe has them back. It was a sorrowful sight, sir, to see him leading four horses with friends over them, but he aims to bury them and with a Christian burial too."

Jack reflected on Samuel's words. "What do you allow about Chandler?"

"Gone, sir. No one knows. Maybe dead."

"Good," said Jack. "He was to be dead soon anyhow."

All the Beckhams went back to the Pacolet the next morning. Jack had slept fitfully, although he never knew it. He talked in his sleep, and his legs thrashed about in the Mabrys' big guest bed. Elizabeth was disturbed by his nocturnal moaning and the incoherent sounds, but she did not awaken him. It was a long and sad good-bye between the two families the next day, but both Jack and Rand felt that it was as safe as it might be. Possibly even more Loyalists might declare an allegiance to the colony, so Grindal Shoals might be safer. At least, Jack and Elizabeth had to try.

They approached their old farm and cabin aware that it might not be there. Jack and John Junior rode ahead to see — and on the chance something might still be amiss. They saw the cabin burned, timbers charred with ribbons of horizontal wood slanting instead of walls. The biggest timbers for the cabin roof were an eerie sight; they appeared larger than the walls that held them up. They seemed defiant, suffering a fiery death that exposed everything beneath them, yet they had held fast. The afternoon sun that played through them cast shadows on the floor that looked like new logs.

Jack stopped and stared at the scene. Fences were gone. Some livestock skeletons remained, but there was no sign of life. The dogs that had gone with Jack to the Mabrys, and had barked at anything approaching them in the night as they first traveled, now trotted past them to their old places. Tobee was with the other dogs, and she sniffed her fireplace hearth where she would first lie down in the evening. Then she meandered to the former kitchen room and did the same. They recognized what had been there with their keen smell.

Jack motioned for John to go back for the others, and they all would ride in. They were prepared for what was there. The girls looked around briefly, and Jack announced matter of factly that they were all off to Aunt Henderson's. They turned, readjusted their baggage on their saddles, and left much as they had when they fled. Most carried younger children as they headed for Colonel William Henderson's plantation and the home where Elizabeth and her family had first come to the Pacolet and Grindal Shoals.

They arrived at Jack's brother-in-law's plantation that afternoon, the second home for his family in the past few weeks. Things had changed in many ways. Colonel Henderson and other officers felt the burden of command now that Sumpter had been wounded severely. The Cow Pens defeat for Tarleton could mean the worst kind of retaliation from the British. It offered the opportunity, however, for the

Americans to pursue and try to win what they could, particularly with Tarleton's force reduced for the time from over four hundred dragoons to about one hundred seventy-five.

Jack, in his mind and body, was war weary to the point of volunteering for as little as possible. He had also to rebuild his cabin home, and he would, with the help of slaves from Hodge's Plantation and Henderson's Plantation. He would also enlist Susan's future husband, Stribling, along with Samuel and other Beckhams. Jack's brother William would surely help.

At the spacious Henderson farm, Elizabeth felt very much at home. Her family had been there for years, given a land grant by Governor Tryon of North Carolina. Then, with surveying, the land fell into the South Carolina colony. Her brother, William, and her brother, John, a Major, had both fought with the Continentals. With William having attained his distinction of Colonel with Sumpter, she did feel a bit uneasy there, for he was more "marked" by certain Tories than John.

They settled in at Aunt Henderson's, and Jack began the mechanics of going back and forth to his own cabin to rebuild it. Often he stayed for three days at the beginning, carrying off burned wood and rebuilding the fences for his livestock first. He would rebuild the barn initially for his horses and sleep there as necessary, while he and slaves carefully hewed the best wood for the cabin.

Jack used mules to pull the fresh cut hard wood to the clearing, and notched the ends to fit. This would take days. Pulling the logs to the cabin might be a hundred yards away, depending on the quality of the timber. Rebuilding the cabin meant rebuilding some fireplaces where stone had fallen, and Jack determined to make the cabin larger to spite those who had fired it.

He would make a two-story structure, but with three rooms downstairs and three rooms upstairs. Six fireplaces would warm the family that had now grown with the addition of Little Maggie. Jack also planned for the marriage of Susan and wanted to have her and Stribling come live with him before they built their own cabin.

After two weeks of going back and forth, spending winter days building his cabin, and with the help of fifteen hands, mostly cutting trees, the cabin became a shelter for the men themselves at night. Fires burned in the almost completed fireplaces that would be the family's way of cooking and staying warm. As of now, the doors and walls were not completed, but the roof was on. The wooden shingles had been set in place with some nails made on the site; others were gifts from the Hendersons and Hodges.

Jack still had men watching for malcontents who were Tories on the run or bent on revenge. The entire perimeter was always being watched by slaves with Samuel in charge. Jack wanted to be at work and insisted on cutting many of the timbers and hewing them, with other men wielding sharp hatchets that were constantly being sharpened.

He was therefore surprised one day when his brother-in-law, John Henderson, showed up escorting Elizabeth, Susan, and Lily-Beth, and with Mr. Stribling accompanying them. Jack was working to fill cracks between the logs in the cabin walls when a slave hailed him to say Elizabeth was coming. Jack stopped his chores and rode out to meet her, fearing bad news or an accident at the Hendersons'. The entourage he met was smiling. His initial fears were put to rest when he saw Elizabeth's face; he knew her so well that he would be able to tell from a distance if it was bad or good news. The look on her face said it was good, that she was eager to share with him some kind of news. Somehow he felt he knew what it might be.

When they met, Elizabeth had a beguiling smile. Jack waited. "John, we have to ask you a question...Mr. Stribling does." Then she and all the others walked back a few paces. Stribling stepped forward as if being formally introduced at a ball Jack once attended at the Hendersons' at Christmas.

"Sir," he said, holding his hat in front of him at his waist and looking very serious, "I knows you know I favors Susan, and we has planned to marry with your blessings. I knows you are building now, but would you consent to our being in matrimony? We are to marry and to ask if we might care for the young baby...uh, Miss Maggie's baby, and to get ready to plant the seed this early spring. There is much to do before we might expect a harvest to help with the food.

"And, sir…I have great affection for her. I will always protect her… sir?"

Jack enjoyed this. He did not answer Stribling but looked hard at him. In the short distance between Jack and Elizabeth, Susan and Lily-Beth, Jack eyed them. They were all straining to see his face for a reaction. Jack would not be disapproving they all felt, but they knew this was the formality, and they burned to have it over and to have his knowledge of their intentions.

"Where are you to live, sir?"

"With your permission, sir, we would be here with you and the Missus, to begin to build a cabin on this property for the short time. Susan wants to care for the baby and to have her sisters for the help as we begin to help with all the chores. I think to be here would be best than to be at my folks'. We do not have the family to help with the baby. But we would do as you directed, sir, and live apart if that is to be."

Jack said, "The big to-do is the Tories. They would come at you, I fear, if you are alone in a woods, no matter how close to us or yours. We has to see this war to its finish. We may has to fight these men and the Cherokee for some time. You would be best to stay at this place with us for the next four seasons. At that, the baby will be bigger."

"May I say this is a yes, sir?"

"Aye, but wait."

Jack raised his hand toward the waiting women and beckoned them to come. Stribling's face did not give a total indication to Susan as she approached, so she still did not know what was to be said. Jack asked her when she was in front of him, "Is this to your liking?"

She beamed. This was her father and his way. "Yes…it be… I have kind feelings for Mr. Stribling, and I would accept his proposal."

Jack said softly, as he had the ability when he wanted to please his children, "Then so be it."

Susan and Stribling reached to hold hands and smile at each other, and Jack looked approvingly at Elizabeth. She said, "John, Lily-Beth has something to say as well."

"Good it is…my sweet Lily…what is it?"

"Papa…I has met a man, and I desire to wed him. May I have him come to you, too?"

Jack was taken back. Now he knew why Elizabeth was so happy…. she had surprised him as had not been done in a long time. Jack could not help but smile broadly and put his hands on his hips in a scornful appearance of shock. "I reckon it! How many more is there? Is Molly Polly been courting, too?"

They all laughed with happiness and relief. Jack could not help but continue this playfulness. "What is this man's name? Is it Cornwallis?"

Lily-Beth gave a demure grin and said, "No. It is Mr. Scoggins near the Mabrys'. His Christian name is Malachi."

"So you were busy helping Mrs. Mabry with her chores, I imagines, and this man just happened to be there?"

"Oh yes. It was Christmas, and I met him at the dance at the Mabrys."

Elizabeth looked knowingly at Jack, and this sealed it. He nodded at Lily-Beth and she hugged him. Jack chided them all again and remarked, "I has to build a larger place and right quickly afore others ask to marry."

Elizabeth walked with him back to the unfinished cabin while the girls and Stribling talked excitedly. She said, as her arm locked inside his when they walked, "Aunt Henderson desires that the girls be married there. It will be a double wedding, and there is much to do about it."

"Aye," Jack nodded. "If this war tolerates William coming home long enough, that is much appreciated. I will thank her myself as well."

In a month, the cabin was completed sufficiently for them to move in. They did so with the knowledge that it would now have to accommodate more people. Jack would welcome a new son-in-law and a new baby. It also marked the beginning of planting season, and the weddings were talked about for April. Not a good time, for everyone was busy with the soil, but time would be taken for a wedding…in fact, two.

It was shortly announced that Mr. Scoggins would visit and ask formal permission to marry Lily-Beth. The entire family of Malachi

Scoggins arrived in late March. Malachi and Jack talked at length and were joined by Malachi's father, Robert. It appeared he was a man of good stock. The family seemed serious and devoted to the Mabrys, a great advantage for them.

The Scogginses brought much to offer Jack and Elizabeth. Malachi was a learned man. He could read and cipher well. He was intent on teaching Lily-Beth to read so they could read together. The Scogginses offered land on Turkey Creek, and an invitation for Malachi and Lily-Beth to own three hundred acres at their wedding, as well as six slaves. Besides all this, the family seemed genuine in their feelings toward Jack's daughter. Mr. Scoggins told Jack in private that he had known of him for some time and much admired him for the things Mabry had told him about Jack.

He asked Jack to move aside with him and then said that three men were buried on his property. He watched Jack for his reaction. Jack looked him hard in the face. "Three men? Was this right late into the month of May or early June of last year?"

"Aye," said Scoggins.

"Men that Mabry 'presented' to you?" asked Jack.

"That it is."

Jack nodded his head. "I fear nothing will grow on top of the ground that has these murderers beneath it. I will say nothing, only to Randolph of this."

"And it is only I that know about it, sir, not even Malachi."

They shook hands, a manly way of exchanging information that would be an honorable bond between them.

Under sprawling trees, the Beckham and Scoggins families feasted on a pig, cooked along with root vegetables, and some wild greens and cider. Jack and the men took turns drinking from a bottle of rye and talked of farming and horse trading. Jack agreed to look at all the Scoggins' horses to give them his advice on their continuing worth and trading value. After a full day, the families went back to their homes. The weddings would be in late spring, it was now decided, at the Henderson home.

One day in their new cabin, Elizabeth, with the big girls, came to Jack and said the weddings would be in the early part of May, and there was a reason for the change. "Aunt Henderson says Colonel Henderson wants to be here. He has sent word that Cornwallis' force was hurt badly, many died and wounded at a courthouse battle in North Carolina, as was Tarleton, all in March.

"Cornwallis is now back to the North Carolina coast. We hears that Camden may be rid of the British soon. Colonel feels he can be here, but many are not to know. We will have a big gathering, but some are not to be here I am afraid."

That evening, Jack and Elizabeth planned to visit Aunt Henderson and her family the next day. It turned out to be a good occasion, for many of the Hendersons were there to plan the wedding and to help. Jack learned much at this visit. He learned that the British were mainly in North Carolina, but holding on to Charlestowne as a large port city and colony capital. But it appeared to Jack that Cornwallis could not hold the backcountry and had not taken back any of the land since Cow Pens.

Jack resolved to have even less to do with the war and to avoid any duties that took him away from his family. He was still weary from months away, and he relished being with John Junior and watching Molly Polly grow.

May came soon. Crops were planted. New livestock filled Jack's fences and barns, and he had spent much time with Elizabeth's horse Derrick to train him even more. He ran Derrick in three races on Grindal Shoals as farmers came together on Sunday afternoons, feeling safer in larger groups of men, with drinking, betting, and horse racing. Jack watched everyone warily and did so with Stribling with him, but the times were more cordial.

Derrick won all his races, and Jack collected some wagers, but none would bet much against him. He earned more from training horses, taking them back to his farm, and working with them in the longer days of spring after farming.

The wedding day neared, and Jack sent word to Mabry to join them. He was asked to come for a special reason. Mabry was close friends of both the Scoggins and Beckhams, and he was practiced in being a Justice that could perform marriages. Many family members would not be there. Samuel, Abner, Johnny, and Kit would all be absent. It would be the families of the brides and grooms by themselves.

In the large room of the Henderson home the families met on that day with the weather being almost hot on the Shoals. Colonel Henderson arrived the day before with an entourage. Word was being told about the plantation was that he might replace the still severely injured Sumpter, and would indeed become a General in the Continental forces. Much was not talked about it but speculation flourished.

Over fifty people gathered in the great room. Slaves filled the porches and windows, looking in and talking much about a special occasion. Mabry took a position in front of the gathering and addressed them. Colonel Henderson and his brother, John, were not in uniform but resplendent in civilian clothes of green and purple and white. The women wore "Sunday" clothes, with Susan wearing red and Lily-Beth blue dresses that flowed out from their bodies and took up much room as they stood beside their new husbands-to-be. Jack stood behind them with Elizabeth, she in her best dress of calico and Jack in his usual black frock with fringe coat, tan breeches, and boots. He held a hat in his hand, more for comfort than for wearing.

Mabry looked out at the families and smiled. He took a book from his pocket, not larger than his hand, and began to read.

"To Almighty God be the glory. I read from our Lord's book.
"It is David's Psalm:
Oh how good and pleasant it is
When brethren gather in unity
It is like fine oil upon the head
That runs down upon the beard
Upon the head of Aaron
And runs down the collar of his robe
It is like the dew of Hermon
That falls upon the hills of Zion
For there the Lord has ordained the blessing:

Life for evermore."

Mabry folded the book and looked at everyone. Jack was mystified. He whispered to Elizabeth. "Who is these people? Mabry has
not mentioned them, this David, Aaron, and Herman; they to be with
Mabry?"

She stared straight ahead and whispered for him to listen. Jack persisted and muttered, "They must be good friends for him to say this."

Mabry looked at the daughters of Jack and Elizabeth. "I will now
marry you and ask that you be good to each other and have many children to love and keep close to the Lord."

Taking the book again, he opened it and read.

"In the name of God, I say to all here that Susan Beckham and
Lily-Beth Beckham have desired to be wed to Mr. George Stribling
and to Mr. Malachi Scoggins as it is. We all witness this and wish for
them to be wed and with God as the chief witness. God the Father,
God the Son, God the Holy Spirit, bless, preserve and keep you; the
Lord mercifully with his favor look upon you, and fill you with all spiri-
tual benediction and grace, that you may faithfully live together in this
life, and in the age to come have life everlasting. Amen.

"You are married."

The slaves burst into applause and praises. Several began to chant
and dance and move to the front yard, where much food was to be
served. Jack and Elizabeth thanked Mabry and embraced their girls.
Molly Polly danced with her two sisters holding their hands and spin-
ning around. She was enjoying this as much as they. Jack asked Mabry
about the people he mentioned in his service.

"What people?"

"The 'David' person and the man, 'Aaron,' who had oil down his
beard and his robe. And 'Herman.'"

Mabry looked at Jack to make sure of Jack's question. Jack really
was questioning. Mabry decided to make a quick explanation. "They
are good men. They have been to weddings like this."

Jack was as sincere as he was honest. "I would sorely like to meet
them."

"*You are married*"

Mabry merely said, "Let us eat and talk to the Colonel."

A significant conversation took place with Jack, Mabry, and Colonel Henderson. Jack learned much about what really was taking place, and he felt great encouragement. Mabry did, too. All felt that many Tories were going to ground and that Bloody Bill Cuningham was able to recruit fewer and fewer. But he still ravaged those he could find. He was a murderer and was the worst of those that killed and took from neighbors.

Henderson said to Jack. "It is a back-handed tribute to you, sir, that you have not engaged this man Cuningham. It appears from what we hear he is not looking to find you with much haste. I also think he believes he will see you at some time, but he does not come here."

"I wish him harm and to die soon," Jack said. "I hopes to be too busy to deal with him."

All grinned at Jack's comment but understood it was more serious than folly.

That summer was the best that Jack could remember. He threw his energy into training race horses and selling wares to many who came to him for both. He oversaw the farming that Stribling was managing for him, along with John Junior. He had not seen Samuel for months now, and Jack had not wandered back to the great falls of the Catawba. He had not seen Soe. Jack had not seen war since Cow Pens and the loss of so many at Hamilton's Ford.

One day in July he spent the day fishing with Molly Polly and John Junior at the Pacolet River streams. They had caught ten large bream and tied them to a stick with a string of linen, dangling them in the water to keep them fresh. Jack and John Junior had enjoyed success when they first came, and the afternoon had dragged pleasantly on until the mid-afternoon when the sun was making the fishing hot.

Molly Polly had caught none. She frowned and walked the bank and fussed about the heat and her lack of fish. Jack and John Junior paid her no mind, but she continued walking, sometimes walking farther away and then coming back to check her lines as if disinterested. She was, however, becoming more aggravated. She caught John grinning at her misfortune, while Jack disguised his smile at the same. She announced that she was going to quit fishing and just ride her horse back home.

Jack finally showed some real interest and pretended to scold her. "You is better off to just jump in and try to swim with them...maybe they will be your friend and go home with you... I fears you are not a good fisher."

She was now offended. She could swear her brother John was laughing at her. She walked down to the water, and looking angry, jumped in and landed on her rear end, splashing her brother. Jack let out a howl of laughter at her, and young John complained that she had ruined the fishing with the disturbance. He looked down and saw that her foot had hit the fish on the string when she leaped in the water and all the fish had managed to get away.

He complained loudly to his Pap, and Jack laughed even more. Molly Polly was swimming away from them as she began to mock young John. Jack simply got up, took six steps back, and ran and jumped into the stream. Now young John, seeing this "madness," ran backwards and then forward again, gaining momentum, and jumped into the water. All three, fully clothed, began to mimic Jack's challenge to Molly Polly and to "dive" for fish. They laughed and came up to the top and splashed each other.

Jack announced, "I has one," as he came back to the top, shaking water from his hair and spitting water. "Let's see," the two said in great innocence. "Here," said Jack..."you can have it," and he handed Molly Polly a rock.

She threw the rock well over his head in a playful manner, and it splashed several yards away. They now all three began to dive for "fish," and they all came up at different times with rocks.

This went on for some time until they all said they were tired, and a father and his two children swam to the bank and lay down, feet still in the water, drenched and laughing.

Jack grinned at his two and said, "We is going to starve."

They all started laughing again. Jack wondered how many times like this he had missed. He felt a pain and then purposely put it out of his head as they began to gather their things and walk their horses back. It was late afternoon and frogs were beginning to welcome the night with their sounds. Cicadas were chirping in trees. The three went back home to their big family with no fish and the children with no logical explanation for their mother.

Before dark that evening, a rider appeared approached the cabin while Jack and Elizabeth walked outside, she holding Henrietta.

"Hail, sir," the man said as he approached.

Jack did not recognize him in the fading light. He shot a glance at Elizabeth and said, "You sees him? You knows him?"

"I think I do. He may be one of William's men. He looks to be an officer with William."

Jack was wary and intrigued. He had his rifle slung to his back. He grabbed it and began to pour powder in the pan. Old fears came back quickly. He was back to another time several months ago. His fear overtook him, and he still raised his gun in defense. Elizabeth looked at him in her own fear. Jack leveled down on the man with his rifle as he passed some trees and momentarily was out of their view.

"Jack?" Elizabeth said.

The man rounded the blind of the tree. Jack had his hand on the rifle trigger. Elizabeth had instinctively turned the baby away, holding it in her arms to protect it front from whatever was to happen. "Dear Lord?" she questioned.

The man came into full view. He had on a 6th Continental uniform and was not threatening. His eyes widened when he confronted Jack with a gun, only twenty yards from him. "No! Sir...hold! I am friendly...a message from Colonel Henderson."

Jack wanted to make sure. He allowed the man to come closer. Still, he feared to be ensnared. His mind was racing.

The man identified himself. "Sir, Captain David Jones, Sir."

Elizabeth said, "He was at the wedding with William."

The man was smiling and approached carefully. "My pardon, Mrs. Beckham. I am truly sorry."

Elizabeth suddenly gasped and said, "My God. Something has happened to William? My brother, sir, is he dead?"

"No, he is well, madam…my apologies," he said as he dismounted. As he did, he held his hands up to Jack in a show of "surrender" or no weapons. Jack lowered his gun, and the man smiled again. "No," he said, bowing to her. "I am to bring a message of some importance to Mr. Beckham. He saluted Jack. "Sir, Colonel Henderson has need to tell you of happenings. He sends his best to you. I have a dispatch."

He handed Jack a parchment, and Elizabeth immediately took it. Thinking quickly, she said, "Sir…this is from my brother?"

"Yes."

"Do us the favor and read it as you please."

The Captain removed the wax and opened the document.

"To my esteemed brother-in-law, I send greetings. Sir, accept this message with the greatest certainty of its value from Captain Jones. I am to tell you of events so that you and Elizabeth are aware and can, in fact, with thanks to our creator for his blessings, be of new joy.

We have, since the time with you at our home, and the weddings of my beautiful nieces, fallen upon Cornwallis and his with much eagerness. Tarleton and others, as well, has suffered.

Herewith are some of the successful actions from our brave men: To wit:

ONE: The British have surrendered their garrison at the Orangeburgh. They have surrendered to Sumpter, to me and ours.

TWO: Marion has captured Fort Motte near the Congaree.

THREE: The British Fort Dreadnought has been captured near the Savannah by Captain Randolph.

FOUR: The British under Maxwell have surrendered to Colonel Henry Lee the Fort Granby on the Congaree.

FIVE: Augusta has been freed after a siege. Samuel performed well there. He has been wounded but he will be well after a time. Doubt not what I tell you. He will recover, in fact is doing so as I write. He is with Elijah Clarke still.

SIX: The British have just evacuated Ninety-Six. This is a greater victory than many. Your area is even safer now. Inform Elizabeth and all ours on Grindal Shoals.

We feel God's hand in turning so much for us. Be encouraged and be ready to help us. I have not a single proposition to make to you, but be aware, be alert, and come to us, if our needs be greater than they are now, as I write this missive to you.

In service to our colony and our Congress.

Faithfully and cheerfully yours, at last.

Your brother-in-law.

William Henderson, Colonel, the 6th Continental Regiment under Thomas Sumpter."

"Sir, is this all?" asked Jack.

"All, sir?"

"I did not mean to short what the Colonel said, but he has been more than kind to send you here."

"It is all true, sir. We will move against the British in other places, and I know he desires that you know all. With having said this I will rejoin a column that is three miles away. Thank you. Shall I send a message back to the Colonel?"

Jack was a hard man. Elizabeth had not seen much of his suspicion and fear. He had also become unsentimental and bitter in his business of spying, along with his increasing prowess at staying alive. He was not convinced. "Let us talk," he said to the man and excused himself from Elizabeth. They walked several paces away. Jack said to him, "What does Colonel Henderson look like to you?"

The Captain described Henderson.

"What is his horse's color and name?"

The man responded, hesitating. The color, sir, I remember is black. I am not sure of markings. I do not recall the name."

Jack said with determination, "You has three miles to ride back to yours. I will ride with you back to them."

Jack talked briefly with Elizabeth and then mounted Derrick to go with the Captain. They rode in silence with Jack observing the man from the corner of his eye. As they reached the view of a camp Jack saw a fire and other men of the 6th gathered there. He stopped and said, looking straight ahead, "Tell my brother-in-law we are well."

The Captain said, "Aye," and he watched as Jack left. He had just experienced Jack Beckham, and he began to believe even more the dire tales he had heard about him.

Jack reached his cabin safely and had trouble resting that night. His old restless self had taken over, and the thoughts of him, Molly Polly, and John Junior fishing and swimming that day seemed long, long ago.

Chapter Twenty Two

A Spy Again

The next months on Grindal Shoals and the Pacolet were as normal as they had been before Jack left to go to Charlestowne almost sixteen months before. He watched August come with its end of the summer harvest of food, with only intermittent reports of skirmishes from farmers who traveled back and forth across the upcolony. He heard much news from gatherings of men at different markets, and he always listened to a few trusted men more than others.

Jack had asked Scoggins to come to him when things happened near Turkey Creek, and this had been the case when Lily-Beth's husband came to Jack's farm in early September. He told him of a skirmish where a Tory, Hezekiah Williams, had attacked Whigs on patrol and then fought with Whig Major Hugh Middleton at a battle on Turkey Creek, all of this near Mabry and Scoggins.

A man from near Mabry's had spent three days with Jack while race horses were being sold on the Shoals. He told Jack and others at the sale about a major battle that had taken place in Eutaw Springs, miles above Charlestowne. As he described it, it was bigger in losses for the Whigs than the battle at the Cow Pens. He surprised Jack by telling him, "Colonel Henderson was wounded at the battle. This has been a costly battle for ours, but I can say we hear Henderson will recover. We also hears that Stuart of the British suffered much. Reports are that

Stuart counts almost seven hundred wounded, captured, missing, or killed.

"We has over five hundred men ourselves inflicted in different ways; that is, officers killed and almost two hundred enlisted killed. Over three hundred of ours are wounded."

The horse trader knew much. He said, "We has lost the field but the British could not pursue."

Jack, when he heard this, asked pointedly, "Are you sure Colonel Henderson is not dead? We has not heard that William is wounded."

They rode back to Jack's cabin, and Elizabeth greeted them. They talked, and Jack saw that the man was able to almost convince her, from what he had heard, that William would recover.

"What think you, John?" she asked.

"I am not proposed to go to Sumpter and find this out. I believe Aunt Henderson would have heard and told you if there was a tragedy. I will ride and tell her what we know."

"And I will ride with you," she said.

Jack and Elizabeth went very shortly to Colonel Henderson's plantation where they were met by a slave, Simon, who greeted them as they rode into the plantation's spacious front yard. "Good day, Massah Jack and Miss Lizabeth." He took their horses, and they were then met unexpectedly by Major John Henderson coming from the large house.

" Brother John!" Elizabeth said in surprise. "Is there trouble here? Is William reported wounded?"

"He is, Elizabeth, but he wanted not to alarm you. Please come in and visit with Leanne. She would welcome you."

Jack and Elizabeth had an unexpected pleasant visit with Leanne Henderson and discovered that William had been wounded in his thigh with a ball that had struck him while riding his horse. His wound had been cauterized and bandaged, and he was walking with a limp, but at worst, he would have a slight limp, possibly none at all.

Jack and Elizabeth continued peaceful days on the upper Pacolet, and he talked often of more hunting and time with Susan and Stribling and Little Maggie. Stribling began to plan for a larger cabin to be built in the spring, for he and Susan were now expecting a child sometime after the new year of 1782.

In mid-October, Jack planned to spend three days in the deep woods hunting for deer. Elizabeth and her family, including Stribling, would know within a one-mile radius where he was going. By a predetermined plan, he would be back in three days, and if they needed him they would go into his woods and fire one shot and wait for a reply. Within a mile he would hear it and move toward it.

Jack planned to kill a deer and fill a haversack with venison, gaining sixty pounds of choice meat before starting back. On this day he waited in an old hollowed-out oak tree for a whole morning for deer to approach. He listened and peered around the massive split in the tree for sounds in the woods. His wait was rewarded in late morning when an eight-pointed buck of some size walked noiselessly from a thicket into plain view. Jack waited for the deer to get closer. He would wait and watch his tail to see if it twitched, a sure sign that the buck was about to look up.

The deer came closer, eating and looking up. It seemed to head directly for the tree where Jack was hidden. He leaned slightly to his right and raised his .50-caliber rifle. He aimed, carefully sighted the deer, and fired. His shot hit the buck just below its neck. It started an awkward run back and then collapsed after twenty yards. Jack was out of the tree trunk with his knife in hand. He ran to kill the deer quickly in the event that it was still dying.

Reaching him, Jack made quick work with his hunting knife and hatchet. He cut one big bone, two ham pieces from the butts, and then the back straps, perhaps the choicest meat of all. Jack cut quickly to minimize blood in the meat and to hurriedly put pounds of venison in the sack. He would leave the remains to the wild animals. After putting the venison over the back of the horse for travel, he stopped to clean his rifle. He put the gun back in the saddle clean and ready for firing.

Now on his way back to the Pacolet, he thought he would arrive a day earlier than planned. On one occasion, Jack saw riders going north, and he stopped, very still, and watched them. They were in a hurry, and he could not tell anything about them. He thought if they looked in his direction he would be seen. There were ten of them moving toward the Spartan district. He slowly backed Derrick straight back so that a ridge blocked the men's view of Jack. He waited until they were well away from him and edged the horse forward to watch them ride away. He still could not tell who they were, but he thought they rode too fast for hunters; they seemed to be trying to get away from someone.

Jack started Derrick in a firm direction of the Pacolet. He had been gone almost two days and was carrying the venison back as quickly as possible for curing. Derrick sensed the "going home" and made unusually good speed across an open plain. Jack would have to cross two rivers before he would be in the Ninety-Six district and finally headed for Grindal Shoals. He was therefore surprised to see three men on horseback at a distance. This was another group like the first, except smaller in number. They were riding to his left, and he, again, did not want to be seen. Jack urged Derrick to move away fast, out of the open plain to woods that would protect him. But he had been seen.

Jack saw the men increase their speed, and all three had guns raised high. They were in pursuit of him. Jack prodded Derrick on, and for the first time thought about Maw in these circumstances and her unmatched speed. Derrick was fast but not as fast as his beloved horse that had been lost to Tarleton's men.

The men behind Jack had stopped. All three fired their guns in the air. Jack stopped and looked again and took out his nautical glass, something he would have done once he had reached the safe haven of the woods. He looked back. They were reloading and firing into the air again. He was happily surprised to see Stribling, John Junior, and Malachi Scoggins.

Jack turned Derrick toward them. He wondered as he rode what would cause them to come looking for him. And why were they all away from his family? They must have exceptional news. Jack tried to think what it could be. Were Samuel and Abner home? Was Colonel Henderson at home? Had anyone been killed? Was his family at home safe? Jack dared think this might mean Tarleton had been killed or Chandler was captured. His mind raced.

As they came closer, Scoggins and Stribling appeared to let John

Junior go in front of them. He would be the first to reach his father. Jack rode faster, as did young John. John began to call to Jack as he got into shouting distance. He was still fifty or more yards away. It sounded almost clear over the horses' hooves, "Pap…the British is …!" His voice faded, and Jack strained to hear what he said next. The young man came closer and Jack saw his expression. "Pap…the British is done…" John came charging up to him with the broadest grin, exclaiming, "The British has surrendered in Virginia…Cornwallis and Tarleton has been captured."

John Junior could not withhold his high spirits at this news. He jumped off his horse and came running to Jack's side. He reached for the reins and waited for his father to climb down from Derrick. "Tell me again," Jack said.

Young John jumped into the air and came down slapping his fist into his open hand. He had seen his Pap do this. "Sir," he said, "Cornwallis and all his army…Tarleton too, has surrendered to General Washington somewhere on the Virginia coast. That is all we know. The British has surrendered." John Junior said it again as if trying to believe it himself.

Jack took hold of his rifle, loaded it with powder, with no ball, and fired. Scoggins and Stribling came up at that time and did the same. They all fired another "false" round, enjoying the noise and making whooping sounds. Jack gave a Catawba yell, a hallo, and they all laughed and shouted wildly. Scoggins produced a bottle of rye, and they celebrated, passing it around to all, and slapping each other's back.

John Junior became his father's full grown son that day. Jack did not treat him any differently than his sons-in-law. They drank another swig of rye and fired off several more shots into the air. Only then did Jack ask questions of the elated men. "When?" he asked.

Stribling said, "About the middle…the nineteenth of October, sir…'bout a week ago."

"Glory to old George Washington," Jack said. "Has they hanged Tarleton yet?"

They all laughed and Jack said, "I am off to Virginia…tell Elizabeth

I am back soon with Tarleton's sword." At last, and seriously, he said, "How is it we know all this?"

John Junior answered, "The man of Colonel Hampton's, who was at Mr. Mabry's...he has come to tell us...he is waiting for you to be back. He is the Colonel Harrington."

Jack stopped suddenly, and only half smiling, said..."That fancy? Does he have an 'opinion' on this. Did he talk so much you left him to talk to himself?"

All of them laughed at Jack's comments. Only John Junior had met the Colonel, but they all smirked. Jack repeated what they had told him. "Harrington is waiting for me?"

"Aye, Sir," said John. "He says he has a message from Hampton for you."

"It has to be joyous news," Stribling volunteered.

"Gentlemen, we are to be gone. I will not wait for you as we ride. Meet me back at the Shoals." Jack started to mount Derrick but stopped and handed the venison to Stribling. "Carry this deer meat. We eats and has a celebration with ours tonight." He was on Derrick without any other words and continued his trip back home. All three of his family followed as well as they could. Jack and John would get there one hour before the others would. Jack often called back to John Junior to "come up," as Jack sped on to the cabin.

Harrington heard the gun shots as Jack and young John began to fire in celebration and to announce their arrival. He was ready for them to arrive, standing in the yard, as was Elizabeth and the children. A welcome celebration took place that night with food and dancing to traditional backcountry music. They danced to the "Swallow Tail Jig" and laughed and talked all evening. Finally Jack and Harrington, with Scoggins beside them, slipped to a corner of the cabin and watched the family dance from several feet away. Little Maggie waddled about and fell down a lot. She was put to her bed a little later than usual, watched over by five-year-old Nancy.

Harrington, ever the astute gentleman, constantly complimented Jack on his competency as a Whig scout and spy, as well as his "fine and gifted, handsome family."

Jack finally said to him "Sir, tells me more of this message to meet Wade."

Harrington said, "Yes, indeed. I wanted to allow you and yours much time to be of wonderful spirit, for the Colonel does desire you to be with him. He has news."

"I will attend to him by the by," said Jack. "I wants to be here for a time. There is some harvest left."

"May I, sir?"

"Be about it," Jack said.

"He desired you to leave on the morrow to be with him near the Congaree in the midlands, at his plantation."

They talked about the importance of this request, and Jack reminded Harrington that his job was finished with Tarleton's capture. "I has failed Wade, but someone of ours in Virginia has him, and Wade is probably just as joyful."

Harrington replied with some urgency in his tone, "I believe he has more news that will be important to him...and to you...so much so that time cannot be wasted."

"If this be so important you cannot allow what it is?"

"That is correct, sir. It is at the pleasure of Colonel Hampton. He wishes to tell you, and it bears some significance to what has happened with the British and their quitting in Virginia."

Jack became more convinced as the Colonel talked. They agreed to leave in the morning. Harrington would spend the night in the large front room, and tomorrow they would leave for the mid-colony.

Jack and Harrington said good-byes to the family, with Molly Polly and brother John riding ahead for the first two miles together, and then leaving to go back to the cabin. It would take a day and a half for the two men to make this trip to celebrate the British surrender with Hampton.

When they arrived at the large plantation Wade met them as soon as he was alerted by a servant that they were there. The yard was occupied by several Continental soldiers on duty and guarding Wade's home. He had on a gray and white brocade coat and white breeches with his riding boots; he looked formal, not military, as he met them. "Gentlemen." he said smiling, and led both of them into a dining room. Hampton put several documents and a large map on the table and then sat down without using them. Jack stared at the paper and tried to perceive their importance. "Jack, we have a British surrender." He then rang a bell, and a servant appeared and brought port wine while Hampton silently poured three glasses. He then toasted with the remark, "To God, our colonies, our leaders, and to men such as you."

"Hear, hear!" said Harrington. He stood up and said, "May I offer a toast, sir?" Jack seemed to groan slightly at what might be a discourse. Hampton nodded agreement.

"To our host and a gentleman Colonel, Mr. Hampton, who did so distinguish himself at Eutaw Springs, and has himself helped bring this unnecessary war to a close."

"Aye" said Jack, still sitting.

"And to my brave friend, Mr. Beckham, and may I say, sir, to those men lost to us…and to that loss of a great race horse of Mr. Beckham's."

Hampton said, "'Tis true…to their memory."

Jack half-stood at the mention of Maw and said nothing, but he raised his glass. Hampton took over, nullifying anymore toasts. "We have a surrender, but not a victory."

Jack looked quizzical. "How is this?"

"Well, sir, Wilmington is in the process of being evacuated as we speak. Savannah will be next. The British evacuated the post at Ninety-Six this summer, but the last place they will leave is Charlestowne.

"Our Capital is still one of the largest ports in the colonies, and they will not easily give up a town where five thousand of ours surrendered in May of last year. Many Loyalists will be leaving their farms… to abandon them, as it is, to go to Charlestowne to board vessels that will take them away. Many are going to Nova Scotia and others will go to the islands off our southern coasts. Barbados and Jamaica will see plenty of the King's servants who are now our neighbors. They will leave from Charlestowne."

"Let 'em leave," snarled Jack.

"It is good," agreed Hampton. "And we have ours, who will try to take over their farms and lands illegally. But that is another problem."

"From where do Tarleton and Cornwallis leave?" asked Harrington.

"New York, and to be exchanged," replied Hampton. "Chesney, the Tory from Grindal Shoals, has already escaped to Europe. We know from our spy in Charlestowne that Bloody Bill Cuningham's men will leave from Charlestowne if they wish, and that Bloody Bill himself has a standing invitation to leave our capital and to go the islands. He will do this before he is captured and hanged. He is one of the worst. We have the names of Cuningham's men here."

He picked up a document and read from it. "They are William Parker; Henry Parker; William Kilmer; Jonathan Kilmer; Hall Foster; Jesse Gray; William Dunahox; Isaac, Aaron, and Curtis Mills; Ned and Dick Turner; Matthew Love; Bill Elmore.

"They are only some of Bloody Bill's who will never stay here.

Hampton queried Jack. "Did you have information of the murder of Captain Samuel Moore by Cuningham?" Not waiting for an answer he continued. "He chased Moore; both were mounted. For miles Cuningham was close to Moore. He was within a sword's length of him for some time, and taunting him to ride faster. He finally killed him, after 'playing' with him and calling him names. He butchered him.

"That is the man and his men that may be in Charlestowne. And there are more like these. We wish to know where they are and to call for some measure of revenge on them, but Charlestowne belongs to the British and this will be hard. It may be impossible. Without the help of one of our finest men, one of our long-time spies, we have no chance. They will have murdered and escaped. And they will take information with them that will do us no good.

"You, Jack, you are being asked by our State Assembly, and our Governor Rutledge in exile, to go to Charlestowne and meet with a man who will assist you.

"What man?" Jack asked innocently.

"Indeed," said Hampton and he lowered his voice. "The spy himself. He will tell you much of what you need to know. Absolutely and to a firm promise, sir!"

Hampton looked around as if others might hear him. "This man knows where several may be. What say you?"

Jack said, "It 'pears this is hard...to git into the Britishers' town and to meet a man and then to do harm to some...maybe many more who are traitors and liars."

"Would it assist if I told you who one of these men may be?" said Hampton, suppressing a grin. Jack held both hands up as if to say "proceed."

"How about the British spy, Elberton Chandler?"

"Good gawd, sir!! He is truly a spy? How is this?"

"We are all to blame. This man has wrecked much among us." He then turned to Harrington and said, "Colonel?"

Harrington stood. "Sir, I know you doubted me and thought me a spy at one time. You are forgiven." Jack looked as if he thought he had been betrayed. At Jack's look at him Harrington said, "Nay, sir, think nothing of it. I should apologize to you."

"Why is it?" asked Jack.

This man's name is not 'Chandler.' In fact, he is an Englishman. He only took the name of Elberton Chandler after he killed the same man. I, sir, am an Englishman and I take great offense at this outrage. I seek some reprisal for my country, albeit I am with you now and the colonies."

"What is this man's name?"

Hampton intervened. "The man you will see, who is ours, will tell you his name. Our spy has access to the list of passengers for the ship on which this man will try to leave. It would do you no good at any time to know his name in advance. You will also know the name of the ship once you agree to do this. I will tell you today. And, sir, I am ordering you on behalf of Governor Rutledge to take Harrington with you...NO! I will not discuss it. Harrington can more easily get you into the city with a contact there, and more importantly, he knows what this 'Chandler' ...this man...looks to be."

"But I knows what he looks like. I has seen him too many times."

"Sir, in all respect you saw him and did not recognize him."

"I beg your pardon, sir."

"No, Beckham, you saw him hang John Craig from a distance and did not recognize him. He was one of the men who charged after you with Tarleton after Blackstock's to kill you at your home, and he was within thirty yards of you…he was with the dragoons that were part of the party that went to Howell's farm where your sister was killed. He was the man, we now know, who came to Elizabeth and tried to get you to stay at your home, so as to kill you and John Junior and others. Elizabeth described this man to you, did she not?"

Jack asked solemnly, "He would have killed Thomas's boys had they been there?"

"Indeed. They would have recognized him for sure and paid the price. No one there had ever seen him. Your Elizabeth and all your children had not until that time. Chandler thought himself very fortunate that he could tell Elizabeth all this and still be undetected.

"Do we doubt that this man killed those brothers as reported to you by Carlisle and his sons? Nay! And, sir, you did not kill Tarleton as you thought. This man alerted him at Hamilton's Ford and you shot a man of straw.

"I say again, Harrington will recognize this man much easier than you. You have many things about you that we need… but if there is a chance Harrington can help you recognize him, we have to take it… and, as said, Drury Harrington here is English….he will be welcomed by an Englishman in the capital and you, my friend, are to pose as a Loyalist…also escaping.

"So…you must do this or refuse to do it. In all respect I have to ask…what say you?"

"I am also more likely to git kilt with this man," said Jack, motioning to Harrington. "I am inclined to say no. Tarleton is trussed like a turkey, I hope. This man, who 'ain't Chandler,' is a coward and a spy, and he did not kill mine. To hell with him. My family is more important on the Shoals than this man."

"Damned it is, Jack, you are a beeve-headed man," said Hampton in a louder voice. "I see with some reservation, I have to 'play the card'

I am holding out to influence you. So be it. This British spy is not the only man to get on this ship. What say you to the Tory, JADROW EDDARDS?"

Jack stood up as if he had been challenged by Hampton. His fists were clinched, his jaw set, his eyes flaming, and he began to curse under his breath. Then he became calmer and looked directly at Hampton. He moved closer to him and said in his face, "Sir, we are long time friends. You knew Elizabeth and her family afore I did. You are honorable. I ask you in spite of these things, on your word, is you saying this to git me to go to Charlestowne? Is this Eddards man really there?"

Jack had questioned Hampton's word. It was a most ungentlemanly thing to do. He had done so in a way that could have resulted in a duel to restore honor had they been different men. But Hampton, out of friendship and patience, and with regard for Jack's proven abilities, walked to the dining table and took a book from it that had been partially covered by documents. He took it and held it out. It was the Bible. Putting his hand on it he swore, "Before God, my maker, to whom I am accountable, Eddards and this man are not only there, they are together."

Jack just shook his head sorrowfully and then reached out to Hampton's hand to clasp it. This reaffirmed their comradeship and this was Jack's "act of contrition." He then did the unexpected. He offered his hand to Harrington, who was holding his glass and staring at this exchange, stunned at the course the discussion had taken. He fumbled his wine glass and almost dropped it, reaching to accept Jack's show of friendship…friendship in this task at least.

Harrington smiled and said, "Sir, I am your servant to do what must be done."

The air was still charged after this interchange, but they sat down and Hampton poured more wine. They all drank silently; these were strange times. To go and do one's duty, to seek death and settling of scores, when the days just passed had been so tame, and peace had for a short time seemed to be the order of the day. Jack spoke first. "Does our spy, this man in Charlestowne, have anything about him that I can know as we sit here?"

Hampton said, nodding, "We have a code name for him, as we often discuss him at length in sessions with our forces. It is 'Saint Peter.' You both will introduce yourselves as 'disciples' when you are directed to do so."

"We are dis…what?"

"Disciples. In the Bible, Jesus had disciples…Peter was one of these. You know my meaning?"

"I has met one of these disciples," said Jack in a matter-of-fact reply, crossing his legs in comfort and looking knowledgeable.

"You have?" asked a curious Harrington.

"Aye, he is Reverend Simpson. He is one of them, I am sure. He has a Bible and he talks a lot about these men…these disciples."

Hampton said, raising his eyebrows in wonderment at this comment, "We are to eat, and you are to be off. You will be told more as we eat."

At the meal, Hampton said once they reached Charlestowne Harrington would assume the role of an English merchant who had been traveling and wished to sail back to England. "His name is on the ship's manifest as 'Thaddeus LeRoy.'"

He continued, "This has been placed there by our 'friend' in Charlestowne. You, Jack, are 'Charles Dunn,' a Loyalist from the upstate. You are friends with Harrington, who will be carrying with him one hundred gold guineas to prove his worth as a successful merchant. It may also help him to 'persuade' any that need it."

Hampton then gave each of them a document from the table. They were letters of transit that identified each of them – using assumed names – for boarding on the British ship. Jack understood it was called the *Palantine* and it sailed from Charlestowne seven days from tomorrow. They had eight days to do their duty or their time in Charlestowne was up, maybe in more ways than intended.

That afternoon they left with plenty of food and with Jack showing the way. They would be four days and three nights on the road to Charlestowne and would wait until mid-morning to enter the main Charlestowne Road. At that time of day many would be going and coming with commerce, and would be in a line to be checked by British guards. They would be met by another Englishman, a local citizen, at a tavern; this waiting man would be present during the day hours, for the next several days, beginning each day in the late morning.

The man was Alexander Burlinn, a prosperous merchant of clothing on King Street. He could at least direct them to another, who could then direct them to the spy called "Saint Peter."

After a non-eventful journey, Jack and Harrington stood on the outskirts of the city. They waited until the flow of people was at a peak, to be even less noticed, near 11 a.m., and then began their entrance to the capital city of Charlestowne.

Jack learned quickly the value of Harrington. They were met by two British red coat guards, who asked for their "letters of travel." One was an officer. He spoke to Harrington, who Jack thought used a more definitive English accent than he had heard before. The officer said to Jack, looking at his document, "You, sir, are Mr. Dunn?"

"Aye," said Jack.

The officer said to him, "You are armed with a rifle, are you not, sir?"

"Indeed, sir. I have been at Hammond's Store, and am blessed to be here after that, and I am also leaving the Ninety-Six now for many days. This piece has fired and kilt rebels, sir."

"And I can attest to that," said Harrington.

Jack said casually, "Would you like to have this rifle, sir?"

Harrington blanched at this remark.

"I would indeed, sir."

"It is well then. I will see you the day before the ship sails, and give it to you. I will have no more use for it. But I dare say, before that, I might see a scoundrel in the city."

The gullible officer laughed and agreed. "It is done. I will be here that day before the *Palantine* sails. Thank you for your kindness, sir."

Harrington quickly said, "God save the King," hoping to move on. Jack nodded, but did not say anything. As they left, Harrington said to Jack out of the side of his mouth, "I do not think King George is well-liked by his men, but certainly he might deserve more than a nod."

They went to the Sir Thomas Tavern; inside, a group of ten or so men who looked quite prosperous were talking animatedly among themselves. This was clearly a tavern where gentlemen met, and Jack felt uncomfortable. They were approached by a handsome young man who was smiling at them. "Ah, you gentlemen look in need of information. You are just into town? We are all disciples of the drink and food here; you are welcome." He laughed heartily. "Would you like to join us in the same?" He looked at them with an anticipating glance as he passed his tankard to the innkeeper to be filled with ale.

"We would indeed, sir," said Harrington. "We will drink good ale, I allow, until Saint Peter calls us home."

The young man laughed and said, "Hear, hear!" With a slight bob of his head to Harrington, he said, "Gentlemen, you have come to the right place."

The three men talked about the weather, the commerce in Charlestowne, the taste of seafood, and how much of it Burlinn had consumed lately. The young man went to great lengths to explain the difference between the shrimp caught in the harbor and those in the creeks around the city. He described what he had that morning for a meal, which included creek shrimp. Jack began to wonder if this was the man. Harrington did not. He was the ultimate listener. Jack, at one point, nudged Harrington after Burlinn had another tankard and said softly, "Is this the gentleman?"

"Oh, indeed, my friend…that is good, is it not?" Harrington laughed hard, disguising what Burlinn and others thought might be another bit of humor, in a room that was growing increasingly louder.

Finally, after encouraging Jack to have another ale, Burlinn said in a pronounced voice for other's ears, "It is loud…I will show you some directions…we can adjourn to the door."

They went out into the afternoon sun, and Burlinn assumed another tone when he said, "Gentleman, your names, please."

Harrington said, "LeRoy, sir."

Jack muttered, "Dunn."

"Good. I am Burlinn, and we will travel into the city to my place. I can direct you from there."

He was stone sober at this point and looked very serious. He was as good an actor as he was a storyteller, and apparently was unaffected by nearly five tankards of ale. Burlinn climbed into a wagon with a bay horse at the front and said to Jack, "What may be the best course, sir, is to put your rifle into this wagon and let us cover it with cloth. Too many British and Jaegers will recognize it, and they will all inquire, I am afraid."

Chapter Twenty Three

The Stone Feather Tavern

They traveled as men of the city, men about their business. Burlinn was known in the streets, and from time to time he saluted someone with a good afternoon and a tip of his hat. He was providing safe passage, through appearances, for Harrington and Jack. Harrington fell into his role of the day and said "good afternoon" to two gentlemen, his clipped English more acceptable in this town than any other in the colony.

They arrived at Burlinn's home on Church Street, and Burlinn ushered them in. He had a beautiful young wife and two daughters less than ten years of age. He introduced them, and Jack was fascinated to learn they were Maggie and Helen. "Well," he said, bending down easily from his waist to their eye level, "I had a sister named Helen Magatha. How are you young ladies?" He sat down and one of the little girls came directly over and sat in his lap.

"I think," said Harrington, " this young one recognizes a man with seven girls of his own." They all laughed at this irony and coincidence.

Burlinn, even with his family in the room, said, "You are close to Broad Street. Indeed you can walk to where you might go. It is 26 Broad, gentlemen, close to the Exchange Building. I suggest you walk and get some flavor of the city. Then we would be pleased to have you back here while I have someone care for your horses. They will be groomed and fed."

"Why there on this Broad Street?" asked Jack

"There you will meet a man who is a Justice. Well-respected. He is expecting you. He will inform you of where you might want to go from his office."

"I agree, sir," said Harrington. "Jack?"

"I think not. I has been here before, and I had to leave right well before I was kilt. That is easy to recall. I would not displeasure you, sir, but I will care for my horse and then ride this short way."

"Not at all displeasured, sir," said the young man. "With no disrespect, you will not be returning here for any time other than to collect your horses. The Justice will have plans for you."

Jack excused himself from the young lady. As she hopped down, he patted her head and gave her a fatherly smile. He went behind the house to the stable and cared for Derrick, feeding him and watering him. Then he collected a waiting Harrington, already on his horse, and they both rode down Church Street. They passed John's Alley, which was familiar to Jack, and then turned north down Broad Street to number 26. They tethered their horses to the post in front of an imposing office and went inside, where a young man came up and introduced himself as Thomas Cook, clerk to Justice William Jay Fisher.

Cook announced the two men to the Justice, who came out of an office and motioned them in. "Gentlemen," he said, glancing up to them and seeing Cook standing behind Jack and Harrington, rolling his eyes at Jack, who looked to be a rough upcountry man. Cook wondered what type of legal matters these two disparate looking men might have with Fisher, a distinguished man of letters.

"Sir, I am Mr. Thaddeus LeRoy, merchant, trading as I have been in the upper colony, and I am listed on the ship *Palantine*, as you know. "This, sir, is Mr. Dunn, a Loyalist, firm to the King. He also is confirmed on the ship."

"Ah," said Fisher, not smiling, taking a seat at his desk and leaning forward on his elbows, "Colonel Harrington and Mr. Beckham. We receive you well into our city."

Harrington laughed. "Well, sir, I assume you had some 'notion' of our presence and, most of all, our purpose here."

"I do," the Justice said. He turned to Jack. "Sir, you may not have knowledge of the fact but you and I are exceptional friends."

Jack missed the meaning but responded. "I am pleased that we are as you say. It is a pleasure to meet you, sir."

"No, I must say, sir, we are meant to be sitting here. Your sister sat in that same chair in 1779, and I constructed a will for her. She signed it. I know that in her death your wife inherits a share in her estate. I know she made Easter Benjamin her legatee also, and I had the painful experience of being part of a proceeding at Camden, when you were exonerated and this 'son of Satan,' Jadrow Eddards, was uncovered. Sir, I have been witness to all this."

Jack was almost speechless. He looked at Fisher again. "Sir, I cannot read. What is this word you said I am at Camden?"

Fisher looked puzzled.

"This exoner…"

"My sincerest apologies. My crucible…uh….my burden… is that I speak in my own language of my profession. Will you accept my apology? The word means you are cleared…you are pardoned, or forgiven."

Jack turned to Harrington and said, "Hellfire. We has found someone who talks as you do."

They laughed except for Fisher. He was a man who measured his time carefully. Fisher said, "I am to direct you to the men you are seeking. I myself have to solicit 'Saint Peter.' My pledge to you is that if these men are here, and indeed they are, we will find the hole they are in before they board this ship. May I propose, gentlemen, that you go to Bay Street and monitor this ship, the *Palantine*. She is lying tied to the docks directly off the Exchange Building. You can almost board her.

"Give me three hours to find and talk to 'Peter.' Then return after the dinner hour this afternoon. We will make plans."

Fisher stood. It seemed the door behind them opened at once, and they were escorted onto the street by Cook. Once on the street, Jack and Harrington walked straight toward the Exchange Building, which was the primary loading and off-loading facility for the city and its goods. There, everything passed through legal processes: tobacco, indigo, lumber, small items, animals, weapons, all things of trade with England and other countries. This building, leading to the wharf and to ships anchored, was the heart of Charlestowne.

Attached directly to the wharf behind the building was the *Palantine*, a vessel of trade and transport for England. All around it were men doing various jobs, preparing her for a long voyage. Cargo was being loaded in the lowest holds on the ship and sailors that would be manning the boat were on and off the long, imposing wooden craft. They stayed off as much as possible, drinking in taverns, gambling, fighting, and carousing until duty or the final call to sail brought them back.

Jack looked with great interest. This was not familiar to him. He missed the woods on Grindal Shoals, the pursuit of game in the upcountry and the streams and rivers he knew so well. Were it not for the evil men who were here, he would not be here. He glanced at Harrington, who was very much enjoying the climate, the salt air, and the chance to be in an English city. Jack secretly resented Harrington and his dependence on him to help identify the man whose name Jack did not know, this schoolmaster that had betrayed him and others.

They walked on and eventually went into a small tavern and had a piece of fish and bread to eat along with some ale. Jack walked with Harrington, holding the reins of Derrick, to Elliot Street and then back onto Church Street. Jack noticed the different colors of homes – blue, yellow, pink, gray – their facades constructed from hard tabby stucco, made with broken sea shells mixed with sand and water.

After a suitable period of time, around the sixth hour of the evening, they were back to Justice Fisher's office, where they were met by Thomas Cook again and led into Fisher. The Justice rose from behind his desk as the door was closed behind them. "Gentlemen, please, be seated. We know where they are."

Jack stood up from his chair at this remark. "Then, sir, let us know and we will 'greet' them and be on our way."

"No, it is not such a simple matter. They are too careful, and they both are in the worst place for us and the best place for them. They are in the Stone Feather Tavern. It is on Cumberland Street, the very center of murder, thievery, and violence in the entire colony. Our own guards and enforcers of our law do not go there. They simply wait until people leave the tavern and try to apprehend them as they go back to a ship, or to leave the port by small boat, or on horseback.

"It is the hell hole I feared they would be in. I give you my promise they will not leave there until the last hour to board the ship. Then they will travel on foot with a pack of men up the streets, hidden in the midst of them, I am sure. In this way they will walk to the ship, board, and be on their way. This is the way. I have seen it many times."

"We will wait until this pack leaves and git them," said Jack. "We will kill anyone who is in our way."

"But Beckham, sir, will you recognize them? You would have to engage more than one man to get to them. All these men are wanted for something, or they are deserters. Some seamen will fight just to be arrested and thrown in the dungeon, so they do not have to sail. They are men that you would want to choose very carefully how you deal with. I fear you may be hurt or killed, and these men you want might simply walk away."

Harrington made his expected suggestion. "Why not hire our own force of men and attack the lot of them? I assume the responsibility of seeing this British spy and making sure we at least get him."

"That is a poor chance, sir," said Fisher. "You may or you may not. If he runs, and you give chase, others may chase you. Our men on duty here, who guard the streets, want nothing to do with this scurrilous lot, and they will not go with you. No. There is only one way."

"And that is?" asked Jack.

"Go to the tavern tonight and try to see them. Our only worry is that we are chased, or worse, set upon by the mad men who are there just for their satisfaction. But I know that tonight they have a special evil pleasure that they will be enjoying…as a crowd. So meet me here at half past the eleventh hour, as the clock will chime at St. Michael's Church. Be here in this office…I will let you in."

Jack asked as he rose, "Has this St. Peter told all this?"

"Aye, and he will be there tonight. There are more men than you seek that will be there. I wish, as it were, that the whole tavern could be fired and burned to the ground."

Harrington said, "We will be at the Bishop's Tavern on John's Alley until that time."

"May I direct you otherwise? I know a place for you to be," said Fisher. "Mr. Beckham, sir. How would you like to meet close friends of your late sister, Maggie? They, in fact, introduced me to your sister. They have had her visit them for several years. They are a young couple with a child and they live close by. Stay there until the hour we are to meet. They will receive you."

Jack nodded, and they all three left the office to go to this house. Justice Fisher, once they were there, introduced Jack to Marcus and Julia Hayes. They welcomed him warmly. Mrs. Hayes embraced Jack with tears in her eyes, something he was unprepared for, and he clumsily held her shoulders in return away from him as she talked about Maggie and asked him to tell her of her death. Mr. Hayes shook Jack's hand and put his hand on his shoulder. Jack took the opportunity to introduce Harrington to break the conversation and the physical contact, and to avoid the questions as long as possible. They all talked informally while standing, and then Justice Fisher gave his good-byes.

Once Fisher had left, the Hayes introduced Jack and Harrington to a guest who was traveling and staying with them, a Mr. Mark Lionnes. "Our friend is from Hillsborough in the middle North Carolina colony," said Hayes. "He is disposed to be here on business."

"My pleasure sir," said Lionnes

They talked and Jack talked "around" the way Maggie died. Jack was struck by the fact that he was in a home where Maggie had stayed with her friends, and he had met Justice Fisher, who knew her and was her legal counsel. Jack's feelings for Maggie were refreshed, painfully so, by people who knew her, and so far from her home. It also smoldered in him why he was in Charlestowne: to avenge her murder.

That night they rode their horses back to Broad Street and met Justice Fisher. He opened the door, and he had completely changed his character. His clothes looked shabby and worn, and he wore a full outer coat that went from a shawl top covering his shoulders, almost to the floor. It covered his boots that were knee-high. His hat was tricorn and was the only distinguished apparel about him.

Harrington said "Sir, we are most grateful to you for going with us and showing us this place. I am sure we will not see you again after you point us to this 'den,' so let me state my appreciation to you."

Fisher said, "Sir, I am not dressed so that I might be among the derelicts we see. I fully intend to be part of this 'party.' Do you take me to be a man who has no taste for these things?"

"I meant no offense, sir, but…"

Jack interrupted and said with some rudeness in his voice, "I mean to offend, sir. Why should I care to protect you in this tavern as you say it is. This appears to be our fight…remove yourself from it, or point us to the way, and we will be gone. I much prefers to be kilt on my own and to run on my own. I am waiting on the street." And Jack turned and walked out.

Fisher called to him and said "Sir, will you indulge me? I wish to show you something that might lessen your ill feelings."

Jack, out of respect, went back inside to find out what was meant by the Justice, and determined that it would not change his mind. Jack intended to tell Harrington to leave with him and to show him the name of the street where the tavern was located. Fisher abruptly threw open his coat and with one sweep of his right arm had his hand on a blunderbuss musket with a six- inch mouth opening. It was strapped to his shoulder, completely hidden until he opened his coat and swung the gun straight out with one motion. The huge mouth of the gun stared at Jack.

"Sir, if I pull this trigger you will have absorbed the impact that could kill several men. I dare say your upper body and your lower part would be separated."

Jack looked at the gun and at Fisher. "That is well and good in this office with your paper and chairs and coverings I see on your floors, but does you have the courage to shoot in a place not so fine as this?"

"I do, sir."

"And Mr. Harrington, and me, with our very lives, has to hope you indeed do…that is what you ask of us?"

"As gentleman to a gentleman, aye. But as a man who knows how to do his duty to the colony and has already done so, I forcefully say the same. I will not burden either of you."

All three men traveled on horseback down Bay Street to Cumberland Street, a lower lying street with sea water partially flooding the way from a previous high tide that had come under the cobblestone streets. They approached a tavern with men standing outside arguing and shouting. Very few horses were in sight; men seemed to have walked to this place. Fisher directed Jack and Harrington to a stable attached to the tavern, and they then made their way through the crowd that actually blocked the door. Jack and Harrington had rifles in their hands, as Fisher had said all men would be armed, mostly with pistols and knives or both. It would be common to see any man with a gun or to know he had one on his person.

As they entered, they went as a group to a wench behind a long table filled with empty tankards. There was overwhelming stench rising from the old pine floor that had been soaked with spilled ale. Men sat at long tables, smoking, playing cards, and laughing. They spat on the floor and were constantly standing up in their places out of their chairs and challenging each other, throwing cards and banging their metal drinking containers on the tables, and pushing each other. It was a controlled brawl and it seemed that it could get out of hand at any time.

Men were passed out and took the chance of being robbed or killed if they lost consciousness in this room of transients and strangers. Others who passed out, if they had friends at all, would be thrown over a shoulder and taken outside to awaken in the clearer air, or be dumped near the building and in the dark.

Fisher threw coins on the table, and the woman filled tankards that had just been used by other men and left them on the table. She never looked up. Fisher handed the tankards to Jack and Harrington. The wench, who had no teeth and still dipped snuff as it ran down her cheeks, cursed and took men's money, and poured more ale into tankards as they were brought to her by a young man.

In the middle of the room was a large open pen. It had slats up to

a man's shoulder and a holding pen with a door. Inside the pen was a
wild boar, a "barrow," the male. Fisher pointed toward the barrow with
his tankard and said to them, "This is their nightly blood sport." In a
short time men gathered around the open pen leaning on the slats and
began an uproar that added to the din in the room. They were getting
louder and louder until a man unlatched the door, and the wild boar
charged out. He looked to be two hundred pounds and he slammed
up against the slats, shaking them. The men stepped back in feigned
horror and continued their coarse laughter.

A man produced a dog of medium size and threw it into the pen
and the boar chased the dog in the pandemonium that followed. He
caught him, speared him with his tusks, shook his head side to side,
and dismembered the dog. He mutilated him and cut him in half to
the delight of the drunken men. Jack tried to look past the hog and
watch the men's faces. He nudged Harrington hard and said, "You sees
anyone we are looking for?" Harrington in the noise tried to talk but
just shook his head no.

Another man came into the room with a sack and with cheers and
urging on from a crowd that followed him from outside. He threw a
large rabbit into the pen and it moved lightning fast around the pen
away from the boar. The boar was no match for the rabbit until the
rabbit jumped toward the slats, got hold of one, and vaulted into the
room among the men. The place went into a complete upheaval. It was
more than deafening. Men stood on tables and shouted, and one drunk
took a pistol and fired at the rabbit, hitting nothing until he himself
was knocked to the floor. The rabbit could not escape among the many
hands reaching for him and was caught and thrown back into the pen
from across the room. Men bellowed again.

This happened twice more. The rabbit was loose and was caught
by one of thirty or more men, stomping and cursing and trying to fall
on the rabbit. It was thrown back to the pen exhausted and killed immediately by the boar, who rushed back and forth slamming against
the wooden slats squealing to the mad delight of the crowd.

As if on a signal, two men brought in two larger dogs, so large they
were holding them against their chests, and threw them into the pen.

The dogs fought the boar, attacking him from the front and back. The boar spun around as the dogs snapped and bit him on his thick skin. The men leaned in so hard on the slats it appeared they would break and unleash the boar among the stumbling drunk men.

In the fight between the hog and dogs Harrington noticed something unusual. Most men were around the pen. But some men paid no attention at all, huddled among themselves at a table in the corner. He motioned to Jack to look. He then caught the eye of Fisher and motioned him to look at the men. He hollered in Jack's and the Justice's ears to be heard over the crowd. "I am going to move so I can better see their faces."

There were four of them, and they appeared to be head-to-head trying to talk above the noise. Harrington had to shove his way around the room; he was the only one going away from the hog pen, and the force of the men against him was like a wave. He positioned himself among other men and peered around them to see those sitting at the table. He did not allow himself to be seen.

He tried to look back at Jack when he saw the men. It was Eddards and this man called Chandler. Harrington was now frantic to communicate. He hoped not to be seen even by an awful draw of luck by the men and at the same time get back to Jack and Fisher.

He almost clawed his way back as the havoc at the pen increased. Men were reaching over the pen and hitting the boar with their hands, throwing tankards at the beast, some trying to hit it with their hands. One drunken and teetering man was standing on the middle slats of the pen urinating on the boar to the crowd's urging. The dogs were wearing down under the weight of being hit by the pig, and at one point the boar caught a dog and flung him into the air and killed him as he fell. The drunken men laughed even louder at this killing.

Harrington got back and breathlessly said, "Aye, gentlemen, it is they with two other men."

Fisher said, "We have to get them outside. There are too many men between us."

Jack said, "I will git to them and knife them in the neck. First, Chandler, then the murderer."

"Sir," said Fisher, "you will not survive. I tell you, you will be killed before you get to the door. The spy whose name is really 'Hughes, Colin Hughes,' will be desperate." For the first time Jack heard this man's name.

Fisher suddenly said, "I will declare him… I will call his name. We will see what he does." He reached into his pocket and pulled out some cloth. "Just do as I ask, gentlemen. Put this in your ears." And he was gone into the crowd.

Jack and Harrington looked at each other. They followed Fisher, who got near and behind the four men after moving through the pressing crowd. He stood feet firmly planted and shouted at them, "HUGHES, COLIN HUGHES!" He shouted several times. Slowly, a man turned with piercing hate-filled eyes. Harrington saw this movement and said to Jack, "LOOK!"

Jack said, "I do not see this man!"

"Look again!"

Jack was looking at the "Hughes" man, but he was not the prim, spectacle-wearing school teacher. Then Jack recognized this man's mouth and the way he had talked when he practically begged Jack for release at Mabry's. Turning also to Fisher was another man. It was Eddards.

Jack saw him immediately and could not help but scream over the crowd, "EDDARDS!"

The man saw Jack. He did not hear his name called but he looked into Jack's face and paled. He stood up from his chair and looked toward the back of the tavern. Jack anticipated his move when the man started to run, and he began to push people aside to get to him.

Eddards saw Jack moving to cut off his exit, and he turned and ran toward the pen to escape through the front door. Hughes began to run in the same direction. Jack hurdled over three men, knocking them to the floor, and as Eddards was passing the masses to escape, he passed the pen where men were not moving.

Jack pulled his knife from his belt, and it flashed in men's faces as he ran toward them. One man thought Jack was going to kill the boar, and he shouted a cheer, "Huzzah!" Jack went past him, and Eddards squeezed through the men at the pen and bolted for the front door. Jack reached out and grabbed him by his neck. Maggie's murderer screamed for help. Men around him thought this more folly in this predatory tavern and laughed. Jack literally picked him up and slammed him to the floor. Men parted, and by separating, gave them space. Jack was suddenly in the middle of the room of men, and they began to cheer this fight. They were even more blood-thirsty after witnessing the boar; now two men might shed blood.

Jack was close to the post of the pen, and he picked Eddards up over his head and purposely threw him into the pen with the boar. The wild hog caught Eddards on the floor and rammed his tusks into his leg, immediately cutting the large artery. Blood splattered across the pen. The mob yelled as if this were a horse race. Jack reached down into the pen and grabbed Eddards' neck and put his arm around it. He was holding Eddards up and beating him from the top of the pen. The boar backed off and charged again and cut Eddards leg so severely with his tusks that it almost severed the lower leg below his knee.

Jack had his knife now turned around, and with its butt was beating Eddards in the face. Jack hit him multiple times, and three of Eddard's front teeth were broken off with one blow. Jack was saying something that could not be understood, and the men were cheering this butchery, with their own primitive lust for blood. All at once, the room was quiet. Everyone was staring at Jack as his voice became the only one heard. He was saying Maggie's name and cursing Eddards. Then suddenly a man yelled, "Kill him," and moved toward Jack.

Several men joined in, their knives drawn. In all this madness, Justice Fisher had appeared behind Jack. The Justice opened his coat and extracted the blunderbuss and aimed it waist level at the men, who paid no attention in their lust for senseless revenge; they kept coming in a blur of movement at Jack.

Fisher fired. It made a singular gun noise unheard before by any of these men. It was a blunderbuss, used for boarding ships by pirating men and was now fired in a close building among many. Its results were unbelievable, even to the hardened criminals in the tavern. Five men were killed or severely wounded instantly, their vital organs punctured

"The blunderbuss was devestating"

by the mass of the charge. Several more lost their hearing temporarily, and they panicked, not knowing what had happened to them. A shot rang out from behind Fisher. It was Harrington, killing a man who had also pulled his knife but hesitated at the sight of this carnage.

One man made it to the door before the others, intent on escaping. It was the spy Hughes. He bowled over more men coming inside in response to the loud report from the blunderbuss. Once outside, Hughes commandeered a horse and rode away.

Jack, Fisher, and Harrington came to their survival senses at once and bolted for the door. They ran as never before while the clogged group of men behind them looked around and began to assimilate what had just happened. They all ran to pursue Jack and his friends, but these men were their own enemy. They could not all get through the door as a throng, and the men on the outside trying to get into the tavern blocked their way.

Jack and his made it to the nearby stables and rode off, just ahead of men milling around in the yard shouting to each other, trying to decide how to chase them for the pure sport of killing men they did not know. The three rode at the direction of Justice Fisher. He looked back, and they followed him without speaking. He raced down Bay to Broad Street to the stables behind his office. There he dismounted and said breathlessly, "The barn and then with me." They left their horses in the barn, with the Justice closing the door securely, and went in through the rear entrance to his office. They all were panting.

Fisher went to the front window and looked out onto Broad Street. In minutes a mob of men came up the street from Bay Street and divided. One group went down Broad and another down Bay. Fisher leaned back against the wall but continued to glance to the street. "We are safe here. They will look for us in taverns and on the waterfront, and they will visit stables; they will look for us to go to the roads from Charlestowne, but not at this place of commerce."

Jack looked at Harrington. "Eddards is a guest of the devil." It would be the last time he would ever mention the man's name.

Fisher said, "But the spy Hughes is away, and he will still try to board the ship; did you recognize him, sir?" He was addressing Jack.

"Just once. He is most likely to git away, I still fear."

"He has become a watch for all of us and my responsibility," said Fisher.

Harrington said, "No, he is my responsibility. I beg to be an honorable person, and I still feel the need to avenge this man's treasonous acts."

Fisher asked Jack about his rifle that he had carried into the tavern. "It is still there or a Tory has it," Jack said.

"My new friend, you have a new gun." The Justice went to a rack in his small private chamber and produced a gun of magnificent quality. "Now, sir, you have the only rifle with a cypress wood stock, I dare say, in the whole of the upcolony." It was a .65-caliber beautiful piece, and Jack was assured it shot accurately. He also provided powder for Jack and several lead balls in a leather bag. He continued listening to Harrington.

"Hughes did not see me in the tavern. He last saw me when Tarleton escaped, as he himself did. In the daylight, we will find the time of day when the ship leaves."

Fisher interrupted. "I can tell you, gentlemen, it is at the one o'clock afternoon hour it leaves. We have only ten hours or less to find this Hughes ."

"Good sir, I will be there, and I will befriend him. He may be shocked. I will tell him I am loyal to the King, and I am boarding. I will show him my letter of transit. He may run. If he does, you will know it is he. If he does not, I will try to find him, and by some signal let you know it is the person. You will be in the crowd that will surely gather to see people off."

Fisher commented, "The crowds have been boisterous of late, some even jeering those boarding."

Harrington replied, "We will get him."

Jack said, "I will shoot him if we do not get our hands on him. He will not leave."

Harrington remarked, "But you must make sure it is the right man. I will get him before he boards and lead him to you. Just be in the crowd. We will restrain him, if we are to be blessed with that opportunity, and take him to be judged."

Jack rebelled at this notion. "We will have to be rightly blessed to take him that many miles to a hanging. I dare say he will not make it."

This sounded chilling to Justice Fisher, who had not experienced the coldness in Jack, but had just witnessed his capacity for violence at the tavern. Fisher brought them back to the task at hand. "You gentlemen have but hours to get this man…I say this again. How do you propose to do this?"

Jack looked at Harrington and took his offer to find Hughes. "I will go to the crowds around the ship. I will stay there, and I will be as 'out of anyone's eyes' as I can be.

"I needs someone to talk with for the next hours while I am there. People don't notice people with others, but one man standing in one place is no good, and walking around may be worse. Hellfire, I might be seen by this man afore I sees him."

Fisher said, "I will send for Mr. Hayes to come and be with you. Thomas Cook, who lives above us here, will assist."

Jack agreed and said, "There is a man staying at Hayes's. Invite him to come and talk with us."

"Gentleman, I have something," added Harrington. He went to the side of the room to his and Jack's haversacks. Out of his he pulled a most unusual surprise, the uniform of a British officer. He also produced a suitable hat. "I will be less noticeable in this. However, if someone from my former unit challenges me, then I may have to make an excuse for a departure."

Fisher had already made plans to leave and had called for Cook to come down now in the early morning. It was close to two a.m. as St. Michael's bells rang. He instructed a sleepy clerk to be at Hayes' home on Elliott Street at dawn and to request his presence and the presence of his guest at the Justice's office at the seven o'clock morning hour.

Jack went to the stable and brought Derrick and Harrington's horse back into the office through a side door. "The horse's stays here tonight," he said to Harrington. "They is too lathered to stay in the barn. The tavern fools might see them and come looking."

That early morning, as Jack and Harrington tried to rest, their horses stood around Justice Fisher's desk, sometimes nuzzling papers and rubbing against each other and at other times bumping into the walls, dislodging oil paintings. It was elegant, small, and safe for two horses of over a thousand pounds inside a law office on Charlestowne's famous Broad Street.

The next morning Hayes, Lionnes, and Cook met at the office of the Justice. Fisher had come at dawn, just after Jack had put the horses back in the barn. Harrington explained to all what was to be done and said, "I am leaving to go and look for this scoundrel. You will be where I can see you?" They nodded.

Hayes said there was an unusual number of hogsheads filled with tobacco on the docks, sometimes stacked two and three high. He suggested that he and Jack, along with Lionnes and Cook, mill around there and be watchful. Justice Fisher agreed to be walking among the crowd and watching Harrington. He was dressed elegantly in a brocade silk coat with a flourishing lace collar and cuffs. He wore silver-buckled shoes and carried a walking stick. Under his coat, however, was the blunderbuss. It was now close to eight a.m. as church bells tolled the quarter hour. The ship sailed in five hours.

Before they left, it was agreed that the "signal" would be any man that Harrington befriended and put his hand on his shoulder in a matter of meeting and friendship. "A hand on the shoulder and perhaps a handclasp, but by all means a hand on this man's shoulder…that is for you to then come to me." These were Harrington's last instructions.

All the men congregated near the docks as planned. Harrington walked among the crowds, his hands behind his back, nodding his head occasionally and not looking to engage any military officer in a long conversation. He and the Justice barely acknowledged each other when they passed in the crowd. Jack and his men were in the middle of the hogsheads as they were being moved to another ship docked beside the *Palatine*. Jack had his back to Bay Street, facing the ship with the others walking around him. They made for small talk, and asked Jack on several occasions if a man they saw, as had been described to them, might be Hughes. He would casually turn and look and nod no.

Harrington tried something. He saw the Justice and walked up to him and "introduced" himself. They both acted out great courtesies to each other. Harrington said, "Tell Jack and others that this man will try to board very late. Right before the plank is pulled aboard. Tell them if it is to be I will wrestle this man down, and tell the others to be closer to us to assist."

Fisher smiled and tipped his hat and began to walk over to the men around the hogsheads.

Time moved closer to the ship sailing, and the men around Jack were all restless with anticipation. They all had muskets except Jack, who had the Justice's rifle. Minutes later they heard St. Michael's church bells ring on the half- hour. It was twelve-thirty. Harrington moved closer to the boarding, with men and women still boarding with assistance from the ship's crew.

Harrington had a horrible thought. What if Hughes was already aboard? What if he were disguised even more? Could he have rowed a boat out last night and climbed on board already? Harrington began to look at those moving toward the ship and those already on board. His eyes went back and forth. It was less than twenty minutes before the ship would be scheduled to sail.

Jack looked intently. He watched every movement of each man going to the ship. He felt a great urge to get closer to Harrington, and he had started to leave his men when he noticed Harrington hail a man. Harrington had seen someone he thought was Hughes. "Sir...sir." The man turned; it was Hughes.

Harrington's mind searched for the right words. He would call him Chandler. "Sir! Mr. Chandler, it is Colonel Harrington. Please, sir, your attention."

The man stopped, and Harrington saw him finger a knife that was a bit obvious. "Sir, I am with the King. This is something I could not tell you. I have been in the King's service for our cause. My deepest apologies for my actions near Grindal Shoals, but I assure you others have paid a great price. Many are dead, and I am back to England." Hughes stopped because of the Colonel's uniform that Harrington wore. He listened but did not comment.

"Sir," said Harrington, "I have been paid well. We can toast our country in a grand way; one hundred guineas, to be exact." He began to pull them from a pouch. Jack saw all this and did not recognize the man. Neither did Fisher. Jack looked at Fisher, and their eyes met. The Justice just gave a slight shrug. Harrington had not shaken the man's hand or shown any friendship or tried to subdue him. Harrington was preparing to show Hughes the coin, and put his hand on his shoulder as he talked, when Hughes bolted. He ran quickly to the ship's officer standing at the gang plank and handed him a letter of correspondence.

Jack was alarmed and Harrington frustrated. He cursed as Hughes ran from him. The Colonel then acted on his own taking a chance how Jack might get to him. He went up to the officer and gave him his transport documents.

"Welcome aboard, Colonel."

As Harrington went up the plank he again called to Hughes, who was moving from him very quickly. "Hold, sir," said Harrington. "I have information for you and bounty to reward you. Let us talk for only a short time, and then we are through for this trip."

Hughes hesitated. He was a cunning man who had lived and survived in the homes of Whigs. He had escaped Jack Beckham and he was close to going back to England, where he already knew he would be rewarded. He eyed Harrington, who called again. Hughes decided to stand on the ship's deck near the rail in plain view of others, looking over the crowd below in case of any trickery on Harrington's part. The Colonel caught up to him and eyed a suspicious man that would either flee or attack him. Harrington again tried to think of words that would buy him time to get close to the man.

As he got closer he said, "This reward is for you. I am to share it with you and others. There are other men on this ship that have done good service as you have. I will introduce them to you, and you can share the information needed to help the cause. London needs to know what we all know. Here, sir, accept these coins and with them my thanks to you for a remarkable task."

Jack was still fifty yards away watching this. He was mystified until

Harrington gave the guineas to Hughes and with them, a firm pat on the shoulder. Jack moved like a cat to a hogshead and leaned on it. There was no time to wait for anything else. He had already prepared Fisher's rifle. It was primed and loaded and ready to fire at only 30 yards away from the ship's mooring. He steadied himself and became very calm. He breathed a small breath and exhaled. He sighted Hughes' chest and then moved the gun upwards.

Suddenly Harrington was blinded. He could not see. He felt a mass of wetness in his face, and he staggered helplessly. He thought he might have been stabbed by Hughes. He struggled to see, to wait for the pain that was sure to come with a wound, and he dropped everything he had in his hand. The gold coins were out of his palms as he took both hands to his face and wiped away the sticky liquid covering him.

He looked at his hands, and they were covered with blood and pieces of fat tissue. At once he felt the man beside him leaning hard on his shoulder and chest. He looked down. It was Hughes, and Harrington was looking straight into the mass of blood and bone that had been his face. Half of his jaw and head seemed to be missing, and blood continued to crawl in thick globs down his remaining face and onto his chest. Jack's shot had blown much of this man's head away.

People on the dock screamed, some women swooned, and merchants and dock hands looked around. Jack was in bad luck. Three British officers and a squad of men had been watching the exodus of ship passengers from the street, and they knew instantly where the shot came from. They charged on foot and on horse to where Jack and his men were. Jack and his men, now mounted, rode from that spot and started down Elliott Street.

As they fled, Jack was trying to reload; he stopped once and did so deliberately. He hollered, "We has to fire." In the middle of the street, with the British on foot ahead of the mounted officers, Jack, Hayes, Lionnes, and Cook all stood and fired together once at the British. Three soldiers fell severely wounded, and one fell with a leg shattered. The officers' horses reared at the sound and sight and trampled two of their own men trying to load and fire.

Jack and all his rode down Longitude Lane, an alley, and followed

Hayes, who took them on a frantic go-round to get away. They went through yards and alleys and onto Meeting Street. They rode toward the Scot's Presbyterian Church and behind it, losing their pursuers.

In the meantime, Harrington had been helped off the ship, covered with blood and sinew, on the pretense of following the man who had caused this murder. He shouted for people to "stop that man." He had seen Jack flee, safely, he thought. Harrington was helped by a citizen, who offered to take him to his place, allow him to wash, and give him a change of clothes. Harrington accepted this kind offer, and he and the citizen, Justice William Jay Fisher, retired unencumbered and without suspicion to the Justice's office.

Chapter Twenty Four

The Resting Ground

Jack and his friends had fled even farther behind the church grave-yard among large tombstones to safety. Only an elderly couple walked among the stones, and they did not look up at them. The four men gathered their horses and talked quietly.

"We is best to leave by one or two," Jack said, still catching his breath.

Hayes volunteered information. "I figure the British may be on the south street nearest the water; I hope they think we take a boat, and search all the way to Mary's Lane. That will take some time. It is best we go back toward King Street and then down Meeting. Mr. Lionnes and me are back to our house on Elliott."

Jack said, "There will be citizens and King's men there to see after the soldiers who are shot. Maybe they will pay you little mind."

The two men left after asking Jack where he would go. "I will take him," Cook answered.

They began to move through the graveyard to King Street. Abruptly, Hayes called back to Jack. "Sir! Come to my house tonight, and we will get you safely back." Jack waved at him.

Cook told Jack he was not married, and they would go to a place he knew where he thought they would be safe. That afternoon they stayed at a brothel near the capitol. Jack and Cook watched the front door and all who came in. Those who did come in were not looking for Jack and his men who had been on the docks.

That evening, as dark came, Cook arranged to have Jack leave that night with the Justice. He went to Justice Fisher's office and told him what had happened. Fisher, in his carriage, left later as he always did. He made a casual stop at the brothel, as if to gather a friend. Jack was watching from behind curtains as the elegant carriage pulled up to the gate of the well-known house.

After tying Derrick's reins onto the back of the carriage, Jack traveled with Fisher to his home on Church Street. Jack would be his guest tonight. Justice Fisher said, "I have arranged to have Mr. Harrington brought here tomorrow morning by Cook. Both of you will have papers signed by me to help you in transit. You are "Dante Gordon," hired by me as a gamesman and hunter. Go back again by the Charlestowne Road. I think the harbor and saltwater creeks will be the most dangerous tonight. But I don't think our British will give too many 'damns' about this man who was shot. I will convey word to influential men that the man killed on the ship was a thief, and that the score was probably settled by another thief. The wounding of the soldiers will be more difficult for the forces here. They will continue to look for you and the others for several days. So you best leave tomorrow about mid-morning."

Jack nodded and Fisher went directly to a desk and made out a letter of transport for him. He looked up and said, "Take care of the rifle; it will do you well as any other you might have or acquire."

"I am much obliged to you, sir."

That night after dinner, Jack went to an impressive room with a bed that was so high it measured four feet from the floor to the top of the mattress. Jack saw the side steps leading up to the mattress and remembered one similar to it at Colonel Henderson's home. As St. Michael's bell struck one, Jack slipped out of the room and down the stairs. He was leaving. He would not wait until morning. As he reached the front door he saw the shadow of a figure move to his right in the room. Jack turned and pulled his knife quickly; dropping the bag he was carrying. He stooped at the same time into a defensive crouch.

"It is me," said Fisher. "Men, I hear say, are waiting to kill you. Don't leave." Fisher looked out the window and pointed to a building across the street. "You have been betrayed, I am afraid, by a woman at the brothel. I gather she is a close 'friend' of a Captain in this town."

Jack muttered in frustration.

"They are reluctant to come here because of my name, I am proud to say. And I don't know that any harm will come to me. They saw me with you earlier. All this I know from Cook, who also is a friend of this woman.

"You can leave from a door that leads to the garden. Spend the next hours in the garden until light. These men are not sure that you are still here, but they think so and that is enough."

Jack was curious. "How does you know all this?"

"I am told by 'Saint Peter.' Today as light comes, go by Meeting Street and make sure to leave that way. That is safer. Many will think you and Harrington will be gone by ferry across the Cooper River past Haddrell's Point. Go by horse, and use the letter of transit."

"Where is Harrington to be?"

"Safe here for the time and then back to where he wants to be. You may not see him again, nor he you."

"Tell the Saint Peter I am right well indebted."

"I will tell him now. You are welcome," said Fisher and smiled.

"Hellfire and damnation," laughed Jack and extended his hand for a firm handshake of friendship. It was his first laugh in days. Jack looked at the sheepish grin on Fisher's face and asked an obvious question. "Why is this name Saint Peter used for you?"

"Ah," Fisher replied, looking almost embarrassed, "that is the humor of Governor Rutledge and Wade Hampton. My name is Fisher and Jesus called Peter, one of his disciples – a fisherman – to witness to men, to be a fisherman of men, if you will. Thus they likened me to Saint Peter."

Jack did not understand the reasoning and looked at the man with part sympathy for him for being awarded this odd distinction, and with puzzlement. Regardless, it did not bear any importance to him, and he left the great room by the side door. Jack spent the rest of the night hiding among the large trees in the Justice's garden. The Justice grew many plants, trees, and flowers, and Jack thought it a large plot of land to be in the city.

The light came and Jack went down Meeting Street as instructed, then turned back toward Broad. He passed 37 Meeting Street, which he knew well, and continued in front of the Presbyterian Church. Jack sauntered past and soon picked up the pace toward Charlestowne Road. He saw guards in the mid-morning, and he fingered the letter inside his frock as he approached. On meeting the guards, he tipped his hat, gave his credentials, and passed through. He did not know how "Saint Peter" knew so much, but he was grateful as he rode swiftly away from the guards.

Jack was back to the Pacolet in seven days. He had ridden hard and felt safe. On approaching his land, he stopped and let Derrick drink long at the river. To Jack this homecoming seemed different, unlike any other he had experienced during these warring times. He made his way to a hill that overlooked his farm. It was a narrow patch of land that quickly gave way to a slope that carried him down to his cabin and its barns, fences, and store houses.

Derrick sensed the barn where he belonged, and he lengthened his stride. Jack proceeded to a spot where he stopped and retrieved his nautical glass and looked in the distance. He saw Nancy and Molly Polly with little Maggie on the river bank, and he was much surprised at how they had grown. Little Maggie did not fall down much as she rambled around on the bank. Molly Polly watched her and rolled pine cones down a hill for her, much to the baby's squealing delight.

Jack studied Molly Polly, who seemed taller; she had on a print dress that she filled out as a young woman. He felt he had been gone so long that his biggest "little" girl was getting away from him. He rode directly to them and called out from a distance. Molly Polly began to run toward him, carrying the baby and holding little Nancy's hand at the same time.

They had a warm reunion of father and daughters but Molly Polly soon became serious. "Papa, Easter is here. She has been here days. She is very sick. Mama says she is dying."

Jack was alarmed. He helped Molly Polly up on his horse, and with her holding the baby in front and Nancy in back, they rode the short distance to the cabin. He dismounted, and they went inside to the family that was gathered there – all except Susan, Stribling, Lily-Beth, and Scoggins. After much joy and picking up children and chatter about the turn of events in the colony, Jack and Elizabeth went in the kitchen to talk alone. No mention was made of Charlestowne, but Jack assured her that what he had seen would be to her liking and that all was as well as might be. He did tell her Wade Hampton said the British were leaving major towns, but Charlestowne would be one of the last. He said he had to find and report to Wade, who probably already knew what Jack had to tell him; however, it would be his duty to leave soon to visit Hampton.

Elizabeth told Jack to stay and see Easter. "She has asked for you," said Elizabeth, stating it in a way that Jack caught her seriousness.

"Where is she? What ails her?" asked Jack.

"She is in the room upstairs where someone can be with her when she is worse. She sleeps much."

"I will see," he said.

They both climbed the stairs, followed by Nancy, John Junior, and Molly Polly carrying little Maggie. Jack saw an emaciated and hollow-eyed Easter in a white gown, lying in a large bed. She had one hand on a cloth beside her and another hand on her chest. Her mouth was slightly open and her eyes closed.

Elizabeth said, "She is weak, and Cat and Abraham both says she has dropsy. John Junior has stayed with her, as has all of us, for ten days since they brought her here. She asked to be here and to see little Maggie again."

That evening, Jack went up to the room and told Susan, who had come to the house from her cabin to see Easter, that he would sit with Easter. He stayed the night, sitting in a chair next to her. He smoked his pipe, stretched his long legs out, and watched Easter closely from time to time. He noticed her hand on the cloth, and he picked up her hand. Under it was the same Bible she had in her cabin when he swore an oath for her.

In the mid-morning she stirred and spoke. She looked at him with glassy eyes and in a weak voice and said, "Massah, is you here? Praise the Lawd, Massah." Her voice trailed off and she drifted again into sleep. Jack looked closely into her face as she breathed a shallow sound. Her fingers flexed on the Bible. Later, she turned to him again and said weakly, "Sir, I has seen my sister, Annalee. She be here!"

Jack looked puzzled and said nothing. Later, Elizabeth came to the room, and Jack asked her about Easter's sister.

"I did not know she had one," said Elizabeth. "Why don't I sit a spell?"

"Nay...I will stay. I am tired, and this is for me now. I is fine," Jack said. He stretched full length again, put his hands on his chest, and closed his eyes. In the middle of the evening, as Jack dozed, Easter turned again, and he heard her.

"Massah, dere is someone's at the door. See what dey wants, Massah."

Jack whispered, "No one is at the door."

Hours later, she roused again, and looking up at the ceiling said, "Lawd...what glorious sounds that be...Massah, where dat be from?"

Jack listened but heard nothing. As the early morning came, Easter stirred again. For the first time, she took her hand off the Bible and put it, bony and cracked from years of work, on Jack's hand. He noticed how cold it was.

Easter sighed, and Jack looked at her closely. Her eyes were fixed open and staring. She had passed. He covered her head and went outside, down toward the river to survey what the family and slaves called "the resting ground." It had been a moonless night and he was unable to determine where Easter would lie. In the slow rising light he walked down further to the river with a shovel, and discovered that a grave had already been dug. A cross of wood was on the edge of the hole, lying on the ground, waiting to be driven into the soil. Flowers were already lying about. Jack was puzzled. How did this happen? Who knew to do this?

He went back and awakened Elizabeth to ask her. "Molly Polly, Stribling, and John Junior did three days ago…before you came."

"Why then?" asked Jack

"Easter told them to," she said. "But she said she was waiting for you to come back. She said you would be here."

Jack sat down and looked straight ahead. He had no words. He waited until the children were down that morning and told them what had happened. They all went outside. Jack carried Easter to the grave. She weighed very little. He placed her in the grave, and all the smaller children filled it with dirt with their hands as John Junior worked with a shovel.

Jack watched them, standing at the grave side. Elizabeth was holding Teressa. The little girls and older girls carried dirt dutifully to the grave and tossed it in. John Junior, Susan, Sarah, and Nancy, and Molly Polly, all had their hands busy filling the site. Little Maggie handed small amounts of dirt to Nancy, who took it from her and tossed it in.

Jack's mind took him back to Maggie, buried in the woods near her farm. He reflected on Easter and her life. It was not one of killing. Jack saw the baby that she had saved now gathering dirt in her tiny hands for this woman's resting ground, and he thought about this twist of fate. He could not forget the war he had been in and the killing in Charlestowne and other places. He wondered – and would never let anyone into these thoughts – who had made the greatest difference in his colony and his family. Was it him, or Easter and her kind?

The grave was filled, and many had left when Jack, John Junior, Sarah, and Molly Polly walked back to the cabin. Molly Polly said to him, in all her innocence, "Pap, will we see Easter again? Will we see her in heaven?"

He did not answer and after a while she asked him again. "Pap, will we see Easter again?"

"Aye" he said. "Aye, we will."

Years later, with her own children, Molly Polly would remember this conversation with her father. It was one of many that would stay with her…the sights and smells, the days and the seasons of the Pacolet. Strange and recurring memories. At times, she wished she could recall certain people, but their faces were gone. Yet she retained many details about her father and events such as this, the walk back to the cabin that day. She remembered that she had not held his hand as usual as they walked. She was a taller girl then, more than fourteen, and she had put her arm around her father's waist for the first time, as a young adult.

Somehow her father's words that day had remained with her. "Aye, we will," he had said. Those words would comfort her for years when she thought about the devout Easter. But they especially comforted her about him, her "Pap," this man Jack Beckham, as he was known to many others but those many others who never knew his soul.

Appendix:

A Brief Historical Perspective Of South Carolina Upcoutry Beckhams, Brigadier General William Henderson, And Colonel Wade Hampton

"John Beckham was a most active Whig and fearful scout." John H. Logan, A.M. <u>A History of the Upper Country of South Carolina, Vol. II</u>

John "Jack" Beckham, Whig scout and spy, actually lived. He lived in what is today Union County, during the American Revolution, in the northern part pointed toward Cowpens, SC. His home on the Pacolet River, Grindal Shoals, and Sandy Run, was approximately twenty miles from the Battle of Blackstock's Plantation, November 20, 1780. It was twenty four miles from the Battle of Cowpens, the southern turning point of the American Revolution on January 17, 1781.

Born December 1, 1736, on Beaver Creek, between Great Falls and Camden, SC in Kershaw County he was the son of William Beckham and Phillis Mackey Beckham. He was the brother of Simon and Thomas, William, Jr., and sisters Phillis and Mary Beckham. He died in 1789 at age fifty three. His brother William is my great, great, great, great grandfather.

Given legendary status in the South Carolina backcountry wars for independence, there are recorded tales about great uncle John "Jack," some courageous and some not too flattering. He was one among eleven Beckham men in the same family who fought in the Revolution in the Carolinas and Georgia, and then later "West Florida," or Louisiana as we now know it. It was not unusual that they lived, served, suffered, and were honored with land grants from the new government of colonies after the American Revolution. Most except Jack; he never filed a pension.

He was a friend of the young, wealthy, and prominent Wade Hampton. He was the brother-in-law of highly regarded Continental officer Colonel (later Brigadier General) William Henderson, who would eventually succeed General Thomas Sumter in 1782, as commandant of all South Carolina troops. Captain Wade Hampton, the same, would in fact serve under then Lieutenant Colonel William Henderson at the Battle of Stono Ferry, near Charleston, SC, June 12,1780. Both Henderson and Hampton would serve in the South Carolina Assembly after the American Revolution, along with Francis Marion and other great patriots. Jack would become a highway "commissioner" in Union County.

Jack is mentioned prominently in at least three books on the American Revolution. Thanks to Pelham Lyles, director of the Fairfield, SC County Museum, we discovered that John H. Logan, A.M., described him as follows in _A History of the Upper Country of South Carolina, Vol. II:_

"John Beckham…was a most active Whig and fearless scout. While Morgan was encamped on Grindal's Shoal, he kept him in constant motion, and he did valuable service. On one occasion, when closely pressed by the Light Horse of Tarleton he plunged headlong down a fearful bank into the river and made his escape. The spot is still well known, and often pointed out. It was on the plantation of old Wm. Hodge, who also was a true Whig. A comrade named Easterwood, from whom the shoals take their name, was with him in this race. Easterwood rode a big clumsy horse and was big and heavy himself. His horse striking against a log, fell sprawling and Easterwood was made prisoner. Beckham's mare, a magnificent animal, soon left them in the rear. He could have got off easier, but stopping at Hodge's to light his pipe, (he was an incessant smoker), the British were close upon him, while he was yet holding the fire. He swore he would light *it before he budged a foot. After gaining the other side of the Pacolet, he slapped his thigh and looking back at his pursuers, 'Shoot and be damned' he cried, his pipe still in his mouth."*

Lieutenant Colonel Banastre Tarleton, of the British Legion, and Jack seemed destined to go against each other. Tarleton occupied the Beckham home on Sandy Run on his march to Cowpens and would have destroyed it completely had it not been for Jack's wife, Elizabeth, urging it be saved. Tarleton captured Jack's closest friend, William Hodge and had him imprisoned in Camden, SC. Hodge was a man to whom Jack had sold four hundred and forty acres of land in 1776, which became known as Hodge's Plantation. It is the very same Hodge plantation where Jack and Elizabeth are both buried.

In the *Union County Miscellaneous Record Book, 1 & 2* the sale information is recorded: "*South Carolina, Ninety Six District: Personally appeared John Hodge and John Grindal Senr., before J. Thompson, J.P.. and state that they saw John Beckham of District aforesaid in the year 1775 or 1776 deliver to William Hodge of Pacolate River and said district, a lease and release for 400 acres. being the plantation wheron the said William Hodge now lives...adj. Robert Colemans, Thomas Draper,27 August 1784. John Hodge, John Grindal. Recorded 3 September 1792.*" (pages 136-137)

Notable among the other Beckham boys was Jack's brother, Thomas, who served under Colonel Leroy Hammond during 1778 and 1779 as a light dragoon. He was present at the siege of Savannah, and captured at the fall of Charlestowne in 1780, the worst single defeat of Americans in the entire revolution. He was paroled ten days later as militia.

Thomas fought at one of the sieges of Augusta, specifically the taking of Brown's Fort and the taking of Gearson's Fort and, still later, he engaged in the American victory at Eutaw Springs near Orangeburg, SC. After Col. Hammond resumed command of a militia unit, Thomas stayed with him as a light dragoon. This militia unit joined General Pickens on a march north of the Broad River where they joined General Nathaniel Greene. Thomas is buried in Edgefield County, SC.

Jack's nephew Samuel was a militia captain and wounded at the first siege of Augusta. Serving under Georgia rifleman Elijah Clark, and as commander of Fort Wilkinson near Milledgeville, he lost his first wife and three children, all killed by marauding Indians. He married again and later commanded Fort Hawkins a militia outpost near Macon, GA.

He was buried with honors at beautiful Memory Hill Cemetery in Milledgeville, GA. An article in *The (Milledgeville) Georgia Journal*, November 8,1825 carried this note about the Revolutionary War soldier: *"On the second of November, at the residence of Albert G. Beckham, Samuel Beckham died, at the age of sixty five years, wanting twenty two days. He was a Revolutionary War soldier who was in actual service during our struggle for liberty, until the close of the war, with the exception of a few months, when he was confined with a wound he received at the siege of Augusta.*

He commanded a rifle company during the greatest part of the war, under general Elijah Clarke, where he was ready to serve his country in any shape that presented itself. His goodness of heart will long be remembered by the hundreds of his countrymen"…

Samuel gave a long oral summary after the Revolutionary War, part of which became known as "The Savannah Papers" and chronicles much of what took place in Georgia, not only from an eye witness but a participator as well.

Jack's nephew Abner, who may have been the closest to Jack in his exploits, was born in Rocky Mount, SC, near an area which became known as "Beckhamville", and in present day is near Great Falls. He served as a captain in the militia fighting in South Carolina and Georgia, and took on a mercenary's task in Western Florida (Louisiana), then under Spanish government control; there he was paid to rid the area of Indians. Abner changed his last name to "Bickham" to assume another legal identity while fighting Indians in Louisiana under the protection of the King of Spain. The adventurer settled and died there but left a legacy in Louisiana of "Bickhams" many of whom are in fact "Beckhams."

Jack's other nephews, Samuel's brothers, Sherwood, Solomon,

Allen, and Laban, as well as cousins Russell and Reuben, all fought as militia. Reuben and Russell served together with Captain Thomas Key and Colonel Leroy Hammond as did the aforementioned Thomas. Oldest brother, Allen became a Major in the militia, serving in the 5th District in Georgia, 2nd Battalion, 2nd Regiment; likewise did Sherwood. Solomon was in brother Samuel's company as part of Elijah Clark's Georgia riflemen.

It was Lieutenant Simon Beckham's duty, another nephew, as a member of Captain William Campbell's Third Rifles in 1815, following the War of 1812, to close the fort at Mt. Dearborn, today's Great Falls, SC, and take final charge of the post's property. This fact of war was written by Daniel Stinson in an article entitled "A Sketch of Mount Dearborn."

The oldest Beckham male of our lineage to be in the revolution was William, Jack's elder brother. Born in 1730 and fifty years old at the time of the fall of Charlestowne, he served as a private in the militia. As mentioned, William was my Revolutionary War great grandfather.

All fought and lived through the revolution. All survived the war and died of natural causes. But none of the Beckham boys was so obvious, so intolerable to the enemy, so productive for the Whig's cause, or so hated by former neighbors and friends, as was the redoubtable Jack. John "Jack" Beckham is one of several colonials written about in another book, Reverend J.D. Bailey's *History of Grindal Shoals*. (Grindal Shoals is now in present day Union County, SC.)

Rev Bailey:

"*Beckham came from North Carolina about 1774 and settled on a part of the Henderson grant on Sandy Run, which is now know as the "Billy" Whitlock place. He engaged in hunting and trapping as game was plentiful. He had a store, which was probably the first in that section. It would be interesting to know what the stock of goods consisted of, and from whence, and how he obtained them.*

"*As a horse trainer, he was considered an expert, and paid a good deal of attention to scout, and did extensive work as a spy. Naturally such a man would suffer much at the hands of British and Tories. Tarleton once made a foray into that section and camped for a night at Beckham's house, and when he left in the morning he took all the bedding except one quilt and soon afterwards, a party of Tories came and took that: hence when the war was over, he had little or nothing left.*

"Subsequently Wade Hampton, who had spent much time in Beckham's home, gave him employment as a trainer of race-horses, but Jack Beckham, ever remained what the old people would call a 'ne'er do well.' At last the faithful old scout who had done his 'bit' in the cause of independence passed away, leaving a poor widow and a house full of daughters. He was buried in the Hodge graveyard, but his grave being unmarked, the exact spot is unknown."

The Wade Hampton connection to the Beckhams is also chronicled in another book. It is recorded by Virginia G. Meynard in *The Venturers : The Hampton, Harrison and Earle Families of Virginia, South Carolina, and Texas,* and describes the Wade Hampton family in SC history.

"Wade (Hampton) also went on trade missions to Grindal Shoals on the Pacolet river (in present Union County) where he lived for some weeks with the John Beckham family. Mrs. Beckham (Elizabeth Henderson) was a relative of Wade's brother-in-law, James Harrison, and Wade had known her in his youth in North Carolina. The Beckhams had come from Granville County, NC, to the Henderson grant at Grindal Shoals about 1774 with her brother, William Henderson, and other members of the family. Henderson was a well educated, prosperous planter and Beckham had opened the first store in the area. He also was in the business of breeding and training horses, and Wade had left several of his stallions with Beckham for that purpose."

Bobby Moss, the prolific historian and author of *Patriots at Cowpens* and *Patriots at Kings Mountain,* said Jack was almost certainly at the Battle of Cowpens. Dr. Moss listed him as "probable" in his book on the patriots at Cowpens while looking for present research and new data to absolutely confirm his presence there. Given Jack's life of stealth and love of confrontation, Dr. Moss interviewed in his home, said with a twinkle in his eye and a smile, "Jack had to be there."

Even Jack's detractors in his own family paid him a backhanded compliment when telling of him. Jack's niece, Angelica Nott, in her recollections of the Revolutionary War in *The History of Grindal Shoals*, page 73, said:

"*My father was one of the first settlers in the country. My mother was a Henderson, a sister of Colonel William Henderson. My father moved to Tennessee before the war. I remained with my aunt, Mrs. Potter, on Sandy Run.*

"*I was related to the Beckhams. Mrs. Beckham and my mother were sisters. I saw Ferguson's army pass the place where Mrs. Harris---saw Ferguson on the occasion, he was a small man.*

"*My aunt suffered much. At the time Tarleton was going to Cowpens some Tories came to my aunt's with whom I lived and burnt the top off our tent. It was a rail pen covered with straw. Tarleton camped at Aunt Beckham's on this march. I recollect Colonel Cunningham came to our house. He came after night with 250 men. They fed their horses on our roasting ears and burnt the rails to roast some for themselves.*"

She later recounted, in the same narrative, almost nonchalantly: "*John Beckham, my uncle, was not distinguished except as a spy; he lived on Sandy Run.*" So Jack, even in service to the colonies as a high risk, certainly a non-paid spy, got only a lukewarm accolade from Mrs. Nott, albeit she was very young in the war. She lived a long life, dying in 1849, nineteen years past her husband.

Jack Beckham's greatest accomplishment may have been that he married well.

On August 12, 1761, he wed Elizabeth Henderson, who came from a much better and notable heritage than the rough-edged rebel. Elizabeth, a woman of bearing and family- connected politicians, bore him eight children, seven girls, one with the unforgettable name of "Molly Polly," as well as a boy, "John Junior." Her family was honored with a large tract of land on Sandy Run, a tract originally in North Carolina, known as Grindal Shoals but presently in Union, SC .The land was granted by Governor William Tryon of North Carolina, who ironically would become known as "The Wolf", and a stooge of the British.

An episode of Elizabeth's character is depicted in Rev. Bailey's book *The History of Grindal Shoals*:

"Elizabeth Beckham was a Henderson, sister to Gen. William and Major John Henderson. She belonged to noted Whig stock and was a woman of remarkable energy and strength of character. Her husband being a drinking and improvident fellow, the burden of making a living fell largely on her and her daughters. This they did bravely and her daughters were worthy of their Mother, fine characters everyone of them. When we think of the bravery and heroism displayed in those trying times, the noble women should not be forgotten.

"When Tarleton encamped at the Beckham home, Mrs. Beckham first saw him while standing in the yard ordering his men to catch her poultry for supper. She spoke civilly to him and hastened to prepare supper for him and suite, as if they had been honored guests. When about to leave in the morning he gave the house up to pillage and ordered it to be burnt; but because of her earnest remonstrance's, he recalled the order.

"Mrs. Beckham once made a trip to Fort Granby * on horseback, a distance of eighty miles. She had a solid gold guinea braided in her hair concealed on the top of her head. With this she bought a bushel of salt and brought it safely home on the saddle.

"Some time after her husband's death she, in looking over his account, found that something was due her from Wade Hampton. She resolved to visit him and see what he would do for her. Her family and friends advised against it; Hampton was now a very rich and distinguished man living in grand style in Columbia. The old lady said she would trust him, that she had known Wade in his youth; her house was then open to him and she could not believe that he would forsake her now. So mounting 'Derrick.' her faithful old horse, she set off to Columbia alone. She made the trip and returned safely. The family, eager to hear the result of her visit, gathered around her. Mrs. Beckham was delighted. 'How did he receive you?' she was asked. 'Receive me! He received me as if I had been a queen; nothing in his grand house was too good for Mrs. Beckham. Child, I was put in a

fine chamber with a great mahogany bedstead covered with a canopy and so high that there were steps to climb into it, and they were carpeted. He paid me and more than paid me."

Elizabeth therefore became noted among early American women, particularly among South Carolina women, just as her husband would be among his enemies and his friends. Her life would be long. Born in 1738 she would live until 1831, dying at the great age of ninety three. She lived an amazing forty years after Jack died, a widow longer than her twenty year marriage.

It would have been a unique opportunity and lesson in oral history in the Beckham-Henderson household, if the conversations of Jack's brother-in- law Colonel, then Brigadier General William Henderson, and Jack and Elizabeth Henderson, had been recorded. It would have been enhanced greatly if their friend Colonel Wade Hampton had been present. There would be the courageous and sophisticated Elizabeth given land by decree, and her military brother in General Henderson, who would eventually take over the "Fighting Gamecock", General Thomas Sumter's command in South Carolina.

General Henderson is described in the <u>South Carolina Roster of Patriots</u> by Dr. Bobby Moss.

...born March 3,1748, he became a Major in the Sixth Regiment and a Lieutenant Colonel on September 16 1776. On February 11, 1780, he was transferred to the Third Regiment and was taken prisoner at the fall of Charleston. He was exchanged during November 1780 and was transferred to the first Regiment on 1 January 1781. He was wounded at the battle of Eutaw Springs on 8 September 1781. On 30 September 1781 he was promoted to Colonel. He served to the close of the war and during 1781 and 1782 he was a Brigadier General of state troops."

(* Present day Columbia, SC)

Listed under *American Leaders The Continental Army* in William Thomas Sherman's book <u>Calendar and Record of the Revolutionary War in the South 1780-1781</u>, he is described:"*Lieut. Col. William Henderson, from Spartanburg County, Sumter's brigade and SC State Troops. Henderson, as an officer in the 6th South Carolina Regiment, was present at the siege of Charleston and there led a gallant and tactically successful sortie. When the city fell he was made prisoner but by early November he was exchanged. He was at Blackstock's, and took charge of Sumter's brigade following Sumter's being wounded in that action. He appears in the record again in May 1781 at the time of the siege of Ninety-Six. When Sumter, under various pressures, resigned temporarily in August 1781, Henderson was put in his place and became commander of the South Carolina Troops, which were created largely from Sumter's now much diminished brigade. He led them at Eutaw Springs where he was wounded. Both his letters and the trust Sumter and Greene bestowed on him show Henderson to have been a truly professional soldier with good sense and sound judgment."*

The distinguishing military maneuver mentioned by Sherman, in fact the most aggressive and successful sortie at the siege of Charlestowne, under Lieutenant Colonel William Henderson's command, is noted by Carl P. Borick, the author of A *Gallant Defense, The Seige of Charleston, 1780,* University of South Carolina Press. He was complimentary of the choice of William Henderson to lead the charge against the British. *"He must have been a neat fellow; he was chosen over Laurens to lead the attack."*

The outstanding exhibit in 2003 at the Charleston Museum of the British siege, a result of Borick's excellent and thoroughly researched book, mentions in cut lines under drawings on display: *"Lt. Colonel William Henderson sallied forth, crossed the canal and charged into the right section of the British third parallel with fixed bayonets. They killed two Jagers, captured 12 other soldiers and forced the others to retreat to the 2nd parallel. Jagers on the left section of the parallel opened fire on Henderson's men and also on their own lines; British artillerymen in the second parallel soon did the same. Shortly thereafter the Americans returned with the prisoners to safety of their own lines."*

In the family discussions that would have taken place, there would certainly be the irreverent rebel John "Jack" Beckham. He, a true guerrilla fighter, and a man who could father eight children and still be gone for long stretches of time, would not have talked about military formations with his brother- in- law. His conversations and contributions were more likely to be suddenness of death and long periods of waiting patiently for vengeance and retribution. Jack, the scout and spy whose very existence depended on stealth, with covert payment for services, changing fortunes of colonists by being ruthless and unsympathetic to neighbors, would have lurid stories to tell. But they would have been typical of violence and hatred in the south, among neighbors, during the American Revolution.

Add to this mix Jack's brothers, nephews, and relatives and the conversations would have seen a cast of characters that could have been written about many times. They were the kind that founded this country. They made it so with all their idiosyncrasies, their lifestyle and their faults.

When the Declaration of Independence was signed Jack was thirty-nine years old, five months short of forty. He had been married for fifteen years with four children for sure. One was born before his marriage to Elizabeth, she being Susan in 1760; and then Elizabeth, who was born in 1762; Molly Polly in 1768; and son John Junior, earlier in 1765.

What Jack must have reveled in most was the ultimate degrading British evacuation onto five hundred ships from Charleston, S C, his own state, in December 1782.

Was he there in Charleston? Probably not. Was he partly responsible for the ultimate British and Tories' defeat, as were many other backcountry hunters, and farmers turned militia? No doubt.

M.C. "Mickey" Beckham, July 4, 2005, the 225th year of many important battles and scrimmages in South Carolina in the American War for Independence.

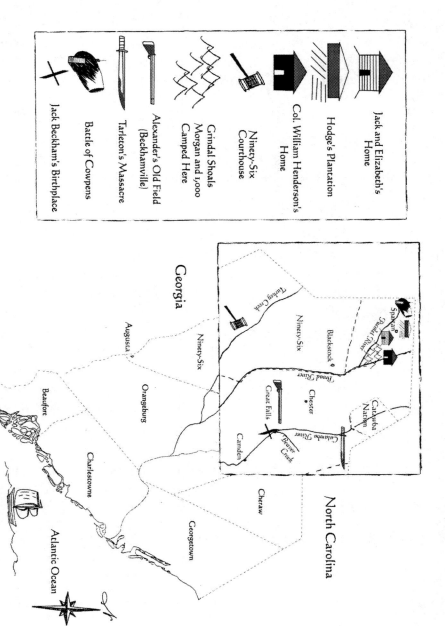

Jack and Elizabeth's Home

Hodge's Plantation

Col. William Henderson's Home

Ninety-Six Courthouse

Grindal Shoals Morgan and 1,000 Camped Here

Alexander's Old Field (Beckhamville)

Tarleton's Massacre

Battle of Cowpens

Jack Beckham's Birthplace

North Carolina

Georgia

Augusta

Beaufort

Orangeburg

Charlestowne

Atlantic Ocean

Ninety-Six

Ninety-Six

Turkey Creek

Blackstock

Broad River

Chester

Great Falls

Catawba River

Beaver Creek

Camden

Catawba Nation

Spartan

Pacolet River

Cheraw

Georgetown